A Convenient Proposal

*Marriage of convenience brings more
than they bargained for!*

By Request

A Convenient Proposal

THE MARRIAGE ARRANGEMENT
by
Helen Bianchin

WIFE BY ARRANGEMENT
by
Lucy Gordon

THE HIRED HUSBAND
by
Kate Walker

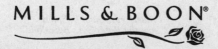

MILLS & BOON®

All the characters in this book have no existence outside the imagination of the author, and have no relation whatsoever to anyone bearing the same name or names. They are not even distantly inspired by any individual known or unknown to the author, and all the incidents are pure invention.

A CONVENIENT PROPOSAL
© by Harlequin Enterprises II B.V., 2004

The Marriage Arrangement, Wife by Arrangement and
The Hired Husband were first published in Great Britain by
Harlequin Mills & Boon Limited in separate, single volumes.

The Marriage Arrangement © Helen Bianchin 2001
Wife by Arrangement © Lucy Gordon 2001
The Hired Husband © Kate Walker 1999

ISBN 0 263 84074 3

05-0904

*Printed and bound in Spain
by Litografia Rosés S.A., Barcelona*

Helen Bianchin was born in New Zealand and travelled to Australia before marrying her Italian-born husband. After three years they moved, returned to New Zealand with their daughter, had two sons, then resettled in Australia. Encouraged by friends to recount anecdotes of her years as a tobacco sharefarmer's wife living in an Italian community, Helen began setting words on paper, and her first novel was published in 1975. An animal lover, she says her terrier and Persian cat regard her study as as much theirs as hers.

**Don't miss Helen Bianchin's powerful new story:
HIS PREGNANCY ULTIMATUM
On sale December 2004, in Modern Romance™!**

THE MARRIAGE ARRANGEMENT
by
Helen Bianchin

CHAPTER ONE

THE grey skies held a heavy electric potency that threatened to unleash cacophonous fury at any moment.

Hannah turned on the car's lights, and flinched as a fork of lightning rent the skyline, followed seconds later by a roll of thunder.

She could almost smell the imminent onset of rain, and seconds later huge drops hit the windscreen in a rapidly increasing deluge that soon made driving hazardous.

A muttered curse escaped her lips. *Great.* A summer storm during peak-hour traffic was just what she needed. As if she weren't already late, with available time minimising by the second.

Miguel *would* be pleased at the delay, she decided grimly.

Almost on cue, her cell-phone rang, and she activated the speaker button.

'Where in *hell* are you?' a slightly accented male voice demanded with chilling softness.

Speak of the devil! 'Your concern is overwhelming,' she returned with silk-edged mockery.

'Answer the question.'

Rain sheeted down, reducing visibility to a point

where she felt cocooned in isolation. 'Caught in traffic.'

There were a few seconds' silence, and she had a mental image of him checking his watch. '*Where*, precisely?'

'Does it matter?' A resort to wicked humour prompted her to add, 'I doubt even you can organise some way to get me out of here.'

Miguel Santanas was a law unto himself, with sufficient wealth and power to command anyone at will.

Andalusian-born, he'd been educated in Paris, and spent several years based in New York managing the North American arm of his father's business empire.

'You could have closed the boutique early, missed the worst of traffic, and been home by now,' Miguel said drily, and she felt anger begin to stir.

The boutique was *hers*. She'd studied art and design, worked in fashion houses in Paris and Rome, only to walk out on a disastrous love affair three years ago and return home. Within months she'd leased premises, stocked the boutique with exclusive designer wear, and at the age of twenty-seven she had built up an exclusive clientele.

'I doubt one of my best clients would have appreciated being shoved out the door,' she returned with marked cynicism.

'Whatever made me think you would assume the mantle of a docile wife?' Miguel offered in a musing drawl.

She drew in a deep breath and released it slowly. 'I didn't promise to *obey*.'

'I vividly recall your insistence the word be deleted from our vows.'

'We made a deal,' she reminded, all too aware of the circumstances that had initiated their marriage.

Two equally prominent, independently wealthy families whose fortunes were interwoven in an international conglomerate. What better method of cementing it and taking it into the next generation than to have the son of one family marry the daughter of the other?

It had taken subtle manipulation to entice the son to relocate to Melbourne from New York, whereupon an intricate strategy had been put in place to ensure Miguel and Hannah were frequent guests at a variety of social functions.

The master parental plan had involved anonymous tips to the media, whose printed speculation had seeded the idea and waived the need for further familial interference.

Hannah, tiring of dealing with some of the city's eligible and not-so-eligible bachelors bent on adding her wealth to their own, was not averse to the security marriage offered, with the proviso she continued to maintain her independence. *Love* wasn't an issue, and it seemed sensible to choose a husband with her head, rather than her heart.

Despite the family business connection, ten years' difference in age, his boarding-school education both in Australia and overseas ensured their paths had rarely met, and she had been only eleven when he'd transferred to New York.

'So we did,' Miguel drawled. 'Have you reason to complain, *amante*?'

'No,' she responded evenly.

Miguel was an attractive man, whose strong masculine features and tall broad-shouldered frame portrayed a leashed strength emphasised by a dramatic mesh of latent sensuality and an animalistic sense of power.

At thirty-seven, he echoed his eminent success in the business arena in the bedroom. She hadn't known his equal as a lover. And wouldn't want to, she added mentally, for he satisfied needs she hadn't been aware existed.

Even thinking about his lovemaking made her nerve-ends curl, and sent heat flaring through her veins.

A sudden horn-blast alerted her attention as the car in front inched forward, then came to a halt.

In the distance she heard the wail of a siren, soon joined by another, and her stomach twisted as she envisaged the probability of a car crash up ahead, the twisted metal, the resultant injuries.

'I think there's been an accident,' Hannah revealed quietly. 'It might take a while for me to get through.'

'Where are you?' Miguel demanded.

'On Toorak Road, about a mile from home.'

'Drive carefully. I'll phone Graziella and tell her we'll be late.'

'Do that,' she responded with dulcet charm. It wouldn't create a drama if they arrived fifteen minutes after the specified time. Their hosts were known to allow up to an hour for their guests to mix and mingle before serving dinner.

The lights changed, and Hannah offered a silent prayer in thanks as the traffic began to move slowly forward.

The Deity, however, was not in a benevolent mood, and consequently it was almost six when she turned into the leafy avenue leading to the remote-controlled gates guarding entrance to Miguel's spacious double-storeyed home.

Landscaped gardens and manicured lawns provided a perfect background for an imposing residence set back from the road. Spanish in design, with thick cream-plastered walls, high arched windows, and a terracotta-tiled roof.

Hannah urged the white Porsche up the curved driveway at speed, and brought the vehicle to a swift halt beneath the wide portico.

Heavy panelled double doors opened the instant she slid from behind the wheel, and she spared the housekeeper Miguel employed a warm smile as she entered the foyer.

'Thanks, Sofia.' It had saved her fumbling for her key and bypassing the security alarm system. 'Would you mind asking Antonio to garage my car?' Sofia's husband took care of the grounds and the cars while Sofia tended to the meals and the house five days out of seven.

'Miguel is already upstairs?' At Sofia's verbal affirmative, she moved quickly towards the wide curving stairs leading to the upper floor.

Seconds later she gained the semi-circular gallery bounded by ornately designed balustrades. Five bedrooms, each with *en suite*, plus a large informal sitting room comprised the upper level. Original paintings were strategically placed on the walls, and there were occasional tables, magnificent ceramic urns and artefacts set in majestic splendour along the entire gallery.

The main bedroom was situated at the front of the house, and she moved quickly towards it, freeing the buttons on her jacket with one hand while slipping off one heeled shoe with the other.

Seconds later she entered the spacious bedroom with its elegant furniture and separate walk-in robes.

Miguel was in the process of fixing a cuff-link, and she took in the look of him, his stance, the superbly tailored trousers, white shirt, his broad, chiselled features, and the dark well-groomed hair.

Beneath his sophisticated façade there lay the heart of a warrior. Compelling, dangerous, she added silently.

At that moment he glanced towards her, caught her expression, and raised one eyebrow in silent query.

Eyes so dark, they were almost black, met hers, and she fought to control the way her blood coursed through her veins like quicksilver.

Was he aware how he affected her? Sexually, without a doubt, she acknowledged wryly. He had the touch, the skill, to turn her into a mindless wanton, for in his arms she lacked the power to be anything else.

Get a grip, she mentally chastised as she crossed towards her wardrobe.

'Twenty minutes?' Hannah intimated, extracting a black knee-length gown with a fine lace-patterned overlay. Stiletto-heeled black shoes, sheer black stockings. The effect would be understated style, and offset her honey-coloured skin and blonde hair.

'Try for fifteen.'

She made it in just under twenty, emerging into the bedroom freshly showered, dressed, her make-up complete. It took only minutes to step into her gown and close the zip fastener, then add minimum jewellery.

'Done.' She caught up an evening purse, and offered Miguel a sparkling smile. 'Shall we leave?'

Together they traversed the gallery and began descending the stairs. Even though she was in heels, her head barely topped his shoulders.

'New perfume?'

Hannah met his faintly quizzical expression and matched it with one of her own. 'A woman's weapon,' she asserted solemnly, and suppressed the feather-light shiver that slid across the surface of her skin as Miguel reached out and traced a slow finger along her collar-bone.

'You have no need of one.'

Her smile tilted the edge of her mouth. 'Are you seducing me?'

One eyebrow arched, and his teeth gleamed white as he slanted her a teasing look. 'Am I succeeding?'

Oh yes. But she wasn't about to tell him so. 'We have a dinner party to attend, remember?'

His husky chuckle almost undid her. 'Anticipation, *querida*,' he drawled. 'Is a game lovers play.'

'Is that how you regard our marriage?' Hannah queried lightly. 'As a game?'

Together they crossed the splendid foyer and made their way along a hallway leading to the internal garage.

'You know better than that.'

'Do I?' The words slipped out before she thought to stop them.

'You want I should show you?' Miguel countered with silky indolence as he paused to face her.

'I imagine you will, later.'

There was something in her voice, some indefinable quality that caused his eyes to narrow slightly and search for something beyond her carefully composed features.

She possessed a vulnerability beneath the sophisticated façade, a genuine empathy that held no artifice. A rare trait among the women of his acquaintance. He doubted she was aware he could define each tone of her voice, every expression, no matter how fleeting.

Tonight, for whatever reason, she was on edge, and he sought to alleviate it a little.

He lifted a hand and cupped her nape, tilting her head, then he covered her mouth with his own in an evocative tasting that brought forth a faint sighing sound as she leaned into him and kissed him back.

How long did it last? Seconds, *minutes*? She had no sense of time, only the feeling of regret as he broke contact.

His eyes were dark, unfathomable, and she was conscious of every breath she took, each beat of her heart as it thudded in her breast.

'There's a difference between sex and lovemaking, *mi mujer*,' Miguel said gently. 'You might do well to remember it.' He smoothed the pad of his thumb along the lower curve of her lip, and proffered a faint smile. 'You have no lipstick.'

Hannah gathered her wits together quickly. 'While you, *hombre*, have a mouth rimmed with *hazelnut noisette*.' She considered him carefully. 'It's not a good look.'

He laughed, a soft, deep, husky sound that curled round her heart and tugged a little. 'Minx. I don't suppose you have a tissue in that minuscule bag you carry?'

'Of course,' she said solemnly, extracting a tissue and handing it to him. 'I am always prepared for any eventuality.'

He used the tissue and discarded it, deactivated the car alarm, then unlocked the door and she slid into the passenger seat. Restoring colour to her lips took only seconds, and it was done by the time Miguel slipped behind the wheel.

Minutes later he eased the powerful Jaguar towards the remote-controlled gates, picking up speed as he gained the street.

Summer daylight saving time bathed their surroundings with a soft golden glow, and while the heat of the day still hovered it was offset by the car's air-conditioning.

The rain-storm had passed, the wet bitumen the only evidence of its brief intensity.

'Who are our fellow guests? Do you know?' Hannah queried idly.

'Forewarned is forearmed?' Miguel posed as he paused at an intersection, and she offered him a faintly wry smile.

'Something like that.' There were a few socialites of her acquaintance who delighted in setting a cat among the pigeons, then observing the result. It was very cleverly orchestrated, and provided amusing entertainment to the perpetrators.

A few years ago *she* had been an object of their speculation. Gossip, she amended, was unavoidable, but she detested any deliberate attempt to hurt or offend.

'Graziella mentioned Angelina and Roberto Moro, Suzanne and Peter Trenton,' Miguel relayed, shooting her a quick glance as the lights changed and traffic began to move. 'Esteban also has an invitation.'

Two partners in a prominent law firm and their wives, Hannah mused, together with Miguel's widowed father.

The del Santos invariably invited between ten and fourteen guests to share their table, and rarely revealed the identity of everyone attending. Graziella always commented that it made the evening interesting.

Hannah wondered who Graziella had invited to partner her charming father-in-law. A widow? Perhaps a divorcee?

'Is there any earth-shattering news I should be aware of?' Hannah queried as the car cleared another intersection.

'In the need to conduct scintillating conversation?'

Hannah bit back a wry retort. 'It negates any nasty little surprises.'

'Such as?'

'The fall of a prominent businessman due to tax avoidance. His wife cranked up her credit card in several élite boutiques.'

Miguel spared her a sharp look. 'Yours was one of them?'

'You got it in one.' It wasn't a fortune, she could write off the loss, but it left a nasty taste in her mouth that someone she trusted had deliberately ripped her off.

'Leave it with me.'

Resentment flared. 'I can handle it.'

'You don't need to,' he responded smoothly.

Hannah wanted to hit him. 'My business,' she said firmly. 'My problem.'

It could wait, Miguel decided, aware that pursuing it now would only exacerbate the situation.

Kew was an old, well-established suburb with large stately mansions, and Miguel turned the car into a leafy avenue, then halted outside an impressive set of gates leading to Graziella and Enrico del Santo's imposing residence.

'We'll discuss this later.' The window slid down and he pressed the intercom, gave his name, then waited as the gates swung open.

'The responsibility is mine, the action *my* decision,' she insisted as he parked the car on a wide pebbled apron adjacent the main entrance.

'Independence in a woman is an admirable quality,' Miguel intoned silkily. 'But there are times when you take it too far.'

He slid from behind the wheel, and she stepped out, then closed the door.

'And a man's indomitable will is a pain in the butt.'

'Pax,' Miguel slanted coolly, and she offered him a brilliant smile.

'Of course, *amante*,' Hannah offered in a deliberately facetious response. 'I wouldn't dream of tarnishing our image.'

'Behave,' he admonished as they mounted the few steps to the massive double entrance doors.

They swung open as they reached them, and a tall well-built man in his fifties offered an affectionate greeting.

'Hannah.' Enrico leant forward and pressed his lips lightly to one cheek, then the other, and pumped Miguel's extended hand. 'Come through to the lounge.'

As they drew close it was possible to hear the light hum of conversation, and Enrico led them into a large spacious room filled with heavy antique chairs and sofas grouped into comfortable facing sets.

Men stood, resplendent in formal dinner suits, and

each of the women resembled a model out of *Vogue*, the epitome in elegance and cosmetic perfection.

Hannah let her gaze skim a few familiar faces, her smile genuinely warm as she moved forward. She was one of them, born into established old money, educated and groomed to become part of an élite social clique. Hell, she'd even married into it.

Graziella enveloped them warmly, then she placed an arm through one each of theirs and drew them towards the centre of the room.

'You know most everyone. Except some dear people I very much want you to meet. They are visiting from Europe this summer.'

Graziella and Enrico had friends in almost every city in the world, and frequently entertained guests in their home.

'Aimee Dalfour, and her niece, Camille,' Graziella indicated in introduction. 'Hannah and Miguel Santanas.'

Camille was tall, slender, and startlingly beautiful, with hair that cascaded way down past her shoulders in a fall of lustrous sable. Exquisitely applied make-up, flawless textured skin, and a body to die for. Add a designer gown and shoes, expensive jewellery, and the result was drop-dead gorgeous.

'Miguel,' Camille purred in a sultry accented drawl. *'C'est opportune.'* She extended her hand and silently dared him to take it, her dark eyes simmering with blatant challenge.

This woman was trouble, Hannah decided with a sinking heart. Camille's fascination with Miguel was glaringly obvious. Also apparent was her intention to charm.

Hannah unconsciously held her breath as instinct caused all her fine body hairs to rise in protective self-defence, watching as Miguel brushed his lips to the manicured fingers, then released them.

'Hannah,' Camille acknowledged with pseudo politeness, and returned her attention to Miguel.

'Enrico will get you a drink,' Graziella informed them, ever the benevolent hostess. 'What would you like?'

Hannah was tempted to request something exotic, but she hadn't eaten since midday and then only a yoghurt followed an hour later by an apple. Alcohol on an empty stomach was not conducive to a clear head.

'Thank you. Orange juice,' she requested, and glimpsed Camille's faint *moue* at her choice.

'You don't drink?' she queried in a tone that indicated not to imbibe was a social *faux pax*.

Hannah inclined her head. 'In this instance I'd prefer to wait and have wine with dinner.'

'You do not have the head for it?'

Hannah chose not to rise to the bait, and merely smiled.

Minutes later she sipped the cool liquid from a stemmed goblet, aware Camille excelled in her role as temptress.

Keep it up, Hannah warned silently, and I'll scratch your eyes out!

At that moment Miguel placed an arm along the

back of her waist. A gesture that didn't seem to have any effect at all.

The brush of beautifully lacquered nails as the Frenchwoman touched Miguel's sleeve. The deliberately seductive smile. The promise lurking beneath those impossibly long curled eyelashes.

Why, she was practically eating him alive!

Hannah decided enough was enough. She didn't have to stand here and *watch* Camille's blatant seduction.

'If you'll excuse me?' She offered Camille a stunning smile, let it drift to settle on her inimitable husband for a few seconds before she moved away a few paces to join her father-in-law.

'May I say you look beautiful tonight?' Esteban complimented lightly as he leaned forward and brushed his lips to her cheek.

'Thank you,' Hannah responded gently. 'It's a few weeks since you've been to the house. You must have dinner with us soon. We don't see enough of you.'

His smile was affectionately warm. *'Gracias.* But you know how it is?' He gave a light shrug, and she couldn't resist teasing him a little.

'A full social calendar,' she said gravely. 'And several women vying for your attention?'

'Ah, you flatter me.'

'No,' she assured him kindly. 'You're a very nice man, of whom I'm very fond.' And one any woman in her right mind would snap up in a minute. Except his late wife Isabella held a special place in his heart, and he had no desire to find a substitute.

A mutual acquaintance joined them, and after a few minutes she moved away.

'I think,' a light feminine voice suggested, 'you might need to sharpen your claws.'

Hannah turned towards Suzanne Trenton. 'Really? And use them on *whom*? Miguel?'

'*Camille*, darling. There are other methods a wife can use to tame her husband.'

It was meaningless repartee, spoken with jesting cynicism for the benefit of mutual amusement.

'Such as?' Hannah ventured, and Suzanne gave a soft laugh.

'Expensive jewellery.'

'Do enlighten me,' Miguel drawled as he threaded his fingers through those of his wife.

Hannah stood perfectly still for a few seconds, then she allowed her gaze to meet his. 'Pink and white diamonds,' she fabricated. 'A drop necklace and matching earrings.' A bewitching smile tilted the edge of her lips. 'They're quite beautiful.'

'Is this a wifely hint?' His mouth slanted into a humorous curve, at variance with the still watchfulness evident as he raked her features, noting the over-bright smile, her tense stance.

At that moment Graziella announced dinner was about to be served, and began directing guests towards the dining room.

'There was no need for you to desert me,' Miguel intoned mildly as they moved across the room.

'You appeared to be doing quite well on your own.'

'Careful, *querida*,' he drawled musingly. 'Your claws are showing.'

She gave him a winsome smile. 'Why, *amante*,' she offered with quiet emphasis, 'I haven't even begun to unsheathe them.'

If Graziella seated them close to Camille, she'd scream. The gods couldn't be that unkind, could they?

It appeared they could.

'I thought I'd place you opposite Camille,' Graziella remarked as she suggested prearranged seating arrangements. 'Hannah studied French and lived in Paris for more than a year,' she informed Camille graciously. 'As you're both in the fashion industry, you'll have much in common.'

Oh, my, this *was* going to be a fun evening!

CHAPTER TWO

'GRAZIELLA tells me you have a boutique on Toorak Road,' Camille began soon after they were seated. 'I must call in and check it out.'

'Please do,' Hannah said civilly, for what else could she say? Miguel was engaged in conversation with Peter Trenton, exploring the mores of legalese.

'Do you carry a range of accessories?'

A hired waitress began serving the first course, a delicate clear broth.

'A small selection of scarves, belts,' Hannah elaborated. 'Exclusive hosiery.'

Camille lifted an expressive eyebrow. 'Miguel has no objection?'

'To what, specifically?' she countered, reluctant to play Camille's game.

'Your little hobby.'

Considering the hours she worked, the responsibility to her clients, the sheer expertise required in running a successful business, the Frenchwoman's words were an insult...as they were meant to be.

Hannah summoned a sweet smile. 'He's relieved I have something constructive to do with my time.'

'Surely he would prefer you to be available for him?'

Hannah looked at the Frenchwoman, caught the avaricious gleam apparent, and opted for blatant honesty. 'On call to accommodate his slightest whim?'

Camille spread her hands expressively. 'Why... naturally, darling. If you don't, there are others who will oblige.'

'Such as you?' There was nothing like going direct for the jugular!

Camille appeared to choose her words with care. 'He's a very wealthy man, is he not?'

'And wealth is everything?'

Camille's smile didn't reach her eyes. 'It wields a power of its own.'

'A reciprocal power.' There was no need for pretence. It was no secret the Santanas-Martinez marriage had been conveniently arranged to legally combine two family fortunes.

'Power versus sexual attraction,' Camille pondered. 'Which would Miguel choose, do you think?'

Hannah held Camille's gaze, and discarded subtlety. 'I would say he already has.'

The other woman glanced at the wide baguette diamond wedding ring adorning Hannah's left hand. 'Most men will stray, given sufficient provocation.'

She wanted to dispute the words. Insist with total knowledge that Miguel was not *most men*, and his fidelity and loyalty to her were a given.

The soup plates were removed and a starter served. Hannah looked at the artistically displayed smoked salmon dribbled with a caper sauce nestling in a nest of finely cut salad, and felt her appetite diminish.

Tension curled inside her stomach, and she took a

sip of wine, then picked up her fork and attempted to do justice to the starter.

Miguel was an attractive man, possessed of a primitive masculinity that drew women like a magnet. There had been occasions when she'd been mildly amused by other women's attempts at coquetry, all too aware the flirtation was merely a harmless game.

Instinct warned her that Camille didn't fit into the *harmless* category, and that bothered her more than she cared to admit, for it raised questions to which she had no answers.

Could Miguel be tempted? Would he be sufficiently cavalier to indulge in an extra-marital affair? Somehow she didn't think so, but did she really *know*?

Theirs was a mutually convenient marriage that had *business* as its base. *Love* wasn't an issue…at least, not on Miguel's part. He cared for her, and she told herself it was enough.

One thing she was sure of—she wanted a relationship built on trust and loyalty. Not fabrication and empty excuses.

'Not hungry?'

Hannah turned towards her husband, met his steady gaze and glimpsed an indefinable quality in the depth of those dark eyes.

She summoned a light smile. 'Concern, Miguel?' His close proximity had a disturbing effect, for it made her aware of his exclusive brand of cologne meshing with freshly laundered cotton. His olive-toned skin was smooth, yet there was the hint of shadow despite the fact he'd only shaved an hour before.

'For you? Always.'

'Protecting your investment,' she ventured quietly, and caught the faintest glimmer of anger evident. So fleeting, she wondered if she'd imagined it.

'Of course,' he agreed silkily, and she tried to view the arrival of a superb paella with enthusiasm.

Camille seemed bent on engaging Miguel in conversation, and Hannah turned to the guest seated next to her and found herself caught up in an animated dissertation on the merits of boarding school education within Australia versus exclusive establishments overseas. Something which lasted until the paella was eaten, the plates removed, and a delicate seafood stew was served.

'Graziella mentioned you have an interest in the fashion scene,' Hannah ventured, in a bid to distract Camille's attention from Miguel.

'I model.'

Two words that supposedly said it all, Hannah reflected. 'Any particular fashion house?'

Camille proffered a haughty smile. 'Whoever offers the highest fee.'

'I was in Paris for the latest season's showing,' she mentioned conversationally, aware she hadn't seen Camille on the catwalks. Such striking looks wouldn't have escaped her notice, she was sure.

'I did Milan and Rome.' Camille lifted a hand and smoothed back a fall of hair in a gesture designed to focus attention on beautifully lacquered nails and her superb facial bone structure.

It had undoubtedly taken her hours to dress and perfect her make-up. Far removed from the nineteen minutes Hannah had allowed herself!

The main course comprised *pescado a la sal* served with a delicious salad, and she ate a small portion of the delicate fish flesh with contrived enjoyment.

'I believe we have a mutual friend,' Camille commented as Hannah finished the last of her salad.

It seemed possible, given their combined knowledge of the European fashion industry. 'I'm sure we have,' Hannah agreed as she lifted her goblet and took a sip of excellent white wine.

'Luc Dubois.' The name silvered the air, no less dramatic for its calculated delivery.

Hannah was conscious of a stillness at the table, as if all conversation had suddenly stopped...or was that just her imagination?

Her fingers tightened fractionally as she slowly set the goblet down onto the table. Miguel didn't move, but she could sense the flex of his body muscles beneath the expensive tailoring.

'Luc is not one of my friends,' she said quietly. 'He lost any claim to that distinction three years ago.'

The Frenchwoman arched an eyebrow in obvious disbelief. 'He particularly asked me to convey his regards.'

She could simply incline her head and retreat. Except such an action would play into Camille's hand, and there was something happening here that warned of a need for confrontation.

'I find that difficult to believe,' Hannah relayed evenly, aware that none of the guests spoke a word. 'We didn't part on good terms.'

'Really? He spoke of you in quite—' she paused deliberately, allowed her eyes to widen, and then appeared to choose her words '—glowingly graphic terms.'

This was a calculated attack, and Hannah felt incredibly angry that Camille had chosen the verbal strike in public. To what purpose?

'Luc was a European playboy who preyed on any woman who could fund his expensive lifestyle,' Hannah relayed with a calm she didn't feel. 'I walked out on him as soon as I discovered he was a superficial leech.' She lifted her shoulders in a light dismissive shrug. 'End of story. The press made much of it at the time.' She even summoned a faint smile, albeit that it held a degree of cynicism. 'The Australian heiress and the French photographer.'

She held Camille's gaze. 'If you want all the details, I'm sure you could look it up in any of the media archives.' So be damned, she concluded silently. It was old news, past news, and her only regret was that she'd been very cleverly fooled by a practised master of deceit.

'Oh, dear,' Camille declared with a stab at contrition. 'I am so sorry. I didn't realise...' She trailed to a halt.

No, you're not, Hannah thought, and yes, you already knew. You just wanted to create an awkward situation.

Miguel covered Hannah's hand with his own, then he leaned towards her and brushed his lips to her temple. *'Brava.'*

His action deflated the air of tension, and within seconds everyone began talking at once.

Dessert was served, and Hannah forced herself to do justice to the *tocino de cielo*, a rich custard. She sipped excellent vintage wine, conversed with fellow guests, and gave every pretence of having a wonderful time.

She laughed at humorous anecdotes, commiserated with the Trentons at the difficulty of getting their two-month-old daughter enrolled into an élite private school, and attempted to ignore Camille's frequent slip in resorting to evocatively delivered French. Did the Frenchwoman imagine no one else understood? Or perhaps she didn't care if they did.

Miguel was fluent in French and Italian, as well as his native Spanish. Hannah had the advantage of the former two, but, even if she'd had no knowledge of the spoken word, the cadence of Camille's voice and its provocative delivery left little doubt Miguel was her target.

To his credit, Miguel did nothing to encourage the attention. But after almost three hours of observing the coveted glances, the blatant verbal seduction, Hannah was tiring of the pretence.

Smiling, when all she wanted to do was render Camille some form of injury. Her jaw *ached* from it, and her palms itched with the need to slap the Frenchwoman's face.

Coffee was served in the lounge, and she didn't know whether to laugh or cry with frustrated irritation when Camille wandered over to join them.

Dear heaven, the woman was persistent!

'It would be so—' Camille paused fractionally '—pleasant,' she stated, 'if you were to include me as a guest, socially.' She gave an expressive smile. 'My aunt, her friends...' She trailed off, and her slender shoulders lifted in a typical Gallic gesture. 'We have different interests, *comprendez-vous*?'

Hardly surprising, considering Camille's sole interest appeared to be Miguel!

'How long will you be staying?' Hannah asked, hoping the visit would be extremely short!

The Frenchwoman lifted an expressive hand, then let it fall. 'I have no immediate plans. A few weeks, several. Who is to say?'

'I am sure Graziella has made arrangements to entertain you,' Miguel drawled, and received a sultry smile.

'One must hope you are also included in such...' she trailed deliberately '...arrangements.'

Not if I can help it, Hannah decided as she endeavoured to subdue her anger.

Miguel took Hannah's empty cup and placed it with his own onto a nearby side-table. His expression was polite as he caught hold of his wife's hand and inclined his head towards Camille.

'If you'll excuse us?'

'You are leaving? It is so early,' the Frenchwoman protested.

'Goodnight,' Miguel bade smoothly, only to discover Camille didn't give up easily.

'You must both be my guests at dinner. Together with Graziella and Enrico, my aunt.' She paused, and offered a sweet smile. 'Miguel, you must bring Esteban.' She cast Miguel a deliberately seductive look. 'We shall make a date, yes?'

'We'll check our social diary and get back to you,' Hannah intimated smoothly, aware this was one engagement she had no intention of keeping.

Camille's expression didn't change, but Hannah glimpsed a brief malevolent gleam in those dark eyes, and felt the beginnings of unease.

Cynical bantering on occasion was part of the game a number of people played, for it formed amusing repartee. But instinct warned Hannah the Frenchwoman played by no one's rules but her own.

'Nothing to say, *querida*?' Miguel drawled as he eased the Jaguar out from the driveway.

She turned towards him, saw the beam of oncoming headlights cast angles and planes to his strong-boned features, and endeavoured to inject amusement into her tone.

'You expect me to *condone* Camille's blatant behaviour?'

'I could almost imagine you are jealous.'

He was amused, damn him!

'Am I supposed to answer that?' she demanded coolly.

He spared her a quick glance, caught the fiery blue glare aimed in his direction, then returned his attention to the road.

'It might be interesting to hear you try,' he declared indolently, and she burst into angry speech.

'What would you have me say?' Her fingers clenched over the clasp of her evening purse. 'That I objected to the way Camille monopolised your attention? *And* flirted outrageously.' She drew in a deep breath and expelled it slowly. 'Dammit, she has designs on you! Anyone would have had to be *blind* not to notice it!'

'Should I be flattered?'

'Are you?' She held her breath waiting for his reply.

'No,' Miguel declared with unruffled ease.

'Hold that thought,' Hannah said darkly.

'Why, *amante*?' he teased mercilessly as he gained the main street. 'What would you do if I succumbed to her charms?'

'Commit grievous bodily harm.' And die a little, she added silently. 'Then divorce you.'

He cast her a sombre glance. 'Extreme measures.'

'What would you do if I showed an interest in another man?' Hannah retorted, unable to resist taunting, 'Turn the cheek and look the other way?'

'I'd kill you.' His voice held a dangerous softness that sent shivers feathering a path down her spine.

'Wonderful,' she remarked facetiously. 'A few

hours in Camille's company, and we're not only arguing, we're threatening divorce and murder.'

The Frenchwoman was a witch, Miguel acknowledged grimly, and, unless he was mistaken, a very dangerous one.

'While we're on this particular subject,' Hannah continued, 'what importance do you place on Camille's deliberate mention of my *bête noir*?'

'Luc Dubois?'

'That's the one,' she conceded.

'Do you still retain an interest in him?'

'No,' Hannah declared vehemently. Even now she found it difficult to accept the Frenchman had penetrated her guard. *She*, who could tag a man's superficial charm in an instant, aware his main interest was her family's wealth, not *her*. Except Luc had been incredibly patient, known which buttons to push, and when. She'd fallen into his arms like a peach ripe for the picking.

'So sure, Hannah?' Miguel pursued silkily.

How could he ask that, when Luc didn't even begin to compare with the man who was now her husband?

'Yes.' She turned towards him. 'You have my word.'

'*Gracias.*'

'Such is the recipe for a happy marriage.'

'Cynicism doesn't suit you, *mi mujer*,' Miguel drawled.

'Ah, but I love this honesty we share. It is *très bonne*, don't you agree?'

'I can think of a more apt description.'

It didn't take long to reach their tree-lined street and traverse the driveway. Minutes later she followed Miguel indoors.

'Get the credit slips from your briefcase,' he instructed as they reached the foyer. At her puzzled look, he elaborated, 'The client who ran up debt all over town. I'll take care of it.'

'No, you won't,' she said emphatically. 'I can do it myself.'

'Why?' he queried steadily. 'When I can do it so much more easily?'

She flung him a baleful glare. 'Because I'm independent.'

'And stubborn,' Miguel added.

'No,' she disagreed. 'Self-sufficient.'

'Tenacious.'

'That, too,' she admitted, then allowed, 'If I have a problem, I promise I'll call on you.'

It would have to suffice, Miguel conceded. 'Are we going to stand here bandying words, or do we go to bed?'

She felt inclined to deny him. To turn her back and ascend the stairs alone. Yet to deny him was to deny herself. And she needed the reassurance of his touch, the possession of her body. To feel, in the darkness of the night, that she meant more to him than just part of his life as a convenient wife. To pretend for a while that the marriage was real, and what they shared was special, not just very good sex.

'Oh, *bed*,' she agreed. 'Definitely.'

'Minx,' he declared. 'What if I'm tired?'

'Are you?' she asked seriously, then wrinkled her nose at him. 'I wouldn't think of overtaxing your strength.'

He laughed, and the sound curled round her nerve-ends as he caught hold of her hand and led her upstairs. 'Let's see who cries *wolf* first, shall we?'

This, Hannah breathed shakily minutes later as Miguel slid the zip fastening free from her gown, was like entering a sensual heaven. He had the touch, the knowledge, the skill, to divine a woman's needs.

And fulfil them, she added with a silent gasp as the gown slid in a silken heap to the floor. The light brush of his fingertips trailed an evocative path over sensitised skin as he eased the silken briefs down over her thighs.

She stepped free of them and at the same time discarded the heeled shoes that added four inches to her height.

He was wearing too many clothes, and she pushed his jacket from his shoulders, tugged at his tie, then freed shirt buttons with restless speed.

His lips settled at the sensitive hollow at the edge of her neck, and sensation arrowed through her body as he used his tongue and his teeth to tease a tantalising kiss that had her arching towards him.

His shirt fell onto the carpet, and her fingers feverishly attacked the buckle on his belt, then tended to the zip on his trousers.

Miguel's contribution to shucking his clothes was to step out of his shoes and pull off his socks.

She reached for his briefs, and slid them free, awed

by the state of his arousal. It fascinated her that such a part of man's anatomy could drive a woman wild, and provide such pleasure.

Unbidden, she drew the pads of her fingers lightly over its silken length, caressing with a sense of captive thrall.

'*Amada,*' Miguel growled softly. 'If you don't want to be tossed down onto the bed and possessed without delay, I suggest you stop that *now.*'

She lifted her head and offered him an infinitely sweet smile. 'Why?'

He uttered a faint groan. '*Madre de Dios.*' The words left his lips in a ragged supplication as he dragged her close.

His mouth covered hers in a kiss that drugged her senses and tore at the very fabric of her soul.

Control, she had none. There were only the man, the moment, and an intensity of emotions so overwhelming she simply held on and joined him as he took her to the heights and beyond before free-falling down to a state of exotic warmth and satiation.

Her body felt like a finely tuned instrument that had been played by a virtuoso. Exultant, still clinging to the sweet sorcery of a master's exquisite touch.

She loved the feel of him, his sheer strength and passion, tempered by a control she sorely wanted to break. What would it be like to experience his unbridled lovemaking? To crash through the barriers of restraint and be taken with a raw primitive hunger that knew no bounds?

Dear Lord. Just thinking about it sent renewed heat

racing through her veins and had her moving restlessly against him.

His lips brushed her temple, almost as if he were attuned to the depths of her innermost needs, and his arms tightened as she found his mouth with her own.

This time it was she who nurtured his desire and sent it spiralling towards hungry passion in a mesmeric coupling that left them both slick with sensual sweat and fighting to regain a steady breath.

'Witch,' Miguel teased huskily as he buried his lips against her breast.

'Hmm,' Hannah murmured with bemused contentment, only to give a tiny gasp as he began teasing the tender peak, alternately with his tongue and the edge of his teeth, taking her to the brink between pleasure and pain.

Then with one fluid movement he slid from the bed, scooped her into his arms, carried her into the *en suite* and stepped into the large shower stall.

Seconds later warm water cascaded from four strategically positioned shower-heads, and Hannah slid to her feet as Miguel reached for the soap.

Evocatively sensual, they lingered for a while, then Miguel closed the water dial, snagged two towels, and once dry, they returned to bed to sleep.

Except after the first few hours Hannah was plagued by dreams that had her tossing restlessly until dawn, followed by a deep fitful sleep as light began filtering through the curtains.

She was unaware of the soothing touch of the man

who lay beside her, or that he curled her body close in to his more than once through the night.

Nor was she aware that he woke early, and propped himself comfortably on his side to watch her sleep.

She had delicate features, and the softest, silkiest skin of any woman he'd had the pleasure to touch, he mused gently. The tousled length of her hair lent an abandoned look, and her lashes were long, curling upwards at the ends. The mouth was lush, the lips softly curved in sleep. Capable hands, slender, displaying the band of diamonds and splendid pear-shaped solitaire that claimed her as his own.

She bore an air of fragility that was deceptive, for she possessed an inner strength, an innate honesty that decried artifice or deceit.

He would have liked to rouse her into wakefulness, to feather light kisses over every inch of her skin until she reached for him, then make long, slow love.

The generosity of her response never failed to move him, physically, mentally, emotionally.

Miguel felt his senses stir, and knew if he remained in bed she wouldn't sleep much longer. With a husky groan he rolled over and slid to his feet, then he walked naked into the *en suite* and stood beneath the shower.

CHAPTER THREE

HANNAH woke late, took one look at the digital clock and raced to the shower, then she dressed and applied basic make-up in record time before running lightly downstairs.

Miguel was in the process of draining the last of his coffee when she entered the kitchen, and heat flared through her veins at the mere sight of him.

It was as if she could still feel his touch, the masculine heat of his possession, the passion...

Dear heaven, she cursed shakily. This was postcoital awareness at its most provocative!

He looked at her and glimpsed the faint tremor that shook her lush mouth. Did she have any conception of her beauty? Something that went far beyond the visual, to the depths of her soul. At this precise moment she was remarkably transparent, and it moved him almost beyond measure.

He watched as she collected a glass and poured herself some fresh orange juice, then she plucked a slice of toast from the rack and spread it with marmalade.

'Why didn't you wake me?' Hannah queried in the quest for normality. She took a bite of the toast and followed it down with black sweet coffee.

He looked every inch the corporate executive, his

tailoring impeccable, a dark silk tie resting against a pristine white shirt.

'I reset the alarm,' Miguel relayed imperturbably, and checked his watch. 'Timed to go off around now.' He cast her a quizzical glance. 'Why don't you sit down?'

Hannah shook her head. 'No time.'

Dammit, he looked good. She wanted to slide her fingers through his hair, lower her head down to his, and kiss him until they both had to pause for breath.

Dangerous thoughts, she perceived as she took a long swallow of coffee. If she gave in to them, she'd be even later for work, and that would never do!

Instead, she finished the toast, downed the last of her coffee, then she extracted a banana and an apple from a silver fruit bowl, caught up her car keys and followed him through to the garage.

Miguel unlocked the door, and regarded her steadily over the top of the Jaguar. 'A restless night, no breakfast to speak of, and food on the run isn't an ideal way to start the day.'

She effected a light shrug. 'So I'll grab coffee and something to eat later.'

He wanted to wring her slender neck. 'See that you do.' He pulled open the door and slid in behind the wheel.

'Yes-sir.'

He shot her a dark speaking glance, freed the electronic garage mechanism, then he fired the engine and eased the car towards the gates.

Hannah's soft curse feathered the air accompanied

by an exasperated sigh. Work beckoned, and there was no time to dally if she was to open the boutique on time.

Seconds later she exited the driveway and headed towards Toorak Road, her mood reflective as she bore with morning peak traffic.

It would have been nice to have woken in Miguel's arms, stirred by his touch, enticed into sex by his passion in an early-morning ritual. She missed the shimmering sensual heat, the electrifying hunger followed by a languid after-play, for it was then they talked awhile before sharing a leisurely shower.

Camille's features sprang all too readily to mind, intrusive and vaguely taunting.

The power of pre-emptive thought? Hannah pondered as she dispelled the Frenchwoman from her mind and focused on the day ahead.

The courier service was scheduled to deliver some new stock this morning, and she mentally selected a stunning ensemble as window display, its accessories, and the rearrangement and placement of existing stock.

By the time she unlocked the boutique Camille temporarily ceased to exist.

Twice during the next hour her hand hovered over the phone. She badly needed to hear Miguel's voice, if only to say 'hi'. Discussing what lay ahead in their respective days had become an early-morning habit. Dammit, she'd ring and ask him to meet her for lunch. Cindy could manage the boutique for an hour, longer if necessary.

Without hesitation she keyed in the digits for his mobile phone, only to have the call go to voice-mail. She left her name and invitation, then busied herself with routine chores.

Cindy, a friend with a flair for fashion who welcomed part-time work while her daughter was in school, arrived at ten, closely followed by the courier.

Unpacking, checking invoices and preparing stock for display took time, and there were the serious clients who came to buy and not-so-serious passers-by who merely wanted to browse.

Then there were the phone calls, none of which was Miguel. Until eleven-thirty, when Hannah had all but given up on him.

'It's *the man*,' Cindy indicated as she extended the cordless handset.

Hannah moved a few paces away. 'I thought we might do lunch.' She drew a slight breath, then released it. 'I can get away any time between now and two.'

'I'm tied up with meetings all afternoon,' Miguel drawled. 'Can it wait until tonight?'

He sounded mildly amused, almost as if he sensed the reason behind her call. 'Of course.'

'*Hasta luego, querida,*' he bade indolently, and cut the line.

'Will you finish doing the window, or shall I?' Cindy queried seconds later, and Hannah gestured towards the clothed mannequin.

'Be my guest.' A cleverly draped scarf, an elegant brooch would add the final touches, together with heeled shoes and matching handbag. Something that would take only minutes to complete.

The end result was stunning, and Hannah was quick to add her compliment. 'Why don't you take a break for lunch?' she suggested, checking her watch. 'I can manage for a while.'

Most of the regular clientele chose to do their shopping mid-morning or mid-afternoon. For the most part, the time between midday and two was spent lunching at any one of several trendy cafés or restaurants in and around the city and its élite suburbs.

Cindy collected her bag and made for the door.

'See you soon.'

Hannah crossed to the CD player, removed the morning selection and inserted sufficient discs to provide soothing unobtrusive background music until closing time.

The electronic buzzer heralded the arrival of a prospective client, and Hannah turned with a welcome smile in place, only to have it momentarily freeze as she caught sight of Camille.

Tall, proportionately slender, the Frenchwoman exuded confidence and a degree of arrogance as she stepped forward. Dressed in designer clothes and wearing expensive perfume, she was elegance personified.

'*Bonjour*, Hannah.' She inclined a perfectly coiffed head, and scanned the carefully arranged racks.

'I thought I might visit.'

Somehow Hannah doubted *clothes* were Camille's main purpose. 'How nice of you to call in.' At what point did politeness cross the line and become a white lie? She indicated a rack of imported designer labels. 'Is there anything in particular I can help you with?' She crossed the floor and extracted a gown that would look stunning on Camille's tall frame.

'Darling, I can get that in Paris.' Her mouth pursed, and her eyes assumed a hardened gleam as she riffled through carefully spaced hangers with total disregard for their existing presentation.

Hannah watched as the Frenchwoman pulled out a hanger, examined the garment with disdainful criticism, then returned it carelessly back onto the rack before moving a pace or two and repeating the process.

There was little doubt as to the deliberateness of the action, and Hannah wondered just how long it would take for Camille to cut to the chase.

Exhausting garments displayed on one side of the boutique, the Frenchwoman crossed the floor and began a similar examination of various silk shirts.

'How does it feel being manipulated into a loveless marriage?'

Four minutes, give or take a few seconds, Hannah calculated. If Camille wanted to conduct a verbal altercation, then so be it. She met the woman's hard stare, and arched a delicate eyebrow. 'Manipulated by whom?'

Camille's gaze narrowed. 'It doesn't bother you Miguel's motivation was born out of *duty*? To his father, and the Sanmar conglomerate?'

Hannah took time to ponder the Frenchwoman's

words. 'For someone who has only been in Melbourne a short time, you seem to have acquired considerable information.'

'Graziella is very discreet. However, my interest in Miguel was captured several weeks ago at a party in Rome,' Camille enlightened with a secretive smile. 'Miguel attended briefly with a business associate.'

Hannah had instant recall. She'd flown in to buy new season's stock, tying the visit in with one of Miguel's Italian business meetings. She even remembered the evening in question, and a wretched migraine that had seen her creep into bed while issuing instructions for Miguel to go on to the party without her.

'I made it my business to discover everything about Miguel Santanas,' Camille continued relentlessly. 'His marriage, his wife, her background.'

This was far more complex than idle curiosity. Almost chilling, Hannah realised silently.

'And your affair with Luc Dubois,' the Frenchwoman revealed, intent on analysing Hannah's expressive features. 'Interesting man.'

Interesting didn't come close. The man was a practised rogue, and it still irked that it had taken her a few months to lose the fantasy and face reality.

'I imagine this is leading somewhere?' Hannah queried coolly.

'Of course, darling. You're hardly naive.'

It didn't take much imagination for it all to fall into place. 'Let me guess,' she began pensively. 'You came here purposely with your aunt, who conveniently happens to be a good friend of the del Santos, aware of their social standing and the opportunity to use them to include you in numerous invitations around the city. Thus ensuring regular social contact with Miguel.'

A tinkling laugh escaped Camille's lips. 'How clever of you, *chérie*. Naturally, the Australian visit was my suggestion.'

Hannah's eyes assumed a fiery sparkle. 'Do we draw battle lines?'

'As long as you understand Miguel is mine.' Camille's smile was entirely lacking in humour.

'Really?' Hannah posed with deliberate sarcasm. 'Aren't you forgetting I have an advantage or two?'

'Miguel might view you as an obligation,' the Frenchwoman relayed with pitiless asperity, 'but, darling, I intend to be his titillation.'

The peal of the telephone came as a welcome interruption, and Hannah crossed to take the call, aware as she did so that the Frenchwoman had turned towards the door. Within seconds she had departed, and Hannah gathered her wits together, answering a client's query, then, when she was done, she set to restoring order to the racks Camille had deliberately disorganised.

Tension knotted her stomach. It was worse, much worse than she'd envisaged. How would Miguel react if she told him? Be amused, probably. But what would lie beneath the humour? Male satisfaction? The thrill of the chase, the challenge? More pertinently, would he indulge in an extra-marital affair?

Dear God, she hoped not. Even the thought that he might almost destroyed her.

The peal of the telephone interrupted her reflection, and she took the call, attended to a client who bought a skirt, two blouses, a beautiful silk scarf, and on Cindy's return she collected her bag and crossed the street to lunch in a trendy café.

Hannah ordered a latte and a salad bagel, sipped the first and picked at the second, only to discard it entirely and order another latte.

Usually she took only sufficient time to eat before returning to the boutique, but today she chose to browse a few shops and view exquisite antique jewellery. A pair of earrings caught her eye, and she entered the shop, tried them on, then bought them in a moment of impulse.

It was almost two when she re-entered the boutique, four when Cindy left for the day, and at five-fifteen she locked up and drove home.

As hard as she tried, it was impossible to dismiss Camille from her mind. What she'd first thought was a transitory game had now proven to hold premeditated intent. Dealing with it could be akin to walking through a minefield.

One thing for sure…Miguel was *hers*. And she intended to fight for him, her marriage, her life, she determined as she garaged the car and made her way into the house.

Sofia was in the kitchen preparing dinner, and Hannah greeted her fondly as she crossed to the refrigerator.

'There are messages for you, and two for the *señor*,' the housekeeper informed her as she wielded a chopping knife with considerable dexterity. 'I put them in the *señor*'s study.'

Hannah extracted a bottle of chilled water and poured some into a glass. 'Thanks. I'll go check them in a minute.' A piquant aroma teased her nostrils. 'Mmm,' she murmured appreciatively. 'Something smells delicious.'

'Seafood,' Sofia enlightened. 'Served with a mixed salad.'

She lifted the glass to her lips and took a long swallow, then moved to the cook-top and lifted the lid on the gently simmering saucepan. The temptation to retrieve a steaming mussel was too great, and she quickly passed the hot shell from one hand to the other as she tore it apart and extracted the succulent flesh.

'You want? I pull some out and put on a plate,' Sofia determined, and Hannah shook her head.

'No, I'll save it for dinner.' Her stomach growled in protest of insufficient sustenance. 'I'll go shower and change. Is Miguel home?'

'The *señor* ring an hour ago. Delayed. I serve dinner at seven. Okay?'

Hannah savoured the mussel flesh, and followed it with yet another glass of water. Maybe she'd go swim a few lengths in the pool first. She had time, and she felt strangely restless with a need to expend some nervous energy.

It took only minutes to reach her bedroom, and a

few more to discard her clothes and don an aqua bikini. Then she caught up a beach towel from the linen closet, quickly retraced her steps and made her way through the wide set of French doors at the rear of the house to the tiled pool area.

Heaven, she breathed a short while later as she cleaved sure strokes through the cool salt-chlorinated water.

She didn't allow herself to think, only focused on the silky feel of the water against her skin, the weightlessness of her body and the measured movement of her arms and legs.

It was so quiet, with no neighbourhood noise to disturb the air. High walls, with tall trees lining the boundaries, lent a secluded atmosphere, making it difficult to believe a large cosmopolitan city hummed with vibrant life mere kilometres away.

She could be anywhere, she mused, intent for a few seconds imagining a place far removed from here, where there were no phones, no social obligations, no distractions. Just her, with Miguel. Lazing in the sun, relaxing. Making love, eating when they felt the need for food, and sleeping when everything else palled.

Except that was a fantasy. Reality was a hurried break in between scheduled meetings…whether it was Paris, Rome, Madrid or Frankfurt. A snatched day here and there, always within reach of a mobile phone and an important call that inevitably broke the spell.

It was life in the fast lane. The need to make and close the next deal. To build and expand, to consolidate and venture into new fields. Always a step ahead of the competitors.

Like a merry-go-round that kept moving, once you were on it was hard to get off.

Maybe she could persuade Miguel to fit a holiday into his schedule. Hawaii. All that sun, surf and sand, where the pace was slower, and the outer islands offered a relaxed, carefree lifestyle.

Hannah didn't hear the faint splash as Miguel dived cleanly into the pool, and it was only when his head broke the surface close by that she became aware she was no longer alone.

She turned towards him and trod water as he reached her side. 'Hi. You're home early.'

Miguel paused to sweep water from his face and smooth both hands over his head, leaving his hair a sleek ebony. 'Impossible, of course, that I might want to be with my wife?'

Hannah tilted her head to one side and cast him a considering look. 'Hmm, maybe.'

'*Gracias, amada,*' he teased lightly. 'For the vote of confidence.' He moved close and cradled her hips, then eased both hands beneath the thin fabric to cup her bottom.

A delicious shiver feathered the length of her spine, and her body arched into his of its own accord, exulting in the touch of hair-roughened thighs against her smooth skin.

Her hands instinctively linked together at his nape, and she angled her mouth as his slanted to capture hers in a sensual tasting that began slowly, sweetly, then began to build into something that became an evocative preliminary to the promise of passion.

She wanted more, much more than this as the slide of his hands wreaked havoc in seeking sensitised pleasure pulses, and a faint groan sighed in her throat at the prospect of what he intended to do.

But not here. She possessed few inhibitions, but making love in the pool in daylight when there was every possibility Sofia might happen into view did much to kill her spontaneity.

Had they been completely alone... Slowly Hannah broke the kiss, and regretfully unwound her hands from his neck. 'Dinner will be ready soon, and we both need to shower and dress.'

Miguel let her go, his eyes dark with lambent emotion. 'I guess we could indulge in a leisurely shower.'

It was her turn to tease. 'Be late for dinner, and ruin Sofia's paella?'

He pressed a quick hard kiss to her parted lips.

'It will keep, *querida*.' And the promise, the erotic wait would present a slow torture...for both of them. Afterwards, she would weep for the release, and cry from the mutual joy of it.

She completed a few side-strokes and reached the tiled ledge, then she pulled herself over it to stand in one lithe movement, aware Miguel mirrored her actions.

In unison they each caught up a towel, removed the excess moisture, then hitched it securely and made their way indoors.

Halfway up the stairs Miguel hoisted her slender

frame over one shoulder and carried her the rest of the way.

'Caveman tactics?' Hannah queried to the broad expanse of his back, and felt rather than heard his faint rumble of laughter.

'You object?'

She clung onto his shoulders, felt the shift and play of powerful muscles as he moved towards the bedroom.

'Would it make any difference?'

Miguel entered their suite, closed the door, then lowered her down to stand in front of him. 'You don't want to play?'

Hannah looked at him carefully, saw the sensual curve of his mouth and glimpsed the darkness in his eyes.

'Yes,' she answered simply, and tried not to wish with all her heart that it was *her* he needed, not just the woman who bore his name.

He made lovemaking an art form, and she told herself she didn't care. It was enough he could make her feel like this. Enough that together they created a sexual magic that transmuted sheer sensation and became exquisite ecstasy.

Desire flared…wild, mesmeric and primitive as instinct met with hunger, and ravaged them both.

Afterwards they showered, then dressed in casual clothes before making their way downstairs, choosing to collect the delectable paella and eat on the patio adjoining the pool.

Occasionally they paused to tempt each other with

a forkful of food, and they sipped a fine white wine, ate crusty bread, and watched the summer sun slowly sink over the horizon.

They took time to discuss the day, and Hannah deliberately made no mention of Camille. Somehow it seemed almost a sacrilege to spoil the moment, and the night.

Outdoor lights provided a soft glow, illuminating the gardens, throwing long shadows from surrounding shrubbery. Moths fluttered around the electric lamps, fascinated by the brightness.

It was a while before they silently collected plates, glassware and cutlery and returned them to the kitchen.

'Tired?'

'A little,' she answered honestly as he mobilised the alarm system.

He held out his hand and she curled her fingers within his as they ascended the stairs. In the bedroom he removed her clothes, then his own, drawing her down onto the bed before gathering her close into the curve of his body.

She succumbed to sleep within minutes, and Miguel lay staring with brooding reflectiveness into the darkness, all too aware of the rhythmic beat of her heart beneath the palm of his hand, the faint muskiness of her feminine scent, the clean, fresh fragrance of her hair as her head nestled close in against the curve of his shoulder.

She moved, snuggling closer, and the hand that rested at the edge of his waist slipped down to his hip. She slept, for her breathing pattern remained unchanged.

He shifted his head slightly to brush his lips to the edge of her forehead and a faint smile softened his mouth as a soft sound sighed from her lips.

Independent, strong, individualistic, he mused as he courted sleep. A generous and passionate lover who matched him with an equal hunger of her own.

His.

CHAPTER FOUR

THE day began badly with a phone call from Cindy's mother to say Cindy had been rushed into hospital for an emergency appendectomy and wouldn't be able to return to work for at least a week.

Hannah felt genuinely upset, for Cindy was a friend as well as someone who worked part-time in the boutique, and she organised flowers to be sent to the hospital, made plans to visit after work, then began ringing the first of two women who made themselves available to work when required.

The first was overseas, the second had a family emergency, and her only recourse was an employment agency. Failing any success there, she could call on her mother, if only to fill in for an hour around midday.

Breakfast was a non-event, with only time to swallow half a glass of orange juice and follow it with a few sips of coffee.

'*Por Dios,*' Miguel swore swiftly as she caught up her bag and slid the strap over one shoulder. '*Sit.*'

He reached out, closed his hand over her arm, and forced her into a nearby chair. 'Eat.' He pushed a plate towards her, split a croissant and spread conserve onto each half.

She threw him a wry look. 'I can't. I'll be late.'

'So be late,' he suggested evenly. 'Five minutes is all it will take. You could easily be caught up in traffic that long.'

'I'm not a child, dammit.'

'You're wasting time,' Miguel said imperturbably.

She *was* hungry, and failing finding someone to fill in, or if Renee wasn't available, she'd have to temporarily close the boutique for the ten minutes it would take to go fetch a sandwich.

Stubborn single-mindedness forbade that she actually *sat*, but she did eat both pieces of the croissant and followed it down with the rest of the fine, hot, sweet coffee.

'Satisfied?'

He cast her a brooding glance. 'No.'

She gathered up her car keys. 'You, of course, rarely suffer emergencies that toss your schedule out the window.'

'Occasionally,' Miguel conceded.

'Don't tell me—you always have a back-up plan,' she responded drily.

'A few minutes ago you couldn't wait to leave,' he drawled, arching an eyebrow. 'Now you want to argue?'

'Why, when I never win?' Hannah flung with exasperation, and threw him a startled glance as he moved swiftly to cup her face.

He angled her mouth to meet his in an evocative kiss that tore at her emotions and made her wish she could take the time to deepen and savour it. Then she was free.

She could only look at him, her eyes wide and unblinking. Just when she thought she could predict how he'd react, he managed to surprise her.

She unconsciously moistened her lips, aware her mouth shook slightly, and saw his eyes flare briefly.

'Go, *querida*. I'll call you through the day.' Hannah turned away from him and moved quickly through the foyer to the garage.

Could the day get any worse? she queried silently as she put a call through to her mother, only to discover Renee was *en route* to the airport to catch a scheduled flight to Sydney.

'I'll be back tonight, darling. Tomorrow is fine, if you need me. I'll ring when I get in.'

Within minutes of opening the boutique she rang the first of two agencies on her list, and felt immeasurably relieved to discover half an hour later they had a suitable salesgirl available to report for work the next day.

Hannah was kept busy all morning as several clients came by to examine the latest delivery of new stock. Telephoned requests to put some items aside for a few hours meant the boutique wasn't empty for long.

At midday she affixed a 'back in ten minutes' sign on the door, locked up and quickly crossed the street to a nearby café. A salad sandwich with coffee to take away would assuage her hunger, and with luck she might even get to eat it without any interruption.

'Hannah.'

The sultry accent caused the hairs to rise on the

back of her neck. *Tell me I'm wrong*, she pleaded silently, only to turn and discover Camille seated at a nearby table.

The Frenchwoman's presence *here* seemed too co-incidental. Another of Camille's ploys to draw attention to her knowledge of Hannah's daily routine?

'Camille,' Hannah acknowledged with forced civility as she stood waiting for her order to be filled.

'Why don't you join me?'

Not if I can help it. 'I have to get back. Perhaps some other time?' An empty suggestion she had no intention of fulfilling.

'I'll call in later.'

Hannah barely resisted the temptation to say *please don't* as the girl behind the counter handed over a capped take-away cup and a plastic container with her sandwich.

'Bye, Camille.' The words were merely a courtesy as she turned towards the door. She didn't want to play *friend* with the stunning Frenchwoman. If she had a choice, she'd prefer not to have anything to do with her at all! However, the chances of that were slim, given Camille's determination.

The phone was ringing when she unlocked the boutique and she hurried forward to answer it. Within minutes of replacing the receiver, it pealed again.

'I've been gifted tickets to a film premiere tonight,' Miguel began without preamble. He named the title and the venue. 'I'll be home at six.'

'*Gracias*,' Hannah declared, and his husky laughter was almost her undoing.

'Take care, *querida*. Don't work too hard.'

Fat chance, Hannah thought as she juggled attending to clients and phone calls in between snatching a bite to eat.

There was satisfaction in selecting beautifully crafted garments to suit a certain occasion for a favoured client. Offering suggestions for footwear, accessories, even jewellery, was something she viewed as an art form. The client's pleasure and continued loyalty was her reward. So much so that when she bought she did so with specific clients in mind.

It wasn't just a job. It never had been. Hannah doubted it ever would be. The prospect of selling the boutique, or retiring and letting a *vendeuse* manage it, hadn't occurred to her. Although there would probably come a time when she considered children. Having a child was an important issue in their marriage, given the main reason for the union was to legally ensure two united family fortunes continued into another generation.

However, *when* this should happen hadn't consciously been decided. Miguel had agreed to her suggestion they wait a year or two, and she had considered maybe thirty might be a good age to discard contraception.

Why was she suddenly given to thinking like this? Because Camille posed a threat?

Dammit, you didn't have a child to use as a bargaining tool, much less a weapon!

The electronic buzzer dispersed her train of

thought, and she endeavoured to keep her smile in place as she recognised Camille.

Talk of the devil!

'I enjoyed a long lunch, then spent an hour or two browsing the boutiques,' Camille informed her as she crossed to where several silk shirts were displayed.

'I caught sight of something here yesterday that I thought I should have.' She slid hangers every which way and a slight frown creased her brow. 'Perhaps you've put it aside?' She described the shirt, named the label, the size, then looked askance at Hannah as if she might conjure it up out of thin air.

'I sold it yesterday afternoon.'

'Order one in for me.'

It was a command, not a request, and Hannah held her breath for a few seconds before slowly releasing it. 'I can try,' she said evenly. 'However, everything here is limited edition stock.'

Camille gave her a long considering look. 'Make the call. I want it.'

Hannah viewed her carefully, then threw politeness out the window. 'You can't always have what you want.'

There was no mistaking her meaning.

The Frenchwoman examined her perfectly manicured nails, then seared Hannah with a vindictive glare.

'You're wrong, *chérie*. I *always* get what I want.'

'Really?' Her cynicism was marked. 'Maybe it's time you didn't.'

Camille resembled a hissing cat about to strike. 'So you intend to fight?'

This could rapidly digress into something feral. 'I won't gift-wrap Miguel and hand him to you on a platter.'

'Why, *chérie*. I don't need for you to gift me anything. I reach out and take what I want.'

She could feel her fingers curling in against each palm, and it was all she could do to stay calm. 'Even if it doesn't belong to you?'

'The fact it doesn't belong to me merely adds to the attraction. Marriage? What is it?' Camille emphasised the point with a Gallic shrug. 'Merely a piece of paper.'

'Try sacred vows citing fidelity, trust and honour,' Hannah cited, and heard the Frenchwoman's pitying laughter.

'Poor *enfant*,' Camille chided. 'So naive and caught up with ideals.'

Ideals, huh? She was as well versed in reality as the next person. More so, because she'd grown up very aware there were those who would adopt any façade if they thought it would work to their advantage. Luc was the only one who'd managed to pull the wool over her eyes.

'What if Miguel won't play your game?' Hannah queried deliberately.

Camille broke into disbelieving laughter and shot her a pitying look. 'That is not an option.'

'You're so *sure* of yourself?'

'Sure of my—' she paused fractionally '—ability, darling.'

'Singular?' Hannah posed with wry cynicism, determined not to concede this verbal match in any way.

'Perhaps we should agree to confer a week from now. You might not be so confident.' With that parting shot, Camille swept out of the boutique and soon disappeared from sight.

Phew! She might not have won that round, but she hadn't exactly lost.

It was after five when she left the boutique, and she drove to the hospital, visited a slightly wan Cindy, then headed home.

Miguel had showered and was in the process of dressing when Hannah entered the bedroom.

His taut, steel-muscled body projected an enviable aura of power. A strength that was also of the mind and spirit, and she would have given anything to be able to go to him, have him enfold her close, and make the world go away.

Well, maybe the *world* was asking too much. All she wanted was for Camille Dalfour to be gone.

'Bad day?'

She lifted her head and threw him a wry look as she shrugged out of her jacket and began unbuttoning her blouse. 'Tomorrow has to be better.'

He reached for his shirt and pulled it on. 'Want to cancel out tonight?'

What she wanted was to relax in the spa-bath for as long as it took for her tense muscles to unknot, then indulge in a long, sweet loving.

'No. The movie received good reviews overseas,' she said evenly.

Miguel's hands stilled at the faint catch in her voice, and he cast her a discerning look, saw the soft shadows beneath her eyes, cheeks that were devoid of colour, and he covered the distance between them in a few easy steps.

He cupped her chin, lifting it so she had no recourse but to meet his gaze. 'Something bothers you?'

Yes, it bothers me like hell. 'As I said,' she prevaricated as both of his thumbs smoothed a soothing pattern along the edge of her jaw, 'a bad day.'

'Hannah.' His voice was a silky drawl. 'Don't take me for a fool. Honesty, remember?'

Well, this was it. There wasn't going to be a better time. 'Camille wants you.'

His eyes darkened, although his expression didn't change. 'She has told you this?' The query held an icy softness. 'When?'

She held his gaze without difficulty. 'Yesterday, and today.' She attempted a smile, and failed miserably. 'You're a marked man.'

'Indeed?' His voice was a cynical drawl.

This time the smile was bright, too bright. 'She's convincing.'

'I'm sure she is.'

'I assured her I possess a few advantages.' She lifted a hand and began counting off her fingers. 'Minor things like a hefty inheritance, a convenient and compatible marriage. *You.*' She cast him a measured look. 'Did I get those in the right order?'

His eyes darkened and became obsidian shards. 'I could shake you.'

'Please don't,' she protested slowly. 'I might shatter.'

Nevertheless he did, gently. 'You sweet fool,' he growled in husky chastisement. 'I am not interested in extra-marital games.' He traced her lower lip with the pad of his thumb, then released her. *'Comprende?'*

'Words, Miguel?' she queried with a hint of sadness. 'Don't insult me by uttering them meaninglessly.'

'Why would I risk our marriage?'

'Exactly.' Something inside her died at the way he obviously regarded their alliance. 'Why would you?'

'Hannah.' The silky warning was evident, but she chose to ignore it.

'To Camille, you're a challenge.'

'Women of Camille's ilk,' Miguel evinced hardly, 'are known to have their own agenda.'

Hannah's eyes sparked with blue fire. 'Well, she can take her agenda and go shove it.'

Amusement lifted the corners of his mouth, and his eyes assumed a humorous gleam. 'At daggers drawn, *querida?'*

'Yes.'

His gaze narrowed slightly. 'You're not in her league.'

'I hope that's a compliment?'

'Without doubt.' He leant down and brushed his lips to her temple. 'Go have your shower.'

Hannah caught up fresh underwear, a wrap, and entered the *en suite*, emerging fifteen minutes later to discover Miguel had already gone downstairs.

She pulled on smart jeans and a rib-knit top, twisted her hair into a knot on top of her head, then she joined Miguel in the dining room.

Sofia had excelled herself with the meal, and an accompanying light white wine provided a relaxing effect.

It took only minutes to clear the table and stack the dishwasher before returning upstairs to change.

Hannah selected an evening trouser suit in brilliant sapphire, brushed her hair loose, and tended to her make-up before adding a knee-length sheer silk evening jacket patterned in green and blue peacock hues. A beaded evening purse completed the outfit.

'*Exquisita,*' Miguel complimented, and she gave him an impish smile.

'*Gracias, hombre.*' She cast his tall frame a considering look, deliberately noting the splendid dark evening suit, the snowy white cotton shirt, the neat black bow tie. 'Not bad.' A mischievous smile curved her generous mouth. 'I guess you'll do.'

'Indeed?' He took in her finely boned features, the petite stature that never failed to stir in him a host of emotions. 'Shall we leave?'

They arrived fifteen minutes before the premiere was due to begin, and walked into the crowded foyer as invited patrons were entering the auditorium.

The film had an unusual premise, one that enchanted the mind, yet held an underlying thread which provided a startling conclusion. The acting was superb, and it was touted that the three main actors would receive Academy Award nominations.

Miguel reached for her hand as the credits rolled, and together they slipped from the darkened theatre ahead of the general exodus.

'Feel like going somewhere for coffee?'

Hannah almost declined, then changed her mind. 'Why not?'

They walked a block, then entered an arcade whose decor was late nineteenth century, and chose a small café specialising in imported coffee and delicate home-made savouries and cakes.

No one seemed to be in a hurry, and it was an ideal niche to relax, unwind, and just *be*.

They both ordered liqueur coffees, and selected a small delicacy to sample.

'My cousin Alejandro and his wife Elise are flying in for the weekend,' Miguel told her as he sweetened his coffee. 'They'll attend the Leukaemia Foundation charity ball as our guests on Saturday evening.'

Hannah offered him a warm smile. She'd only met Elise a few times since the wedding, but they shared a friendly empathy. 'How long are they staying?'

'Only a few days. Elise is leaving the two boys with a nanny and flying north to spend time with friends while Alejandro is in Perth.'

'You're going with him.' It was a statement, not a query, and Miguel glimpsed the fleeting emotions evident in her expressive features.

'You could join me.'

Hannah almost said *yes*. Then she remembered Cindy was unavailable, and leaving the boutique in a stranger's hands wasn't an option. 'I'd love to,' she said regretfully. 'But I can't.' She gave a resigned shrug. 'How long will you be away?'

'Two, maybe three days.'

Two lonely nights. She could go visit her parents, connect with a few friends and organise a night at the theatre, take in a movie, maybe go out to dinner. Numerous possibilities to occupy her time. Except she'd miss him like crazy.

Did he possess an inkling how much he meant to her? Somehow she doubted it. Fondness and affection didn't equate to *love*. And duty was an empty substitute.

'The boutique—'

'Is important to you.'

She looked at him carefully, silently imploring him to understand. 'We agreed—'

'I know.'

'It's the one thing I've done totally on my own,' she said simply.

'I'm not questioning your ability to achieve success in your own right.'

'No. But you want me to choose.'

'The social circuit in favour of the boutique?' He arched a quizzical eyebrow. 'Not your style, Hannah.'

'What are you suggesting?'

'Give Cindy a promotion. Elevate her to manageress, cultivate two relieving saleswomen who can work in your place.'

'Thus leaving me available to travel with you at short notice?'

'I would prefer to have you with me, than leave you at home.'

A concession? An admission of sorts? 'I'll give it serious thought,' she conceded, and saw his gleaming smile.

'Do that, *amada*.' He drained what remained of his coffee. 'Shall we leave?'

It was late when Miguel garaged the car, and on entering their bedroom Hannah removed her clothes, her make-up, and slid between the cool percale sheets.

She fell asleep within minutes, drifting effortlessly into oblivion where scattered dreams invaded her subconscious mind until the early hours, when the light brush of fingers trailing the indentations of her spine brought her slowly into a state of lazy wakefulness.

Hannah arched her body in a feline stretch, then turned towards the man who was bent on creating havoc with her senses.

With deliberate playfulness she traced a teasing pattern over the dark whorls of hair that smattered his chest, dipping the tips of her nails and gently dragging them across his pectoral muscles before trailing to his navel.

She heard his faint intake of breath, and explored lower, barely touching the engorged tumescent shaft as she sought the apex between his thighs.

In one fluid movement she rose into a sitting position and swept aside the bedcovers, aware of his hands as they caressed her breasts, bringing the dusky peaks into tingling arousal.

Her hair was loose, its length tousled from sleep, and she bent her head so that it brushed against the most sensitised part of his body in a movement that brought him to the brink.

With a soft growl he closed his hands over her waist as he deftly swung her round to sit astride him, and she gasped out loud as his fingers touched her intimately.

Sensation arrowed through her body as he gently rocked her back and forth, until it was she who cried out his name and begged for his possession.

He gave it, lifting her so that she slowly took him deep inside as her body lowered onto him, and then it was she who held the power, she who set the pace, until he removed it from her and took over.

Together they sought the pinnacle and soared the heights in perfect accord. A slow, beautiful sharing of the ultimate meshing of mind, body and soul.

Such attuned sensuality robbed her of the ability to speak, even to move for what seemed an age, then she gently subsided against his chest, nuzzling her lips into the curve of his neck.

His hands brushed the length of her back, caressed her buttocks, returned to slide through the length of her hair as he angled her head towards his, seeking her mouth in a kiss that made her want to weep with its gentle evocativeness.

He traced a path over every inch of her skin, lingering over pleasure pulses, teasing them into vibrant life until she pleaded for him to stop.

'Are you sure you want me to?' Miguel teased in a soft accented drawl, and he gave a low husky laugh at her denial.

What followed was a tantalisingly slow loving as he followed the trail of his hand with his mouth, using it as an erotic instrument that made her totally *his*. Passion flared as he surged into her, raw and primitive, an exotic hunger that was libidinous and almost beyond control.

Afterwards they slept a little, exhausted, until dawn filtered silvered fingers of light through the diminishing darkness, slowly painting soft muted colour over land and sea until the emerging sun feathered a faint golden glow, giving substance to shadows as it heralded a new day.

Hannah woke to an awareness of weightlessness and the knowledge she was being carried. There was also the faint hum of tumbling water, and the slight scent of aromatic oils.

Within seconds Miguel lowered her into the pulsing spa-bath, then stepped in to sit opposite.

He looked far too vibrant for her peace of mind, and she scooped up a handful of water and aimed it at him, watching his gleaming smile as he returned the favour.

With automatic movements she twisted the length of her hair atop her head and secured it with a pin from a nearby shell-shaped dish.

It was a perfect way to begin the day. All of it.

The lovemaking, which she refused at this moment to call *sex*, the sheer bliss of curling into her lover's arms, and now the shared luxury of gently pulsing jets to ease away the slight pull of overused muscles.

She wanted to lean her head back, close her eyes, and stay here for hours. Perhaps enjoy a champagne breakfast, with fresh strawberries followed by eggs Benedict, crispy bacon and two cups of strong black sweet coffee. Then crawl back to bed and sleep beneath the covers until the sun rose to its zenith.

Sadly, it was the wrong day. The weekend didn't begin until tomorrow, and the boutique awaited, as did the replacement saleswoman. And then there was *Camille*.

Slowly she opened her eyes.

'Where did you go?' Miguel queried gently, and she smiled at him.

'You don't want to know.'

'If you tell me, I can—'

'Wave your magic wand?'

'Make a few calls, pull a string or two.'

'Ah, I believe you would. But it's not that simple. Besides, this one's mine, *querido*.' She reached out a hand and snagged a towel, then stepped out from the spa-bath.

It wasn't nearly as late as she'd thought, she discovered as she dressed in the exquisitely tailored gear she chose to wear to work.

There was time for a leisurely breakfast before catching hold of her briefcase and following Miguel through to the garage.

The automatic door lifted, and almost in unison they unlocked each vehicle, slid in behind the wheels, engaged the ignitions, and at Miguel's signal Hannah reversed out ahead of him.

At the end of the street, she lifted a hand and waved, glancing in her rear-vision mirror as she turned in the opposite direction.

The replacement salesgirl arrived late, and, although her credentials appeared satisfactory, she was more suited to the teen section in a department store than catering to a very particular clientele demanding exclusive and expensive designer labels.

Hannah did her best to provide a crash course in haute couture, but after one disastrous clash with a client she relegated Chantal to menial tasks, and had her fetch lunch.

By mid-afternoon Hannah had a tension headache, Chantal had called it quits, which meant another call to the agency, impressing very specific needs, and a desperate call to Renee who willingly agreed to fill in for a few hours the next day.

There was a brief moment when Hannah seriously considered Miguel's suggestion to promote Cindy. But first, she decided a trifle grimly, she had to get through the next week or two.

CHAPTER FIVE

THE gown Hannah chose to wear for the evening's soirée was a full-length slim-fitting creation in ice-blue silk with a halter-neck and flaring into soft folds from the knee. A soft cowl effect provided an attractive *décolletage*. Matching blue stiletto-heeled shoes and a gem-encrusted evening purse completed the outfit.

Jewellery was confined to a diamond tear-drop necklace suspended on a slim gold chain, with earrings to match, and a diamond tennis bracelet at her wrist.

Make-up was kept to a minimum, with emphasis on her eyes, a light rose colouring her lips, and she swept her hair into a sleek chignon.

The prestigious charity event owed its success to an active and imaginative committee, a guest-list of the city's social élite, a luxurious venue, fine food and wine, and top-line entertainment.

This particular end-of-year function numbered as the jewel in the crown of charity events, with the funds raised being donated to the Leukaemia Foundation.

Miguel looked resplendent in a formal black dinner suit, white shirt and black bow-tie. Superb tailoring accentuated his breadth of shoulder and tall muscular frame. He presented a forceful image that combined a dramatic mesh of latent sensuality and elemental ruthlessness. Add an enviable aura of power, and the effect was lethal.

'Ready?'

Hannah offered him a sparkling smile. 'To go do battle?'

His husky chuckle caused a shivery sensation to slither down her spine.

'Is that how you see tonight's social event?'

She wrinkled her nose, and resorted to humour.

'It'll be a dazzling occasion, with the usual players.'

Including Camille, she added silently, offering a fervent prayer the society princess wasn't included in the guests seated at their particular table.

The Deity wasn't listening, she determined an hour later as she slid into reserved seating and saw Camille's name on a place-card next to Miguel.

Damn. Could she surreptitiously switch it? Suiting thought to deed, she quickly transposed the place-card with that of a guest seated opposite.

Alejandro and Elise were a welcome inclusion, and anyone seeing Miguel and Alejandro together could not fail to note they shared relatives in common. They were of a similar height and possessed the same breadth of shoulder, the same physically fit stature and ease of movement. Even their facial features bore a certain similarity, the sculpted angles and planes, piercing dark eyes, that beautifully moulded sensual mouth.

Their respective fathers were brothers who had each left the land of their birth to seek a fortune in another country, succeeded, married and produced one son.

Alejandro resided in Sydney, with his wife Elise and two young children. The Santanas name was well respected in the business arena, and both Alejandro and Miguel shared a mutual stake in a few financial ventures.

Hannah embraced Elise warmly. 'It's so good to see you. When did you arrive?'

'Midday. Alejandro has only used the cell-phone once, and has yet to open the laptop.' She gave an irrepressible smile. 'And I've only checked with the nanny twice.'

Hannah's eyes twinkled with humour. 'This is the first time you've left them at home?'

'Second,' Elise owned. 'It doesn't get any easier.'

'She has a compulsive need to check on the children's welfare,' Alejandro drawled as he leant forward to brush a kiss to Hannah's cheek.

'Of course,' Elise acceded, sending her husband a long glance of the kind that made Hannah's nerves shimmer with envy.

'We're seated together,' Hannah indicated, and watched as Elise slid into a chair, then patted the one next to her.

'Sit beside me. We have so much to catch up on.'

There was background music, and the majority of guests were already seated.

There were only two empty seats at their table, and

Hannah had to concede Camille made a stunning entrance, clothed in a deep red creation that covered her perfect body like a second skin.

Hannah's gaze slid to Camille's partner, and froze in shocked disbelief for all of three seconds before she quickly masked her expression.

Luc Dubois.

Dear heaven. It was three years since she'd last seen him.

Then, he'd been a charming rake whose main occupation was insinuating himself into the lives of wealthy women. Young, not so young, it hadn't seemed to bother him. A photographic professional who used his skill to gain entry into the realm of the rich and famous.

She should know. For three months in Paris he'd exercised his considerable charms on *her*. Wined, dined, and eventually swept her off her feet and into his arms.

Now, Hannah watched as Camille began weaving her way towards them with Luc in tow, and she forced herself to maintain a polite smile as they drew close.

Had Miguel noted their entrance? Recognised Luc?

Apprehension scudded down her spine at the thought of his reaction when he did.

Although it was possible, she wasn't sure the two men had ever met. A hysterical bubble of laughter rose and died in her throat.

Dear heaven. Camille *and* Luc seated at their table? How cruel could fate be?

Hannah was aware the instant Miguel caught sight

of them, and could only wonder if anyone else noticed the way his body uncoiled and then became frighteningly still. Like a jungle animal scenting an enemy and assessing when to strike.

'Miguel, Hannah.' Camille resembled an aristocratic cat who'd just snacked on caviare and cream.

All it took was one glance at Camille's bland expression to guess that Luc's invitation had been deliberately orchestrated.

'Camille.' She thought her face would crack with the strain of keeping a smile pinned on her face as she acknowledged the Frenchwoman.

What was Luc doing here? Not so much Australia, or even Melbourne, but *this* particular charity event, *and* partnering Camille?

It didn't take a genius to arrive at the correct answer, Hannah decided wryly. Even the most kindly disposed person would suspect Camille of mischief-making. Luc's appearance *here* simply reinforced Hannah's belief that Camille was not only serious in her pursuit of Miguel, but she'd stop at nothing to gain her objective.

So it was *war*. Well, she was very good at self-protection. She had years of experience in dealing with it. If Camille thought snaring Miguel would be a walkover, she had another think coming!

'You know each other, of course,' Camille purred as she slid into her seat, and Hannah opted for confrontational strategy.

'The media made much of it at the time.' She

looked at Luc, wanting to sear him to a burnt frizzle on the spot. 'I hope they paid you well.'

'Handsomely.' His smile would have melted many a hardened female heart.

But not hers. 'Let me introduce my husband, Miguel Santanas.'

Miguel was incredibly polite. Anyone who knew him would have blanched at the icy silkiness apparent in his voice.

Luc, however, seemed totally oblivious.

Wine stewards began serving drinks, and the event began with an introductory speech by the charity chairwoman, followed by the MC who outlined the evening's entertainment.

The organisation was very smooth as models strutted the catwalk to funky music while waiters served the starter.

Hannah looked at the artistically arranged seafood in a bed of salad greens, and merely forked a few morsels, her appetite seriously impaired by the presence of not one enemy, but *two*, in her immediate vicinity.

She would have given anything to be able to walk out of the ballroom and take a taxi home. Except that would amount to running away, and her pride forbade such an option.

Pretend, a tiny voice urged, and act as if you don't have a care in the world.

Miguel ordered champagne, and indicated that the steward should fill her flute. Hannah cast him an enquiring glance and caught the faint smile curving the edge of his mouth, the steady gleam apparent as he raised his glass in a silent salute.

He knew, of course, exactly who Luc Dubois was, and the part Luc had played in her life.

'What is this in aid of?' Hannah queried quietly, slanting one eyebrow in quizzical humour as she touched the rim of her flute to his. 'Courage?'

'Do you need it?'

She inclined her head slightly, and offered with soft-edged mockery, 'This is going to be one hell of an evening.'

'Do you want to leave?'

Her eyes widened. He'd do that for her? 'No.' Her voice was steady, but inside her heart missed a beat.

The models concluded showing the after-five segment, and the MC announced a well-known comedian who delivered a few amusing and occasionally risqué anecdotes while an army of waiters removed plates and the stewards tended to the guests' drinking needs.

Two singers performed two numbers, after which the models returned to the catwalk with a comprehensive display of evening wear.

It was while the main course was being served that Camille chose to engage Miguel's attention with a flirtatious coquetry that made Hannah barely refrain from grinding her teeth in angry vexation.

'Am I missing something here?' Elise ventured, *sotto voce*. 'Or is the beautiful Camille on a flirting mission with Miguel?'

'If he responds,' Hannah murmured, 'he's dead meat.'

'Luc is the smokescreen, or the ammunition?'

'Both, I imagine.'

Elise's features softened in empathy. 'Tread carefully.'

Now would be a good time to utilise the powder room, and with a murmured excuse she slipped out from her chair.

Miguel could indulge in polite conversation with Camille if he chose, but *she* didn't have to stay and watch Camille's play-acting!

'I'll come with you.' Elise rose to her feet and together they began making their way towards one of the exits.

Hannah paused to greet a few friends as she threaded her way through the ballroom, and she took unnecessary time freshening her make-up.

Elise joined her after using the facilities, and she pressed a hand to her waist, then groaned and vanished into a stall, only to emerge looking slightly pale and wan.

Comprehension was immediate. 'You're pregnant?'

Elise managed a faint smile. 'After two sons, *this* one has to be a girl. Already she's exerting her personality in a way neither of the two boys did.'

'Uh huh,' Hannah conceded with an impish grin. 'I gather Alejandro knows?'

'He finds it incredibly amusing.'

'Naturally, he'll be captivated from the instant she's born and be hers to command within minutes.'

Elise's gaze misted. 'He's a wonderful father.'

'Are you okay?'

'Oh, yes. I get to throw up on a regular basis half-way through breakfast and dinner.' She opened her evening purse and produced a toothbrush and paste. 'Before and after, I'm fine.'

Minutes later, their make-up restored, they moved towards the door, only to see Alejandro standing immediately outside in the vestibule.

Oh, my, Hannah breathed silently. Elise was his most precious possession. It was evident in the way he looked at her, the protective arm that immediately circled her waist. Body language that was intense and evocative.

It must be wonderful to share that kind of emotion, to be twin halves of a whole, and so complete. Together they returned to their table, and Miguel cast her a discerning look as she regained her seat. She was willing to swear she caught a glimmer of amusement evident as she reached for her wine.

'Your meal has cooled.' He beckoned a waiter and instructed another plate be served. Something that was done with alacrity.

'I'm not really hungry.'

'Nevertheless you will eat something,' Miguel chastised silkily, and saw her eyes widen as he lifted a hand and brushed the edge of her cheek with his fingers.

'What are you doing?'

His mouth formed a sensual curve. 'It's called re-assurance.'

'The attentive husband bit, huh?' Hannah queried with a touch of mockery.

'Something like that.'

'For Camille's benefit?'

'Yours.'

Oh, he was good. Very, very good. She doubted anyone present observing their byplay could be in doubt as to his feelings. She could almost hear the unspoken comments...*fifteen months into the marriage, and look at them.*

She offered him a brilliant smile. 'Careful, *querido*, you're in danger of reaching overkill.'

He touched a thumb-pad to her lips. 'Think so?'

The lights dimmed, a spotlight hit the MC, and the charity organiser announced the amount of money raised for the night's function, alerted guests to the next gala evening, and indicated a return of the comedian.

Somehow Camille had managed to manoeuvre the seating so she occupied a chair next to Miguel, and Hannah had to commend her determination while silently condemning her to hell.

Hannah picked at the decorative fare on her plate, forked a few mouthfuls, then pushed the plate aside.

Camille took every opportunity to engage Miguel's attention with a light trail of red-lacquered nails on his sleeve, a touch to his hand, and her smile was a work of art in the seduction stakes.

The models took the catwalk for the final round while dessert was being served, and afterwards the waiters brought coffee while the singing duo closed the entertainment for the evening.

A DJ switched on special lighting effects, set the first of several CDs playing, and background music and recorded vocals encouraged those inclined to dance to take to the floor.

Now was the time for guests to mingle, table-hop and socialise with friends who were also present.

Alejandro and Elise communicated their intention to leave. 'Tomorrow,' Elise promised quietly. 'We'll catch up. I have photos, and the men have organised a day cruise and a picnic lunch.'

As they left a colleague crossed to their table to talk to Miguel, Camille slipped through the crowd heading for the ballroom exit, Miguel excused himself briefly and moved a few steps away as a friend joined the colleague, and within seconds Hannah was aware of someone taking Miguel's seat.

'How are you, Hannah?'

The male voice was familiar, and she turned slowly to face the man to whom it belonged.

'Luc,' she acknowledged coolly. 'Believe me, there is no need to observe the social niceties. I have nothing to say to you.'

'So cool,' Luc mocked. 'Still the ice princess, I see.'

'You expect me to believe your presence here is purely coincidental?'

He inclined his head in a gesture of musing cynicism. 'We could enjoy a conversation. Three years, Hannah. We have some catching up to do.'

'No,' she denied. 'We don't.'

'Why, *chérie*?' His smile aimed to melt her heart. 'It was good while it lasted.'

She could feel the anger begin to burn deep inside. 'Strange,' she remarked coolly. 'Our memories don't match.'

She fixed him with an icy glare. 'So let's cut the pretence, shall we?'

He spread his hands in an expressive gesture. 'Who's pretending? I was very fond of you.'

'Words,' Hannah dismissed. 'Suppose you tell me exactly why you're here?'

'This event?'

'Oh, for heaven's sake. Cut the game-playing. You know very well what I mean.'

'Are you ready for the facts, *chérie*?'

As ready as I'll ever be! She didn't bother answering, just sent him a fulminating look that spoke volumes.

He gave a voluble sigh. 'It will cost you.'

'No, it won't,' Hannah denied heartlessly. 'You owe me. For living the good life at the expense of my foolish generosity.'

He proffered a mocking smile. 'When did you become so cynical?'

'Three years ago.'

'All right, *chérie*. This one is on me, for old times' sake.'

'*Merci*,' she acknowledged in a voice as cold as an arctic ice floe.

'Camille sought me out, paid my air fare, and is

footing my accommodation,' he revealed, and she arched one eyebrow.

'And you're bent on playing both ends against the middle?'

He gave a negligent shrug. 'Your words, not mine.'

Hannah looked at him carefully, saw the handsome features, the rakish gleam evident in his expression, and wondered how on earth she could have been swayed by his charm. His megawatt smile had no effect whatsoever.

'Go get a life, Luc.'

'A word of warning, sweetheart,' he offered quietly. 'Camille is on a mission.'

'As if I didn't know?'

'Dance with me, and I could be persuaded to tell you more.'

He was unbelievable! 'Not even if my life depended on it!'

One eyebrow lifted in cynical amusement. 'Perhaps you're right.' He cast a glance in Miguel's direction.

'Miguel Santanas doesn't look the type of man who would willingly share.'

No, Hannah agreed, suppressing a slight shiver. Miguel's ownership was total.

'Maybe we could share a coffee somewhere and talk about old times.'

'You can't be serious?' He had such a thick skin, it was almost laughable. 'Yes, you are,' she acknowledged with a shake of her head.

'No hard feelings?'

She faced him squarely, her eyes steady. 'When

you report to Camille, tell her she doesn't stand a snowflake's chance in hell.' She stood to her feet, needing a change of scene, if only for a few minutes.

She turned from the table and saw Miguel's tall frame a few feet distant. He looked totally relaxed, his strong masculine features portraying interest as he listened to whatever his colleague had to say.

One glance at the expression in his eyes was sufficient for Hannah to realise he hadn't missed a thing. There was a darkness evident, a latent anger that was almost frightening.

She moved towards him, pausing as she reached his side while he performed an introduction, and she stood perfectly still as he reached for her hand and linked his fingers through her own.

Support? Protection? she wondered. Or was he merely staking a claim, making a statement?

The colleague excused himself and returned to a nearby table.

'Shall we leave?' Miguel queried with a faintly inflected drawl.

Hannah offered him a stunning smile, then lifted a hand and traced a light path along the edge of his jaw.

'And spoil Camille's fun?'

He caught her fingers and pressed an open-mouthed kiss to her palm, observing the way her eyes darkened in dilation. Her lips trembled slightly, and for one infinitesimal second she looked acutely vulnerable.

'You resemble a piece of fragile glass on the point of shattering,' Miguel said gently. 'Home, I think.'

Her chin tilted fractionally. 'I'm really very resilient.' She summoned a smile. 'Besides, there's music, and we should dance.'

They did, for a while, moving to the funky beat, then when it changed to something slower Miguel pulled her into his arms and held her close.

It was heaven. She could almost forget where they were, the time, the place, everything except the man and the emotions he was able to arouse.

She felt his lips brush the top of her head, then linger at her temple, and she made a sound in her throat as they settled just beneath one earlobe.

They fitted together so well, and this close she could feel his powerful thigh muscles, the strength of his arousal.

'I think we should go home.'

His soft laughter feathered sensation over the surface of her skin, and heat unfurled within, warming her body to fever pitch.

'Do you need to return to the table?'

She shook her head, and together they made their way towards the ballroom exit, pausing from time to time to speak to acquaintances. They were about to pass through the large double doors when they came face to face with Camille.

'You're not leaving?'

Hannah offered a polite smile. 'We both have an early start tomorrow.'

'Tired, darling?' Her expression was deliberately bland. 'Miguel must find your lack of stamina a little—' she paused slightly '—tiresome.'

'Perhaps *tired* is just a polite euphemism,' Hannah ventured sweetly, and almost held her breath at the sheer venom evident in Camille's gaze before it was quickly masked. 'Goodnight, Camille.'

There was little the striking brunette could do other than make a graceful retreat. However there was the promise—no, *threat*, Hannah amended as she walked at Miguel's side to the lift, that this was only the beginning of Camille's campaign.

She sat in silence as Miguel eased the car through the city streets, lost in contemplative thought.

Media speculation had run rife at the time of her engagement to Miguel, and the caption above their wedding photos had given allusion to it being an arranged union. Something that aroused public conjecture, and added fuel to the social gossip columns.

However, more than a year down the track, the conjecture had lessened, they'd settled easily into the pattern of marriage, work and social commitments.

'You're quiet.'

Hannah glanced at Miguel and could determine little from his expression in the car's dim interior.

'How perceptive,' she afforded wryly, and incurred his brief glance.

'Camille bothers you?'

'Clever, too.'

He waited a beat. 'And Luc?'

She didn't even have to think. 'Is ancient history.'

'Not from where I was standing.'

Hannah took a deep breath, then released it slowly. 'You should have stood closer.' She bit back a humourless laugh. 'Then you would have heard me tell him to go get a life and stay out of mine.'

'That was the extent of your conversation?' They reached Toorak and turned into a select residential avenue.

'Oh, there's just one other detail,' she revealed as he took another turn and slowed before the impressive set of gates guarding the entrance to their home. 'He revealed Camille has *you* firmly in her sights, and she'll go to any lengths to get you.' She watched as Miguel activated the remote, opening the gates, and the car eased forward onto the wide sweeping drive. The garage doors slid up automatically at the touch of another remote, then closed seconds later when he cut the engine.

Hannah slid out and walked to the door leading into the house, waited while Miguel tended to the lock, then she moved through to the foyer.

'Indeed?' he drawled with ill-disguised mockery. He paused at the foot of the beautiful staircase and subjected her to a searching appraisal. 'Is his role that of accomplice in Camille's diabolical scheme?'

'Yes.'

'Be careful, *querida*,' he warned silkily. 'He hurt you once. I won't tolerate him hurting you again.'

'*You* won't tolerate it?' She strove to conquer a complex mix of emotions. 'There's no need to play the jealous husband!'

'I prefer…protective.'

He didn't move, but she had the impression his

body tensed, and apprehension slithered over the surface of her skin.

'Luc—'

'Occupied a small part of your life before you committed to me,' Miguel drawled in a dangerously quiet voice.

Just as several women undoubtedly occupied his. A hollow feeling settled low in her stomach and radiated towards her heart. Dear heaven, just thinking about who they were and how many there might have been made her feel ill.

Hannah held his gaze for several long seconds, then she brushed past him and moved quickly up the stairs.

A hollow feeling settled round her heart as she traversed the gallery to their room, and inside she began removing her ear-studs, then she reached for the catch on her necklace.

Miguel entered the room and shrugged off his dinner jacket, loosened his shoes, and discarded his socks. The bow-tie came next, then he undid and removed his shirt.

Dammit, what was the matter with the catch? She cursed it beneath her breath, and followed it with another as Miguel crossed to her side.

'Stand still.'

She was incredibly aware of him, the raw primitive aura combined with the subtle scent of his skin and the sensual warmth of his body. There was a part of her that wanted to sink in against him and lift her face for his kiss, while another part wanted to pummel his chest with her fists.

Didn't he know how vulnerable she felt? How much of a threat she knew Camille to be? As to Luc…she wouldn't trust him as far as she could throw him.

Miguel freed the catch in a second, and he dropped the chain into her hand before placing a thumb and forefinger on her chin, lifting it so she had no choice but to look at him.

'*Por Dios.*' His eyes darkened, and a muscle bunched at the edge of his jaw. 'You think I cannot see what Camille is?' He traced a thumb along her jaw, then slid a hand to capture her nape. 'Credit me with some intelligence, *mi mujer.*'

'It's your libido she's aiming at,' Hannah returned succinctly. 'Not your intelligence.'

'You imagine I would slip easily into another woman's bed?' Miguel queried with chilling softness.

All she could do was look at him, her mind filled with haunting images that drove her almost to the brink of sanity.

'We promised each other fidelity,' she managed quietly.

'You have no reason to doubt my word.'

'Nor mine.'

His gaze seared hers, seeing beyond the surface, aware of her vulnerability, its cause, and he silently damned Camille for deliberately setting out to undermine it.

He moved his fingers to the zip fastening on her gown, releasing it slowly, then he slipped each shoulder strap free so the beaded silk slithered to a heap at her feet. All she wore beneath it was a pair of lacy satin briefs, and his hands skimmed to her waist, settled, then slid up to shape her breasts.

He slanted his head down to hers and took her mouth in a slow, drugging kiss that was wholly sensual, tasting, exploring, teasing, until she wound her arms round his neck and kissed him back.

She loved the feel of him, the glide of her fingers as she traced strong muscle and sinew. The silk-smooth skin, the powerful breadth of shoulder, the hard ribcage, his taut midriff.

He was wearing too many clothes, and she reached for his belt buckle, undid it, then set about freeing his trousers.

Hannah felt the need pulse through her body, heating her senses to fever pitch.

Now, dammit. *Now.* Hard and fast, and wild. She didn't want his restraint, only his passion.

Had she said the words aloud? She was past knowing, beyond caring. There was only the moment, and she cried out, urging him on as he lifted her into his arms, then swept aside the bedcovers and tossed her onto the sheets, shielding her body from his weight as he followed her down.

With one hard, long thrust he entered her, felt the customary tightness as she closed like smooth silk around him, taking him in with a series of tiny gasps at his size.

Never before had he resorted to quite this degree of unbridled savagery. Her gaze clung to his, mesmerised by the primitive hunger that sculpted his features into something wild and untamed. His head was flung back, his neck muscles corded, his jaw clenched.

Then he began to move, slowly at first, almost withdrawing before plunging in, again and again, faster and faster, in a rhythm as old as time.

She became caught up in it, swept along on a roaring tide that crashed, then receded, only to gather force and crash again.

There was only the man, the electrifying primeval emotion, and need.

The control he inevitably maintained was gone, and in its place was something incredibly primitive. A hunger so intense it surpassed passion and became raw desire. Brazen, mesmeric, libidinous.

It was as if she was possessed, held captive by a driven overwhelming need, and she abandoned herself to it, to him, allowing him to take her wherever he chose to lead, exulting in the journey.

She had wondered what it would be like to have him lose all semblance of constraint, to be caught up in his total abandonment. A tiny smile curved the swollen fullness of her mouth. *Wild*, she reflected silently. Incredibly, inexplicably wild.

There was a sense of bewitching satisfaction at having the power to cause a man to lose control so completely in her arms.

Hannah sensed the moment he regained a measure of control, felt the heave of his chest as he dragged in air and steadied his breathing, heard it catch in his throat as his body shuddered in emotive reaction, and she simply held him as he uttered a stream of self-castigating words in whispered Spanish.

She wanted to reassure him, to somehow convey for the first time she truly felt a woman's sensual power, and that she was completely swept away by it.

With a tentative touch, she stroked her fingers lightly over his back, felt the tautened muscles and tense sinew beneath her tactile caress, and attempted to soothe them. Gently she traversed his waist, and traced the rigid outline of his buttocks, squeezing them slightly before trailing slowly up over his rib-cage to rest on his shoulders, then capturing his head and bringing his mouth down to hers.

It was she who kissed him, savouring his lips, his mouth, sweeping her tongue in an evocative dance with his, encouraging, beguiling in a brazen invitation.

Afterwards he held her close, his arms a protective cage as he cradled her, and she felt his lips on her hair, at the edge of her cheek, caressing her temple, then nuzzling the soft hollow at the curve of her neck.

'*Madre de Dios,*' Miguel breathed tautly. 'Did I hurt you?'

Hannah pressed her mouth to his throat. 'No.'

It had been passion at its most elemental, for both of them.

His lips found hers, in a kiss that was so incredibly gentle it almost brought her to tears.

'Rest, *amada*,' he bade gently.

She felt the beat of his heart beneath her cheek,

and in the security of his arms she simply closed her eyes and drifted into a dreamless somnolence.

At some stage during the early pre-dawn hours she stirred, felt the lack of human warmth and reached for him, only to find the bed empty. Cautiously she lifted her head and searched the shadowy room. It was then she saw him, silhouetted against the partly drawn curtains, looking out over the shadowed garden.

Slowly she slid from the bed and crossed to stand behind him, aware from his slight movement that he had heard the rustle of the sheets, the almost silent pad of her feet.

Hannah linked her arms around his waist and leaned in against him, holding him close. Long minutes later he gathered her into his arms and carried her into the *en suite*. There, he filled the spa-bath, switched on the jets, then he stepped in and lowered her down in front of him.

She simply closed her eyes and let the pulsing warm water provide a soothing relaxation. It would be so easy just to drift to sleep, and she almost did, only to open her eyes wide when Miguel scooped her out and wrapped her in a huge bath-towel.

Dry, they returned to the bedroom, and she made no protest when he drew her down onto the bed. With exquisite care he began an erotic tasting that took her to the edge of sensual nirvana, then tipped her over.

Would it always be like this? Hannah wondered on the edge of sleep.

Beautiful, glorious, heart-wrenching sex. Affection, fondness, respect. But not love.

She, who had sworn never to become emotionally involved with another man, had no choice.

Her heart belonged to Miguel. It always had, always would, whether he wanted it or not.

CHAPTER SIX

'WONDERFUL,' Elise murmured as she relaxed beneath the canopied section of the comfortable cruiser Miguel had hired for the day.

Hannah adjusted her sunglasses and smiled as Elise pulled the brim of her hat down to shade her face from the sun's strong rays.

Together they'd driven down to Williamstown at ten this morning, where Miguel had organised to hire a luxury cruiser and captain to cruise the sparkling waters, then return mid-afternoon.

'It's nice to get away somewhere quiet,' Elise said appreciatively. 'No phones, no visitors, no one-hundred-and-one things to do.'

And no way a certain very persistent Frenchwoman could intrude, Hannah added silently, unable to prevent herself from wondering what Camille's next move might be.

Miguel and Alejandro were seated at the stern, both casually attired in pale chinos and a polo shirt. Both wore sunglasses and baseball caps, and resembled, Hannah decided, two businessmen relaxing on a rare day off.

All she had to do was *look* at Miguel to feel her insides begin to melt. Traitorous desire flared, and spread stealthily through her body, heating her blood and sensitising every nerve-end into pulsing life.

It was impossible not to relive the cataclysmic passion they'd shared less than twelve hours before, and, as crazy as it seemed, she was willing to swear she could still *feel* him inside her. Sensitive tissues throbbed a little from his possession, and there was a part of her that ached for his touch.

At that moment he turned and cast her a long measured glance, and for an instant she could almost imagine he'd read her mind. Then his mouth curved into a slow, infinitely sensual smile that tore her composure to shreds.

'Lunch,' Elise stated with evident relish, 'might be a good idea.'

'Junior is hungry?' Hannah queried musingly, and found herself laughing at Elise's expression.

'Little missy has very definite ideas on when and what I should eat.' She stood to her feet and smoothed her hands over her barely perceptible bulge. 'Today, I have a craving for ham, mayonnaise, gherkins and pineapple.'

Fortunately Sofia had packed a wide selection into a picnic hamper, together with crunchy bread rolls, salmon, chicken, and a variety of salads.

Hannah went inside the cabin and retrieved the hamper, then with Elise's help she set it out on the table, added bottled water, soft drinks and wine, and called the men to eat.

The fresh air, the faint breeze, made for a very pleasant few hours, and they disembarked and then took the coastal road down to the Port Phillip before returning to Toorak.

A seafood barbecue as the heat of the afternoon sun began to wane completed a relaxing day in good company, and Hannah stacked plates and dishes onto a tray and carried them indoors.

Elise followed her, and together they rinsed and stacked them into the dishwasher in record time.

Hannah wiped down the bench, then paused as Elise touched her arm.

'May I say something?'

'Of course.' Hannah turned and gave Elise her full attention.

'Alejandro had a woman chase him when I was pregnant with our first son. Savannah made a complete nuisance of herself and caused me immeasurable grief at the time.' She smiled a little at the memory. 'Unless I'm reading things wrong, you have a similar nemesis in Camille.' She drew in a deep breath, then released it slowly. 'One thing I learned that might help. The Santanas men are one-woman men.'

'So don't worry about Camille?' Hannah queried wryly.

'Don't worry about Miguel,' Elise corrected gently. Her features momentarily clouded. 'Here we go again,' she groaned, rolling her eyes an instant before she quickly exited the kitchen.

Miguel and Alejandro entered the house as Elise returned from her mercy dash, and Hannah set the coffee filtering as she extracted cups, sugar and milk.

'Tea for me,' Elise requested, and Hannah extracted a tray.

'Why don't you go sit by the pool and I'll bring it out in a few minutes?'

It was pleasant to relax in the quiet evening air and watch the sun go down. The garden lights sprung to life by automatic control, and recessed lighting around the pool area added a luminous glow that was highlighted by underwater pool lighting.

A private fairyland, secluded, peaceful, and a relaxing way to end a lovely day.

Elise voiced the words, and Hannah had to agree.

'Time to go, *querida*,' Alejandro commanded quietly as he stood to his feet. 'You're tired.'

'I am?' Her eyes assumed a musing gleam. 'If you say so.'

How many years had they been married? Hannah posed. Six, seven? Yet the intense passion was there, burning just beneath the surface. Somehow she could imagine it would always be so. Yet it hadn't been in the beginning, she reflected as she stood with Miguel at the front door and watched the tail-lights of their hire car glow in the darkness. An arranged marriage that had gone wrong, with Elise escaping only to find herself involved in a car crash and suffering memory loss.

'More coffee?' Hannah queried as she turned away from the door.

'No,' Miguel refused as he locked up and set the security alarm. 'I need to pack. Alejandro is picking me up at seven-thirty *en route* to the airport.'

Where the Sanmar company Lear jet would fly them across the vast Australian continent to Perth.

Without a word she crossed the foyer with him and ascended the stairs to their room where she watched in silence as Miguel extracted a leather holdall and rapidly tossed in a few shirts, a pair of trousers, together with other essentials.

The thought of him being absent for a few days didn't thrill her at all, and she gathered up a silky nightshirt, then entered the *en suite* to shower.

Miguel joined her there minutes later, and she felt acutely vulnerable as he took the soap from her hand, using it gently over every inch of her body before extending it to her to return the favour.

For a second she hesitated, and the breath caught in her throat as he cupped her face and slanted his mouth down to cover her own in a kiss that was so tender it was all she could do not to cry.

It was a while before they both emerged, and towelled dry, re-entered the bedroom and slipped beneath the covers.

He reached for her, and she went to him willingly, curving her arms round his neck as she pulled his head down to hers.

Miguel indulged her, allowing her to take the initiative, until he stilled her hands and held them.

'*Amante*, no. As much as I want you, last night—'

'Was wonderful,' Hannah assured. 'Earth-shattering.'

'I don't think—'

'Don't,' she pleaded. 'Think, I mean,' she added

quickly. 'Just feel. *Please.*' She extricated her hands and ran light fingers down his chest, traced a pattern over his navel, then moved low. 'I want to make love with you.'

And she did, with exquisite care, rising above him as she took in his length, feeling acute pleasure, enclosing him tightly she began to move.

Yet it was Miguel who took control and measured the pace, making it a slow erotic dance that shattered them both with its intensity. Then he brought her down to him and held her long after her breathing returned to normal and she slept.

Saying goodbye was harder than it had ever been before, and she wanted to say *don't go.* Except the words never found voice, and she managed the semblance of a warm smile as he kissed her briefly before moving quickly out to the car and slipped into the front seat beside Alejandro.

Fortunately there wasn't much time to reflect on Miguel's departure as she returned to the dining room to finish the last of her breakfast and skim the daily newspaper before ascending the stairs to get ready for work.

The replacement salesgirl sent by the agency proved to be a dramatic improvement on Chantal, and Hannah began to relax as the morning progressed.

Renee rang to check how the new girl was shaping up, and Miguel called to say they'd landed in Perth.

When the phone rang again minutes later Hannah

automatically lifted the receiver and intoned her usual greeting.

'*Bonjour*, Hannah.'

The voice on the other end of the phone was familiar. Far too familiar, and not one she wanted to hear.

'How did you get my number?' A silly question, she silently castigated herself the instant the words slipped from her lips.

'Dearest Hannah,' Luc drawled with cynical humour. 'Your boutique has a name, which is listed in the telephone directory.'

The connection to Camille was obvious. 'What do you want?'

'Ah, *chérie*,' he chastised softly. 'Straight to the point.'

'I don't have time to chat.' Her voice was distant, formal.

'Meet me for coffee.'

'I don't think so.'

'You have to break for lunch, surely?'

'Yes, but I don't intend to have it with you.'

'Afraid, *chérie*?'

Had he always been this insufferably arrogant? She almost cringed at the thought she'd once been attracted to him. 'Of you? No.' She replaced the receiver, and turned towards the sheaf of invoices waiting to claim her attention.

A client entered the boutique, and Hannah watched surreptitiously as Elaine moved forward with a practised greeting. In only a matter of hours the girl was showing her worth, and Hannah felt cautiously hopeful she'd work out.

Elaine took a lunch break at midday, and on her return an hour later Hannah crossed the street to the café she usually frequented. The food was good, the coffee superb.

Big mistake, she realised within seconds of entering the busy eatery. Being a creature of habit had its downfall, for anyone familiar with her regular routine would be aware this particular café was her favourite haunt for lunch...whether she chose food to take away, or took the time to eat in.

Seated at a table overlooking the street was Luc Dubois, looking the relaxed urbane sophisticate he aspired to be.

Now why wasn't she surprised to see him there? Luc did nothing without motivation. It made her feel distinctly wary.

'*Bonjour, chérie,*' Luc greeted with deliberate warmth. 'I knew if I sat here long enough it would be only a matter of time before you arrived.'

'I must remember to change my eating venue.' Without a further word she turned on her heel and walked out again.

The entire street held several equally trendy eating places. She'd go somewhere else.

Five minutes later she was seated at a table and had just given her order when someone slid into the seat opposite.

'Whatever the lady ordered,' Luc instructed the waiter, 'make it two.'

Hannah cast him an arctic glare. 'Just what in hell are you trying to pull?'

Luc extended one arm in a sweeping gesture. 'We're in public,' he indicated with an eloquent shrug. 'Why not combine lunch with a little reminiscing?'

Hannah arched one eyebrow. 'To what purpose?'

He tried to look hurt. 'Why, *chérie*. We shared some good times together.'

She spared him a bitter smile. 'It took me three months to discover your charm was only an act.'

'Not all the time.'

'Oh…p-l-e-a-s-e,' she discounted wearily.

'The attraction was Daddy's bank account and my healthy annuity. *I* was irrelevant.' Every instinct told her to get up and walk out *now*.

The waiter delivered two lattes, and against her better judgement she tore open a sugar tube and tipped the contents into the milky froth. Luc did the same.

She cut straight to the chase. 'What has Camille paid you to do?'

He spread both hands in a conciliatory gesture.

'Why should Camille have anything to do with me wanting to share a coffee with you?'

She speared him with a look. 'Don't take me for a fool.'

The waiter arrived with two plates, each containing a salad sandwich. As he turned away a flash bulb exploded nearby, and she caught a brief glimpse of a photographer making a rapid exit.

'Pay dirt,' Luc informed with a cynical smile.

It all clicked into place in an instant, and Hannah rose to her feet in one angry movement, extracted a note from her purse, then flung it down onto the table and walked out into the street.

Dammit, she should have seen it coming! Luc played a tune to the highest bidder. In this instance, Camille. Another step down a diabolical path towards Camille's main goal…Miguel. Now, there was photographic evidence Hannah had shared a meal with Luc. It didn't take a genius to work out how Camille intended to use the photograph.

A car horn blared, and she halted mid-step. Dear God, she whispered shakily as realisation hit that she'd stepped off the footpath onto the road. Get a grip!

Minutes later she entered the boutique, caught Elaine's surprised look, and offered a humourless smile. 'That bad, huh?'

'Are you okay?'

Hannah attempted to downplay the past thirty minutes. 'Something disagreed with me.'

'Or someone?'

'You're good,' Hannah accorded wryly. 'Any problems while I was gone?'

'I sold two shirts, a scarf, and took two orders.'

'Well done.'

'You weren't away long. Did you get to eat?'

'I lost my appetite.' Wasn't that the truth!

It was after six when she arrived home, and she ate the meal Sofia had prepared for her, then she retreated to the study and keyed in the digits to connect with Miguel's mobile, only to get his voice-mail.

Maybe he and Alejandro were out to dinner. She left a message, then took a shower and changed into jeans and a singlet top.

Her mother called, and Hannah accepted an invitation to dinner the following evening. They chatted for a while, catching up on each other's news, and afterwards she watched a television movie before opting to indulge herself by reading in bed.

It was almost eleven when the sudden peal of the telephone startled her into dropping the book, and she caught up the receiver, uttered a brief curse as it slipped from her fingers.

Seconds later she managed an articulate greeting, and heard Miguel's husky voice on the line.

'Did I wake you?'

'No,' Hannah said at once. 'I was reading.'

His soft chuckle set all her fine body hairs standing on end. 'You left a message to call.'

'I—' She hesitated, then opted for the banal. 'How are things going?'

'What is it?' Miguel demanded in a dangerously quiet tone.

'What makes you think something's wrong?'

'*Querida,*' he drawled with deceptive mildness. 'Don't stall.'

'Luc came into the café opposite the boutique during my lunch break.' She could almost *see* his features harden. 'I refused to join him.'

'There's more to the story?'

'Try having him follow me, sit down at the same

table after I'd ordered, then, just as the waiter delivered the food, a photographer appears from nowhere and captured the two of us apparently sharing a meal.'

'He set you up.'

'I should have seen it coming,' Hannah said wretchedly.

'I'll take care of him.' His voice was tensile steel and just as dangerous.

'What are you going to do?'

Miguel smiled grimly on the other end of the line. 'Ensure he doesn't come near you again.' He waited a beat. 'Or he will answer to me.'

Hannah shivered. 'Miguel—'

'Tomorrow there will be someone to shadow your every move.'

Comprehension dawned. 'I don't need a bodyguard!'

There was a brief silence, then he said hardly, 'My decision, Hannah.'

'Shouldn't it also be mine?'

'Accept it as a protective precaution.'

'And if I choose not to?' she pursued, angered by his high-handedness.

'The bodyguard stays.'

She took a deep breath and released it slowly. 'I don't like tyrannical men.'

'Tough,' Miguel reiterated succinctly. 'Alejandro can wrap up the deal. I'll be on the late afternoon flight Wednesday.'

Now she was getting steamed. 'Don't cut an important business deal short on my account.'

'*You, amante*, are more important than any business deal.'

'Me, or my vested interest in the Martinez half of the Sanmar corporation?'

'It's as well the breadth of a continent separates us,' Miguel declared with chilling softness, 'or I would take you to task.'

'For daring to speak the truth?'

She had the distinct impression he was actively controlling his temper. 'It will keep.'

Hannah had had enough. 'Goodnight, Miguel.' She cut the connection, and replaced the receiver.

Overbearing, autocratic man! A *bodyguard*? Was he mad?

She picked up the book and tried to get back into the characters, the story, only to close the cover and toss it down onto the bed.

A protective precaution, indeed! Her teeth worried the soft part of her lower lip. Luc was unlikely to do her physical harm. She doubted he'd risk life or limb or arrest, no matter what price Camille offered him. Or could she be wrong?

It wasn't a comfortable thought, and one that kept her awake long after she'd switched off the bedside lamp.

Dreams invaded her subconscious, a series of scary sequences where she was mysteriously pushed from behind into the path of an oncoming vehicle, and worse, driving a car with brakes that didn't respond when she most needed them.

CHAPTER SEVEN

HANNAH was in the middle of eating breakfast when the 'phone rang, and she answered it on the third ring.

'*Buenos días.*' Miguel's faintly accented voice curled round her nerve-ends and tugged at something she was loath to analyse. 'You slept well?'

No, and I missed you like hell. 'Thank you.'

'That's not an answer,' he reproved. Would it help her to know he'd lain awake until almost dawn?

'It's all I'm prepared to give.'

'Be as angry as hell, *querida*,' he warned silkily. 'It won't make any difference.'

'That's an ambiguous statement. I imagine there's a purpose for your call?'

He didn't know whether to laugh or repress the need to wring her neck. 'Remind me to beat you.'

'Lay one hand on me, and I'll…'

'Lost for words?'

'Too many choices,' Hannah reiterated with crushing cynicism.

At the risk of having her hang up on him, he relayed pertinent details of the man he'd hired to take care of her.

'Rodney Spears is thirty-two, ex-police, average height, bulky frame, fair hair, blue eyes. He's driving a late model dark blue Holden sedan.' He gave the registration number. 'He'll be at the house in ten minutes to introduce himself.'

The bodyguard. Hannah clenched the receiver, and threw the cat stretched out on the tiles nearby such a dark look the poor animal leapt to its feet and ran from the room.

'Next you'll tell me he's an expert in unarmed combat and a sharp marksman.'

Miguel didn't answer, which in her mind was an admission by avoidance. 'Apart from the initial introduction this morning, he'll remain unobtrusively in the background. You won't notice him. Nor will anyone else.'

'This is beginning to sound like a scene from a cheap detective movie,' she alluded cynically.

'Indulge me.'

'How long is this subterfuge to continue?'

'For as long as it takes.'

'Do I entertain him for breakfast and dinner?'

Miguel's faint laughter sent goose bumps scudding down her spine. 'He has the days, *querida*. I get to take care of you at night.'

'My guardian angel,' Hannah remarked in droll tones.

'You could thank me.'

'I'm more likely to hit you,' she retaliated fiercely.

'Do you have any plans for tonight?'

'Dinner with my parents.'

'Why don't you stay with them overnight?'

This was too much. *He* was too much! 'I'm way past the age of requiring a babysitter.' She took in a deep breath in an effort to control her anger. 'Aren't you taking this *protection* thing just a bit too far?'

'No,' Miguel declared with hard inflexibility. 'Do as I ask. Please.'

'I'll think about it.'

He wanted to reach down the line and *shake* her. Stubborn independence didn't come close! Yet it was those very qualities he admired in her. But not when he was several thousand miles away.

'I don't want to see you upset or hurt.' His voice deepened slightly. *'Comprende?'*

'Okay, you've made your point,' she conceded, and heard him expel a faint sigh.

'Gracias.'

Sofia escorted a man fitting the bodyguard's description into the breakfast room, and Hannah lowered her voice.

'The cavalry has arrived.'

'I'll call you later.'

He did, and she was able to report Luc hadn't telephoned or shown up at the café.

The day had gone well, with new stock snapped up by various clients. Renee called to say there would be a change of plan and they'd eat at a restaurant.

'I'll go home and change first, then meet you there. Six-thirty?'

Should she alert Rodney Spears? Just as she thought about dialling his mobile, he rang through to confirm her evening plans, and carefully noted the changes.

Hannah checked her rear-vision mirror as she

pulled out from the car park, and glimpsed a dark blue sedan follow at a discreet distance.

Then she lost him in the flow of traffic, and she didn't catch sight of the sedan until an hour later when she left the house *en route* to the restaurant.

It was, she reflected silently, totally unnecessary for him to shadow her every move. When did the man eat, for heaven's sake? Hamburgers and fries at a drive-through? And he had to sleep some time, surely?

Miguel was probably paying him a small fortune, but that didn't stop her from offering Rodney a one-hundred-dollar bill to eat in the restaurant.

'Look on it as a bonus,' she advised when he offered a protest. 'I'll go ahead and ensure you get a table.'

She did, and she'd only been seated a few minutes when Renee and Carlo entered the foyer.

'Darling, have you been waiting long?' Renee greeted anxiously. 'We got held up in traffic.'

It was a pleasant evening. The food was superb, each course presented with flair and artistry. Hannah sipped a half-glass of wine throughout the meal, and together they caught up on each other's news.

'How is Cindy?' Renee broached as she forked a few morsels of salad, then speared a sliver of chicken.

'She was discharged this morning.'

Renee looked at her daughter carefully. 'One imagines Luc's appearance at the Leukaemia Charity Ball was deliberate, rather than a chance circumstance?'

'I have no idea,' Hannah indicated with a slight shrug. 'Nor do I care.'

'It doesn't bother you that he's in town?'

'Why should it? He's a bad memory I'd prefer to forget.'

'He hasn't attempted to contact you?'

'What is this?' she queried lightly. 'The third degree?'

'You would tell us if he proves to be a nuisance?' her father countered insistently.

'He won't get the opportunity.' Her omnipotent husband was taking care of it. She spared a glance towards the bodyguard's table, and saw that he was just finishing up.

She could confide in her parents, but what was the point in worrying them unnecessarily? She opted not to suggest she follow them home and stay overnight. She hadn't done so before on any of the other occasions Miguel had been away. If she suggested it now, their suspicions would be aroused. And what was the point? In her opinion, Miguel's precautions were way over the top. Besides, the house and grounds were secure with a state-of-the-art security system.

When the waiter cleared their plates Hannah declined dessert, the cheeseboard, and settled for coffee. It had been a leisurely meal, and nice to catch up with her parents away from the social scene.

'We should discuss Christmas, darling,' Renee ventured. 'I thought I'd do lunch this year, and invite Esteban.'

Christmas? Why, that was—

'Nine weeks away, darling,' her mother reminded. 'The first of the pre-Christmas social festivities begins next week.'

Heavens, it was that close? 'I'll check with Miguel, but I'm sure lunch will be fine.'

'Well, this is a nice surprise.'

Hannah heard her father's words an instant before she felt a hand touch her shoulder.

'What will you check with me, *querida*?'

She turned her head at the sound of that deep, faintly accented drawl, and felt the floor drop away.

Miguel?

'I didn't expect you back until tomorrow night,' she managed an instant before his mouth closed over hers in a brief, tantalising kiss. The quick sweep of his tongue wreaked havoc with her senses, and it took a few seconds to regain her scattered thoughts.

Why was he *here* at this restaurant?

'I caught a taxi from the airport.'

'Have you eaten?' Renee queried warmly as he took the chair next to Hannah.

'On the plane,' Miguel confirmed. 'However, I'll join you for coffee.' He caught hold of her hand and lifted it to his lips, then he linked his fingers through her own and rested them on his thigh.

His smile left her breathless, the faint teasing quality stirring her emotions to fever pitch within seconds.

'What will you check with me?' he repeated, giving Hannah his total attention.

It wasn't fair that one man should possess such

devastating sensuality, or that she could be rendered so intensely vulnerable by his look, his touch.

From somewhere she restored order to her scattered thoughts. 'Christmas. Renee mentioned lunch, if it suits your father to join us for dinner.'

How did Miguel know she'd be dining at this restaurant?

Rodney Spears, Hannah concluded. The bodyguard had obviously reported the change in venue to Miguel. But what had occurred to influence Miguel to drop everything and fly home at a moment's notice?

Whatever it was, it had to wait until they were alone, and she toyed with her coffee, stirring it unnecessarily, then she sipped the contents without registering the excellent espresso blend.

The next hour seemed to be one of the longest in her life, and she breathed an inward sigh of relief when Miguel indicated they would leave.

Hannah burst into speech the instant they were inside the car, and Miguel effectively silenced her by placing a hand over her mouth.

'It'll keep until we get home.' He put the car in gear and reversed out before heading towards the exit.

'The hell it will,' she said fiercely as he joined the flow of traffic and headed towards Toorak.

Miguel slanted her a long glance as he drew to a temporary halt at a set of lights. 'The thought that I might have cut my trip short just to be here with you does not please you?'

'I'm still mad at you over the bodyguard bit.' She

met his gaze and held it, then the lights changed and he gave the road his attention. 'I take it I have Rodney to thank for reporting to you my every move?'

'That's what I pay him to do.'

'A case of total overkill.'

'You may change your mind when you see what I have to show you.'

Something in his tone stilled the retort she was about to utter. A cold hand closed round her heart, and she searched his features, noting the hard set of his jaw, the serious expression which didn't bode well.

'It's Camille, isn't it?' Hannah queried quietly. 'What has she done?'

Miguel turned the car into their driveway, paused while the electronically controlled gates swung open, then he headed towards the house. Within minutes he entered the garage and cut the engine.

He popped the boot and removed a bag and his briefcase. 'Let's go indoors, shall we?'

He led her into the study, dropped his bag to the floor, then he placed the briefcase on the desk, unlocked it, and extracted a large manila envelope.

'A scanned copy of these was sent to me by e-mail today.' He withdrew six colour prints and spread them out on the desk. 'Look at them carefully.'

There was no mistaking the first three prints. They featured herself and Luc sharing lunch. The second three prints were something else entirely.

Miguel and Camille seated at a table together.

Worse, they were looking into each other's eyes with an expression only lovers shared.

Hannah felt sick, and it was all she could do to regulate her breathing. Dear heaven. Miguel and *Camille*?

'Look at them very carefully, *querida*,' Miguel prompted gently. He was almost afraid to touch her for fear she might shatter. A silent rage reasserted itself, and he consciously held it in check. 'They are not quite what they seem.'

'They look real enough to me.'

'As they are meant to.' He picked up one print and pointed to Camille. 'If you look very carefully, you will see there is a slight difference in the reflection of light.' He picked up a pen and pointed its tip to the print. 'Here. Do you see?'

The texture wasn't quite the same, the shade of light reflecting from one set of features compared to the other was fractionally different.

'The original photograph has been digitally enhanced on a computer. In this particular print your image has been removed, and Camille's image superimposed. I had it checked out.' He picked up a sheet of paper and handed it to her. 'This report confirms it.'

Hannah was silent as she examined the prints again, then she read the in-depth report noting the technical irregularities.

'What do you think Camille's next step will be?' she queried slowly, trying to dispel the ache that had settled round her heart.

'At a guess, Camille will ensure you receive the second set of prints some time tomorrow.'

'Delivered personally, with verbal embellishment.' Hannah predicted. 'Will she take it further, do you think?'

Miguel arched one eyebrow. 'The media? She may try. However, these prints will never be used.' He had influence, and a copy of the technician's report had already been faxed to various sources.

'I owe you an apology.'

He took the prints and the report from her hand and locked them in his briefcase.

'For what, precisely?'

'Accusing you of overreacting,' Hannah said simply. 'And I want to thank you for ensuring I saw those—' she indicated his briefcase '—before Camille dredged every ounce of shock value from them tomorrow.'

She died a thousand deaths just thinking about it.

Miguel lifted a hand and trailed his fingers down her cheek. 'Camille is about to learn I will not tolerate any form of invasion.'

She looked at him, taking in his strength, the power he exuded, and felt infinitely relieved she wasn't his enemy. 'I see.'

His mouth curved slightly. 'Do you?'

'Yes.' It was all about preserving the image, professionally and personally. She told herself she understood. Hadn't she been reared to be aware of *image*? The private-school education, extra-curricular activities, the social niceties? Luc had been her only transgression…if believing the false words of a cad could be termed a transgression.

'I doubt that you do,' Miguel denied silkily. 'Verbal abuse is difficult to prove without an independent witness. So is slander.' His expression hardened. 'However, these prints and the report prove Camille's intent to defame.'

'You intend to confront her?'

'Not personally.' His voice was clipped, he was watching her expressive features. 'In the only way she will understand.'

'Legal action?'

'Yes.'

There was a ruthlessness apparent that boded ill for anyone daring to cross him, and Hannah shivered, caught up in a mix of complex emotions.

He wanted it done. Camille and her obsessive behaviour out of their lives. As to Luc… It would be as well if he never caught sight of him again. To do so would incite the possibility of physical assault, he decided grimly.

Hannah took in a deep breath, then released it. 'What do you want me to do?'

'Nothing. Absolutely nothing, do you understand? We must wait for her next move.' His gaze speared hers, dark and incredibly formidable. 'No heroics, Hannah. Rodney Spears will be close at all times.'

Miguel reached forward and caught hold of her shoulders, sliding his hands down her back as he pressed her body close in against his own. He angled his head and nuzzled her earlobe, then feathered a trail of kisses down the edge of her neck. 'Miss me?'

Dear heaven, *yes*. She didn't like sleeping alone in their bed. She'd turn over in her sleep, subconsciously searching for the warmth of his body, seeking the touch of his hands, the reassuring brush of his lips…only to discover a cool empty space.

'Uh-huh.' His mouth was playing havoc with her senses. The blood sang in her veins, heating all the pleasure pulses and creating a fast-pacing tempo that demanded more, much more than the touch of his lips.

Hannah gave a faint gasp as an arm skimmed beneath her knees and Miguel lifted her against his chest. Her eyes were almost on a level with his own as he carried her into the foyer and began ascending the stairs.

She saw the passion smouldering in those dark depths and felt the thrill of anticipated pleasure as he gained the gallery and strode towards their bedroom.

When he lowered her down to her feet she simply wound her arms round his neck and brought his mouth down to her own.

She was hardly aware of him divesting her of her clothes, or that her fingers dispensed with shirt buttons, took care of his belt and the zip on his trousers.

There was only the need to feel skin on skin, the ecstasy of their joined bodies moving in perfect harmony as they created the ultimate pleasure.

Something they sought and achieved again in the

early dawn hours before sleep claimed them for a brief hour.

The need to rise and face the new day saw them shower, dress, share breakfast and depart the house in separate cars *en route* to their respective places of business.

CHAPTER EIGHT

How long would it take Camille to stage her confrontation?

It had to be today, Hannah estimated, for if the Frenchwoman had gone to such pains to discover Miguel's plans, she'd be aware he was due to return home tonight.

Anticipating the time and place made her edgy, and by midday she was fast becoming a nervous wreck. It made sense that Camille would choose a time when Hannah was alone, which meant the hour Elaine went on lunch break, or immediately afterwards when Hannah visited the café.

Knowing Rodney Spears remained unobtrusively on duty provided reassurance.

Hannah checked her watch, and indicated Elaine should go to lunch, during which the phone rang three times, three clients called in to collect orders, two people opted to browse, and Camille was a no-show.

The nervous tension mounted with every passing minute as she ordered a Caesar salad and carrot juice at the café counter, paid, then selected one of three empty tables and took a seat.

The salad was delectable, she knew, because she frequently ordered the dish. However, today she could have been eating chalk, and her appetite was non-existent.

Hannah sat there for more than half an hour, then she ordered bottled water and slowly sipped it over the next fifteen minutes. Camille was nowhere to be seen.

At ten to two, Hannah walked out onto the street, visited a nearby newsagent and selected a card to send to Cindy, then she retraced her steps to the boutique.

Elaine left at four, and an hour later Hannah checked the locks, set the alarm, closed up and walked to the car park.

She slid into the Porsche and closed the door, inserted the key into the ignition, then gasped in shocked surprise as the door opened from the outside.

Camille leant forward and dropped a large envelope onto her lap. 'I thought you should have these.' She stood back and prepared to close the door. 'By the way, Perth was fun, darling.'

Where had she come from? Hannah questioned silently. Then she heard the sound of an engine, and she turned to see Camille behind the wheel of a car as it moved quickly towards the exit.

Seconds later Rodney Spears appeared out of nowhere. 'Are you okay?'

'I'm fine.'

He didn't appear convinced. 'I'll report in to Mr Santanas.'

Hannah tried for a smile, and almost made it.

Rodney Spears had already hit the rapid dial key and was talking into the phone. 'The perpetrator dropped off a package. One minute contact. Yes, your wife is fine. I'll follow her home.' He cut the connection. 'Are you okay to go now, ma'am?'

She was about as okay as she would ever be. 'Sure.' Seconds later she cleared the exit and joined the line of cars crawling along Toorak Road.

Perth? Why had Camille mentioned Perth?

It took several minutes to reach the turn-off, and she moved freely through various residential streets before entering her own.

Miguel's Jaguar was parked outside the front door, and she drew the Porsche to a halt behind it.

No sooner had she entered the foyer than he was there, tall and brooding, his eyes compellingly dark as he raked her petite frame.

His gaze shifted to the large envelope in her hand, and he took it from her, then he cupped her chin and kissed her, hard.

'Let's take this into the study.' Miguel caught hold of her hand and led the way. 'I think we could both do with a drink.'

And then some, Hannah echoed silently as she entered the large book-lined room, watching as he opened a bottle of chilled white wine and filled two goblets with the golden liquid.

She accepted one and took a long sip of the contents as he leaned one hip against the desk.

Hannah indicated the envelope. 'Aren't you going to open that?'

'In a minute. First, there's something you need to know.'

She held his gaze, then said slowly, 'I don't think I want to hear this.'

'Camille apparently discovered I would be in Perth, and she not only caught an earlier flight, she also booked into the same hotel.'

He caught the fleeting stricken look before she successfully controlled it, and he felt moved to violence at the lengths Camille was prepared to go to wreak destruction.

'Don't tell me,' Hannah said bitterly. 'Not only does that envelope contain doctored photographs we've already seen, but shots taken of the hotel with the date function exposed.' Her gaze lanced his. 'What else? You leaving your hotel room? Camille posing in the hallway with the room number showing, should I want to check it out?'

'Worse. Camille lying almost naked in an unmade bed. The fact it isn't *my* bed is immaterial, as most of the rooms are identical.'

She stood up and carefully placed the goblet down onto the desk. *Calm*, a tiny voice soothed. Stay calm. Just go look at the prints. Examine them carefully. And don't say a word until you're done.

With slow deliberation she slit the edge of the envelope and extracted the prints. One by one she discarded them onto the desk until she came to the final six.

As she anticipated, there was a photo taken of the hotel exterior, another of the reception area with a clear view of Camille checking in. The hallway, displaying a room number on the door. Miguel emerging from the same room. And the final two showing Camille sprawled in differing poses among rumpled sheets looking dreamily sated and incredibly seductive.

Hannah's first inclination was to rip them in half and throw them in the waste bin. It sickened her to look at them, and she felt positively ill at the mental image of Miguel pleasuring another woman. Even if it hadn't happened, just the thought was enough to kill her.

'Look at the date.'

Miguel's voice penetrated the dark void into which she'd mentally retreated, and she shook her head.

'Por Dios.' The husky imprecation sounded like silk being razed by razor-sharp steel. *'Look.'*

It was today's date. *Today?* But—

'I was here last night,' Miguel relayed inexorably. 'With you.'

Irrefutable proof. 'Just as well,' Hannah ventured with a shaky smile. 'Otherwise I'd have killed you, or worse.'

He appeared vaguely amused. 'Then it's fortunate I have an alibi for Monday evening.'

'I hope it's watertight.'

'It is. Alejandro will confirm.' His voice became hard, his expression inflexible. 'Camille will be served with an interim injunction. If she chooses to disregard it, she'll be charged, independently of existing harassment charges.' He paused fractionally. 'Then there's scientific proof regarding tampering of photographic prints.' His gaze speared hers. 'If she's wise, she'll take the first flight out of here.'

And their lives would revert to normal. Until the next time, Hannah added cynically. Although many women coveted Miguel, none had gone to such extraordinary lengths as Camille. Because the woman was obsessive? A practised man-stealer who derived her satisfaction from setting the scene and playing a devious game?

It made Hannah feel fiercely territorial. And possessive. About Miguel, her marriage, her home... *everything* she held sacred.

There were a few what if's tumbling around in her mind, and she felt sickened at the thought that Camille's plan had almost worked.

Don't go there, she silently cautioned. A partnership, a marriage, had to be built on trust. If there wasn't trust, there was nothing.

She reached for her goblet and took a generous sip of wine. It curled round her stomach and seeped into her veins, gradually lessening the tension.

A few weeks ago she hadn't known of Camille Dalfour's existence. Yet in the past week the Frenchwoman had managed to create chaos.

Miguel could take whatever action he chose. But *she* intended to instigate a strategy of her own.

In an impulsive move she drained the remaining wine in a long swallow, then replaced the empty goblet down onto the desk.

'I feel like a swim before dinner.'

Miguel let her go, and when the door closed behind

her he slid the prints back into the envelope and locked them in the wall safe. Then he picked up the phone and dialled his lawyer's number.

Hannah slipped out of her clothes and stepped into a stunning deep aqua one-piece, then she pinned up her hair, snagged a towel and ran lightly down the stairs.

The pool looked inviting, the water clear and sparkling in the early evening sunlight. The heat of the day had diminished slightly, but it was still hot, and she dived cleanly in at the deep end and when she surfaced she struck out with leisurely strokes, one lap after another, until she'd counted to fifty, then she turned onto her back and lay there, held buoyant by the crystal water.

She could feel the sun on her face, her limbs, and she closed her eyes, becoming lost in reflective thought.

Soon she would need to emerge, go upstairs, shower and change ready for dinner. But, for now, she was bent on enjoying the quietness and the solitude.

Five minutes later she rolled onto her stomach in one fluid movement and made her way to the tiled ledge.

The strategy took shape as she showered, then she dried her hair and slipped into a casual pencil-slim skirt and top. Minimum make-up, a touch of lipstick and she was ready.

Dinner was timed for six-thirty, and a quick glance

at her watch revealed she had just five minutes to set the plan in motion.

Rather than use the house line, she extracted her cell-phone and punched in a series of numbers.

'Graziella?' She exchanged pleasantries, then voiced her request. 'Could I speak to Camille, if she's there?'

If Camille was surprised at the identity of her caller, she didn't show it.

'Hannah, how charming, *chérie*.' Her tone was pure feline.

'Let's do lunch tomorrow.' Hannah named an up-market restaurant a block from the boutique. 'One o'clock. Be there.' She cut the connection before Camille had a chance to utter a further word.

Dinner was a simple meal of chicken served with piquant rice and a delectable salad with fresh fruit to follow. Hannah declined wine in favour of a lemon spritzer, and admired Miguel's appetite while she merely picked at the food on her plate.

'Not hungry?'

She met Miguel's steady gaze and effected a light shrug. 'A client brought in a platter of fresh grapes, crackers and cheese. Elaine and I nibbled all afternoon.'

'You haven't forgotten we have tickets for the opening of David Williamson's new play tomorrow night?'

She'd been so preoccupied with Camille, she hadn't checked her social diary for days. 'No, of course not.'

'I have some work to do on the laptop for an hour or so,' Miguel declared as Hannah pushed her plate to one side.

'Likewise.' End-of-month invoices, stock receipts, and she also needed to check catalogues from several different fashion houses. 'I should make a start on it.'

'You load the dishwasher,' he instructed, rising to his feet. 'I'll make coffee.'

There was a part of her that wanted the comfort of his touch, the warmth of his arms and the feel of his mouth on hers. In reassurance? It didn't help to feel this needy. Yet they shared a marriage, had created a bond, and what more natural than to go to him, wind her arms round his neck and pull his head down to hers?

She couldn't do it. Not here, not now. Camille stood like a spectre between them, a living, breathing entity that seemed to sap her natural warmth and spontaneity.

When the coffee was made, she poured it into two cups and carried hers through to the comfortable room next to Miguel's study. It wasn't as large as his, but it held an antique desk, bookshelves, filing cabinet, and a laptop.

For the next two hours she worked diligently, and when the paperwork was up to date she fired off a few e-mails to friends, which mostly took care of personal correspondence.

'Not finished yet?'

Hannah looked up and saw Miguel's tall frame leaning against the door-jamb. He'd removed cuff-links and rolled back his shirt-sleeves. The top few buttons on his shirt were loosened, and he looked as if he'd raked fingers through his hair more than once.

'Five minutes.'

'Want to watch a video?'

Why not? 'Okay.'

'Comedy? Action? Drama?'

She wrinkled her nose and gave him an impish grin. 'Surprise me.'

When she entered the entertainment room he sat sprawled on the leather couch, a half-magnum of chilled champagne rested in an ice-bucket, there was a packet of crisps waiting to be opened, the lights were dimmed, and the television screen was running previews prior to the main movie.

Miguel patted the space beside him and extended a hand. His eyes were dark and his mouth curved into a sensual smile. 'Come here.'

'That sounds like an invitation,' she murmured as she crossed the room, and his smile broadened.

'Do you need one?'

Hannah indicated the ice-bucket. 'Are we celebrating?'

He caught hold of her hand and pulled her down to him. He leaned forward, eased the cork from the bottle, then poured the contents into two flutes and handed her one. 'Salut.'

Miguel took a sip of excellent vintage champagne and watched as she mirrored his action, then he took the flute from her hand and gave her his.

It was a deliberately sensual gesture, and she held

his gaze for a few seconds, all too aware of the exigent sexual chemistry between them.

Liquid fire coursed through her veins, awakening each separate sensory nerve-end until her body became one pulsing ache in anticipation of his touch.

With considerable effort she dragged her gaze away and looked blindly at the television screen, focusing on the Technicolor images as the movie began to unfold.

The champagne was superb and she sipped the contents slowly, aware of the shift in Miguel's frame as he draped an arm along the back of the couch bare inches above her shoulders.

It was a relationship film, the acting excellent, and if she remembered correctly both male and female leads had earned Oscar nominations for the parts they played.

Hannah gradually became absorbed in the plot, and relaxed a little. She finished her champagne and Miguel took the empty flute from her fingers, placed it on a nearby low table, then settled back.

Minutes later she was aware of his fingers playing idly with her hair, gradually loosening the pins that held the smooth twist neatly together.

Her concentration was shot to hell as he leaned close and nuzzled her earlobe, then began pressing light kisses along the edge of her neck. When he savoured the sensitive hollow at its base, it was all she could do not to groan out loud.

'You want to see this movie?' she questioned huskily, and heard his soft chuckle.

'You watch it, *querida*.' His fingers slipped open one shirt button and slid beneath her lacy bra to tease one burgeoning peak. 'I have something else in mind.'

'Here?'

A hand covered her thigh and began a slow upward slide. 'We'll eventually make the bedroom.' He released another shirt button. 'But for now, enjoy.'

Five minutes was all it took for her to twist her fingers into the folds of his shirt and pull him hard against her. It was her mouth that sought his with hungry passion, eliciting a husky chuckle as his arms bound her close.

With urgent hands she sought his waist, wrenching the buckle open in her quest to touch him as he had caressed her.

She felt shameless, utterly wanton, in the need for his possession, and she gasped as he reared to his feet in one easy movement and strode towards the stairs.

On reaching the bedroom they helped remove each other's clothes, then Miguel took her down onto the bed with him and subjected her to such exquisite lovemaking she wept from the joy of it.

Later, much later, it was she who initiated a slow, sensual journey that had him breathing deeply as he fought for control, only to lose it as she rode him to a tumultuous climax that left their bodies slick with sensual sweat and sated emotions.

CHAPTER NINE

THE day began with rain, which diminished to light showers and by midday the city was bathed in steamy heat and high humidity.

Hannah had dressed to kill in a tailored lightweight black suit that shrieked *class*. The deep V of the buttoned jacket showed a tantalising glimpse of cleavage. Black stiletto-heeled shoes added extra height to her petite frame and sheer black stockings showcased slender calves. Her hair was smoothed into a sleek chignon, and she wore minimum jewellery.

The overall look was one of a woman who was self-confident with high self-esteem. It hardly mattered that inside she felt like jelly as she entered the chosen restaurant a deliberate few minutes late.

It appeared Camille intended to play the same game, for she was nowhere in sight, and Hannah allowed the *maître d'* to escort her to a reserved table where she ordered a light spritzer and sipped it slowly as the minutes ticked on.

The waiting increased her nervous tension, and after ten minutes she summoned the waiter and placed her order. If Camille intended to be a no-show—

'Hannah. My apologies.' The voice was as fake as the smile Camille offered as she slid into the seat opposite. 'I was held up on the phone.' She lifted a hand in an expressive Gallic gesture. 'Parking, you know how it is.'

Begin as you mean to go on, a tiny voice prompted. 'I've already ordered. I can only spare an hour.'

The wine steward appeared and Camille ordered *Dom Perignon*. 'I thought we'd celebrate, darling.'

'And the occasion is?' Hannah queried with a lift of one eyebrow.

'Why—*life*.' Camille's smile didn't reach her eyes. 'Isn't that enough reason?'

'Not,' she countered firmly, 'when you're determined to interfere in mine.'

The waiter presented the menu and Camille spared it the briefest of glances, ordered a salad, then flipped Hannah a hard, calculated look. 'Haven't you learnt I am a formidable adversary?'

'A very foolish one.'

Camille's gaze narrowed. 'What did you think of the prints, darling?'

'The digitally altered ones?' Hannah posed silkily. 'Or the few of you sprawled among the sheets in a state of *déshabillé*?'

The calculation evident intensified into something that was almost dangerous. 'How else would I be, when Miguel had just left my bed?'

'Wrong, Camille,' she corrected with deceptive quietness. 'Miguel was never in your bed.'

Camille's expression didn't change. 'Failing to face up to reality, darling?'

Hannah speared a succulent asparagus, dipped the tip in the river of hollandaise sauce on her plate, and took time to savour it. 'It is *you* who needs a reality check,' she offered seconds later.

'The prints were explicit.'

She looked at the Frenchwoman, and almost felt sorry for her. 'A fantasy, Camille.'

Camille's lips tightened. 'Irrefutable proof. The date function does not lie.'

'No,' Hannah agreed. 'You made just one small mistake.'

'And what was that?'

She took her time in answering. 'Miguel flew home Tuesday evening.'

'Impossible. The suite was still occupied.'

'By Alejandro,' she confirmed. 'You were just too clever in activating the camera date function. It made a mockery of Miguel being in your bed, when he was already in mine.'

'What of Monday night, Hannah?' Camille queried hatefully, and Hannah fought back the desire to slap the Frenchwoman's cheek.

'Camille, give it up. You played what you thought was your trump card, and it proved to be the joker.'

Red lacquered nails on one hand curled round the table napkin. 'You invited me to lunch to tell me this?'

'No,' she denied. 'I wanted the opportunity to warn you in person that I won't tolerate your attempts to interfere in my life, or my marriage.'

Camille pressed a hand against the region of her heart. 'I am so afraid.'

The degree of dramatic mockery was almost laughable, if Hannah was inclined to see humour in the situation. 'Be afraid,' she warned inflexibly. 'I can have you charged with harassment and stalking.' Her gaze was direct, her tone icy with intent. She waited a beat, then added, 'I doubt your aunt will be impressed. Nor, I imagine, will Graziella and Enrico del Santo.'

Camille's eyes glittered with dark malevolence.

'I am not finished with you yet. Miguel—'

'Finds you as much of a nuisance as I do,' Hannah intercepted smoothly. 'Go get a life, Camille. And get out of mine.'

A venomous stream of French issued from Camille's perfectly outlined mouth in a pithy, street-gutter diatribe that left those who comprehended the language in little doubt of an attack on Hannah's parentage, status and character.

Two things happened simultaneously, and Hannah had the briefest warning of both.

Camille's hand snaked out and caught her cheek a stinging slap. Champagne spilled across the damask tablecloth. Then Rodney Spears appeared from nowhere and held the Frenchwoman's flailing arms in a restraining grip.

What happened next was almost comedic, as the waiter almost flew to the table, followed close on his heels by the *maître d'*. Fellow patrons looked alarmed, others merely curious, and throughout it all Camille continued to demean every one of Hannah's relatives, both living and those who had passed on.

It almost contained a surreal quality, like something out of a movie.

'You wish me to call the police, *madame*?' the *maître d'* queried with concern. He was all too aware of Hannah's identity and her connection to two of the city's wealthiest families.

Hannah ignored Rodney Spears' nod of assent. 'No.'

'You are sure, *madame*?' he repeated anxiously. 'You are not hurt?'

The left side of her face stung, emotionally she was a little shaken up, but that was all. 'I'm fine.'

'There will, of course, be no charge for the meal. Can I get you something to drink?'

'I will take care of Mrs Santanas,' Rodney asserted in a tone that brooked no argument. 'Just as soon as I have escorted this woman from the premises.'

He shot Hannah a direct look. 'You are quite sure you don't want her detained?'

She turned towards Camille, who resembled a spitting cat waiting for another opportunity to lash out. 'Come within ten metres of me again, and I'll slap you with every charge in the book,' she warned with quiet dignity. Difficult, when inside she felt like a nervous wreck.

Rodney strong-armed the Frenchwoman from the restaurant, and Hannah viewed the table, the spilled champagne, the scattered food.

'I apologise,' she offered simply, and had her words immediately waved aside. She gathered up her purse and withdrew her credit card.

'No, no, *madame*.' He waved aside the card. 'There is no need to leave. Let me arrange another meal.'

'Thank you, but I must get back to work.' She had to get out of here and breathe in some fresh air.

'You should wait for the detective to return.'

The bodyguard. Oh, hell, that meant Rodney would report to Miguel, and then, she grimaced, there would be hell to pay.

It didn't take long. Ten minutes, Hannah counted, checking her watch as her cell-phone rang.

'What in *hell* are you playing at?' Miguel demanded the instant she acknowledged the call.

'Protecting my own turf,' she relayed imperturbably, and heard his soft curse.

'Don't be facetious.'

'The cavalry arrived just in time.'

'Hannah,' he growled. 'I am far from being amused.'

'I wasn't exactly laughing, myself.'

'Close the boutique and go home.'

'Why? I'm fine.'

'Hannah—'

'If you must conduct a post-mortem, it can wait until tonight.'

The answering silence was palpable, and she could almost *hear* him summoning control. 'Tonight,' he conceded hardly. 'Meantime, Rodney stays close. *Comprende?*'

Rodney's instructions were explicit, for he took *close* to mean his presence inside the boutique in full view of any clientele who happened to wander in and peruse the stock.

Elaine was fascinated by the drama, concerned at the reddened patch on Hannah's cheek, applied an ice-pack, and insisted on staying until closing time.

Of Camille there was neither sign nor word, and Hannah suffered Rodney escorting her to the car park, then following so close behind his bumper was almost touching her car.

Miguel greeted her at the door, and she cast him an exasperated look as he took her face between both hands and conducted a tactile examination of the affected cheek.

There was a slight bruise just beginning to appear over the cheekbone, and his gentle probing made it difficult not to wince.

'Talk to me,' Miguel commanded. 'Does it hurt when you move your jaw?'

She effected a light shrug, and saw his gaze narrow. 'Not too much.'

He took hold of her arm and led her into the study, closed the door, then he turned to face her.

'Now, suppose you tell me how you happened to lunch with Camille?'

Oh, my, the third degree. The simple truth was the only way to go. 'I rang and invited her.'

His features assumed a brooding study. Without a word he crossed to the desk and leaned a hip against its edge.

'What in heaven's name possessed you to do that?'

The query was silk-smooth and dangerous, and she viewed him with open defiance.

'I tired of being a victim. Camille was running all the action. I figured it was about time she was told enough was enough.'

'Even knowing I had already instigated legal action and the matter was in hand?' His gaze was direct and analytical. 'Aware,' he continued with an infinite degree of cynicism, 'that the woman was unpredictable, and therefore dangerous?'

'I wasn't alone with her,' Hannah defended. 'And, thanks to you, the inestimable Rodney was on hand.'

His gaze speared hers. 'Did it occur to you what might have happened if he hadn't been there?'

She drew herself up to her full height and glared at him. 'If you're done with the inquisition, I'm going to have a shower and change.'

Miguel uncoiled his length and reached her before she had taken more than a step. His hands closed over her shoulders, then he cupped her chin and tilted her head. 'Give me your word there'll be no more attempts at independent heroics.'

He was close, much too close. A pulse thudded at the base of her throat, and she just stood still, looking at him as he examined her features with daunting scrutiny.

The breath seemed to catch in her throat, and her eyes clung to his, bright, angry, yet intensely vulnerable. 'I'll give it some thought.'

His husky imprecation acted like a catalyst.

'Are you done?' She tried to wrench away from him and failed. 'Let me go, damn you!'

His eyes assumed an inexorable bleakness. 'Dinner will be ready in half an hour.' He brushed the pad of his thumb along her lower lip, felt it quiver, and wanted to *shake* her. 'We're due at the theatre at seven-thirty.'

Oh, Lord. She almost groaned out loud. The play. The producer was a personal friend. Not to appear would be the height of impoliteness.

'I'm not hungry.'

Emotional upheaval and nerves were hell and damnation. Heaven knew she'd experienced enough of both in the past week to last her for ages.

'If you're not in the dining room in half an hour, I'll come get you.'

Her eyes widened, deepening to a brilliant sapphire. 'Don't play the heavy husband,' she warned, and saw his eyes harden.

'Hannah.' His voice held a silky warning she chose not to heed.

'Don't,' she retaliated angrily. 'Just—*don't*.'

Miguel released her without a further word, and she walked from the room.

A leisurely shower did much to restore her equilibrium, and, donning fresh underwear, she pulled on smart jeans and a top, blow-dried her hair, then she went downstairs.

Sofia had prepared a succulent beef stew with crunchy bread rolls and a salad. The pervasive aroma tempted Hannah's appetite, and she ate with enjoyment.

She thought of a few topics of conversation, then abandoned each of them.

'Nothing to say?'

She glanced at him, met his gaze and held it, then she forked some rice and speared a plump prawn. 'What would you suggest? My contretemps with Camille has been done to death.'

'Renee rang. She assured me it was of no importance, and indicated she'll have the opportunity to speak with you tonight.'

Hannah looked at him sharply. 'You didn't tell her about today?'

'No. Why would I worry her unnecessarily?'

Her mother would freak if she discovered the extent of Camille's campaign and the repercussions it had caused.

Opening night at the theatre meant dressing up, and Hannah chose an ensemble that comprised a high-waisted skirt with alternating bands of cyclamen-pink and burnt orange and a strapless fitted top in burnt orange. A long wrap in cyclamen-pink completed the outfit, and she selected minimum jewellery, choosing to twist her hair into a fashionable knot atop her head.

Members of the city's social élite were in attendance, and it came as no surprise to discover Graziella and Enrico del Santo mingling among the guests in the auditorium. Also present were their friends, Aimee Dalfour, *and*, Hannah noted, Camille and Luc.

Somehow, the 'cat among the pigeons' allegory

didn't even begin to cover it. Admittedly, the harassment injunction Miguel had applied for wouldn't be served until the following day, but, given Camille was no fool, her appearance here tonight was nothing short of blatant arrogance.

Dressed to kill, the Frenchwoman looked positively sinful in a designer gown that was strapless, backless, and moulded her curves like a second skin.

A last-ditch attempt to show Miguel what he was missing?

Impossible, of course, that they could slip through the foyer unnoticed. Nor could they ignore the del Santos' presence.

Act, Hannah prompted silently as Miguel enfolded her hand within his own.

'Hannah, Miguel. How nice to see you,' Graziella greeted with enthusiasm. 'You remember Aimee, of course. Camille, Luc.'

How could they forget? They exchanged polite meaningless pleasantries and Hannah endeavoured to ignore Camille's sultry appraisal of Miguel. It was a wonder he didn't *burn* at the sensual pouting of her lips and the wicked promise portrayed in the provocative depths of her gaze.

If they were seated close together, she'd *scream,* Hannah decided, and was immeasurably relieved to see her parents moving towards them.

'Oh, my,' Renee murmured minutes later as the del Santo party moved away. 'Is there an apt word for such exhibitionism?'

'Not one utterable in polite company,' Hannah acknowledged with a touch of cynical amusement.

Within minutes the auditorium doors were opened, and the guests began making their way forward to take up reserved seating. Hannah attempted to extricate her hand from Miguel's firm clasp, and failed. Was he making a statement, or seeking to provide her with reassurance? Maybe both?

Hell, now she was being paranoid!

As they took their seats she was thankful there was no sign of the del Santo party within the immediate vicinity, and she began to relax.

The play was superbly acted, the sets, the characters magnificent, and Hannah took pleasure in losing herself in the excellence of the script, the cast, the production.

The interval provided the opportunity for patrons to mix and mingle in the foyer, have a drink or coffee at the bar, or choose to remain in their seats.

'Let's go out for coffee, shall we?' Renee suggested. 'Miguel and Carlo can opt for something stronger—' she flashed Hannah a conspiratorial smile '—while we check out the fashions other women are wearing.'

Why not? Hannah rose to her feet and felt the light touch of Miguel's hand at the back of her waist as they moved into the aisle.

His close proximity stirred her senses, and she felt the return of nervous tension as they entered the foyer.

There were people she knew, a few clients and their

partners, friends, and she paused briefly to exchange a greeting as they crossed to the bar.

'Renee, Carlo. Please join us.'

Hannah momentarily closed her eyes, then opened them again. Enrico del Santo indicated four chairs empty at their table. This was not her evening! How long did the interval last? Ten to fifteen minutes? She could survive that long in Camille and Luc's company, surely?

Miguel deliberately placed Hannah next to Renee and took the adjoining seat. He was charming to Graziella, conversed with Carlo and Enrico, and chose a polite façade whenever Camille commanded his attention.

A frequent occurrence, Hannah noticed, as she was meant to. It all became a bit much, and in a bid to escape she excused herself and headed towards the powder room.

Big mistake, she realised minutes later as Camille quickly joined her. A queue was inevitable, given the number of stalls, and Hannah stood stiffly as she waited for Camille to strike.

She wasn't disappointed. 'Don't imagine you can hide behind a bodyguard. I suppose you think you're very clever.'

Hannah turned slightly to look at the Frenchwoman. 'Not at all,' she responded lightly. 'And the bodyguard is there at Miguel's instigation.'

Camille's expression became an icy mask. 'Protecting his business investment.'

'Of course.' It was the truth, so why deny it?

'But there is a bonus,' Hannah continued quietly. 'I get to share his bed, his life, and bear his children.'

She took a shallow breath and released it. 'Admit you failed, Camille, and go look for another rich man who's not averse to your game-playing.' She paused fractionally. 'And take Luc with you.'

'He's a practised lover,' the Frenchwoman intimated with deliberate maliciousness.

'Do you think so?' Hannah contrived a slight frown. 'I found his foreplay technique reasonable, but his application needed work.' She managed a careless shrug. 'Maybe he's improved.'

Camille swung her hand in a vicious arc, except this time Hannah was prepared, and she took a quick sidestep so the slap didn't connect.

Hannah was aware of a few surprised gasps, then Renee was there, her normally composed features fierce with anger.

'You've said quite enough, Camille! Now get out of here at once. There is another set of facilities if you must use them.' She turned towards her daughter. 'Darling, are you all right?'

'Yes. Thanks,' she added, and couldn't help wondering if Miguel had sent Renee to her rescue.

'Come, let's go back to—'

'The table?' She shook her head. 'I really do need to freshen up. Tell Miguel I'll go straight to our seats.'

'I'll stay,' Renee said firmly.

'Then we'll have both our men sending out a

search party.' She could almost see the humour in the situation. 'Really, I'm fine.'

'Well,' her mother said doubtfully. 'If you're sure?'

A stall became vacant, and Hannah moved into it. Minutes later she paused in front of the long mirror to freshen her lipstick, then she emerged into the foyer.

She hadn't taken two steps when Miguel fell in beside her, and she shot him a steady look as he caught hold of her arm. 'First Renee, now *you*?'

'Another minute, and I'd have fetched you personally.'

'Entered a known *women's* domain? How brave.'

'Don't push it, *querida*,' he warned in sibilant anger.

They weren't moving in the direction of the auditorium. 'We're going the wrong way.'

'I'm taking you home.'

'The hell you are!' She resolutely refused to move. Her eyes sparked blue fire as she confronted him. 'I'm not missing the rest of the play.' She balled one hand into a fist and connected with his ribs. 'The only way you'll get me away from here is to toss me over your shoulder and carry me out!'

He was caught between laughter and voluble anger. 'Don't tempt me,' he bit back with a husky growl.

Hannah wrenched her arm from his grasp and marched, as well as four-inch stiletto heels would allow, towards the auditorium.

By the time she reached a set of double doors he

was beside her, and together they entered the dimmed theatre, located their seats, and slid into them.

Almost immediately the curtain rose and the next act commenced.

Hannah focused on the actors and their lines in a determined effort to forget Camille, Luc, and her inimitable husband. She succeeded, almost, rising from her seat with the audience to applaud the playwright, the cast, and the producer.

The exodus of patrons took a little while, and it was almost eleven when Miguel eased the Jaguar through the city streets. A shower of rain wet the bitumen, and she watched the automated swish of the windscreen wipers as the car turned into Toorak Road.

The headache that had niggled away at her temple for the past hour seemed to intensify, and as soon as he brought the car to a halt inside the garage she slid from her seat and preceded him into the house.

They reached the foyer, and his gaze sharpened as he took in her pale features. 'Take something for that headache, and go to bed.'

'Don't tell me what to do.'

'*Querida,*' Miguel drawled. 'You want to fight?'

'Yes, damn you!'

'There's a punch bag in the downstairs gym. Why don't you go try it out?'

He was amused, damn him. She threw him a dark glare. 'I might do that!'

'Just one thing,' he ventured indolently. 'Go and change first.'

She didn't even pause to think, she just bent one knee, pulled off a heeled shoe and threw it at him.

Miguel palmed it neatly, placed it carefully down onto a nearby side-table, and turned back towards her.

'Want to try again?'

This time it was her evening purse that flew through the air, and she cried out with rage as he scooped her into his arms and carried her upstairs.

Hannah hit out at his shoulders, his arms, anywhere she could connect, and groaned with angry frustration when she didn't seem to make any impression at all.

He reached the bedroom and entered it, kicking the door shut behind him, then he released her down onto the floor.

'Okay,' he growled huskily. 'That's enough.'

'Do you know how I feel?' she demanded vengefully.

'I'd say it's mutual.' He caught hold of her shoulders and held her still. 'Stop it.'

'Right at this moment, I think I hate you.'

'For being a target for some woman's warped mind?'

'I want to go to bed. Alone.' *Fool*, a tiny voice derided. You're taking your anger out on the wrong person. Except she wasn't being rational.

Miguel released her slowly. 'Then go to bed.' He turned and walked from the room, closing the door quietly behind him.

She looked at the door, and almost wished he'd slammed it. It would have made more sense.

Slowly she crossed to the window and looked out

over the darkened gardens. The moon was high, a large round white orb that cast a milky light onto the earth below, making long shadows of small shrubs, the trees, and duplicating the shape of the house. Somewhere in the distance a dog barked, and another joined it in a howling canine melody.

Hannah closed the curtains, then slowly undressed, removed her make-up, then she pulled on the silky slip she wore to bed and slid between the sheets, snapped off the bedside lamp, and lay staring into the darkness. Images filled her mind, prominent and intrusive, and her eyes swam until tears spilled and trickled slowly towards her ears, then dripped onto the pillow.

She brushed them away, twice, then determinedly closed her eyes in a bid to summon sleep.

Except she was still awake when Miguel entered the room a long time later. She heard him discard his clothes, and felt the faint depression of the mattress as he slid into bed.

Hold me, she silently begged him. Except the words wouldn't find voice, and she lay still, listening to his breathing steady and become slow and even in sleep. It would have been so easy to touch him. All she had to do was slide her hand until it encountered the warmth of his body.

Except she couldn't do it. Be honest, she silently castigated. You're afraid. Afraid that he might ignore the gesture or, worse, refuse it. And how would she feel if he did?

Shattered.

CHAPTER TEN

HANNAH woke to the sound of the shower running in the adjoining *en suite*, and she rolled over to check the digital clock. Seven.

She slid out of bed, gathered up fresh underwear, her robe, and adjourned to the next bedroom where she showered and changed.

It would have been easy to join Miguel, just pull open the glass door and step in beside him as she did every morning. Except today she couldn't, not after last night.

And whose fault was that? a silent voice taunted.

She drew a deep breath, then returned to their room to see Miguel in the process of dressing.

He cast her a long measured look, which she returned, then she discarded her nightwear onto the bed and crossed to her walk-in wardrobe to select something to wear.

'Do you intend sulking for long?' His voice was a slightly inflected drawl, which she ignored as she stepped into sheer black stockings, then selected one of three black suits she chose to wear to the boutique.

When she emerged, he was standing in her path, and she just looked at him.

'Hannah,' he warned silkily.

'I am *not* sulking!' She *never* sulked; it wasn't in her nature.

And I don't hate you, she added silently, unable to say the words aloud. Dear heaven, what had possessed her to say such a thing? Reaction, angry tension. But words, once said, were difficult to retract. Except the longer she left the anger to simmer, the harder it would be to explain.

'What do you want me to say?' Her eyes darkened and became stormy. 'I'm sorry I acted like a bitch last night? Okay, I apologise.'

'Apology accepted.'

Hannah looked at him sharply. 'Don't patronise me.'

'Stop it right there,' Miguel warned.

'I'm not a child, dammit!' What was she doing, for heaven's sake? She was like a runaway train that couldn't stop.

'Then don't behave like one.'

'You'll forgive me if I don't join you for breakfast,' Hannah said stiffly. 'I'll stop off at a café for coffee and a croissant.'

She moved past him and entered the *en suite*. She picked up the hairbrush and attacked her hair, stroking the brush through its length until her scalp tingled, then she applied minimum make-up.

Her eyes widened as she caught sight of Miguel via mirrored reflection as he moved in to stand behind her, and her fingers faltered and tightened around the tube of lipstick.

She felt like a finely tuned string that was about to

snap as he turned her round to face him, and she was powerless to move as his head descended.

'This, *this*,' Miguel breathed close to her mouth, 'is important. Nothing else.' And he kissed her, thoroughly, until her head spun. Then he released her, and walked from the room.

Hannah gripped hold of the marbled vanity unit and tried to regain her breath. Dear heaven, what was the matter with her?

She had no idea how long she stood there, only that it seemed an age before she gathered up her bag, slid her feet into heeled shoes, and made her way downstairs to the garage.

Ten minutes later she parked the Porsche, then crossed the road, bought a daily newspaper, entered a coffee bar and joined the patrons enjoying breakfast.

At nine she unlocked the boutique and spent the next half-hour on the phone chasing a courier who had been supposed to deliver late the previous afternoon, and hadn't.

The morning dragged, and trying to continually pin a smile on her face began to take its toll. How could she pretend to be happy when inside she was breaking into a thousand pieces?

'Are you ill?' Elaine enquired with concern at midday.

'No.'

An inquisitive smile curved her attractive mouth. 'Pregnant?'

'No.'

'You sound hesitant,' Elaine teased. 'Could that be a maybe, but it's too soon to tell?'

Hannah simply shook her head. 'Go take your lunch break.' She extracted her purse and took out a note. 'Can you bring me back a chicken and salad sandwich and bottled water?' Today she'd eat in the small back room instead of spending her usual half-hour break at a nearby café.

Elaine finished at four, and the afternoon seemed to drag as Hannah checked her stock list, then made a few phone calls. A fax came through alerting that a special order would be despatched by overnight courier, and she made a note to phone the client.

Miguel's forceful image haunted her, as it had all morning, only now it was worse, for there was no one to talk to, no client entering the boutique to attract her attention, and the phone didn't ring.

Thinking about last night made her stomach twist into a painful knot. Somehow Miguel's controlled anger had been worse than if he'd let fly a string of pithy oaths, or thrown something, yelled at her. Instead he'd reduced her angry outburst to a childish tantrum, and that irked and angered her more than she wanted to admit.

The electronic buzzer sounded, alerting her to someone entering the boutique, and she summoned a warm smile as she moved out from behind the desk.

'Hannah, darling.'

'Mother.' Renee always rang before calling in. Always. The fact she hadn't this time caused Hannah's forehead to crease into a slight frown.

'I know, I should have phoned first. But I was close by…' She trailed off, before launching into an explanation, 'Lunch with an old friend, darling. And I thought I'd just pop in and say hello.'

'It's great to see you.' She injected enthusiasm into her voice and crossed the floor to bestow the customary air-kiss to each cheek. 'The scarves arrived this morning. I put a few aside that I thought you might like. Would you like to see them?'

Business. If she could keep everything on a business footing, maybe Renee wouldn't notice the fine cracks in her daughter's façade.

'Oh, please, darling.'

Hannah retrieved the box, extracted three scarves and spread them across the counter. They were pure silk, exquisitely patterned, and an attractive fashion accessory.

Renee selected two, then crossed to the blouse rack, chose one, then moved to the desk. 'I'll take these, darling.' She gave a soft exclamation, and followed it with a ladylike curse. 'I don't believe it. I've left my bag in the car.'

'Locked, I hope,' Hannah said at once, concern marring her features.

'Of course, locked, darling. I have my keys.' She held them up in plain sight. 'I remember activating the alarm.'

'Where are you parked?'

'This side of the street, just a few cars down.' She held out the keys. 'Would you mind fetching it for me?' She cast the empty boutique a cursory glance. 'It'll only take a minute.'

Maybe a breath of fresh air might lift her mood, Hannah determined as she accepted the keys and made for the door.

It was hot outside, the sun's brightness intense after the air-conditioned coolness indoors. A few cars down meant she met the worst of the glare as she walked towards her mother's car, and she lifted a hand to shade her eyes. Only to come to a dead halt at the sight of a familiar tall frame standing beside Renee's Lexus.

Miguel. Looking totally relaxed and at ease, his expression shaded behind dark sunglasses. A deceptive pose, for she had no doubt beneath that calm exterior lay the coiled strength of a predator.

There was a part of her that wanted to turn back and return to the boutique, where her mother's presence would ensure civility was maintained. Yet she refused to take the easy way out. Whatever they needed to say to each other had to be said.

Miguel saw the moment she mentally squared her shoulders, witnessed the slight lift of her chin, and accurately defined the expression in her clear blue eyes.

It was her nature to confront, resolve, and move forward. He was bargaining on her doing just that.

'It's four thirty,' Hannah said evenly as she took the necessary steps to reach the Lexus. 'What are you doing here?'

He pulled back the cuff of his jacket, checked his

watch, then trapped her gaze. 'A few minutes past that, if you want total accuracy.'

Miguel didn't shift position, and she was forced to move in close as she deactivated the alarm, unlocked the passenger door, retrieved her mother's bag, then reversed the security process.

'Shall we return Renee's bag?' he queried mildly, and she threw him a measured look.

'We?'

He caught hold of her elbow, firming his grasp as she made to wrench away. *'We,'* he reiterated firmly.

'Miguel—'

'There's the easy way where we walk back to the boutique. Or I can hoist you over one shoulder and carry you. Which would you prefer?'

Her eyes sparked angry fire. 'You're giving me a choice?'

He brushed his thumb over the generous curve of her mouth. 'No.'

Her palms itched with the urge to slap him.

'Don't.' The warning was silky soft and curled round her nerve-ends.

Without a word she turned and made her way back to the boutique, aware of an explosive electric force field that surrounded them.

Hannah was startlingly aware of him, his proximity, the faint aroma of his aftershave, the clean smell of his clothes. His grasp on her elbow would tighten in a heartbeat if she attempted to pull free.

Four shop fronts, a matter of mere metres, and they reached the boutique. She didn't even question his intention to enter, for it was clearly evident he meant to.

She paused, her features strained, her eyes too dark. 'Is there a purpose to this?'

'Yes.'

Hannah extended her hand to open the door, only to have it swing inward.

'Ah, there you are,' Renee declared, her features carefully schooled. 'There was one phone call, which I dealt with.'

Hannah looked from one to the other, and settled on Miguel, suspicion uppermost. 'You set this up.' She turned towards her mother. 'Didn't you?'

'Guilty.'

'Why?' Hannah demanded, sorely tried.

'Go get your bag,' Miguel instructed. 'We're leaving.'

'I'll stay and close the boutique,' Renee informed before her daughter had a chance to protest.

'No.' Hannah threw Miguel a vengeful glare. 'And if you try any macho tactics, I'll call the police.'

'Call them.' It took two seconds to sweep an arm beneath her knees and lift her against his chest.

Renee crossed quickly to the desk, opened a cupboard, retrieved Hannah's bag, and handed it to Miguel.

'I'll never forgive you for this,' Hannah vented as she closed her fingers into a fist and set a bruising punch to his shoulder.

He turned and walked out the door, traversed the

pavement to where his car was parked, unlocked the door, then he thrust her into the passenger seat.

The next instant he crossed round to the driver's side, then slid in behind the wheel.

The engine fired and settled into a soft purr as he eased the car out of its parking space and into the flow of traffic along Toorak Road.

Hannah didn't trust herself to speak. There was too much anger to bother with meaningless words.

Instead, she looked beyond the windscreen, noting the traffic, people walking, children, mothers laughing, scolding. Movement, life. Outside, the world continued to evolve, along with people's lives.

From inside, somehow it didn't seem real. She might as well have been viewing the scene on television.

Familiar streets, familiar locale. She passed by here five days out of seven.

But not quite this far, she suddenly realised.

'You've missed the turn.'

'We're not going home.' Miguel's voice was a faintly inflected drawl, and she looked at him carefully, seeing the strength and sense of purpose evident.

'Perhaps you'd care to enlighten me exactly where we *are* going?'

He slanted her a quick glance. 'Wait and see.'

'Oh, for heaven's sake,' Hannah dismissed angrily, and refrained from offering so much as another word.

The flow of traffic intensified as they neared the city, and she contained her surprise as Miguel swung the car into the entrance of one of the inner city's most exclusive hotels.

The porter opened her door, leaving her little recourse but to slip out from the passenger seat.

What on earth were they doing here? In a hotel, for God's sake, when they had a beautiful luxurious home less than fifteen minutes distant? It was crazy. Even more puzzling was the fact Miguel had apparently checked in, for he led the way to the bank of lifts adjacent the foyer.

Hannah spared him a level glance as they rode the lift to a high floor, and within minutes Miguel ushered her into a spacious, elegantly appointed suite.

She crossed to the wide plate-glass window and parted the filmy day curtains to look at the view, then she slowly turned back to face him.

He had removed his jacket, and was in the process of loosening his tie.

'You owe me an explanation.'

Miguel discarded the tie, undid the top few buttons of his shirt, removed cuff-links from each sleeve, then he crossed to the bar-fridge.

'What would you like to drink?'

She was angry and on edge. 'Stop playing the gentleman.'

He paused, and she had the impression of harnessed strength and immeasurable control. For some reason it made her feel apprehensive.

His eyes held an expression she didn't care to define. 'What would you have me play, *amante*?'

She was reminded of silk being razed by steel, and

she crossed her arms, hugging them against her midriff in a unconscious protective gesture.

'The savage?' he posed. 'A husband who is moved to such anger, it is all he can do not to strangle his beautiful wife's neck?' He extracted bottled water, unscrewed the cap, filled a glass and handed it to her, then he took out a can of cola, pulled the tab, and drained some of the contents.

'Or perhaps I should beat you.' He lifted the can and took a long swallow. 'Believe I am sorely tempted to do both.'

'Try it,' Hannah said tightly.

He cast her a long dark look that sent shivers scudding down the length of her spine. 'Don't push me.'

Without thinking she threw the contents of her glass in his face, watching with a sense of mesmerised disbelief as the cold water splashed from his broad features down onto his shirt, leaving a huge wet patch that was impossible to ignore.

She didn't move, despite a terrible sense of panic that urged her to run as far and as fast as she could.

Instead, she stood glaring at him in silent defiance.

His eyes didn't leave hers as he set the can aside, then in seeming slow motion he pulled the shirt free from his trousers, undid the buttons, then he shrugged it off and draped it over a nearby chair before turning to face her.

With deliberate movements he reached for a neatly folded towel displayed in plain sight and removed the excess moisture from his face, then he tossed the towel onto the bed.

He was an impressive sight. Olive skin stretched over hard musculature, the liberal sprinkle of dark hair at his chest, a tight stomach, firm waist, with not a spare ounce of flesh in evidence.

'Are you done?'

'It depends.'

He took a step towards her, and she stood her ground.

'So brave,' Miguel mocked silkily, watching her pupils dilate as he drew close.

She was damned if she'd beg, and the single word emerged as a warning. 'Don't.'

He didn't touch her. 'Don't—*what*, specifically?'

'I'll fight you,' she said fiercely, unaware that her hands had tightened into fists, or that her stance had altered slightly preparatory for attack.

'You can't win.'

'I can try.' She would, too. Self defence was an art form she'd studied to a degree, and she had the element of surprise on her side.

He saw the slight lift of her chin, the muscle flex at the edge of her jaw, the anger, the fire so close to the surface.

'Do you want to so badly?'

'Yes,' Hannah vented, and saw him slide a hand into each trouser pocket.

'Then go ahead.'

Hit him? For all the times she'd wanted to, for the few occasions she actually had...now that he was placing himself at her mercy, she found she couldn't do it.

Miguel caught each fleeting expression on her mobile features, and accurately defined every one of them.

'I guess we need to talk,' she offered slowly.

'We did that. It didn't resolve anything.'

Her face paled as she recalled the explosive scene they'd shared early this morning.

'Miguel—'

Whatever else she might have said remained locked in her throat as his mouth slanted down to cover hers in a kiss that tore at the very roots of her emotional foundation.

There was nothing punishing about it, just intense evocative passion that seemed to plunder the depths of her soul, dragging something from her she was reluctant to give.

She didn't *want* to respond. Dear heaven, how could she, when there was so much hurt and anguish?

It was almost as if he was trying to tap into her fragile heart, to instil something so infinitely precious that meant more, so much more than mere words could convey.

His mouth was the only part of his body touching her. He could easily have drawn her into his arms, used his hands to mould her slender frame to his, his heavy arousal in evidence. Employed sensual body heat to tantalise her senses, to touch and tease with such skilful expertise she would soon shatter into a thousand pieces. *His.*

Yet he did none of those things. There was just his

mouth, and the mesmeric intoxication of heat and passion.

She hated the distance between them, and it took tremendous strength of will not to sink into him. *This*, after all, was the one level of communication at which they excelled.

Sex. Really great sex.

She'd thought it was enough. She'd even managed to convince herself that *love* didn't matter. But it did, and a little part of her had slowly died with each passing day.

Sensation flared, spiralling through her body, filling it with a sweet sorcery only Miguel had the power to wield.

A faint sob rose and died in her throat, a slight compulsive movement he felt rather than heard, and he sensed the way her hands rose, then fell again as she sought control.

The long slow sweep of his tongue against her own almost caused her to lose it, and she began to shake beneath the emotional weight of resisting him.

He sensed the moment she ignored her mind and went with her heart, felt the first tentative touch of her hands as they crept to his shoulders and twined together round his neck.

Something within him convulsed, and a deep shudder raked his powerful frame as he drew her close in against him.

His kiss deepened, possessing with shameless hunger as he led her down a path towards sensual conflagration.

Hannah lost track of time and a sense of place in the need to be part of him. The rest of his clothes, hers, were an unwanted intrusion, and her fingers sought the buckle fastening the belt on his trousers, only to have him shift slightly and cover her hand with his own before gently placing her at arm's length.

Her eyes widened and seemed too large in her face. Uncertain, she edged the tip of her tongue along the swollen curve of her lip. The gesture was unbidden, and she saw his eyes flare, then become incredibly dark.

He placed a finger over her lips, felt the faint tremble, and cupped her jaw.

'You are my life,' Miguel said gently. '*Amada*, the very air that I breathe. Everything.' A finger traced the pulsing cord to the base of her throat and settled in the sensitive hollow above the rapid beat of her pulse. 'You have my heart, all that I am.' His smile held a warmth that made her breath hitch. 'Always.'

Hannah wasn't capable of uttering a word.

'From the beginning,' he added. 'I took one look, and there could be no one else. Only *you*.'

She found her voice with difficulty. 'But we—'

'Married to please our respective parents, ensure the business *stayed in the family*?' He brushed a thumb along the curve of her lower lip. 'Do you really believe that?'

Her mouth quivered. 'You said—'

'I asked you to marry me.'

'I thought—'

'You think too much,' Miguel chastised gently. 'I love you. *You*,' he emphasised. 'For everything you are.'

'You loved me?' she queried as hope began to unfurl. 'From the beginning?'

'Do you really believe I'm the kind of man who would tie himself legally to a woman, contemplate making her the mother of my children—' He broke off, and shook his head. '*Querida*, haven't you come to know me better than that?'

Yes, she had. Or, at least, she'd thought she had before Camille had begun playing her games.

'Camille—'

'I barely refrained from strangling her. As to Luc—' A muscle tensed at the edge of his jaw, and his eyes took on a dangerous gleam. 'The temptation to break his jaw was never far from my mind.'

Something that had been evident on occasion, Hannah reflected. Although at the time she'd thought Miguel was simply playing the part expected of him.

And Camille?

'Notice that an interim apprehended violence order would be filed against Camille was issued yesterday. I understand she chose to take the option of dropped charges if she remove herself from the state and the country within twenty-four hours,' Miguel informed her, reading her mind.

His words were so clipped and hard, Hannah didn't doubt *he* had delivered the ultimatum in a manner Camille couldn't fail to understand.

'I see,' she said slowly.

One eyebrow slanted with musing humour. 'What do you see, *amante*?'

She lifted a hand, then let it fall to her side.

'Where do we go from here?'

'Now?' Miguel pulled her gently back into his arms, and nuzzled the delicate curve at the base of her neck. 'I'm going to make love with my wife.' He drew the soft skin into his mouth and grazed it with his teeth.

A tremor shook her slender frame as liquid fire flooded her veins, heating her body to fever pitch.

'Show her how infinitely precious she is to me.' Slowly and with infinite care, he freed the buttons on her blouse, then slid it from her arms and discarded it. Next came the zip fastening on her skirt, and he skimmed slip and briefs over her hips in one easy movement. Hannah stepped out of her heeled shoes as he unfastened the clip of her bra.

'And ensure she never has reason to doubt my love for her.' He traced the curve of one breast, then brushed his fingers back and forth across a rosy peak, watching as the bud protruded before lowering his head to capture it in his mouth.

Her body arched as he suckled, and a gasp emerged from her throat when he rolled the tender bud with the edge of his teeth, leaving her teetering on the brink between pleasure and pain.

'This isn't fair,' she inclined, reaching for the buckle on his trousers, then the zip, and seconds later he kicked aside his trousers and briefs.

'Better?'

'Much.'

'I intended to take you to dinner,' Miguel informed her as she began a subtle exploration that soon promised to have dangerous consequences.

'Maybe later.'

'With champagne,' he added for good measure, then drew in a deep breath and held it as she enclosed him.

'Room service,' Hannah offered an instant before he carried her down onto the bed.

CHAPTER ELEVEN

THEY did eat, well after the witching hour of midnight.

The lovemaking had been hard and fast, then afterwards they'd indulged themselves with a sensual feast that surpassed anything they'd previously shared. Vibrant, erotic, it was sensual magic at its most primitive.

Following a leisurely shower they donned courtesy robes, and sipped fine French champagne while they waited for room service.

When they finished the food, she leaned back in her chair. There were questions she wanted to ask. Words she needed to say. *Now*, a tiny voice prompted. Say them now.

There were tiny lines fanning out from the corners of his eyes, and his features showed evidence of emerging dark stubble.

She looked at him carefully, seeing the strength, the aura of power he projected, and knew that it would always be there. For her.

'I love you,' she revealed with quiet sincerity, and saw his features soften.

His eyes were dark, so very dark, their expression unguarded so as to almost make her catch her breath at the wealth of emotion evident. *'Gracias, mi mujer,'* he acknowledged gently.

'I always have. If I hadn't,' Hannah assured him, 'I would never have agreed to marry you.' She swallowed a small lump that suddenly rose in her throat. 'You're everything I need. All I could ever want.' Her eyes became luminous with shimmering tears. 'My life.'

Was it possible for a heart to stop beating? That emotion could be so intense it could cut off the ability to speak?

Miguel stood and pulled her into his arms. His mouth was an erotic instrument as he kissed her, gently at first, then with increasing passion.

Hannah became lost, adrift in a sea of emotion and she simply held onto his shoulders as she met and matched his fervour.

How long did they stand there, locked in each other's arms? She had no recollection of time.

Slowly he eased his mouth from hers, pressing soft kisses to her swollen lips as she sighed in protest, and she groaned a little when he disengaged her arms and crossed the room.

She watched idly as he extracted something from his jacket pocket, and returned to press a slim jeweller's case into her hand.

'I have something for you.'

'Miguel—'

'Open it.'

She did so, carefully, and felt the sudden prick of tears. Nestled in a bed of velvet was an exquisite drop necklace and matching earrings. Beautifully delicate, it linked Argyle pink and white diamonds alternately with a pear-shaped pink diamond at the base of the drop.

'They're beautiful,' Hannah whispered, feeling the moisture well, then spill to run down each cheek in a slow rivulet that paused momentarily at the edge of her jaw. 'Thank you.'

'Tears, Hannah?'

At his teasing query she blinked them away, and brushed shaky fingers across each cheek. 'I can't seem to stop.'

Miguel removed the necklace, placed it in position and fastened the safety clip. Then he leant down and brushed his lips to her temple.

The intricate centre star-burst lay just beneath the hollow of her throat, with its single line of pink sapphires and diamonds dropping several inches towards the soft swell of her breasts.

The fact he had remembered was one thing. Since the description had been her own and didn't refer to anything she'd seen, it meant he'd consigned a jeweller to craft it to this specific design.

'Don't you want to see how it looks?'

Hannah shook her head. 'It's the most beautiful thing I've ever owned,' she said softly. 'Special,' she added, aware he knew just how much the gift meant to her.

She reached for the clasp, only to have him still her hands.

'Leave it on.'

Without a further word she drew his head down to hers and initiated a kiss that proved so evocative it could have only one ending.

Later, much later, Miguel curved her in against him and pressed a light kiss to her temple. 'Sleep, *amante*. Tomorrow is another day.'

Hannah woke to the peal of the doorbell, and Miguel ushered in the waiter delivering room service breakfast.

What time was it? She cast a hurried glance at the digital clock on the bedside pedestal, and gave a groan.

Eight-fifteen! Dear heaven, she was due to open the boutique at nine, and she needed to shower, dress, get home and collect a fresh change of clothes...

With rapid movements she thrust aside the covers and slid to her feet. The shower...

'*Amada*, slow down,' Miguel growled in husky chastisement, and she cast him a harried glance.

'The boutique— You should have woken me...'

'Come and have breakfast.' He sounded indolently amused. 'You're not going anywhere.'

'What do you mean I'm not going anywhere? It's late—'

His dark musing expression held warm appreciation of her nudity, and she quickly caught up a robe, thrust her arms through the sleeves and hurriedly caught the silk edges together.

He extended a hand, caught hold of hers, and pulled her close.

'Miguel,' she protested in exasperation. 'We don't have time—'

'Yes, we do.'

'No, we don't.' She dragged fingers through the tousled length of her hair, and made an effort to free her hand.

Except she didn't stand a chance as his mouth covered hers in a lingering kiss that almost destroyed the will to move. Almost. It was she who pulled away first, and only, she suspected, because he allowed it.

He could, he knew, slide the silk from her shoulders and pull her down onto the bed. Early morning lovemaking was a mutual indulgence that made for a great start to the day. Today, however, it would have to wait.

'Renee will open the boutique this morning.'

She stilled, and gave him a searching look. 'Why?'

Miguel led her towards the table where the waiter had laid out their breakfast. 'Sit down and we'll eat.'

'I'm not doing a thing until you tell me what's going on.'

'Okay,' Miguel said easily. 'We're due to board an international flight in a few hours.'

She stilled, and her eyes were wide as she looked at him. 'What did you say?'

He reached out an arm and drew her forward and into a chair, then he took the seat opposite. 'You heard.'

'How?'

He cast her a musing glance. 'The usual way, I imagine.'

'I mean, how can we get away at such short notice?'

'Delegate.'

'I can't—'

'Yes, you can.' He drank half of his orange juice in one long swallow. 'Cindy returns to work on Monday, she will manage the boutique with Elaine's help, and Renee will go in at four each afternoon to close.'

'But—'

'The world as we know it won't end if we take time out,' Miguel relayed quietly.

He was right, it wouldn't. It was just so...*sudden*. So unexpected.

Hannah took a sip of orange juice, then another. 'Where are we going?'

'Hawaii.'

Oh, my, did he possess some kind of mind-reading gift? She mentally pictured white sand, blue sea, and white-crested surf, sunshine, and tranquillity. Lazy days, long, languid nights. Heaven.

She almost dared not ask. 'How long?'

'A week in Honolulu, and a week on Maui.'

'Honolulu?' she queried, a slow, sweet smile curving her lips. Maui. She didn't know which held the most appeal. 'Really?' Her eyes acquired a gleam. '*Today?*'

His mouth twitched with wry amusement. 'Don't look at me like that. Or we won't get out of this suite, let alone catch a scheduled flight.'

Hannah laughed, a light-hearted sound that stole round his heart and tugged a little. 'You think so?'

He reached out a hand and placed a finger over her lips. 'Breakfast, *querida*.'

'Okay,' she acquiesced. She held up one hand and began counting off her fingers. 'Hmm. A nine-hour flight.' Her eyes acquired a devilish sparkle. 'That gives me plenty of time to plan exactly how I intend to reward you.'

'Minx,' he said, tempted to discard breakfast altogether.

'Pity we need to go home to pack.'

'No,' Miguel discounted. 'We don't. I have our bags in the boot of the car.'

She couldn't restrain an incredulous smile. '*You* packed for me?'

'I have as much as you need,' he said with musing solemnity. 'Anything else you can buy there. Besides,' he added indolently, 'I don't plan on having you wear much at all most of the time.'

Hannah leaned across the table and pressed a finger to his lips. 'Well, I have news for you, *amante*. I plan to swim, lie in the sun, go for long walks, and read. And a pleasant meal among fellow diners is also a prerequisite.' Her eyes sparkled and acquired the hue of brilliant blue topaz. 'If you've only tossed briefs and a robe into my bag, you're in serious trouble.'

'Try…an evening suit, a dress or two, shorts, a few tops, bikini, shoes…' Miguel trailed off, then opened his mouth and playfully nipped her finger with the edge of his teeth before releasing it.

'Food,' she mocked gently, and began doing justice to cereal and fruit, following it with toast and strong black coffee.

They made the flight with only minutes to spare, and Hannah divided her attention between the pages of a spellbinding murder mystery and the movies offered on-screen.

It was late when they landed in Honolulu, and almost midnight by the time they checked into their hotel.

The luxury suite on a high floor overlooking Waikiki beach was superb, and Hannah crossed to the wide expanse of plate glass and slid open doors onto the lanai.

A gentle breeze wafted in from the ocean, and the air held the fresh smell of the sea. Twinkling lights outlined the mainland arching towards Diamond Head.

Miguel moved in close behind her and linked his arms around her waist. His chin rested on top of her head as she leaned back against him.

'It's magical,' she murmured softly. Melbourne, home, *Camille*, seemed so far away. Like a bad dream from which she'd just awoken. 'Thank you.'

'For what, precisely?'

'Bringing me here,' she said simply. Taking affirmative action, believing in me...*us*, she added silently.

Miguel's hands tightened fractionally, and he lowered his head to savour the vulnerable hollow at the base of her neck. 'My pleasure.'

'I've reached a decision,' Hannah said slowly, feeling the heat slipping through her body at his touch. It was like an aphrodisiac, powerful, potent, and electric. She felt malleable, *his*. 'If you approve.'

'Are you asking, or telling me?' he teased, aware of her quickening heartbeat, the way her body was poised between want and surrender.

'I thought—' She paused, and dragged in a quick breath as his hand cupped her breast and began caressing its vulnerable peak.

'Hmm?' he queried musingly. 'What did you think, *querida*?'

'After Christmas might be a good time to promote Cindy.'

'A sensible decision.'

'I think I'll keep Elaine on part-time, just to help out.'

'I assume this is leading somewhere?' Miguel prompted leisurely.

'Babies,' Hannah ventured with a soft smile. 'How do you feel about starting our own family?'

He felt as if someone had punched him in the solar plexus. A child? His mind leapt ahead to a blonde angel the mirror image of her mother. Maybe a dark-haired son who would drive his mother mad with boyish pranks... *Por Dios*, Hannah heavy with child, the birth... He went pale at the thought of her in pain.

'Are you sure about this?'

She twisted in his arms as she turned to face him. 'You're not?' She searched his features in the half-light, and glimpsed something evident she couldn't define.

'I can't think of anything more special, other than you, that you could gift me,' Miguel declared fervently.

Hannah felt the slight tremor that ran through his large body, and she wound her arms round his waist and pulled him close.

'Maybe we should go inside,' she teased lightly, 'and practise a little.' A warm chuckle emerged from her throat. 'Besides, I have a particular reward to bestow.'

Together they re-entered the suite, closed the door to the lanai, then drew the curtains.

Their own private world, Hannah mused as she removed her outer clothes and entered the shower. Miguel joined her, and they took their time, enjoying the promise, the anticipation of the loving they would always share.

During the following few days they delighted in playing tourist. They rode the tramcar, hired a limousine for the day and toured the island.

Midweek they took a flight out to Maui, and spent a wonderfully relaxing six days in a hotel right on the beach overlooking the ocean. Lovely sunny days walking on the beach, lazing beneath the spread of palm trees reading, listening to music on the Walkman. They swam in the ocean, frequented the hotel pool, played tennis, then dined in one of several restaurants, before retiring to their suite to make long, sweet love through the night.

Miguel rose early in the morning to use the laptop for an hour, and checked his cell-phone before they went to dinner each evening as a brief concession to the outside business world.

Hannah didn't mind. It was enough they were to-gether in a wonderfully idyllic part of the world.

On their return to Honolulu they shopped in several exclusive boutiques. 'Retail therapy,' Hannah teased as she added yet another brightly coloured designer bag to the few Miguel indulgently carried in each hand.

There were gifts to select for Renee, Carlo and Esteban, as well as something for Cindy and Elaine.

In one shop she caught sight of the most exquisite little dress for a baby girl, and bought it with Elise in mind.

'Are you done?' Miguel queried musingly as she emerged from yet another boutique.

'Not quite.' She had something very special in mind. 'I don't suppose you'll take those packages back to the hotel and give me an hour to shop alone?'

'Not a chance.'

'Okay,' Hannah said with resignation. 'But there are conditions.'

His eyes gleamed and his mouth moved to form a generous smile. 'And what would those be, *querida*?'

She sent him a sparkling glance as she lifted a hand and began ticking off each finger in turn. 'You won't question which shop I enter. You'll remain outside and won't look through the window. And under no circumstances will you come inside.'

He tilted his head slightly and regarded her thoughtfully. 'Bar there being a robbery, or some strange man attempts to chat you up.'

'Hmm,' she conceded, sending him an impish grin. 'That sounds fair.'

She looked no more than sixteen, Miguel ruminated musingly. Her hair was caught together at her nape, sunglasses rested atop her head, her make-up was minimal, her skin glowed a soft honey gold, and, attired in casual linen shorts and a singlet top, she didn't resemble anyone's wife.

Except she was his. The light of his life, his reason for living. It was something he gave grateful thanks to the good *Dios* for every day. He hadn't thought it possible to give up your life for another human being. But he'd give up his, for her, in a nanosecond.

Hannah paused outside an exclusive jewellery store, and turned towards him, her expression serious.

'Remember, you promised?'

'Go, *amante*.'

She did, earning circumspect interest from two male staff until she explained what she wanted, indicated a price range, and had their interest immediately switch to respect.

It took a while to make her selection. It took even longer to persuade them to have one of their craftsman engrave an inscription. A huge tip helped.

She had it placed in a beautiful velvet-lined box, gift-wrapped, charged to her own personal credit card, and she emerged through the glass doors with a satisfied smile.

It was their last evening in this beautiful paradise, and they'd dined at an exclusive restaurant in Honolulu's 'Pink Palace'. The food was delicious, the champagne superb, and the view out over the darkened ocean provided a peaceful backdrop.

Together they lingered, each reluctant to bring the evening to a close. For soon they'd have to return to their suite, call the porter to take their bags down to Reception, from where a cab would deliver them to the airport in order to catch the midnight flight home.

The waiter served coffee, and while Miguel signed the credit slip Hannah retrieved the gift-wrapped case from her bag and placed it on the table.

'For you,' she said gently as the waiter disappeared, and Miguel regarded her carefully for several seconds before reaching for the package.

He undid the gold ribbon, broke the seal, removed the wrapping, and opened the case.

Inside nestled in a bed of velvet lay a beautiful gold fob-watch with an attached chain.

'Hannah—'

'There's an inscription. Read it,' she encouraged, watching as he removed the watch and turned it over to read what had been engraved on the back.

Miguel, my heart, my soul. Hannah.

'*Dios,*' he breathed, momentarily speechless.

'There's a place inside for a photo,' she relayed softly. One that would change from year to year as they added to their family.

'*Gracias, amada.*' He rose to his feet and crossed round to kiss her.

Very thoroughly, Hannah mused long seconds later.

Together they left the table and made their way back to their suite.

A long flight lay ahead, and there was little time to spare.

'One lifetime won't be enough,' Miguel said gently as he drew her into his arms.

'Not nearly enough,' Hannah whispered an instant before she pulled his head down to hers.

The insistent peal of the telephone caused them to reluctantly draw apart, and Miguel picked up the handset, listened, then added a brief few words.

'The porter is on his way up, and the cab is waiting downstairs,' he relayed with something akin to regret, and her mouth curved into a warm smile.

'We'll be home tomorrow.'

His answering smile held a certain musing wryness. 'That's no help at all.'

A soft laugh emerged from her lips. 'Patience, querido, is good for the soul.'

He bent his head and kissed her with such gentle evocativeness, she wanted to cry. 'I'll remind you of that, later.'

They had the rest of their lives, and together they would make each day count. For ever

EPILOGUE

ALEXINA KATHLYN SANTANAS was born eleven months, three weeks and four days later. A joy to her mother, and cherished with idolatry awe by her father.

Family and close friends attended the christening and returned to Miguel and Hannah's Toorak home to offer congratulations and toast the blonde-haired angel's health and future happiness.

The sun shone brightly that day, and there was much laughter as everyone celebrated the event.

The guests departed early evening, and it was almost nine when Hannah retreated to the nursery to feed her daughter.

It had been a magical day, Hannah reflected as she changed Alexina and prepared to put her to the breast. She was a placid child, except at moments when she required sustenance or needed changing. Now, she was hungry, and her tiny fists beat an agitated dance before she latched on to suckle strongly.

Hannah looked at the perfect tiny features, the fine textured skin, and felt her heart swell with maternal pride. She really was the sweetest little thing. A precious gift.

What a difference a year made, she decided dreamily. Together she and Miguel had travelled to Rome, toured Italy and spent time in Andalusia. Cindy now ran the Toorak boutique with Elaine's help.

Life, she decided, was very sweet.

'How is she?'

Hannah had been so rapt in her own thoughts she hadn't noticed Miguel had quietly entered the room. She lifted her head and gave him the sort of smile that took hold of his heart and made it beat a whole lot faster.

Did she know how much he loved her? Couldn't fail to, he mused silently as he crossed to her side and stood watching while she disengaged their daughter and handed her to him to burp.

Minutes later he laid Alexina down carefully in her cot, drew the covers, then enfolded Hannah close to his side as they stood watching their daughter sleep.

'She's beautiful,' Miguel said softly. 'Just like her mother.' He turned as Hannah leant her head against his chest, and brushed his lips to her forehead. 'Time for us, *querida*.'

'Mmm,' she responded witchingly. 'Sounds interesting.' She lifted her head to look at him. 'What do you have in mind?'

He adjusted the baby monitor, then led her into their bedroom. 'Pleasuring you.'

'Isn't that a bit one-sided?'

He slowly undid the buttons on her top, and freed the rest of her clothes. His mouth slanted down to capture hers, and she kissed him back, swept away by the tide of passion as he gently pressed her down onto the bed.

'Later,' Miguel murmured. 'You get to have your turn.'

She did, although not for long. A thin reedy cry came through the baby monitor, and she stilled, waiting for another to follow it. When it did, she pressed a light kiss to her husband's thigh, then slid from the bed.

'Our daughter has no sense of timing,' Miguel groaned huskily as Hannah pulled on a robe.

'I'll be back,' she promised, and she was, several minutes later after soothing Alexina to sleep.

'Wind,' she enlightened succinctly as she slipped into bed and reached for him. 'Now, where were we?'

'I would say,' Miguel evinced huskily, 'just about there.' His breath caught, then hissed between his teeth as she caressed an acutely sensitive part of his male appendage.

It didn't take long for him to break, and Hannah exulted in the way he took control, entering her in one long thrust that soon settled into a rhythm as old as time.

A shimmering sensual feast shared by two people who loved to the depths of their souls. Without reason, other than they were twin halves of a whole. Beyond mortal life, for all eternity.

Lucy Gordon cut her writing teeth on magazine journalism, interviewing many of the world's most interesting men, including Warren Beatty, Richard Chamberlain, Sir Roger Moore, Sir Alec Guinness and Sir John Gielgud. She also camped out with lions in Africa, and had many other unusual experiences which have often provided the background for her books. She is married to a Venetian, whom she met while on holiday in Venice. They got engaged within two days.

Two of her books have won the Romance Writers of America RITA award, SONG OF THE LORELEI in 1990, and HIS BROTHER'S CHILD in 1998 in the Best Traditional Romance category. You can visit her website at www.zyworld.com/LucyGordon

Look out for Lucy Gordon's latest intense, emotional title: THE MONTE CARLO PROPOSAL Coming in December 2004, in Tender Romance™!

WIFE BY
ARRANGEMENT
by
Lucy Gordon

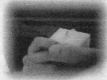

This book is for Nikki Little
who gave generously of her time

CHAPTER ONE

'HEY, Heather—your Sicilian lover is here.'

Heather looked up self-consciously. 'Lorenzo isn't my lover!' she insisted. 'Just—just—'

'Just good friends?' Sally suggested wickedly. 'Well, if the man out there isn't your lover, he ought to be. Big and sexy with "come to bed" eyes. If he was mine, I wouldn't waste time *not* sleeping with him.'

'Will you keep your voice down?' Heather said frantically, aware that every woman in the staff room was regarding her with interest. She was taking her afternoon break from the perfume counter of Gossways, London's most luxurious department store. The worldly-wise Sally was on the next counter.

Heather got to her feet, smiling at the thought of Lorenzo Martelli, the light-hearted, handsome young man who had swept into her life a month ago and made her head spin.

'I didn't know you knew Lorenzo by sight,' she told Sally.

'I don't, but he asked for you. Besides, he looks just like a Sicilian should: incredibly sensual, as if he'd take a woman to bed as soon as look at her. Hurry up and get out there, or I'll have him myself!'

Heather chuckled and returned to her counter, eager to see Lorenzo. He'd come to England on a business trip that was supposed to last two weeks, but he'd been enchanted by Heather's quiet charm and stayed on, unable to tear himself away from her. They were going out together tonight. Now she was delighted at the thought of seeing him early.

But it wasn't Lorenzo.

Lorenzo was tall, fair, curly-haired, in his late twenties. This man was past thirty. There was a slight scar on one side of his face and his features, which were too irregular to be handsome, were marred by a touch of harshness.

He was tall and heavily built, his shoulders wide, his hair black. He had the dark eyes and olive skin of the southern Italian, but he had something more. Heather couldn't put a name to it, but she knew at once why Sally, who judged each man by his bedworthiness, had reacted strongly. It was because he judged every woman the same way. It was there in his eyes, that were lazy without ever quite being off guard: the instinctive question—do I want to sleep with her? Yes? No? Probably yes. How much of a challenge would she be?

Heather was startled to receive such a look. Her fine features were pretty without being beautiful. Her hair was very light brown, but not exactly blonde, and although her slim figure was graceful it wasn't voluptuous. At twenty-three she'd never known the tribute of a wolf whistle, and no man had ever raked her up and down as this one was doing.

'Are you the gentleman who was asking for me?' she asked.

He glanced at the nameplate pinned to her white blouse. 'I am.'

His voice was dark and deep, with an accent that coloured the words without obscuring them. Not like Lorenzo's light, teasing tones.

'You were recommended by a friend of mine whom you served—a Mr Charles Smith, but you won't remember him among so many customers. I'm buying for several ladies, including my mother. She's in her sixties, very respectable, but perhaps secretly wishing her life had been a little more exciting.'

'I know what she'd like,' Heather said, producing a fragrance that was a little daring, but not outrageous. She was touched and impressed by this man's understanding of his mother.

'That will suit her perfectly,' he said. 'But now we come to the more delicate part of the business. I have a lady-friend—beautiful, sensual, with very expensive tastes. Her name is Elena, and her personality is extravagant, mysterious and passionate.' His eyes met hers. 'I'm sure you understand.'

In a flash she found herself understanding all sorts of things. For instance, how Elena would be very drawn to this man who, despite his lack of conventional beauty, had an impressiveness that—she put a firm brake on her thoughts.

'Perfectly, sir,' she said crisply. 'I'd suggest "Deep of the Night".'

'It sounds just like her,' he agreed shamelessly.

She rubbed a drop of the perfume on her wrist and held it out to him. He inhaled slowly, then took her wrist between his fingers and brought it close to his face. She had a sudden impression of fierce, controlled power behind his civilised manner, as though she'd been strolling through a sedate garden and seen a tiger lurking behind the leaves, ready to spring. She resisted the impulse to snatch her hand back.

'Admirable,' he said. 'I'll take the large flagon.'

Heather almost gasped. The large flagon was the costliest item in a very costly range. Her commission on this sale was beginning to look very good. Perhaps even good enough to buy a really beautiful wedding dress…

She stopped that thought in its tracks. It was undignified to hope for something that probably wouldn't happen.

'Now, another lady, with a different personality—light-hearted and fun.'

'"Summer Dance" might suit her. It's fresh and flowery—'

'But not naive?' he asked anxiously.

'Certainly not. Insouciant but sophisticated.'

She tested it on the other arm and again he took her wrist, holding it a quarter-inch from his face. Heather could feel his warm breath against her skin and she wished he would let her go. But that was an absurd over-reaction, she told herself sensibly. He wasn't looking at her. His eyes were closed and he was in a faraway world, with his various mistresses. His hold on her wrist was quite impersonal.

But then the thought crept in that nothing was impersonal with him. This was a man with whom everything—every kind word, every cruel one, every insult, every wound to his pride, every gesture of love—would be taken deeply personally. And for that reason he was very, very dangerous: perhaps the most dangerous man she had ever encountered. When he opened his eyes and looked at her she realised that she'd been holding her breath.

'Perfetto,' he murmured. 'How well we understand each other.'

He released her and she felt as though she were awakening from a dream. She could still feel the pressure on her wrist where he'd held it with such soft, yet irresistible power. She pulled herself firmly together.

'I try to understand all my customers, signore,' she replied. 'It's my job.'

He made a face of appreciation. 'Signore? So you understand Italian?'

She smiled. 'I know some Italian and about ten words of Sicilian.'

She didn't know what had made her mention Sicilian, except perhaps a desire to know if this man really did come from the same part of the world as Lorenzo. It seemed that he did.

He regarded her with amused curiosity, murmuring, 'I wonder why you are learning my dialect.'

'I'm not exactly learning it,' she disclaimed hastily. 'I just picked up a few words from a friend.'

'And doubtless your friend is a handsome young man. Has he yet told you that you are *grazziusu*?'

'I think we should concentrate on your purchases,' Heather said, hoping she wasn't blushing. Lorenzo had used exactly that word to her only the night before, explaining that it was one of the many Sicilian words for beautiful. She shouldn't be talking like this with a stranger. But he was like a magician, who could twist the conversation this way and that with a wave of an invisible wand. He had said *grazziusu* with a soft, seductive power that even Lorenzo, in his ardour, hadn't matched.

'I see that you understand the word, and not from a dictionary,' he observed. 'I'm glad your lover appreciates you.'

No wonder this man had several mistresses if he went about talking like this. Doubtless she too was supposed to be flattered. But she refused to go weak at the knees. It had been a long day, and her legs were tired. That was all.

'Shall we return to the matter in hand?' she asked.

'If we must. What next?'

Heather regarded him levelly. 'Let me get this clear, *signore*. Just how many lady-friends are you trying to— er—keep happy?'

He grinned shamelessly, giving an eloquent shrug. 'Is it important?'

'It is if they have different personalities.'

'Very different,' he confirmed. 'I like one to suit each mood. Minetta is light-hearted, Julia is musical, and Elena is darkly sensual.'

He was trying to unsettle her; there was no doubt of it. His eyes spoke meanings that went far beyond what his lips were saying. She observed briskly, 'Well, that should make things nice and simple.'

'Simple?'

'A man of only three moods.'

She was startled at herself. A good sales assistant thought only of the sale. She didn't backchat the customer and risk offending him. But he wasn't offended. He even seemed amused at her swift riposte.

'You're quite right,' he said. 'Three isn't enough. I have a vacancy for a witty lady, which you could fill perfectly.'

'Oh, I wouldn't suit you at all,' she fenced.

'I'm not so sure about that.'

'*I* am. Completely sure.'

'I wonder why.' He was laughing.

Heather laughed back. She was beginning to take his measure. 'Well, for a start, I'd never agree to be part of a crowd. You'd have to get rid of all the others.'

'I'm sure you'd make it worth my while.'

'If I felt that *you* were worth it,' she said daringly. 'But you wouldn't be, because I'm not in the market.'

'Ah, yes, of course! You already have a lover.'

There was that word again. Why was the whole world harping on lovers all of a sudden?

'Let's just say that I have a young man who suits me.'

'And he comes from Sicily, since you are learning his

language. Which also means that you're hoping to marry him.'

To her dismay Heather felt a revealing blush creep over her face. To cover it she spoke sharply. 'If you mean that I've set my cap at him, you're wrong. And this conversation is over.'

'Forgive me. It's not my business.'

'Indeed it isn't.'

'But I hope he isn't leading you on a fool's dance, seducing you with hints of marriage, and then vanishing back to his own country.'

'I'm not that easily seduced. Neither by him nor—by anyone,' she finished hastily, wondering why her mind had scurried down that particular by-path.

'Then you haven't allowed him into your bed. That's either very neglectful of him, or very clever of you. I wonder which.'

Indignantly she challenged him with a direct gaze, and what she saw startled her. Despite the teasing sensuality of his words, his eyes held the same dispassionate calculation he would have shown to a high-priced purchase.

'You don't dress like the others,' he remarked. 'Why?'

It was true. Heather was perfectly made-up and her long hair was elegantly styled, courtesy of the store's beauty parlour. But whereas the other assistants, with their employer's encouragement, dressed in slightly provocative styles, Heather stuck firmly to conventional clothes. Her skirt was black, her blouse was snow-white and fresh. Her boss had suggested that she might 'put herself about more', but she had refused, and since her sales figures were excellent the matter had been allowed to drop.

'I think,' the man persisted, 'it's because you're a proud and subtle woman—too proud to put everything in the window. And subtle enough to know that when a woman holds back she's at her most alluring. By covering your-self up you make a man wonder how you would look without clothes.'

It was a direct, frontal attack from a man with all the nerve in the world, and something in Heather was wryly appreciative even while something else warned her to put him firmly in his place.

'Can I interest you in anything more, sir?' she asked primly.

'You could interest me in a good deal,' he responded at once. 'Let me take you to dinner, and we can discuss my interest in you.'

'That wasn't what I—still, I suppose I could have phrased that question more cleverly, couldn't I?'

'I thought you phrased it perfectly. I'm interested; I've made that plain. And I'm a generous man. I doubt your boyfriend will marry you. He'll disappear, leaving you with a broken heart.'

'And you'll leave me dancing for joy, I suppose?' she couldn't resist answering.

'It depends what makes you dance for joy. Shall we say ten thousand pounds to start with? Play your cards right, and I think you could do very well out of me.'

'And I think the sooner you leave you the better. I'm not interested in you or your money, and if you say an-other word I shall call Security.'

'Twenty thousand pounds.'

'Shall I gift-wrap these items for you, sir, or have you changed your mind now you know you'll get nothing from me?'

'What do you think?'

'I think you'd better find a woman who's selling her-self. I'm only selling perfume. I take it you don't want these.'

He shrugged. 'There'd hardly be any point, would there? Of course, it's a shame about the commission you would have earned.'

'Commission be blowed!' Heather said very deliberately. 'The store is about to close. Goodbye! Don't come back!'

He gave her a grin that contained a hint of challenge, and walked out with the air of a man who'd achieved something, although for the life of her she couldn't think what.

She was furious, both with him and herself. He'd raised false hopes for her pay packet, and he'd insulted her. But, far worse, for a brief moment he'd persuaded her to find him charming. Part of her had enjoyed the light-hearted game she'd thought they were playing. But then she'd seen the cold calculation in his eyes, and she'd known that the woman who went to this man's bed for money would be a fool. And the woman who did it for love would be an even greater fool.

She hurried home. Her flatmate was out so she had the place to herself as she prepared for the evening ahead with Lorenzo Martelli, the young man Sally called 'her lover'. He wasn't her lover, nor had he tried to urge her into bed, for which she liked him more.

In the month she'd known him she seemed to have been under a spell, something lovelier than reality, with none of reality's pain and trouble. She didn't call it love, because the word 'love' summoned up Peter, and a wilderness of suffering at the brutal way he'd dumped her. She only knew that Lorenzo had charmed her out of her sadness.

She'd met him through a buyer in the Gossways Food Hall. The Martellis dealt in Sicilian fruit and vegetables, much of which they grew on the vast family estates around Palermo. What they couldn't supply themselves they bought in from other growers, taking nothing but the very best. Even so, Gossways had a special deal under which it accepted only produce grown by the Martellis themselves. Lorenzo had recently been appointed export manager of the business, and was visiting customers, introducing himself.

He lived like a young king at the Ritz Hotel. Sometimes he took her to eat there; sometimes they found a tiny place by the river. But always there was a gift, sometimes valuable, sometimes silly, given with a tribute in his eyes. She didn't know what it might mean for the future. Lorenzo had a touch of the playboy whose charm and looks won his way through life. She guessed that back in Sicily there were a dozen young women who would be disappointed if he were to marry. Of course, she wasn't counting on marriage. She told herself that many times. She knew that his charm and admiration were doing her a world of good, and when he left without her she would cope somehow.

Tonight she found his message on the answer-machine, urging her to wear the pale blue silk dress he'd bought for her, which brought out the dark blue of her eyes. They were large eyes, and they gave her face distinction, even beauty.

As always he arrived five minutes before the agreed time, with a red rose, which he gave her with a flourish, and a pearl necklace which he'd bought to go with the dress.

The sight of him made her smile with happiness. He was a handsome young giant, six foot two, with a booming laugh and good-natured grin that invited the whole world to share his pleasure.

'Tonight is a great occasion,' he told her. 'My older brother, Renato, has arrived from Sicily.' He added ruefully, 'I should have gone home two weeks ago. He knows I stayed because of you, and now he wants to meet you. We are his guests at the Ritz tonight.'

'But we were going to the theatre—'

'Could you bear not to? I have rather neglected business recently—' he flicked her cheek gently '—all your fault.'

'Tossing me into the lions' den, huh?' she asked with a chuckle.

He put his arm around her. 'We'll go in together.'

On the short journey to the Ritz he talked about his brother, who ran the vast family estates in Sicily. By hard work and shrewd dealing he'd transformed the vineyards and olive groves, making them produce three times as much, buying up land, expanding, making Martelli the top name in fine produce in every luxury store and hotel throughout the world.

'He thinks of nothing but work,' Lorenzo complained. 'How he can make more money, and more money. Me, I prefer spending it.'

'I'm sure he knows that. He wants to see who you're spending it on.' She touched the pearls, which were elegant and restrained, but clearly expensive.

'He's ready to like you. Trust me.' As they reached the Ritz and he handed her from the taxi, Lorenzo murmured, 'Don't be afraid of him.'

'I'm not. Are *you* afraid of him?'

'No way. But he's the head of the family, and in Sicily that's very important. However fierce he was, he was always my wonderful big brother who'd stick by me, help sort out my problems—'

'Deal with the girls' fathers?' Heather suggested mischievously.

Lorenzo cleared his throat. 'That's all in the past. Let's go in.'

Heather was curious to meet this man who was so important in Lorenzo's life. She looked around at the luxurious restaurant with its elegant marble and floor-to-ceiling French windows, hung with heavy red curtains.

On the far side a man sat alone at a table. He rose as they approached him, a polite smile of welcome on his face. Heather strove to match it through the tide of indignation that welled up in her.

'Good evening, *signorina*,' Renato Martelli said, giving her a courteous little bow. 'It is a pleasure to meet you.'

'You mean, meet me *again*, don't you?' she asked coolly. 'You surely can't have forgotten our encounter in Gossways this afternoon?'

'What's this?' Lorenzo asked. 'You've met before?'

'Earlier today,' Renato Martelli confirmed. 'I was impatient to see the lady of whom I've heard so much, so I adopted a subterfuge, for which I hope I'll be forgiven.' He was smiling as he raised her hand to his lips.

Heather regarded him wryly. 'I'll think about it,' she said.

Renato gallantly pulled out a gilt-and-plush chair for her, and the three of them sat down.

'What subterfuge?' Lorenzo asked, looking from one to the other.

'Your brother came to my counter, posing as a customer,' Heather told him.

'I thought we could assess each other in a more natural atmosphere,' Renato explained.

'Each other?' she murmured.

'I'm sure you formed your own opinion of me.'

'Oh, yes,' she assured him. 'I certainly did.'

She left it there. She was far from finished but she didn't want to look as though she were sulking. A waiter appeared with the menu and when he'd given the order Renato added, 'And a bottle of your very finest champagne.'

At this hint of approval Lorenzo grinned. Perversely Heather found herself even more annoyed. Was she supposed to jump for joy because Renato Martelli had tossed her a crumb of favour?

She would never have guessed they were brothers. She knew that over the centuries the island of Sicily had been invaded so often that many racial types—Greek, Arab, Italian, French, Spanish, Celtic—were mixed in its inhabitants. There was something Greek in Lorenzo's fine looks, blue eyes and light brown curly hair. Despite his size his movements were graceful.

She guessed Renato was one of those men who had come to manhood in his early teens. It was hard to picture him as a boy. Perhaps an Italian ancestor had given him those vivid looks, but the air of haughty pride came from a Spaniard, and there was something Celtic in the mobility of his face, the sensuality of his wide mouth.

His features were fierce and irregular, and at first sight he was put in the shade by his beautiful younger brother. But there was a dark glitter in his eyes that compelled attention, and he had an extra something that made looks irrelevant. In a room full of handsome men, Renato Martelli would be the one women looked at, and wondered about.

He was powerfully built, with a massiveness about him that reminded Heather of a bull. Yet he carried no extra weight. His body was hard and athletic, the heavy muscles pressing against the expensive cloth of his suit, as though formal clothes didn't come naturally to him. He was a man made for the outdoor life, riding a horse, surveying his acres, or anything he could do in shirtsleeves.

The champagne was served in tall crystal glasses. Renato raised his in salute. 'To the pleasure of meeting you,' he told Heather.

'To our meeting,' she replied, significantly changing the words. There was the briefest flicker on Renato's face that might have been acknowledgement.

Over cream of cauliflower soup with ribbons of smoked salmon, he talked about Lorenzo and his lengthened visit to England.

'He should have left two weeks ago, but always there are excuses, and I start to understand that some great power is holding him here. And that power comes from a woman. For the first time he is talking about marriage—'

'Renato—' Lorenzo groaned.

'Ignore him,' Heather said. 'He's trying to disconcert you.'

'You seem to understand me by instinct, *signorina*,' Renato said, impressed.

'I don't need instinct. Experience will do. You spent the afternoon trying to disconcert *me*. You like to wrong-foot people.'

He raised his champagne glass in ironic salute, but his eyes, over the rim, were suddenly harder, alert. *'Touché!'* he said. 'I see I shall have to beware of you.'

'What a good idea,' she agreed sweetly. 'Do go on. Lorenzo was talking about marriage and you rushed to England to see if I was good enough.'

'I came to discover if you were as wonderful as he says,' he corrected smoothly. 'And I find that you are.'

It was charmingly said but she wasn't fooled. This was a man who did nothing except for his own reasons. But if he thought she was going to make it easy for him he had another think coming.

'Let's be frank,' she said with a challenging smile. 'Lorenzo is a Martelli. He could marry an heiress. When you found him paying attention to a humble shop assistant it set your alarm bells ringing. That, Signor Martelli, is the truth. The rest is just fancy talk.'

Lorenzo groaned and dropped his head in his hands. Renato reddened slightly. 'Now it is you who are trying to disconcert me.'

'And I'm not doing too badly either,' she murmured.

His response was a grin that blazed out suddenly, taking her by surprise. It was brilliant, intensely masculine, and it came from a fire deep within him.

'Then I too will be frank,' he told her. 'Humble shop assistant! That is nonsense. You feel no more humble than I do. You're a strong woman, even an arrogant one, who thinks she could take on the world, and win. You certainly believe you could get the better of me. You might even be right.'

'Always assuming that I'll need to fight you,' she said lightly. 'But will I?'

'I don't know. I haven't finally decided.'

'I await your decision in fear and trembling,' she told him in an ironic tone that conveyed just the opposite.

He raised his glass in salute. Heather raised hers in return, but she was still on her guard.

'That's the spirit, darling,' Lorenzo said. 'Don't let him scare you.'

'Let her fight her own battles,' Renato told him. 'She's more than capable of it. You see,' he added to Heather, 'I know a lot about you. You left school at sixteen and got a job in a paper shop. For the next four years you went from job to job, always behind a counter, always climbing a little higher, until three years ago you came to work at Gossways.

'You sought a place on their training programme that leads to management, but Gossways refused, saying they take only college graduates. So you set out to prove them wrong. You worked hard, studied languages, badgered them. At last, impressed by your persistence and your splendid sales figures, they gave in, and offered you a place on the next programme. Humble shop assistant! You're a formidable woman.'

'Hey, I didn't know all that,' Lorenzo said.

'Your brother has been asking Gossways Head Office about me,' Heather explained. 'Snooping.'

'Gathering intelligence,' Renato suggested.

'Snooping,' she said firmly. 'And it was very rude.'

'Yes, it was,' Lorenzo said. 'You don't think *I* did anything like that, do you, darling?'

'*You* didn't think of it,' Renato informed him scathingly.

Heather felt a sudden need to get away from the two men, so that she could breathe freely. 'Excuse me, gentlemen,' she said, rising.

She found the powder room and sat gazing at her own reflection in an ornate gilt mirror, wondering why the world always seemed to be the wrong way up. She was being wined and dined at the Ritz, by two attractive men who were giving her their whole attention. That should have made her a woman to be envied, and if she'd been alone with Lorenzo she would have thought so too.

But Renato Martelli made her very, very suspicious.

CHAPTER TWO

WHEN Heather was out of earshot Renato said, 'My compliments. She's charming.'

'You really like her?' Lorenzo asked.

'Yes, I think she's admirable. I admit that I expected a floozy, but she's a *lady*, which must be a first for you. It's time you settled down.'

'Now wait,' Lorenzo said hastily. 'You're rushing me. Why did you tell her I mentioned marriage?'

'Because you did.'

'I said *if* I was thinking about marriage it would be to someone like her. It's a very big step.'

'All the more reason to take it while you're young enough to be influenced by a good woman.'

'*You* didn't.'

Renato gave a wolfish grin. 'Apart from our mother no woman has ever influenced me.'

'That's not what I heard. Wasn't her name Magdalena—? All right, all right,' he finished hastily, looking at his brother's expression.

'Magdalena Conti didn't *influence* me,' Renato said coldly. 'She merely taught me that permanent relationships are not for me. But it's different with you. Beneath your irresponsible ways you have the makings of an excellent husband.'

'Oh, no! I see your game. One of us has to marry and provide a Martelli heir, and you've cast me as the sacrificial lamb. Well, to hell with you, brother! You're the eldest. You do it.'

21

'Forget it. I'm past praying for.'

'And you don't want to give up your nice enjoyable life with all those accommodating ladies,' Lorenzo said indignantly.

'Fidelity has no charms for me,' Renato admitted.

'Why can't Bernardo do the family duty? He's our brother.'

'Our half-brother. He carries our father's blood but not his name, owing to the circumstances of his birth. Besides, he isn't Mamma's son, and his children wouldn't be her grandchildren. No, it has to be one of us, and you're the one who's in love.'

'Yes, but—'

'Hush, she's coming back. Don't be a fool. Make sure of her while you can.'

They rose to greet Heather and Lorenzo kissed her hand. She'd recovered her poise and accepted his tribute with a smile, but inwardly she was still wary.

During the main course a number of visitors came to their table, all of whom eyed Heather curiously, and she began to be self conscious. It was like dipping a toe in shallow water and finding yourself swept away by a tidal wave. Something was happening here that she didn't understand.

At last the visitors had all gone. As Heather was enjoying her chocolate mousse Renato said, 'Lorenzo, I see Felipe di Stefano over there. He's a man you need to speak to.'

When Lorenzo had gone they looked at each other. 'I thought you'd appreciate the chance to tell me exactly what you think of me,' Renato said.

'If I did that we'd be here all night.'

He laughed. 'Go on, say it.'

'Where do I start? Where would it end? Your impertinence in checking up on me with my employers, and then this afternoon—Charles Smith never existed, did he?'

'I'm afraid not.'

'You were *auditioning* me, sizing me up to see if I was "suitable".'

'Certainly I was curious about the woman who's made such an impression on my brother. If I'd told you who I was you wouldn't have acted naturally. I wanted to see you when you weren't trying to impress me.'

'Your conceit is past belief. What makes you think I'd have been trying to impress you?'

'I credit you with enough intelligence to know that you can't marry my brother without impressing me first.'

'Always assuming that I want to marry Lorenzo. I don't think I do, not if it means being related to you.'

'I admit I was a little clumsy. But perhaps you'll forgive me when you hear what I have to say. I admired your behaviour greatly, especially when I abandoned the sale and you lost a large commission. You controlled yourself splendidly.'

'You—did—that—on—purpose?' she breathed.

'Of course. And you passed with flying colours. Lorenzo tends to be emotional and impulsive. Your cool, northern efficiency will be good for him. My congratulations. You've gone the right way to earn my respect.'

'And you're going the right way to earn a chocolate mousse over your head,' she threatened, not in the least appeased by these compliments. 'You actually—you actually—?'

'The lady has finished eating,' Renato said to a waiter, hastily removing her plate with his own hands. 'You may bring the coffee— No—' He corrected himself on seeing the glint in Heather's eyes. 'Best leave the coffee until later.'

When they were alone again he turned to her. 'Please don't be angry. I promise you, the opinion I formed of you was entirely favourable.'

'The opinion that *I* formed of *you* was far from favourable. The things you said to me—'

'I wanted to see if you'd respond to my money—'

'If I was a fortune-hunter!' she snapped.

'The choice of words is yours, but the meaning is the same.'

Heather prided herself on her practical common sense, but this man annoyed her enough to make her toss it aside and take risks instead. The next words seemed to come out of their own accord.

'You'd have looked silly if I'd said yes, wouldn't you?' she said coolly.

'Why? Are you saying that you wouldn't have delivered? I doubt it. I think you're a woman of your word. If you'd promised to sleep with me, you'd have slept with me. We'd have enjoyed a mutually pleasurable experience—'

'*Oh, really?*'

'I promise you it would have been.'

'Perhaps you'd like to give me signed testimonials from Elena and all the other fictitious ladies.'

'They're real enough, and I think they'd vouch for me—although not, perhaps, under these circumstances—'

'At the price you offer I should hope they'd vouch for you under all circumstances. Otherwise they wouldn't be giving what you pay them for, would they?'

That flicked him on the raw, she was glad to notice. His eyes glittered with a strange, dark light. 'Perhaps I've only myself to blame if you sharpen your claws on me,' he said after a moment. 'Let it be. I made you a genuine offer—'

'And never mind what it did to Lorenzo.'

'If you'd accepted I'd have been doing him a favour, and he'd have seen that.'

'People always see things your way, do they?'

'With time and persuasion.'

She regarded him wryly. 'Does that mean that, given time and persuasion, you think you could have seduced me?'

He was suddenly alert. 'I don't know,' he said slowly. 'I simply don't know.'

It was like playing chess, she found, and suddenly very thrilling. Shrewdly she moved her queen into the centre of the board, inviting attack. 'Perhaps you just didn't raise the price high enough,' she murmured.

'What are you saying?'

'Don't you know that a woman who seems honest can charge twice as much as her more blatant sisters?'

'Oh, yes,' he said softly. 'I know that. What now?'

'Come a little nearer, and I'll tell you.'

Slowly he moved his head closer to her. Heather leaned forward until her hair lightly brushed his face, and her breath fanned his cheek.

'I wouldn't want you if you were the last man on earth,' she whispered. *'Go and jump in the river, and take your money with you!'*

He turned his head so that his eyes looked directly into hers. They were hard with astonishment, cold, appraising. 'You are a very unexpected lady,' he said. 'And a very brave one.'

'I don't need to be brave. You can't harm me because you have nothing that I want.'

'Except that I hold your marriage to Lorenzo in my hands. I'm particular about who I take into my family—'

'Then you'll be relieved to know that you won't be

asked to accept me,' she said, drawing back and facing him with furious eyes. 'Let me make my position plain. I hope Lorenzo wasn't planning to propose, because my answer would be no, and *you* are the reason.'

'Heather—' came Lorenzo's dismayed voice from behind her. He had returned in time to hear the last words.

She jumped to her feet. 'I'm sorry, Lorenzo, but it's over. We had a lovely romance but it was just a fairy tale. Now it's reality time, and your reality is your very unpleasant brother.'

He seized her arms. 'Don't go like this. I love you.'

'And I love you, but I'm saying goodbye.'

'Because of *him*? Why?'

'Ask him. Let him tell you if he dares.'

She pulled free and stormed away. Lorenzo started after her but Renato growled, 'Leave this to me.'

Anger gave speed to Heather's feet and she'd already whisked herself halfway down the Long Gallery before Renato had caught up with her.

'This is ridiculous,' he said, reaching for her arm.

'Don't call me ridiculous,' she seethed, shaking him off. 'What's ridiculous is you thinking you can move people like pawns on a chess board.'

'I haven't had much difficulty so far,' he was rash enough to say.

'So I guessed. But you hadn't met me then.'

'Indeed I hadn't—'

'It's been a short acquaintance, not a pleasant one. This is where it ends.'

She turned away sharply and headed for the street. Outside, the night traffic of Piccadilly honked and blared. Renato caught up with her at the door, taking her arm again. 'Please, Heather, come back inside and let's discuss this calmly.'

'I don't feel calm. I feel like throwing something at your head.'

'You're punishing Lorenzo because you're mad at me, and that isn't fair.'

'Not, it's not fair. It's not fair that he has you for a brother, but he's stuck with you. I'm not, however, and I intend to keep it that way.'

'All right, insult me if it gives you pleasure—'

'After the way you've insulted me, it gives me more pleasure than I can say!'

'But don't do this to Lorenzo.'

'I'm doing it *for* Lorenzo. We'd only make each other unhappy. Now, will you please let me go, or do I have to scream for a policeman?'

She pulled free and stormed out onto the pavement, heading straight across the road to where she could see a taxi approaching. She was too angry for caution. Through the noise of the traffic she thought she heard Renato's horrified voice shouting her name. She didn't see the car bearing down on her, only the glare of the headlights against the darkness. Then Renato seized her and swung her violently sideways. Somebody screamed, there was an ugly sound of brakes, and the next moment she was lying in the road.

For a moment she couldn't breathe. But she didn't seem to be injured. A crowd was gathering around her, hands outstretched. Lorenzo burst through, crying, 'Heather, my God! *Oh, my God!*'

His voice rose on a note of horror and she realised that he wasn't looking at her but at his brother. Renato lay in the road, bleeding from a wound in his arm. With a terrible sick feeling Heather saw why Lorenzo had cried out. Renato looked as though he'd severed an artery. Blood was streaming from his arm in a river, and if something wasn't done fast he had little time left.

'Give me your tie,' she told Lorenzo. 'Quickly!'

He wrenched it off, while she fumbled in her bag for her pen. Her head was spinning but she fought to clear it while her hands moved swiftly, wrapping the tie around Renato's arm above the wound, knotting it, slipping the pen through and twisting it. Renato's eyes were open and he was looking at her, but she tried to think of nothing but what she was doing, twisting, twisting, while the tourniquet around his arm grew tighter and tighter, until at last—oh, thank God!—the bleeding lessened and stopped as the vein was closed.

'Lorenzo—' she gasped.

'Yes,' he said, taking the tourniquet from her. 'I'll hold it now.'

'Thank you—I'm feeling a little—' Her head was swimming.

'No, you're not going to faint,' Renato murmured.

'Aren't I?'

'A woman like you doesn't faint. She takes over and gives orders, but she never weakens.' His voice was almost inaudible, but she heard every word.

'Let us through, please.'

Suddenly an ambulance was there, the crew urging their way through the crowd, taking over. There were police too, talking to the motorist who was wringing his hands and protesting his innocence. Heather forced her head to clear. She still had something to do.

'It wasn't his fault,' she said urgently to the policeman. 'I ran out in front of him.'

'All right, miss, we'll talk at the hospital,' the young constable said.

Lorenzo helped her into the ambulance and sat beside

her, pulling off his jacket and wrapping it around her, warming her against the shock. Renato presented a ghastly sight, covered in blood and with a pallor on his face that suggested death hadn't been far off. One of the crew was giving him oxygen, and at last he opened his eyes over the mask. His gaze wandered to Heather, then to Lorenzo. His expression was intent, as though he were sending a silent message to one of them. Or perhaps both.

At the hospital Renato was hurried away for emergency treatment, while Heather's grazes were tended. She emerged to find Lorenzo sitting in the corridor with two policemen. She repeated what she'd said before, exonerating the driver. At last they left, satisfied, and she could be alone with Lorenzo.

He put his arms about her. 'Are you all right, darling?'

'Yes, it was just scratches. What about Renato?'

'He's in there.' He indicated the opposite door. 'They've stopped the bleeding and given him a transfusion. He's got to stay here a few days, but he's going to be all right.'

A doctor emerged. 'You can come in for a minute. Just one of you.'

'I'm his brother,' Lorenzo said, 'but this is my fiancée—please.'

'All right, but try to be quiet.'

Renato looked less alarming without his blood-stained clothes, but still very pale. He was lying with his eyes closed, not moving but for the light rise and fall of his chest.

'I've never seen him this still,' Lorenzo said. 'Usually he's striding about, giving orders. What did he say to make you storm out like that?'

'I can hardly remember. Whatever it was, I shouldn't have put his life in danger.'

'I only know that he was bleeding to death and you saved him. Thank you, *amor mia*. I know he can be a bear, but he's a good fellow really. Thank God you were there!'

'If I hadn't been there it wouldn't have happened,' she said, touched by his belief in her, but feeling guilty at the same time.

Lorenzo slipped an arm about her shoulders. She rested her head against him and they sat together, exchanging warmth and comfort.

'Are you angry that I called you my fiancée?' he asked after a while.

'No, I'm not angry.'

'Do you love me enough to forgive Renato, and take me on?'

Renato's eyes had opened and he was watching them. 'Say yes,' he urged her. 'Don't turn us down.'

'Us?'

'If you marry one Martelli, you get the whole pack of us.'

'I'll be a good husband,' Lorenzo vowed. 'Good enough to make up for Renato.'

'What more do you need to hear than that?' Renato asked.

'Nothing,' she said with a smile. 'I guess I can take the risk!'

Suddenly everything was happening fast. The traumatic evening had swept her up in a fierce tide of emotion, and under its influence she'd promised to marry Lorenzo.

In an instant, it seemed she was part of the Martelli family. Renato had stretched out his good hand and clasped hers, weakly, but with warmth. 'Now I shall have a sister.'

Within twenty-four hours her left hand bore a ring with a large diamond. Two days later she saw the brothers off from Heathrow Airport, knowing that her own ticket was booked for a month ahead.

Now she was on the flight to Palermo, still wondering what had come over her. Beside her sat Dr Angela Wenham: Angie, her closest friend and flatmate, who was enjoying a well-earned holiday.

'I'm so glad you asked me to come with you as bridesmaid,' Angie said now. 'I'm looking forward to a few days just living for pleasure.'

Besides being brainy and hard working Angie was also pretty, daintily built, and a social butterfly. Her recent stint on hospital night duty had severely restricted her romantic life, and she was intent on making up for it, if the smile on her delightful, impish face was anything to go by.

'Fancy you being swept off your feet,' Angie chuckled 'Much more my style than yours.'

'Yes, it's not like sturdy, dependable me, is it?' Heather mused. 'And the way I acted that night—I swear I didn't know myself. Normally I'm a quiet sort of person, but I was ranting and raving, telling him where to get off—'

Angie collapsed with laughter. '*You?* Ranting and raving? How I wish I'd been there to see that!'

'I swear it's true. I even told him I disliked him enough to turn Lorenzo down.'

'Wasn't that true?'

'No, it wasn't. But he got me so mad I said the first thing that came into my head.'

Angie looked mischievous. 'You did say he had two brothers, didn't you?'

'You're incorrigible,' Heather laughed. 'I've only met Renato.'

'Ah, yes, the monster Renato.'

'I have to be fair. He's not a monster. I was mad at the way he inspected me, but he could have died because of me. He's welcomed me into the family, and he actually restored his cancelled order afterwards. Someone turned up from the Ritz and collected it.'

'Tell me about the other one.'

'There's also a half-brother, called Bernardo. Their father had an affair with a woman from one of the mountain villages, and Bernardo was their son. They were together in the car crash that killed them both, and Lorenzo's mother took the boy in and raised him with her own sons.'

'What an incredible woman!'

'I know. Her name's Baptista, and if I'm worried about anything, it's how she's going to view me.'

'But you showed me the letter she wrote you. It was lovely.'

'It's just that someone who can put her own feelings aside to do what she saw as her duty—well, you'd never really know what she was thinking, would you?'

'It's what Lorenzo thinks about you that counts,' Angie said staunchly. 'Hey, isn't that Sicily, down there?'

From here they could see the triangular island: close to Italy, yet apart from it, separated only by a narrow strip of water, the Straits of Messina, yet with its own distinct identity.

'A Sicilian,' Lorenzo had told her, 'is always a Sicilian first and an Italian afterwards. Sometimes he is barely an Italian at all. So many races meet in us that we think of ourselves as a race apart, doing things our own way.'

She was searching for him as soon as she and Angie left Customs. And there he was, with another man. He waved eagerly to her and broke into a run. Heather hastened towards him, while Angie brought up the rear, smiling, pushing the baggage trolley, and eyeing the second man with pleasurable speculation.

Lorenzo hugged his bride, kissing her between words. 'It's been such—a long—time, my darling.'

'Yes—yes,' she said kissing him back.

It was marvellous how certain she was now that she was here. Within a few minutes of landing in Sicily Heather knew she had come home. Everything about this place felt perfect, even before she'd discovered the details. And that could only mean that she was doing the right thing in marrying Lorenzo.

'This is my brother, Bernardo,' Lorenzo said at last, indicating the man with him.

'Half-brother,' murmured the man.

'Bernardo, meet Heather, my bride-to-be.'

She introduced Angie to Lorenzo. But when he tried to present Bernardo his brother waved him away with a grin. 'We've already introduced ourselves,' he said, 'while you two were—er—saying hello.'

This caused general laughter. Bernardo took charge of the trolley and they made their way to the car, where he invited Angie to sit in the front with him.

'They won't want to be disturbed,' he said, smiling.

So many sensations were converging on Heather that she had only a confused impression of the most brilliant colours she had ever seen, the bluest sky, the sweetest air. Bernardo swung the car around the outskirts of Palermo and down the coast, and soon the Residenza Martelli came into sight.

Heather sat up to watch it eagerly. Lorenzo had told her about his home, how it was built on an incline, over-looking the sea, but no words had conveyed its beauty. It rose before them, tier upon tier, balcony on balcony, each one a sea of blooms. Geraniums, jasmine, white and red oleanders, clematis and bougainvillaea danced together in a dizzying riot of colour that was always in perfect harmony.

Then they were on a winding road that twisted and turned, bringing the villa nearer until at last they swung into a courtyard. A flight of broad steps led up to a wide, arched entrance, with a door that was being opened from the inside. Through it came a small, elderly woman, making her way slowly with the aid of a walking stick. She took her place on the top step.

'That's my mother,' Lorenzo said, taking Heather's hand to lead her up the stairs.

Baptista looked imperious, despite her evident frailty and the fact that she barely came up to Lorenzo's shoulder. She was in her early sixties, but illness had aged her and she looked older. Beneath her shining white hair her face was sharp, and her brilliant blue eyes missed nothing. But Heather saw the warmth in those eyes, and when the thin arms went around her she felt the unexpected strength in the old woman's embrace.

'Welcome, my dear,' Baptista said. 'Welcome to the family.'

She was beaming, her expression full of kindness. She greeted Angie equally warmly. 'When you have seen your room, then we can take a little refreshment together.'

Although the house bore the modest title of Residenza, it might more aptly have been called a palace. It was built in medieval style, of beautiful yellow stone, with long tile and mosaic corridors. The rooms were lined sometimes with marble, sometimes with tapestries. Everywhere Heather saw wealth, beauty, elegance, and an inbred assumption of authority.

She and Angie were sharing a huge room. It bore two large four-poster beds hung with white net curtains which matched those at the tall windows leading onto the broad terrace, facing inland. Beneath it was the huge garden, and beyond that the land stretched away until it rose into dark, misty mountains on the horizon. Everywhere the colours had a vividness Heather had never seen before. After the pastel shades of England their sheer depth and brightness overwhelmed her.

A maid helped them unpack, then showed them out onto the terrace that went all around the house, and led them to the front, where Baptista was seated at a small rustic table, looking out over the bay. Bernardo and Lorenzo were there, and immediately drew out chairs, and when they were seated filled their glasses with Marsala. A larger table nearby was laden with Sicilian cheesecake, zabaglione, coffee ice with whipped cream, candied fruit ring, and several other things that they were too dazed to take in.

'I wasn't sure of your preferences, so I ordered a variety,' Baptista murmured.

The food and wine were delicious. Overhead a flowered awning sheltered them from the bright sun, and a soft breeze was springing up. Heather wondered how she had ever lived before coming to this perfect place. Lorenzo kept catching her eye and smiling, and his smile was irresistible, making her return it.

'That's enough,' Baptista said imperiously, tapping his hand. 'You'll have plenty of time to play the fool, my son. Go away now, and let me get to know your bride.'

CHAPTER THREE

WHEN Lorenzo had vanished, and Bernardo was showing Angie the garden, Baptista refilled Heather's glass. 'Renato told me how your prompt action saved his life,' she said. 'You and I have been friends from that moment.'

'You're very kind,' Heather said, 'but didn't he also tell you that it was my fault he was ever in danger?'

'I think he was largely to blame. He made you angry with his high-handedness. I've spoken to him very severely.'

Heather concealed a smile. The idea of the domineering Renato being alarmed by anything his frail mother might say was charming, but unconvincing.

'You are going to be very important to this family,' Baptista continued. 'More important than perhaps you can imagine. Lorenzo says you have no family of your own.'

'I was an only child. My mother died when I was six. My father couldn't cope without her.' Heather paused. She seldom talked about this because it seemed a betrayal of the sweet-natured, confused little man who'd longed only to follow his wife. But suddenly she wanted to confide in Baptista. 'He drank rather more than he ought,' she said. 'In the end he couldn't keep a job.'

'And so you looked after him,' Baptista said gently.

'We sort of looked after each other. He was kind and I loved him. When I was sixteen he caught pneumonia and just faded away. The last thing he said to me was, "Sorry, love."'

She'd sobbed over her father's grave, unable to voice

the real pain: the knowledge that she hadn't been enough for him. The practical difficulties had followed—lack of money, the abandonment of her dream of college, seizing the first job she could find. She explained in as few words as possible, and had the feeling that Baptista understood.

They talked for an hour, and each moment Heather felt herself grow closer to this regal but kindly woman. When Lorenzo poked his head out through the net curtains with a questioning look on his face, both women welcomed him with a smile. Laughing, he joined them, bringing fresh cakes.

From inside the house they heard Renato's voice, and suddenly he appeared through the long white curtains. When she'd seen him and Lorenzo off at the airport in England he'd looked pale, his arm in a sling. Now he moved freely and his look of vibrant health had returned.

She felt a slight shock. She had forgotten his massiveness, the heavy muscles of his neck, his air of being about to charge. Here in his native land, amid the fierce sun and the bright colours, that effect was reinforced.

Renato went first to his mother, greeting her with a mixture of affection and respect that caught Heather's attention. Then he turned to her.

'Welcome to my sister,' he said, placing a hand lightly on her shoulder and kissing her cheek. She had a moment's intense awareness of his spicy male scent. Then he moved away and greeted Lorenzo with a mock punch to the chin. Lorenzo returned the compliment and for a moment the two brothers engaged in a light-hearted tussle, as lively as young stallions, their voices rich with laughter. It ended with them thumping each other on the back in a way that suggested their mutual affection.

Baptista met Heather's eye, inviting her to share her pride and pleasure in her magnificent sons. Heather nodded, thinking that one day it would be her turn. At least, she hoped so.

At last Renato seated himself opposite her, smiling self-consciously. He was dressed informally, in fawn trousers and a short-sleeved shirt. Against the white material his skin, tanned to dark brown, showed up sharply. His black hair was tousled, and grew more so when he ran his hand through it after brushing the damp from his forehead. Heather had the feeling that everything else had grown pale. Just by being there, leaning back, half sprawled in his chair, he made everything revolve around him.

The light was fading. Someone asked where Bernardo and Angie were, and Lorenzo went to find them, amid good-natured laughter. Heather recalled Angie's laughing words on the plane, and hoped her friend hadn't been carried away by her impulsive romantic tendencies.

When it was time to get ready for dinner Heather went to her room and Angie appeared a moment later, her eyes shining. 'Have a nice time?' Heather asked.

'Lovely, thank you,' Angie said with suspicious innocence.

Just as they finished dressing there was a knock on the door and Baptista swept regally in, carrying a black box.

'Perfect,' she said, smiling at the wedding dress which Heather had set up on a stand near the window. 'And this will go with it.' She opened the box, revealing a tiara made of flawless pearls. 'Legend says that it once adorned the head of Queen Marie Antoinette,' she said. 'Later it passed to the Martelli family, and for generations it has been given to a bride for her wedding veil.'

'But—it's kind of you—but this is too much for me. What about when Renato marries? Won't he expect—?'

'That is no matter,' Baptista observed imperiously. 'If

he's so stupid and stubborn about marriage he has only himself to blame. Come, try it on.'

The tiara was perfect when set on Heather's luxuriant fair hair, but best of all was the way Baptista accepted her. She thanked her but was relieved when Baptista offered to keep the jewels in her safe until the wedding.

Seeing the glories of the Residenza, Heather was glad she'd splashed out on some expensive clothes—or, at least, they would have been expensive if she hadn't bought them at Gossways, heavily discounted. She was popular, and friends on many floors had slashed prices to the bone for her.

As a result she was able to appear in the medieval dining room in an off-the-shoulder pale yellow silk that followed the contours of her body without being obviously seductive. For sheer splendour she was outdone by Angie, a sizzling peacock in blues and greens that seemed almost to flame. But Lorenzo had eyes only for her, and Renato too seemed struck by the sight of her.

Baptista took her by the hand and led her forward, saying, 'Here is our guest of honour,' to be introduced to some local dignitaries. Then she was seated at the head of the table, between Lorenzo and Baptista, becoming uneasily aware that everyone was deferring to her, like a queen.

It was delightful but it made her nervous to have every dish presented for her approval. The meal was practically a banquet, and Baptista explained that the kitchen was practising for the wedding reception. The finest Sicilian cuisine was on offer. To start with, a choice of stuffed baked tomatoes, orange salad, stuffed rice ball fritters, bean fritters. Then the rice and pasta dishes, Sicilian rice, rice with artichokes, pasta with sardines, pasta with cauliflower, and the main dishes still to come.

By the time they reached the braised lamb, stuffed beef roll, and rabbit in sweet and sour sauce Heather was running out of appetite. But she knew that to say so would cause offence to those who had laboured to bring forth this feast in her honour, so she ploughed on valiantly.

'Perhaps you would rather have no more,' Baptista suggested gently, seeming to understand.

'But I must try those sweet dishes,' Heather said. 'They look so delicious.'

Watermelon jelly, fried pastries with ricotta cheese and candied fruit, pistachio cakes, nougat—she took a mouthful of each, and was rewarded by the looks of approval from every direction.

But the reward that touched her heart the most was when Baptista whispered, 'Well done, my daughter.'

She couldn't help being struck by the three brothers. All elegantly dressed in dinner jackets, they made an impressive sight: Lorenzo, the tallest, the most handsome; Bernardo, lean and dark with a gravity that made his rare smiles breathtaking—and Renato, dour, forceful, with his air of giving no quarter and asking none. He would be a difficult man to get to know, she thought, despite his evident intention of making her welcome.

Twice during the meal Renato was summoned from the table to take a phone call. In the gathering that followed Angie murmured, 'Bernardo says that Renato is the worker of the family and Lorenzo the charmer.'

'And what is Bernardo?' Heather wanted to know.

Angie's eyes twinkled. 'Tell you later.'

As the guests began to leave Lorenzo took her hand, whispering, 'Come with me,' and drawing her out of the room.

Hand in hand they ran up the stairs and along a corridor, until he reached a pair of oak double doors. He flung them open, revealing a large austerely beautiful room, hung with tapestries. 'There are going to be three uncles sleeping in this room,' he said. 'But after that—oh, come here!'

He pulled her into his arms and in the tenderness of his kiss she forgot everything else. It felt so good to be here, knowing that she'd come home.

'Excuse me,' came a voice from behind them. They jumped apart and saw Renato in the doorway, grinning. 'Sorry to disturb you,' he said. 'How do you like your apartment?'

'Our what?'

'This set of rooms is almost self-contained,' Lorenzo explained. 'It would be just perfect for us.'

'You mean—live here, instead of having a home of our own?' Heather asked, dismayed.

'But this *will* be a home of our own.'

'No, it won't. We'll be right next to your brother.'

'A terrible fate,' Renato agreed.

'It's nothing personal—' she started to say.

'Oh, I think it is,' he said, meeting her eyes. 'If we're here, Lorenzo will be at your beck and call. I dare say that's how you prefer it—'

'But will you have time to arrange a house before you marry in just over a week?' Renato asked reasonably. 'Of course Lorenzo could have chosen something already, but I thought you'd prefer to do that yourself. Why do you assume the worst of me?'

'Instinct,' she said, not mincing matters.

He grinned, unashamed. 'You wrong me.'

'No, I don't.' But she couldn't help smiling back at him. He was a devil, but he could be a disastrously engaging devil.

'You can start househunting later,' Renato assured her. 'Meanwhile, these rooms will be comfortable.'

It all sounded so reasonable, but her warning signals were flashing. Renato liked to keep people where he wanted them, and sounding reasonable was just another way of doing it. His teasing look showed that he followed her thought processes perfectly.

'Just for a little while, then,' she said at last. 'As soon as we return from honeymoon—'

'Not quite that soon,' Renato said. 'Lorenzo has a trip scheduled for New York—'

'Oh, really—' she began, up in arms again.

'And I naturally assumed that you'd want to go with him.'

Her weapons clattered uselessly to the floor. She would die for a trip to New York.

'That only leaves your honeymoon,' Renato said.

'Don't tell me you've arranged that too!'

'I thought you might borrow my boat for a couple of weeks' cruising. The crew will do the work; all you need do is enjoy yourself.'

'It's a beautiful boat, darling,' Lorenzo broke in eagerly. 'A sloop, with air-conditioning and—'

'And the two of you have settled it. Suppose I don't like sailing? Suppose I get seasick?'

'Do you?' Renato enquired.

'I don't know. I've never been on a boat.'

'Then the sooner you do, the better. Tomorrow Lorenzo has to go to Stockholm, to catch up on his delayed schedule. I shall take you out on the boat and you can let me know your decision.'

Heather had half expected Angie to come with them on the boat trip, but she was spending the day with Bernardo.

'He's going to show me his home village in the mountains.'

'You only met him yesterday,' Heather protested.

'I know.' Angie's chuckle was full of delight.

'You be careful.'

But Angie glowed with the self-confidence of a young woman who'd always been able to win any man she chose. She laughed merrily, and a moment later Heather heard her singing in the shower.

There was no mistaking the *Santa Maria*, a beautiful single-masted boat, over a hundred feet long, dominating everything in the little harbour of Mondello. Renato parked the car and handed her out. 'What do you think of her?' he asked in a voice full of love and pride.

'She's lovely,' Heather admitted.

He leapt lightly down onto the deck and reached up to settle both hands about her waist. The next moment she was swinging through the air to land beside him. 'All right?' he asked.

'Yes,' she said breathlessly. The sudden movement had taken her by surprise.

He introduced the crew, who were lined up to greet her.

'This is Alfonso, my captain, Gianni and Carlo, the crew. And this,' he added, indicating a little man, 'is Fredo the cook. He can manage anything from the fastest snacks to *cordon bleu*.'

The sun was bright and warm, a strong breeze whisked across the water, and soon they were edging out of the harbour into the wide sea beyond. After a few minutes Heather became used to the movement, and even began to find it pleasant.

'Well?' Renato asked, watching her face. 'Do you want

to go back, throw yourself overboard, throw *me* over-board—?'

'That last one sounds nice,' she said, laughing.

He shared her laughter, showing strong white teeth against his tanned skin. After the tense, argumentative man she'd met in England, this was a transformation. His clothes, too, were different. The elegant formality of last night was replaced by blue shorts and a white short-sleeved shirt, that was unbuttoned all the way. He looked powerful, glowing with life, intensely masculine.

'Let me show you your kingdom,' Renato said, taking her hand.

Below, it was like a little palace. In the galley Fredo, surrounded by the most modern equipment, was furiously at work on a feast. Along the narrow corridor was the master bedroom, complete with luxurious private bath-room. Everywhere was panelled with gleaming honey-coloured birchwood. At the centre was a huge double bed, the perfect place for lovers on their wedding night.

'This is yours for today,' Renato told her. 'Why not change into a swimsuit?'

'I don't even own one.'

He pulled open a wardrobe to display a series of swim-suits on hangers. Heather stared. There must have been about ten, in all colours, styles, and varying degrees of daringness.

'But how come you—?' She checked as she saw the wicked humour in his eyes. 'I'm not even going to ask.'

'You don't really need to, do you?' he asked.

His sexuality was so frank, his appetites so shameless that she didn't know where to look. She began to rifle through some pastel-coloured costumes, but Renato's big hand came out of nowhere and stilled hers.

'Not those,' he said. 'This one.'

He held up a bikini but she instinctively shook her head. 'No, I can't—'

'Why not? It's very modest.'

That was true. As bikinis went it was unfashionably modest. The lower part would cover most of her behind, and the upper part would enclose her breasts satisfactorily. But Heather had always seen herself as a once-piece person.

'And I can't wear cerise,' she argued. 'I'm too fair.'

'There's no law to stop you wearing reds. Risk it.'

'Right, I will.'

When he'd gone she changed, realising that in this place the dramatic colour seemed natural. She found a matching scarf in the wardrobe and tied it around her head, letting her hair fall free behind it. To cover her semi-nakedness she slipped on a robe of white lacy silk.

Back on deck she found Renato in the stern section, with a table that bore snacks and tall glasses. Above him a striped awning offered shelter from the sun. He handed her gallantly to her seat, and served her. The chilled wine was delicious; the little almond cakes were superb. Heather began to feel that she could easily get used to this.

'Sicily's at the centre of the Mediterranean,' Renato explained. 'So the boat can take you anywhere, easily. You can go across to Tunisia, or head the other way to Greece, or sail up the coast of Italy.'

'Where are we going today?'

'Just part of the way around the island, and then back. We'll find a quiet bay, take a swim. Are you feeling sea-sick yet?'

'Not at all,' she admitted. 'In fact, it feels wonderful.' She took a deep breath of salty air. 'Mmm!'

He grinned. 'We'll make a sailor of you yet.'

They toasted each other and she ate some of the little marzipan fruits, which looked so perfect that at first she thought they were the real thing. Then Renato took the helm and she stood beside him with the wind in her hair and the soft mist of water in her face, suddenly possessed by happiness and well-being.

'Why not sunbathe?' he suggested. 'But first rub in some sun cream—your skin is very fair and you must protect it.'

'The sun never touches me,' she said, a little regretfully.

'English sun,' Renato said dismissively. 'What do you know of the heat in my country? Even on land it can be fierce, but here the water reflects the sun back and doubles its strength. There's sun block in your cabin.'

She chose one of the luxurious lotions in her little bathroom, and went back up on deck to stretch out. Renato watched as she smoothed the silky liquid over her arms and legs. 'Turn over and let me do your back,' he said. 'Think how my brother would blame me if you went to your wedding looking like a lobster! I tremble at the prospect.'

'Tremble?' she chuckled. 'You?'

'I assure you that under this grim exterior beats the heart of a mouse.'

She gave in and rolled over onto her stomach. The touch of Renato's fingertips on her spine was unexpectedly light, not forceful, but almost delicate. She rested her head on her hands and began to relax as he worked on the back of her neck, kneading the cream in thoroughly with both hands.

Through half-closed eyes she watched the sun slanting on the deck. The hypnotic rhythm of his hands, strong yet sensitive, was making the edges of the world blur, so that

she couldn't tell where one thing ended and another began, or where she ended and the world began. The blood
was pulsing slowly, blissfully through her veins...

Suddenly she was awake, forcing herself back to reality
through clouds of contented sensation. Somewhere there
were seagulls calling, the waves lashing noisily against
the side of the boat, but her heart was beating so loudly
that it blotted out these sounds. She turned sharply and
found Renato looking at her with something in his eyes
that might have been shock.

'I must return to the helm,' he said, his voice coming
from a long way off.

'Yes,' she replied vaguely. 'You must.'

To her relief he left her. She looked around, finding to
her surprise that everything was in its normal place. Her
heart was pounding, but gradually it slowed to a soft throb
of pleasure. She was breathless, as though she'd been running. And Renato had been the same, she recalled. She
lay down again, meaning to puzzle it out, but contentment
overcame her, and a moment later she was asleep.

Renato's light touch on her shoulder awoke her. 'We've
dropped anchor,' he said. 'Just over there is a little bay.'

The *Santa Maria* had a small dinghy, already loaded
with a picnic hamper and being lowered to the water.
Renato handed her into it and they were away, headed for
a small golden beach where there was nobody else in
sight.

'Let's swim before we eat,' he suggested. 'Come.' He
seized her hand and they ran down the yellow sand.

The shock of the cool water was delicious. She plunged
in and together they swam out to deep water. She'd never
swum so far from shore before, and she wasn't a strong
swimmer, but she felt full of confidence as long as Renato

was there. They swam for half an hour, then headed back, side by side.

'Let's stay in a bit longer,' he said as their feet touched ground.

'No, I'll unpack the picnic. You go back if you want another swim.'

He raced away and plunged back into the water while she dried off her hair, and swung it in the sun for a moment. When she looked out to sea again he'd vanished. The water was clear and level, and there wasn't a sign of Renato.

Slowly she got to her feet, feeling as though a dark cloud had covered the sun. It was like waking in a lunar landscape where everything was bare and desolate, and no life would ever live again.

Then his head broke the surface and the world was bathed in her relief. He waved and she waved back, discovering that she'd been holding her breath.

'You scared me,' she accused him as he walked up the beach.

He grinned. 'Sorry. I like to swim under water for as long as I can.'

He towelled himself dry, and sat down beside her. The movement gave her a good view of the ugly scar near his wrist, and she shuddered.

'It's nothing,' he said. 'It's healed. See.'

He held out his hand and she took it between hers, turning it to see the scar better. As he'd said, it had healed beautifully, but now she saw how large the wound had been, how close he had come to death. His big, forceful hand looked strange against her slim, delicate ones. By tightening it he could have crushed her, but he let it lie there while she gently brushed the sand from it.

'I always said no woman would ever leave a permanent mark on me,' he mused. 'But now one has.'

'It's not really funny.' Something inside her chest was aching.

'All right, then I'll tell you something serious. What happened that night told me all about you. One minute you were telling me to jump in the river. The next you were saving my life as cool as a cucumber, despite having been knocked about yourself. And when you did weaken, just a little, you pulled yourself together so that you could clear the driver.'

'That's my English reserve and efficiency,' she teased. 'We're well known for keeping our cool.'

'Does anything throw you off balance?'

'Probably nothing you could think of,' she said with a smile.

'By God, I did the right thing bringing you here!' he said suddenly.

'You? It was Lorenzo who brought me here.'

'Of course, of course. I think we should eat now.'

The picnic was magnificent and Renato explained that Fredo had outdone himself in her honour. As they sipped the cool wine, the slight movement of his face drew her attention to another scar. It made him look as though he'd tangled with a wild animal and emerged battered. She wondered how the animal would look. He caught her gaze and he rubbed it self consciously.

'I'm sorry,' she said, horrified at herself.

He shrugged. 'It makes no difference. Nature didn't make me a beauty to start with. Then I played the fool on a motorbike and got what I deserved.'

'You did that on a motorbike?'

'I was wild as a boy. I bought a fast bike and rode it to the limit. The police warned me time and again, but I was a Martelli and that has its privileges. Then I took a mountain bend at an insane speed and nearly killed myself. Luckily nobody else got hurt, and I was left with this scar on my face as a reminder not to be a damned fool.'

'I can't picture you wild, somehow. You seem so much in control.'

'I learned the consequences of not being in control the hard way. Besides, my father was dead by then, and the firm was being run by an uncle who wasn't very good at it. Somebody had to get a grip while there was still time.'

'So the firm had to become your life?'

'It's a more useful life than dashing about getting myself half killed. And now I find it very satisfying.'

She noticed that 'now' and wondered how hard it had been for a young man addicted to excitement to put on a suit and chain himself to a desk.

He said casually, 'My mother told me that you were reluctant to accept her gift yesterday.'

'The pearl tiara, yes. It's a family heirloom. You're the eldest son. Surely it should go to your wife?'

'Who doesn't exist, and never will. The single life suits me too well to give up.'

'Oh, yes, Elena, Julia and the rest of the crowd. I don't believe it. It sounds so immature, and I don't think you *are* immature.'

He grimaced wryly. 'I didn't always feel this way. There was a lady once—her name was Magdalena Conti—the story is nauseatingly sentimental. I was much younger, and I believed in things I don't believe in now. She taught me a lesson in reality from which I benefited enormously.'

'Is she why you think all women are fortune-hunters?'

He shrugged. 'Possibly. She was beautiful, tender, loving. She was also greedy, manipulative and deadly. She aimed her arrows at me for money. I fell for it. She told me she was pregnant. I asked her to marry me. I'd have asked her anyway, but fatherhood thrilled me. I indulged in many dreams in those days.'

He fell silent, looking out over the sea. His eyes might have been fixed on the horizon, or maybe on some other horizon, inside himself.

'And then?' Heather asked softly.

'Then she met another man, much richer, and in films, which she found exciting. At our final meeting I learned for the first time how much I bored her. Then she went off with him.'

'And your baby?'

'She never gave birth. I know that much. Perhaps the child was an invention, or perhaps she—' He shrugged. 'I prefer to think she was lying about the pregnancy, but the truth is that I shall never know.'

Heather was silent. There was nothing she could have said that wouldn't have sounded like a mockery of his pain. And the pain was unmistakable, even after so long. Suddenly the air about her was jagged with suffering. At the same time she was wondering about the woman who could be bored by this man.

'Now the only woman I trust is my mother,' he finished. 'Lorenzo is fortunate to have found you.'

'So you think I can be trusted? Then surely, other women can?'

'Lorenzo still knows how to *give* trust. But I don't. I would invite betrayal by expecting it, and—forgive me—such expectations are always fulfilled in the end. I made my decision, and I'll stick to it. Take my mother's gift. No woman will ever challenge you for it.'

She refilled his glass and he accepted it with a slightly forced smile.

'Do you think you'll be happy here, Heather?' he asked quietly.

'I've known it from the first moment. It's not like me to be so impulsive, but Lorenzo made me feel so wanted.'

He looked at her intently. 'Had nobody ever made you feel that way before?'

'There was someone else, quite recently. We were engaged for a year, and he called it all off a week before the wedding. I suppose it left me feeling a bit bruised and rejected.'

Then a dreadful thought occurred to her. 'But don't think I accepted Lorenzo on the rebound. It's not just because of Peter. It's Lorenzo himself, the way he is—so loving and warm-hearted.'

To her surprise Renato was frowning as though something troubled him deeply. At last he said, 'Heather, if ever you're in trouble, promise that you will come to me.'

'But why should I when I can go to him?'

'He's a fine fellow, but if you need an older brother's help, please remember that I'm here.'

She would have turned the moment aside with a laugh, but something in Renato's manner stopped her. There was a strange intensity in his eyes.

'Promise me, *miu soru*,' he urged.

'What was that you called me?'

'*Miu soru.* It's Sicilian. It means, "my sister", for that's what you must be now.'

'And what is "my brother"?'

'*Miu frati.* Promise your brother. Give him your word.'

There was something in his urgency that was as puzzling as his frown had been. 'All right, I promise,' she said. '*Miu frati.*'

'Shake?'

'Shake.' Her hand was engulfed in his big one, and for

a moment she could feel the power flowing through him, power that he'd just offered to put at her service.

'And to show that I'm really your brother,' he added, 'may I give you away at your wedding?'

She was touched. 'Thank you. That's very kind.'

'For my sister, nothing is too much,' he said gravely, raising her hand and brushing his lips against the back of it. Suddenly a stillness came over both of them. It was so total that Heather could hear and feel her heart thumping. She had the odd sensation that the whole world was pulsing with it.

Abruptly, he released her hand. Heather stared at it, wondering what had happened. Why did she have this strange feeling that the world had changed, that the sun had grown dark and the heat more intense?

'We should go back now.' Renato's voice was strange.

'Yes,' she replied, not knowing what she said.

But by the time they'd packed everything into the dinghy the brief sensation had passed and she was chiding herself for imagining things. The whole Martelli family had opened their arms to her in welcome, and the sensation was so unfamiliar that it was distorting her perceptions. As the little boat sped across the water the rushing wind blew the last crazy thoughts from her head.

CHAPTER FOUR

ON THE journey home Heather took a fascinated look at the stern, where a jet ski, big enough for two people, was fixed.

'Would you care to try it?' Renato asked.

'I'd love to,' she said eagerly.

Slowly the jet ski was winched down to the water. Renato leapt down and took the front seat, and Heather eased her way into the seat behind him. She had just time to wrap her arms about him before they roared away across the water. The speed, noise and vibration took her by surprise and she tightened her arms, turning her head sideways and pressing herself against Renato's broad back.

'All right?' Renato roared back at her.

She could barely make out the words through the noise, but she yelled back, *'Fine!'*

It was true. The vibration was taking her over, coming up through every part of her flesh, her thighs, her stomach, her breasts where they were pressed against Renato's back. The water rushed by, lashing her with white foam, whipping up her excitement in the most physically exhilarating experience of her life. Renato's body was like a strong column in her arms. She clung onto him, eyes closed, relishing his warmth.

At last he slowed and brought the jet ski to a halt.

'Wahooo!' she cried.

'You enjoyed it, then?' he said, turning his head and grinning at her.

'Oh, yes!' she said happily. 'Oh, yes, I did! Where are

we?' She caught sight of the boat, which looked tiny in the distance. 'It's miles away.'

'These things travel very fast. Another few minutes and we'd have been out of sight of the boat.'

A mad impulse seized her. 'Let's!'

'You want to go on?'

'And on and on and on!' she cried out, throwing her head back and carolling up to the sky.

'Heather, what's got into you?' He was laughing, but he sounded half alarmed at something wild and uncontrolled about her.

'Nothing. Everything. The whole world!'

'I think we should go back.'

'Never. I want to go forward. Start her up.'

'*Right!*' Something he'd heard in her voice got to him and he kicked the engine into life, swinging away towards the horizon, then driving forward across the endless water.

Soon the *Santa Maria* was out of sight. For some reason Heather found that knowledge thrilling, as though she had cut loose from all safety and restraint in a way she'd never felt able to do in her life before. The sense of freedom was mindblowing. She unwrapped her arms from Renato's body and rested her hands lightly on his shoulders. Now she felt quite safe this way. She was invincible. Nothing could happen to her.

But the next moment they swerved sharply. Caught off guard, she tried to grip his shoulders more tightly, but it was too late. There was nothing to hold onto, and then she was flying through the air to land in the water with a crash.

At this speed it was like slamming into a brick wall. For a dreadful moment everything went black. She was half unconscious, sinking, sinking into the depths that went on for ever, and the horror was engulfing her. Somehow she managed to fight back to the surface, but she was still dizzy and fighting for consciousness. Through water-logged eyes she glimpsed Renato speeding away from her, unaware that she'd vanished. She screamed after him, knowing he couldn't hear her. Then she was sinking again, into deep, deadly water, and despair.

She fought back up again, but she knew she could drown before he even knew that she'd gone. When he returned it would be too late. She felt her consciousness start to fade as weights dragged her down for the last time, and the world grew darker....

The arms that seized her seemed to come from no-where. She could see nothing, but she could feel herself being forced upwards. There was light above, air, gasping relief. She had her arms about Renato's neck, clinging to him.

'I looked back and you were gone,' he said, his voice hoarse with fear. 'What happened—?'

'I don't know—I can't—'

'Never mind. Thank God you're safe.'

The jet ski was a little way off, having stopped when he dived into the water for her. Now he swam over, using his one free arm, and clambered aboard, keeping firm hold of her with one hand. Then he hauled her up in front. 'I want you where I can see you,' he growled. 'You vanished beneath the water—*and I didn't know where to look.*'

His horror matched her own. She clung to him, trembling violently. 'I thought nobody would ever find me,' she gasped.

'It's all right, hold onto to me. Hold on tightly to—' a shudder racked him '*—to your brother.*'

He made a moderate pace back to the ship, with Heather sitting sideways, clinging onto him. She was beyond thought. She just didn't want to let him go. Her consciousness was coming and going in waves. At last she felt herself being hauled aboard, then Renato lifting her and carrying her below to her cabin, then darkness.

When she awoke, Angie was there with her.

'Hello,' her friend said, smiling. 'Surprised to see me? Renato called Bernardo on his mobile, and asked him to bring me to the harbour. I came on board a couple of minutes ago. Trust you to get in the wars.'

Heather was recovered enough to say wickedly, 'I hope you weren't interrupted at too difficult a moment.'

Angie's smile was both impish and mysterious. 'There'll be others. Let me help you get dressed and we'll go ashore.'

'I'll just put something over my swimsuit—'

'What swimsuit?'

Then Heather realised that she was wearing a towelling robe and nothing else. She tried to remember taking off her bathing costume, but her last memory was of Renato laying her down on the bed and kicking the door shut.

'Did you—?'

'Not me,' Angie said. 'You were like that when I got here.' Her face was demure but her eyes were mischievous. 'It's all right. I won't tell Lorenzo.'

'Don't be ridiculous,' Heather said hastily, feeling a blush start in her face and spread all over her body. 'Let's just go home.'

On Angie's orders Heather spent the next day in bed. She slept like a log and awoke feeling good. But when Baptista or Angie dropped in, she thought she sensed a certain tension that they wouldn't talk about. She couldn't ask Renato, because he didn't come to see her at all.

At last Angie explained. 'Renato called Lorenzo in Stockholm to tell him to come home, but he'd never checked into his hotel and nobody knew where he was. So everyone got a little uptight. But it turned out that he was already heading this way.'

'He was coming home anyway?' Heather asked.

'I guess he couldn't bear being away from you. He'll be here later today.'

The knowledge galvanised her to get up, and by afternoon she was looking her best for Lorenzo. As soon as the car stopped he hurried up the steps to clasp her in his arms. He seemed tense and distraught, but she put that down to concern for her safety, and when he said, 'Where's Renato? I have to talk to him, *now*,' she guessed he was going to berate him for allowing her into danger.

'Darling, I'm all right,' she said.

'We'll talk later,' he told her. 'Later. *Renato*.'

He vanished into the house and she didn't see him again that day. Angie and Baptista made her go to bed early, and when she awoke next day the sun was up and Lorenzo was waiting for her at breakfast. He was pale but composed, and he smiled as he promised her he hadn't quarrelled with his brother.

They saw little of each other after that. Renato didn't send him abroad again, but kept him at Head Office in Palermo. Each morning the two of them would leave early for work, and return late.

Heather had no time to miss him. She was enjoying her flowering relationship with Baptista. The old woman showed her all over the house, and she began to understand a little better the family into which she was marrying. Renato had said, 'If you marry one Martelli, you get the whole pack of us,' and it was true.

Looking through photograph albums, she saw the wedding pictures of the young Baptista and Vincente Martelli, the extravagantly beautiful bride barely coming up to the shoulder of her unsmiling groom. He looked several years older, and stood straight and uncomfortable. His face was uncannily like that of Renato today.

Then the early pictures of Renato himself, always looking straight into camera, his dark eyes full of challenge, his mouth uncompromising. Right from the first this had been a young man who knew who he was, what he wanted, and how he was going to get it.

Then Lorenzo appeared, curly-haired, angelic, bringing forth Heather's answering smile. At last there was Bernardo, grave-faced, always standing a little apart, looking as though he wanted to be anywhere else.

'And soon there will be more photographs,' Baptista said, 'when we welcome you into the family.'

Baptista suffered from a weak heart, and spent much of her time resting, but one morning she appeared at breakfast looking strong and cheerful, and invited Heather to take a short trip with her, although wouldn't say where they were going.

'I would have invited Angie as well,' she said as the car took them inland, 'but she and Bernardo had already made plans.' She gave a conspiratorial smile.

'I've never seen Angie like this before,' Heather admitted. 'Usually she's a bit—well—'

'Love 'em and leave 'em,' said Baptista robustly. She was proud of her grasp of English idiom.

'Yes, but she seems really absorbed in Bernardo. I wonder about him, though.'

'He's a very difficult man, but since Angie has been here I've seen him happier than ever before. She may have more to contend with than she imagines, but it will be so nice for all of us if it works out.'

Inland Sicily was more sparsely populated than the coast. Now they were in the rural heartland, where goats grazed within sight of the ruins of a Greek temple. Their way was briefly barred by a flock of sheep, driven by a little nut-brown man with a gap-toothed grin. He nudged his flock to the side and hailed Baptista, who hailed him back.

'We're on my land now,' she explained. 'I have a small estate, a village, some olive groves, and a little villa. It was my dowry.'

At last they saw the village, called Ellona, clinging to the side of the hill. It was a medieval place with cobblestones, tiny houses and only two buildings of note. One was the church, and the other a pink stone villa with two staircases curving up the outside.

The midday heat was at its height, and they sat just inside the house, at a French door looking out onto a terrace, with the net curtains moving gently in the faint breeze.

'I ordered English tea in your honour,' Baptista said, with a note of triumph.

'It's delicious,' Heather said, sipping the Earl Grey. *'Deliziusu.'* She pronounced the Sicilian word very deliberately, to differentiate it from the Italian, *delicioso.* Baptista smiled.

'Already you are becoming a Sicilian,' she said.

'Well, I learned some Italian to get on in the store, and Sicilian isn't too hard if you remember how often it uses "u" where Italian uses "o". I'll get the hang of it.'

'What matters is that you are working hard to become one of us, just as I knew you would.'

'I'll tell you something,' Heather said impulsively. 'I've only been in Sicily a few days, but as soon as I arrived I had such a feeling of—of *rightness.* I don't know how else to say it, but it's as though everything was conspiring to tell me that this is where I belong. I've never had that sense before.'

'Then you have come to the right place, and the right people.' Baptista made a sweep of her hand, indicating the sunlit landscape, down the valley, across to Palermo, with a faint glimpse of the sea beyond. 'See, the very land welcomes you.'

'This place is so beautiful. Did you live here when you were a child?'

'No, but we visited sometimes in the summer, when the city was too hot. It was my property, to be kept in good condition so that it could be a fine dowry when my marriage was arranged.'

'Arranged?' Heather echoed, not sure she'd heard correctly. 'An *arranged* marriage?'

Baptista chuckled. 'Of course. Arranged marriages were very common, and even today—where there is property—' she gave an eloquent shrug. 'They often work out very well, despite what you think.'

'But what about love?'

A faraway look came into Baptista's eyes. 'I was in love once,' she said softly. 'His name was Federico. I called him Fede. He was a fine-looking boy, tall and strong with dark, speaking eyes, and hands that could hold a woman so gently.'

She smiled, looking at something deep inside herself. 'Of course, a well brought up young girl wasn't supposed to notice things like that, but he was the most handsome young man in Sicily. All the girls were crazy for him, but I was the one he loved.'

'What happened?' Heather asked.

'Oh, we never had a chance. He was a gardener, and in those days rich girls didn't marry gardeners. In fact they still don't. He used to work here and grow such beautiful roses, just for me. He said that whenever he saw a rose, he thought of me.'

'What happened?'

'My parents separated us. He was sent away and I never saw or heard of him again. I tried to find out what had become of him, for I thought if only I could know that he was well I might find a sort of peace. But I never managed to discover anything. He had vanished into a void. That was the hardest thing of all to bear.'

'Vanished?' Heather echoed, shocked. 'Do you mean that—?'

'I don't know,' Baptista said quickly. 'He vanished. It would be nice to know, one way or the other, but I suppose now I never will.'

'You still think of him—after all these years?'

'He was my one true love, and no woman ever forgets the man who is that,' Baptista murmured with a touch of wistfulness. 'I cried for weeks, and was sure my life was over. My parents arranged marriages for me and I refused them all. After several years they were growing worried. I was already twenty-five, a late age for a girl of my generation to marry. Finally they suggested Vincente. He was a good man, although very dull. But I wanted children. So I married him, and I was glad.'

'You fell in love?'

'No, not I with him, nor he with me. But we became dear friends.' She gave Heather an impish smile. 'How easy it is to embarrass the young. You are wondering if I knew about my husband and Bernardo's mother. Of course I did, and it wasn't the end of the world. I'd had my love, and the happiness I knew in that short time will stay with me all my days. I was glad Vincente could also be happy.'

'But are you saying that—that love doesn't matter in marriage?'

'I'm saying there is more than one kind of love. Vincente was my dearest friend. As friends we loved each other, and our marriage was strong. When our little girl died we wept in each other's arms.'

'You had a daughter?'

'Our first child. She died when she was six months old. Her name was Doretta.' Baptista took her hand. 'If she had lived, I hope she would have grown up like you, gentle, sweet-natured and strong.'

Heather laid her other hand over Baptista's and looked at her with eyes that were suddenly blurred.

'We haven't known each other very long,' Baptista said, 'but sometimes a few days is enough—as you and Lorenzo have discovered. I knew from the first that you were the daughter of my heart, as surely as if I'd given birth to you. Bella Rosaria would have been Doretta's dowry. Now it will be yours.'

'You mean—you're giving it to Lorenzo—?'

'No. I am giving it to you.'

'But—I couldn't possibly—'

'If you refuse, you will break my heart,' Baptista said simply.

'And I wouldn't hurt you for the world,' Heather said at once. 'Thank you.'

After all, she thought, the property would return to the family on her wedding day. And that was so close now that the gift probably wouldn't happen until the actual wedding.

But Baptista had another surprise for her. She rapped on the floor with her walking stick, and when a maid looked in spoke a few words in Sicilian. A moment later two grave-looking men, dressed in black, entered the room, carrying papers.

'This is my lawyer and his assistant,' Baptista explained. 'The papers are all ready for signature, and they will act as witnesses.'

'You mean now?' Heather asked, slightly aghast.

'There will never be a better time,' Baptista said calmly taking up a pen.

'*Signora*—' Heather said urgently.

'In a few days it will be right for you to call me Mamma,' Baptista observed. 'Why not now? It would make me so happy.'

'And me—Mamma.'

'*Bene!* Now be a dutiful daughter and don't argue.'

A few moments later Heather found herself the owner of an estate. They all marked the occasion with a glass of Marsala, and the lawyers departed.

'Now I'm feeling a little tired,' Baptista announced. 'I'll go and lie down for a while, and you can look over your property.'

As she wandered through the rooms of the elegant little villa Heather knew she'd found the true home she wanted. It was the perfect size for two people in love, and just close enough to Palermo to make it feasible for her and Lorenzo to live here.

Plans were forming in her mind. Since she could travel with him it would be easy for her to involve herself in his work. Baptista had a seat on the board, and was all for Heather taking an interest in the firm. She and Lorenzo could work together and then retreat to this magic place and make their own world.

And when their world began to grow she knew exactly the room she wanted for a nursery. It was at the back of the house, overlooking the magnificent, flower-filled gar-

dens. She stood at the window a moment, mentally re-
decorating this room in pastel shades, then hurried down
to explore the grounds.

Here the air was heady with a thousand scents. Tall
trees shaded her progress and birds called overhead as she
wandered in a place of pure enchantment. Always she was
within sound of rushing water, and sometimes she came
upon little fountains, cut into the walls.

Suddenly the path widened into a small arbour, almost
separate from the rest of the garden. Everywhere she
looked there were roses, pink, white, yellow, climbing
roses, trailing roses, full blooms and small tight buds. And
in the centre a bush of brilliant crimson blooms that was
in itself a declaration of love.

'I thought you would find this place,' Baptista said.

Heather turned and saw her standing there, leaning
slightly on her stick.

'I saw you from my window, and wanted to show you
my special place myself.'

'Did he—?'

'Yes, Fede began it for me. It was his way of saying
what he dared not say in words.'

She indicated a small wooden bench and they sat there
together.

'Over the years I have tended this place with love and
it has grown. I've protected the plants so that they survived the winters, taking them into greenhouses, or even
the house. Some are still the original plants that he put
here. Some are from cuttings.

'And I have taken cuttings to the Residenza, and put
them in my garden there. But here, in this spot, was where
he said to me that no other woman would ever exist for
him besides me.'

She pointed to the glorious red blooms. 'We planted

that together, and I have never let it die,' she said softly. 'If he came back now, I could show him that bush and say, "See how I have loved it for your sake."'

'And I shall love it for yours,' Heather said softly.

'I knew you would. And when they bury me, and my coffin is piled high with formal tributes from people I cared nothing about, will you make sure a single bloom from this bush lies hidden there somewhere?'

'Of course I will. But don't you want Lorenzo or Renato to do that for you?'

She shook her head. 'When the time comes Lorenzo will sob and forget everything but his grief. You will have to be strong for him then. And Renato is a good man, but there are things about the heart that he doesn't understand.'

'Just about everything, I should think,' Heather said, and the two women exchanged a smile. 'Of course I'll do this for you,' she promised.

'Then I can be peaceful, for it was troubling me that there was nobody I could rely on to do this.'

'You still love him, after so long?'

'Not as I think you mean it. Passion is long dead. What matters then is someone to sit with you in the evening sun: someone who will talk and hold your hand, and smile at you with eyes that say, "Let us go, unafraid, into the twilight together." Sometimes at dusk I'll come and sit here, and remember. But always I sit alone. I am growing old, my dear daughter, and my heart aches for what I shall never have.'

She tucked her hand in Heather's arm, and slowly they made their way back to the house.

Lorenzo's reaction later that night was strange. After the first surprise and pleasure, he said, 'I wonder how

Renato will take this. He always hoped to own Bella Rosaria one day.'

After which Heather braced herself for recriminations, but Renato went up to his room without giving her more than a brief nod.

CHAPTER FIVE

RELATIVES were beginning to converge on Palermo, some to stay in the Residenza, others to occupy the biggest suites in the best hotels. Heather was astonished by the legions of aunts, uncles, cousins that made up the far reaching branches of the Martelli family.

She met people until she was giddy. The ones she enjoyed the most were Enrico and Giuseppe. They were first cousins to each other, and distant cousins to Baptista, and long ago they had both been in love with her. When she married Vincente Martelli, they had consoled each other's broken hearts. Forty years later they were still bachelors, still competing for the honour of escorting her. She was allowing them both to squire her to the wedding. Otherwise there would have been a riot.

Two days before the wedding the great house was gleaming in readiness for the wedding ball. In their bedroom upstairs, Angie and Heather prepared for an evening of dancing.

After her day on the boat Heather had tanned to a pale biscuit colour that was very becoming. It was a pity, she thought, as she stepped out of the shower, that she couldn't be the same perfect colour all over. But that would have meant sunbathing naked...

Suddenly she could feel Renato's hands gliding over her shoulders and down her spine, lulling her into a warm, hypnotic daze that made everything else unimportant. And later he'd stripped her naked in the cabin. She pressed her hands against her cheeks, which were suddenly burning, wishing desperately that these strange fancies would cease tormenting her.

'Hurry up!' Angie called.

'Coming,' she said with relief.

Lorenzo kissed her hand when he saw her in pale lavender embroidered silk. 'Every man there will envy me,' he declared. Despite his gallant words his air was abstracted. But they were all under a strain, she thought.

There was a burst of applause as they opened the ball together, making the first circuit of the floor alone before the others joined them. Heather had the feeling that everything was happening in slow motion, so that as she whirled in Lorenzo's arms she had time to see the faces watching them. There was Baptista, flanked by her two cavaliers, smiling contentedly as she saw her dream come true. There were Angie and Bernardo, already looking like a settled couple. Everything was wonderful.

Then she noticed Renato standing close to the most extravagantly lovely woman she had ever seen. She was a ripe brunette in the full summer of her beauty. Her mouth was ripe and luscious, her dark eyes were as huge and vacant as a cow's. Everything about her proclaimed lasciviousness, including the speaking look she was directing up at Renato.

'Careful,' Lorenzo said, tightening his grip on her. 'You nearly stumbled.'

'Sorry,' she said breathlessly.

'You were miles away. What were you thinking of?'

'Why—our wedding, of course,' she said with a bright laugh. 'I think of it all the time.'

'So do I—the day after tomorrow—and then we'll tie the knot for ever.'

'Yes—for ever.'

'Thank goodness the others are starting to dance. I don't feel so conspicuous.'

'Who's that woman with Renato?'

'That's Elena Alante, she's a widow. Renato prefers them married, divorced or widowed. Experienced, anyway. The one over there is Minetta, and just behind her is the Contessa Julia Bennotti. All three of them are—well, Renato is—'

'A brave man,' Heather suggested lightly.

'Very brave to have them all here at once. I wonder what possessed him.'

Heather wondered too when she finally came face to face with Renato. He looked more tense and edgy than she'd seen him before, like a man with a fiend sitting on his shoulder. He greeted Heather with a nod and a smile that seemed to take a lot of effort, and introduced her to Elena. As the two women inclined their heads in greeting Heather became aware of something that made her smile.

'Allow me to congratulate you on your perfume, *signora*,' she murmured. 'It's delightful.'

'Dear Renato bought it for me recently,' Elena cooed. 'It's called "Deep In The Night". I keep telling him he shouldn't buy me so many expensive gifts, but he says I'm special to him.'

'And for a special friend a man buys a special gift,' Heather murmured. 'I'm sure he took a lot of trouble to choose exactly the right perfume for you.'

'I think it's time I had the privilege of dancing with the bride,' Renato said curtly, taking her hand. Heather let him lead her onto the floor, where another waltz was just beginning.

'That's enough of your tricks,' he growled.

'I was only being polite. It really is a lovely perfume.

And since you had the nerve to flaunt your harem, surely you shouldn't be shy about them?'

'There are some things best not talked about,' he growled, a warning light in his eyes.

'Not a guilty conscience, surely?'

'No, just a sense of propriety,' he snapped.

A bitter demon drove her to say, 'Propriety? You? I wish I'd been a fly on the wall when you gave Elena that perfume, with a gallant speech about how she haunted your thoughts while you were in London—that is, the thoughts you could spare from Julia and Minetta, and, of course, when you weren't propositioning your brother's girlfriend—'

His hand in the small of her back tightened. 'Stop it,' he whispered. 'Don't dare to talk like that.'

'I—' It was suddenly hard to breathe. 'I was only making small talk.' She pulled herself together. 'I haven't yet thanked you for a delightful day out. You were right about spending our honeymoon on your boat.' She was spinning words, any words, barely knowing what she said.

'One thing I wasn't right about,' he grated. 'You and Lorenzo must find somewhere else to live.'

'But you said—'

'I've changed my mind. *You can't live here.*'

No need to ask why. She'd been wrong about the fiend. It wasn't on his shoulder, but in his heart. It looked out from his eyes and told her that he was on hot coals. Just as she was.

She became aware that he was breathing harshly. She tried to tell herself that it was merely the exertion of dancing, but the truth was there between them. If they had been alone he would have kissed her. And then he would have kissed her again, long, hard and passionately. And she would have kissed him back in the way they'd both foreseen on that long ago day when he'd come to her counter and the air had been jagged between them from the first moment.

It was all wrong. She loved Lorenzo dearly, so how could she be on fire at the thought of laying her lips against Renato's and feeling his arms about her? How could it be his body she ached to feel pressed against hers, his hands on her skin with the purposeful yet sensitive touch she'd felt once before? It had haunted her every moment since. She could admit that now.

It would have been easier if she'd stayed hostile to him, but their moment of sympathy on the beach had destroyed that. She'd discovered that she could like him, even be sad for him. That was even more dangerous than her body's wayward reaction.

'I shouldn't dance with you,' she blurted out in sudden dread.

'I know,' he said quietly.

'I meant—I have so many duty dances to do. I shouldn't waste one with *miu frati*.'

But the words were a mistake. They recalled the picnic when he'd spoken to her with a quiet intensity she suddenly didn't want to remember.

'You're right,' he said. 'You must return to your duty, and I must return to my "harem". They suit me. They cause me no problems.'

'I'm sure nobody could cause you a problem that you couldn't solve, Renato.'

'Once I thought so too. The dance is ending. Goodnight—until I lead you to the altar to marry my brother.'

She turned away to meet one of the many Martelli relations who mustn't be overlooked. After him there was another, and so her whole evening was taken up, and she didn't have to look at Renato, or wonder who he was dancing with.

The world was shrouded in mist. Through it she was vaguely aware of strong arms carrying her down steps, laying her on a bed, hands moving over her bikini, stripping it from her body. She felt the slight breeze on her naked flesh, a towel dabbing her dry, her breasts, her thighs—

And then, piercing the mist, the man's face, his eyes defenceless, appalled at his own thoughts.

Suddenly it all vanished, and Heather found she was sitting up in bed, shuddering, her body alive with unwanted sensation. 'No,' she gasped. *'No!'*

'What is it?' Angie asked, scrambling out of her own bed and hurrying to her. 'Heather, what's the matter?'

'Nothing—just a dream—'

Just a dream in which the memory she'd fiercely suppressed had forced its way into view. She hadn't dared remember how she'd lain naked in Renato's arms, or how he'd looked at her. But part of her would never forget.

'I'm going for a walk,' she said.

'Shall I come with you?'

'No, thank you. I—I need to be alone.'

Throwing a light robe over her nightdress, she slipped out onto the terrace. The house was quiet and dark, and here in the cool night air she might soothe the fever that consumed her. It was two in the morning. Her wedding day. And she had been wrenched awake by a dream of another man.

In her heart she'd always known Renato was dangerous. But it would pass once she was married. In Lorenzo's arms, in his bed, she would forget everything else. She *must!*

She looked over the terrace rail to the one below and what she saw filled her with relief. 'Lorenzo,' she called in a whisper. 'I'm coming down.'

She returned through her room and slipped out, along the corridor, down the stairs. He was waiting for her in the hall, his arms open to receive her as she flung herself against him.

'What is it, darling? What's wrong?'

'Nothing. I just wanted to say how much I love you— love you—*love you*—'

'There's no need to sound so upset about it.'

'I'm not upset. Everything's perfect. But I had to tell you that I love you.'

'And I love you, so everything's all right.'

He kissed her. Heather gave herself up to that kiss, trying to find in it everything she wanted. But no kiss could give that. They were both too full of tension. Things would be different when they were on the boat, drifting beneath the moonlight.

She jumped at a sudden sound from the darkness. 'What was that?'

'Only Renato. That's his study. He's actually in there, working.'

'Could he have heard us?'

'Probably. What does it matter? Forget him. Why, darling, you're trembling.' Lorenzo's arms went around her. 'Let me take you upstairs. Just a few more hours, and we'll belong to each other for ever.'

The wedding dress was made of silk-satin, designed in a subtly medieval style, with the skirt falling in heavy folds from her waist, and the slight fullness coming from the huge amount of material that had been used. At the back it stretched out into a long train embellished around the hem with French lace. The sleeves were plain to the elbows, then flared into more lace. The veil stretched almost down to the floor, held in place by the pearl tiara. The effect of it with the dress was elegant and breathtaking.

The sensation of becoming a new person, that had come upon her gradually since she'd been here, was stronger now. Her day on the boat had bleached her light brown hair to gold; her lightly tanned skin made the whites of her eyes glow with brilliant effect. For the first time in her life she was not merely pretty but beautiful, even glamorous.

The heat of Sicily had done this to her, as it had also warmed her body, awakening her to physical sensations that had lain dormant in the mists of England. It was the heat of the furnace, and some northerners wilted in it. But Heather had flowered.

As bridesmaid, Angie wore a simple cream silk that brought out the glow of her skin and her dark eyes, full of pleasurable anticipation. Heather smiled at her.

'I believe some Sicilian wedding customs are the same as those in England,' she teased. 'Like the one about the bridesmaid and the best man.' Bernardo was the best man.

There was a knock on the door, and Renato called. 'Everyone has gone to the cathedral. Bernardo and Lorenzo left several minutes ago. I'm waiting for you downstairs.'

Angie presented Heather with her bouquet of white roses. 'You look fantastic. Lorenzo will keel over when he sees you.'

Heather smiled. In the bright sunlight her troubling fancies had faded. She loved Lorenzo and he loved her. That was all that mattered.

They made a slow procession along the corridor, then a slight turn so that Heather was looking down the broad staircase. Every servant in the house seemed to be gathered there to see her entrance, all beaming up at her with approval. And there was Renato, gazing up as the bride began her stately descent. His face bore a rigid look, as though he was holding his breath. Then he stepped forward, extending his hand. She placed her own hand in it, and he steadied her down the last few steps, while the servants applauded.

The limousine was waiting. Heather climbed carefully into the back and sat while Angie settled her dress and veil perfectly about her, then got in beside her. Renato joined them, and they were ready to go.

At first she looked out of the window at the scenery as they glided slowly down towards Palermo, trying to take in that this was really happening to her. Renato was silent, and she thought he too must be preoccupied, but when she turned to him she found his gaze fixed on her. In his eyes was the same stunned look she'd seen earlier.

They had reached the outskirts of Palermo and the car was making its way through the streets until at last the great cathedral was in sight. Both cars were drawing to a halt, the doors were opening.

She stood in the bright sunlight while Angie straightened her dress, then fell into place behind her. There was a little crowd nearby. They stopped to look at the wedding party. Some of them applauded, and Heather heard the whisper, *'Grazziusu.'* Beautiful.

Renato looked at her.

'Are you ready?'

'Quite ready.'

'No doubts?'

'Why do you ask that?' she cried.

'I don't know,' he said abruptly. 'Let's go.'

She took the arm he offered, and they walked across the piazza and into the cathedral together.

After the brilliance outside the dim light was like darkness, but then her eyes focused on the magnificent interior full of guests, all turning to watch her arrive. Beyond them she could see the choir, and the archbishop waiting by the altar to marry her to Lorenzo.

High overhead the organ pealed out. She took a deep breath, her hand tightened unconsciously on Renato's arm, and she prepared for the first step.

'Wait,' Renato said softly.

Then she saw Bernardo hurrying down the aisle towards them. He looked worried. 'Not yet,' he said in a low, urgent voice. 'Lorenzo isn't here.'

'What do you mean?' Renato demanded. 'You arrived together, didn't you?'

'Yes, but then he slipped away. He said he needed to have a word with someone, and he'd be back in a moment but when I went to look for him, nobody knew where he was, and—'

'And what?' Renato asked harshly, for Bernardo seemed unwilling to continue.

'I spoke to a woman outside. She'd seen a young man get into a taxi. From the description—but it might have been anyone, of course—'

'Of course it might,' Renato broke in. 'A storm in a teacup. Lorenzo will return in a minute.'

But behind the apparent conviction Heather heard the uneasy note in his voice, and she saw that Bernardo couldn't meet her eye.

Even so, it wasn't real. She felt as though she were floating in a place where there was no sensation, and from where she could look down on a woman in a bridal gown, staring disaster in the face. It was somebody else.

'What has happened? Where is Lorenzo?'

Nobody had seen Baptista approach down the aisle. Now she was there, a tiny, commanding figure, clinging to Enrico's arm, looking from one to the other. 'Where is Lorenzo?' she repeated.

For a ghastly moment nobody knew how to answer her. Then there was a small commotion outside, and a boy of about sixteen hurried in and came to a nervous halt at the sight of the group. He gulped, thrust a sheet of paper into the bridal bouquet, and ran for his life.

She was floating again, watching the bride carefully remove the paper and hand the beautiful flowers to the bridesmaid. There wasn't even an envelope, just something in pencil on a sheet. It was scrawled, as though it had been written in a hurry, or great agitation, or both.

Dearest, darling Heather,

Please forgive me. I wouldn't have done it like this if there had been any other way, but Renato was so set on this marriage that I haven't known whether I was coming or going.

I do love you—I think. And maybe if things had happened naturally between us we would have married anyway, in time. We had a lovely romance, didn't we? If only it could have stayed that way. But Renato descended on us in London. It suited him for us to marry, and you know the rest.

And then he was injured and you saved him. You looked so marvellous to me that night that marriage didn't seem so bad any more. And suddenly everything was arranged and I was practically an old married man before I'd had time to enjoy being young.

I came back from Stockholm early to talk to you,

*explain why we ought to postpone everything for a
while, but Renato made me 'see reason' (his words).*

*So I suppose when I set out this morning I really
meant to go through with it. But when I was sitting in
the cathedral I suddenly knew I couldn't.*

Try to forgive me. I still think you're wonderful.
Lorenzo.

The silence seemed to be singing in Heather's ears, but
it was a strange kind of silence that sounded almost like
laughing. The whole world was laughing. Slowly she lowered the sheet of paper, staring into space.

Lorenzo wasn't coming. He'd never loved her very
much, never truly wanted to marry her at all. Renato had
wanted their marriage, 'because it suited him.' For his
own convenience he'd moved them around like puppets,
pulling strings here, bending the truth a little there. No
wonder he'd welcomed her so enthusiastically.

Behind her she heard Renato's furious Sicilian curse,
'Malediri!' and understood that he'd read the letter over
her shoulder. As if drawn by a magnet she turned to look
at him and saw his eyes full of shock. It had drained the
colour from beneath his tan, so that he looked almost the
same as in the ambulance, the night he'd nearly died.

He met her gaze. For once he wasn't in command. He
looked as she felt, like someone who'd received a savage
blow in the stomach. Later Heather was to remember that,
but now it made little impact. She still had the sense of
floating above everything.

Curious relatives had started to drift up the aisle to get
a better look. More and more of them came as the news
whispered through the congregation that something had
gone horribly, excitingly wrong.

'What does he say?' Angie whispered.

Receiving no answer, she took the page from Heather's nerveless fingers. Bernardo too contrived to read it, then raised his head to meet Renato's eyes, his own angry and astonished. 'I'll find him, bring him back—'

'No!' Heather said violently. Her head cleared and she looked round at them. 'Do you think I'd marry him now?'

'Heather, he doesn't really mean it,' Bernardo pleaded.

'*I* mean it. Do you think I'm so desperate for a wedding ring that I'll marry a man at gunpoint? How dare you!'

He nodded. 'Forgive me! It was a foolish thing to say.'

Her strength was coming back. Inwardly she was screaming, and some time very soon there would be bitter tears. But right now she seemed to be made of pure pride, and it would sustain her until she was alone. If only she could run away now, and hide from the crowd who'd witnessed her humiliation. But she wouldn't run. She wouldn't hide. She would face them with her head up.

'Right,' she said calmly. 'That's that, then. We'd better go home.' She looked Renato in the eye. 'You brought me. You can take me back.'

There was a look of pure admiration in his eyes, if she hadn't been too angry to see it. But her anger faded as she looked at Baptista, who had been standing there in silence. The old woman looked wretchedly ill and frail.

'I'm sorry, Mamma. This is terrible for you too.'

Baptista managed a tired smile. 'Try to forgive my son, if you can. He means well, but he always did what was easiest. I spoiled and indulged him, and this is the result.'

'None of this is your fault,' Heather said emphatically. She looked directly at Renato, but didn't underline the look with words.

'You're very kind, my dear,' Baptista said faintly. 'Very kind—' she swayed and her eyes closed.

'Mamma!' Renato said sharply, and put his arms out just in time.

'Lay her down,' Angie said, turning in a moment from a bridesmaid into a doctor. She knelt beside Baptista, felt her heart, frowning.

'Is it a heart attack?' Renato asked tensely, kneeling on the other side.

'I'm not sure. It may not be too serious, but she needs to get to the hospital.'

Renato raised his mother in his arms. 'Mamma,' he said urgently. 'Mamma! *Miu Diu!*' Still carrying her, he strode to the door. 'The hospital is close. We'll go straight there.'

'Leave the guests to us,' Enrico said. 'We'll take them home, see they're fed, and get rid of them.'

'Thank you,' Bernardo said fervently, following his brother.

'What do we do?' Angie asked Heather.

'We follow,' Heather said firmly. 'I love her too.'

Outside they commandeered one of the wedding cars and directed the driver. They reached the hospital to find Bernardo and Renato in the corridor, pacing about.

'Is there any news?' Heather asked, not looking at Renato. She wanted to pretend that he didn't exist. Her mind was so full of misery and turmoil that it was only by concentrating on Baptista that she could keep from screaming.

'Not yet, but I'm sure she'll be all right,' Bernardo said. 'She's had giddy spells before, and always recovered.'

'But each one brings her closer to the end,' Renato said wretchedly. 'Her heart could give out at any time; we've always known that.'

'I think you're being too gloomy,' Angie said firmly. 'It didn't look like a heart attack to me. Just a faint. And I am a doctor, don't forget.'

Bernardo threw her a grateful look, and Heather didn't miss the way he squeezed Angie's hand, or the reassuring smiles they exchanged. How right they seemed together: as perfect for each other as she had once thought she and Lorenzo—

A shuddering gasp broke from her, and for a moment her eyes filled with tears. Through the blur she could see the magnificence of her dress swirling around her. At this moment she should be kneeling before the altar at Lorenzo's side, while the priest intoned the words that made them each other's for ever. Instead it had all been a mockery. And the man who'd schemed and manipulated to bring this disaster down on all their heads was Renato.

Heather had never hated any human being before in her life, but at this moment the taste of hatred was bitter in her mouth. She looked up to find Renato watching her, and knew that he'd read her thoughts. She wanted to hurl bitter accusations at his head, but the sight of his ravaged face stopped her. Angrily she brushed the tears away from her eyes. His mother was ill. She wouldn't curse him, but neither would she let him see her weeping, or showing any sign of weakness.

'Darling,' Angie whispered, reaching out to her.

'I'm all right,' Heather said firmly, pulling herself together. 'Bernardo, I should like to ask you a favour.'

'Of course,' he said at once.

'Would you telephone home, please, and speak to Baptista's maid? Ask her to bring me some day clothes to change into.'

'And me,' Angie said quickly.

He nodded and moved away to a quiet corner, taking out his mobile. Heather went to the window and stood looking out. If she didn't have to look at Renato she might just about endure this.

Bernardo returned to say the maid was on her way, just as a doctor appeared.

'She's stable,' he said. 'You can see her just for a moment.'

The two men departed. Angie and Heather sat in silence until the clothes arrived. Within a few minutes they were plainly dressed, and nobody could have told that there was ever going to be a wedding.

Renato emerged into the corridor. Beneath his tan his face had a kind of greyish pallor and his voice sounded strained. 'My mother would like to see you,' he told Heather.

'How is she?'

'Suffering terribly. She blames herself for this disaster.'

'That's nonsense. I know who's to blame and it isn't her.'

'Then tell her that. Tell her anything you like, but for God's sake stop her torturing herself. You're the only one who can help her now.'

Heather slipped past him into Baptista's room. Bernardo rose from the bed and backed away as she approached. Renato came just inside the room and stood there, watching as Heather approached the bed.

Only a short time ago the old woman had looked magnificent and indomitable in black satin, lace and diamonds. Now she looked frail and tiny, lying against the white sheets, her face drained of colour. She turned her head towards Heather. Her eyes were tired and anxious.

'Forgive me,' she whispered. 'Forgive me...'

'There's nothing to forgive,' Heather said quickly. 'This isn't your fault.'

'My son—has dishonoured you—'

'No,' Heather said firmly. 'I can only be dishonoured by my own actions. Not somebody else's. There is no dishonour. This will pass, and life will go on.' She took Baptista's hand. 'For you too.'

Baptista searched her face. 'I think you have—a great heart—' she murmured. 'My son is a fool.'

Heather leaned closer, smiling into the old woman's eyes, trying to reassure her. 'Most men are fools,' she said. 'We know that, don't we? But we don't have to be affected by their foolishness.'

Baptista's face relaxed, and she seemed drawn into the kindly female conspiracy Heather was offering her. 'Bless you,' she whispered. 'Don't go.'

'Not just yet,' Heather agreed. 'Not until I know you're on the mend.'

'I'll be home soon. Promise me that I'll find you there.' Baptista's voice grew urgent. 'Promise me.'

Heather stared at her in dismay. All she wanted was to flee Sicily.

'Please—' she started to say, 'I can't—'

'Promise her!' Renato said violently.

Baptista was growing dangerously agitated. Heather spoke quickly. 'I promise,' she said. 'I'll be there when you come home. But I'll go now so that you can be alone with your family.'

'You will be there,' Baptista repeated. 'You have given your word.'

'And I'm a woman of my word. Don't worry.' She slipped out.

'What is it?' Angie asked quickly, seeing her pale face.

'I can't believe what I've done.' Briefly she told Angie what had happened.

'You didn't have any choice.'

'No, I didn't. But how do I live in the same house with Renato without telling him how much I hate him?'

CHAPTER SIX

THE Residenza was eerily quiet. The vast hordes of guests had swarmed all over it, devouring the feast, hungrier and thirstier for the excitement of having something horrifying to talk about. Now they were all gone, save for one or two who lived too far away to depart that night. In the morning they too would vanish.

The wedding cake remained uneaten, because everyone had been too superstitious to touch it. It stood tall and beautiful in its white, shimmering glory, celebrating a lovers' union that would never be.

Heather stood in the semi-darkness of the great hall, looking at the cake, with its tiny bride and groom on the topmost tier. She was trapped in limbo, unable to go forward or back. The way back involved too many painful thoughts. The way forward was blocked by her promise.

She felt slightly giddy, and recalled that she'd eaten nothing since the night before. This morning she'd refused breakfast. Too excited. She would eat later, at the reception, she'd thought. And when they cut the cake she'd planned to take the two little figures from the top and treasure them always. Well, they were still there, if she wanted them.

Suddenly she broke. All day she'd used Baptista's illness to fend off the truth, but now there was nothing to protect her from it. Lorenzo didn't love her, had deserted her in front of the whole cathedral. The dream of love that she'd believed in had turned out to be a monstrous, sickening farce.

At this moment she forgot the doubts that had plagued her only the night before. They belonged in the realm of reason and common sense and it was too soon to heed them.

What tortured her now were memories of the time when Lorenzo had been the young man who charmed her and made life sweet with his kindness, his cheerful good nature, and his adoration. Her feelings for him might have turned out to be no more than infatuation, but they had been real enough in their way, and now they were bitterly painful. She covered her eyes with her hand and leaned forward, swaying against the table, while anguish shook her. Tears threatened but she fought them back.

I will not cry. *I will not cry.*

At least, not now. Not until she could be alone, away from this house, away from this island, away from Renato Martelli.

A footstep made her whirl around. Renato stood there, watching her. Furious at his intrusion, she pulled herself together and spoke as calmly as she could. 'How is your mother?'

'Asleep when I left her. The doctors think it was just a giddy spell.'

'And she's in no danger?'

'She has a bad heart. But this wasn't a heart attack.'

'Fine. Then I can go soon?'

'If you want to hurt her. She has welcomed you as her daughter—'

'But I'm not her daughter,' Heather said harshly, 'nor will I ever be—'

'You don't understand. I'm not talking about legalities. I'm saying that she loves you. From the moment you arrived she opened her arms to you. Didn't you feel that?'

'Yes, I did, and it meant the world to me, but now—'

'Now you'll turn your back on her? Is that how you repay her kindness?'

'I've said I'll stay until she returns home. I can't promise further than that.'

The sound of her own voice startled her. It sounded hard with the effort of suppressing all emotion, not like herself at all. Or perhaps this stern, dry-eyed, controlled woman was who she was now.

One of the family maids was hovering uneasily. She asked Renato something in Sicilian. 'She wants to know what she should do with the cake,' he said.

Heather stared at him, aghast. She was starving, devastated, with every nerve at breaking point, and her exhausted mind on the edge of hallucinating. The prosaic question caught her off guard and almost sent her into hysterics. 'How would I know?' she asked wildly. 'I've never been in this situation before. Oddly enough, the books of wedding etiquette don't cover it. You suggest something. You're the man who has an answer for every problem, *even if some of your answers fall apart at awkward moments.*'

He flinched but stayed calm. 'I'll tell her to send it to the children's home.'

'Good idea. But not the top tier. Ask her to take that down now and give it to me.'

Renato did so. The maid climbed on a chair and reached up to lift down the tiny cake, adorned with the figures under a flowered arch. But her hand shook and the little bridegroom fell to the floor and broke in two. Renato gave her a nod of reassurance, and she hurried away.

'Why do you want that?' he asked as Heather surveyed the small top tier.

'To eat, of course. I think the bride should have some of her own wedding cake, don't you?' She took up a sharp knife and cut into the ornately decorated icing. 'Have some with me.'

'I don't think—'

'Then pour me some champagne. You're not going to deny me wedding cake and champagne on my big day, are you?'

He found two glasses and filled them. 'When did you last eat?'

'Yesterday. I couldn't manage anything this morning.'

'You'll regret drinking champagne on an empty stomach.'

She poured two glasses and thrust one at him. 'Drink it with me. Let's toast the day you brought about.'

'Heather, I know you must hate me—'

'And try contempt and loathing. Especially contempt.'

She drained her champagne glass and refilled it. 'I want to know how much of Lorenzo's letter was true. When he returned from Stockholm early—that was why? To tell you that he wanted to call it all off?'

'Look—'

'Tell me, damn you!'

'Yes,' he said reluctantly. 'He said that.'

'And you kept it to yourself?'

'Why should I tell you what could hurt you? I talked to Lorenzo and—' He seemed to have trouble going on.

'"Made him see reason," was his charming expression. You mean you told him he had to marry me whether he liked it or not. *How dare you?* What do you think I am? Some helpless bird-brain with no guts or independence?'

'No, but after what you told me—about your previous fiancé—'

'You told him *that*?' she cried, aghast. 'Oh, you've done everything you can to humiliate me, haven't you? I can just hear you—"You can't walk out on her, Lorenzo.

The poor creature's already been deserted once. You've got to see it through, however much you'd rather not.'''

'Would I have done better to let him walk away from his obligations?'

Eyes flashing, she whirled on him. 'He *did* walk away. You just made sure he did it at the worst possible moment. And why obligations? I was marrying for love and I thought he was doing the same. I don't want a husband who's only doing his duty.

'If we'd broken up in London I could have coped. I'd still have had my job, my friends, my life there. But you wanted our marriage, to suit yourself. You had to play God with people's lives, *to suit yourself.* And now Lorenzo has vanished, I'm stranded and your mother is ill, all because Renato Martelli has to have his own way.'

He didn't answer, but there was a drawn look about his face that checked her. 'I'm sorry,' she said wearily. 'I didn't mean to throw your mother's illness up at you.'

'Why not? It's true.'

'Yes, but I shouldn't have said it. I shouldn't—' Her voice thickened, and she set her jaw. She would not weep. She *would not.*

'Heather—' He reached for her but she backed off, eyes flashing.

'I'm warning you, Renato—if you touch me, there'll be violence.'

He checked himself. 'Perhaps enough has been said for tonight,' he sighed. 'I'm sure you'd prefer me to leave you.'

She didn't answer. Her face was unyielding. As he left her Renato felt a flash of some emotion he could hardly identify. He was a man who feared nothing, so his own dread took him by surprise. He didn't know this woman who looked as though a stone lay where her heart should be. He only knew that he was guilty of some terrible crime.

Next morning, when the last guest had left, Renato sought out Heather and said, 'I thought you should know that I've traced Lorenzo. He's staying with friends in Naples.'

He didn't look directly at her as he spoke. That way he didn't have to notice her pallor, or the signs that she hadn't slept. But he couldn't help knowing that she tensed at the sound of Lorenzo's name.

'Does he know that his mother is ill?' Heather asked quietly.

'No, I haven't spoken to him.'

'You must. He ought to return and see her.'

'There's no need for that,' he said sharply. 'It's not serious. She'll be home tomorrow.'

'But it would mean a lot to her to see him.'

'It might also strain her.'

'I think you're wrong,' Heather said firmly. 'It's much harder for her to wonder about him.'

After a moment's silence she looked up to see Renato regarding her strangely. 'You're very determined to fetch him back,' he said quietly.

Once she'd hardly been aware of having a temper. Now a word from Renato could trigger it. 'If you mean what I think you do, you should be ashamed. It's all over between Lorenzo and me. I'd never marry him now.'

'Perhaps you think you mean that. But if he came back and turned on the charm—'

'Well, you should know all about the power of Lorenzo's charm,' she said bleakly. 'It was you who told him to give me the full blast of it for your own ends.'

She heard the slight intake of his breath and knew she'd

struck home. She was glad, she told herself angrily. Let him suffer as she suffered.

'Besides,' she added, 'he's not very likely to try to win me back, is he? Not after all the trouble he took to escape me.'

Try as she might, she couldn't stop her voice shaking on the last words, and it made Renato say more gently, 'It wasn't you he was escaping, but me. And I know my brother better than you. He values things more when he's lost them.'

She gave him the cool, defiant look that was her way of coping. 'So there's hope yet,' she said ironically. 'Lorenzo will make a play for me, and I'll be fool enough to fall for it. Cue wedding bells, summon all the guests back, and—hey presto! Renato Martelli gets his own way again.'

'*For pity's sake!*' he shouted. 'Can't you under-stand—?' He checked himself. 'I'm sorry. I just wish I could find the right words to say to you.'

'Does it occur to you that there aren't any?'

'I'm beginning to be afraid that you're right. Heather, won't you let me ask your pardon? I never dreamed of anything like this happening.'

'No, you wanted life arranged your way, and to hell with anyone else. I did a lot of thinking last night, and several things came back to me. Chiefly the fact that no-body mentioned marriage until you did, that night in London. You said Lorenzo was talking about marriage, but that came as news to him. I saw his face. I thought his expression was embarrassment but actually it was sur-prise.'

'He had told me that if he thought of marriage it would be to you—' Renato said unwillingly.

'*If*? But it was a very big if. I'm almost as angry about

what you've done to Lorenzo as I am about what you've done to me. You pushed him into something he wasn't ready for, and now he's the one who looks bad.'

'He could have stood up to me and refused,' Renato said angrily.

'Oh, please! Who stands up to you?'

'You do.'

'And much good it does me! Now, I think you should get him back here to see his mother. Tell him there'll be no tears or reproaches from me. He's not the one I blame.'

'Not blame him? After what he did to you—?'

'After what *you* did to me. Lorenzo tried to tell me honestly about his doubts, but you stopped him. If he and I could have talked I'd have released him at once, quietly, here at home, instead of having to do it in public. That was your doing, not his. So tell him not to worry.'

After a moment he said, 'If we could talk naturally I could tell you how much I admire you for the dignity and spirit you've shown in this. But I know that my admiration will only provoke your contempt.'

'Right first time,' she said crisply. 'Now, please, go and make that call.'

She spent the day at the hospital. Baptista slept a good deal but when she awoke her eyes sought Heather, always finding her in a chair by the window, and she smiled with relief. When Renato arrived Heather rose to go, but before she could do so she heard him say in a low voice, 'Lorenzo will be home this evening, Mamma.'

She left the room before she could become too aware of them looking at her, and went to have a coffee. Before he left Renato joined her.

'You were right,' he said. 'The news has cheered her

up. It was generous of you to insist. I hope it won't come too hard on you.'

'I have no feelings one way or the other,' she assured him.

'I wish I knew if that were true.'

'Does it matter? It's your mother who counts.'

'But you count too. We need to talk very soon—'

'I don't think so.'

'Surely you can see that matters can't be left like this?'

'Of course. When she's better I'll arrange to return Bella Rosaria, and then I'll go back to England.'

'That wasn't what I meant. There are other things—'

'No, Renato, there's nothing else. I'll go back to her now.

Towards evening Baptista became wakeful, growing alert at every sound.

'He'll be here soon,' Heather promised.

'My dear, will it break your heart to see him?'

'Hearts don't break that easily,' she said with a determined smile.

'I think they do—at least for a while.'

'I'll tell you something,' Heather said in a rush. 'It's not just losing Lorenzo—it's losing everything. That day we went to Bella Rosaria, I told you how right it's all felt since I arrived. I was so sure that fate had brought me to the right place to marry the right man.' She gave an ironic little laugh. 'It just shows you how wrong you can be.'

'I don't think you were wrong,' Baptista said.

'I must have been. I misread every signal, even my own. I'm different. I can't recognise my own reactions. Once this would have made me cry my heart out. Now I just want to do something forceful, to show people that I'm not to be trifled with.'

'That's a very Sicilian reaction, my dear,' Baptista said.

'That feeling of rightness you had when you arrived—it was a true feeling. But it wasn't Lorenzo who caused it. It was Sicily, telling you that you'd come home.'

'What a charming theory—'

'But you believe it's just an old woman's fancy. My dear, *think*. Forget Lorenzo, and think of the land. I've seen you standing on the terrace, watching it, when you thought nobody knew. Think of it in the morning when the mist is rising, or at noon when the shadows are deep and sharp—'

'Or in the early evening when the light is that strange soft gold that happens nowhere else,' Heather mused, half to herself.

'And the language that you're learning so easily,' Baptista reminded her. 'In fact, everything about this country comes easily to you. Even the heat.'

Yes, Heather thought. She'd flowered in the sun and it had relaxed all her instincts, blurring the edges of her personality, making her feel things that otherwise…

But that was all over now. The trauma she'd suffered in the cathedral had been like a blow to the head, knocking out emotion and sensation, so that she could function calmly. With any luck it would remain that way until she returned to England, and became herself again. And what she suffered there would be nobody's business but her own.

'I'm English, Mamma,' she said now. 'I belong there.'

'No, you belong here,' Baptista said firmly. 'And you must remain.'

A shocking suspicion swept Heather. 'No! If you're thinking what I think you are—I could never marry Lorenzo now.'

'Of course not.' She stopped, alerted by a step in the corridor outside. The door opened and Heather stiffened as she saw Lorenzo. The next moment there was a glad cry from Baptista, and she opened her arms to her son. He was across the room in a moment to embrace his mother.

She tried to leave before he saw her, but at that moment he looked up and a deep flush spread over his face. 'I'll leave you two alone,' she said. She kissed Baptista and departed quickly.

The little scene was over too fast for her to be aware of feeling anything. It was only when she was walking down the corridor that a wave of emotion swept her. Her head might tell her that their marriage would never have worked, but it was too soon for her to see Lorenzo without hurt. She checked her steps and leaned against the wall, pressing her hand against her mouth.

'Heather!' It was Renato's voice.

She looked up. 'Your brother has arrived,' she said. 'I've left them together.'

'Are you all right?'

She gave a little puzzled laugh. 'Why on earth wouldn't I be all right? I'm going home now. Goodnight.'

It was a bad night to be thinking of lovers and honeymoons. The full moon was exquisitely reflected in the sea, and turned the land to pure silver. A sensible woman would go in right now, not sit here on the terrace, thinking of how she and her husband should be on a boat, cruising beneath that moon, lost in each other. And she *was* a sensible woman. It was being sensible that had enabled her to survive the last few days.

She heard a sound behind her and turned to find Lorenzo standing in the shadows. She sensed him take a deep breath and straighten his shoulders before he stepped forward.

She tried to use anticipation to suppress the pain of seeing his face, but nothing could change the fact that it was the one she'd fallen in love with, and whose smile had brightened her life.

'I've come to ask your forgiveness, and to listen to whatever you have to say to me,' he said quietly.

She raised her chin and confronted him with a bright manner. She even managed a touch of cheerfulness. 'What are you expecting?' she asked. 'A tirade crashing about your ears? Reproaches, tears—"How could you do this to me?" Let's take all that as read. I don't have the energy for a big dramatic scene.'

'But you must be angry with me.'

'Must I? Well, I suppose I am, a bit. You should have told me the truth earlier.'

'I meant to, when I came back from Stockholm, but Renato said—'

'Stop right there. The less said about Renato, the better.' After a moment she sighed. 'He's injured us both, and if there's one good thing about this mess it's that I shan't have to be related to him.' She gave an ironic laugh. 'The night we met I told him that I'd never marry you because of him. I should have stuck to that. Ah, well! I didn't. My mistake. Let's not make a tragedy of it.'

'How strong and brave you are!' he said quietly. 'You make me ashamed.'

Heather regarded him askance, a faint touch of amusement in her eyes. 'Did you expect me to go into a decline because you ran away? Don't flatter yourself. You just weren't ready for marriage, and I've got better use for my tears than to waste them on you.'

'You really don't care for me any more?'

'Luckily for us both, I don't.'

'But the night before our w—the other night—you

flung yourself into my arms and told me again and again how much you loved me—'

'That's enough,' she said sharply. 'The past is the past. Believe me, you wouldn't really want me swooning all over you and telling you that you'd broken my heart. You'd find that very uncomfortable.'

'Yes, yes, of course,' he said hastily. Then a hint of his charming smile crept over his face and he asked ruefully, 'Just the same, couldn't you flatter my vanity by being just a little bit sad?'

'Not even a little bit. Now be off with you.'

He turned to go, but stopped suddenly and said, 'If things had been different—if we'd been allowed to go at our own pace—I might not have proposed marriage just then, but when we'd parted I'd have missed you unbearably, and—'

'Stop,' she said, suddenly unable to bear any more, for this was the thought that tormented her. 'Don't talk like that. Go away, Lorenzo, please.'

'Darling—'

'Don't call me that!'

'I really was falling in love with you,' he said huskily. 'If only we'd been granted a little time—'

'Go!' she said fiercely.

She kept her face away from him, and didn't move until the fading footsteps told her that he'd gone. She was more hurt than she wanted to admit to herself. Their love was over. She could never marry Lorenzo now. But the habit of affection lingered and the misery was still sharp.

Lorenzo found both his brothers in Renato's study, pouring whisky.

'Come in,' Renato told him. 'Here.' He held out a glass.

'Thanks, I need it.' Lorenzo downed the malt in one gulp and held out his glass for more.

'You only got what you asked for,' Bernardo observed.

'Actually, I didn't. I thought it would be dreadful— tears and reproaches—'

'Then you don't know the woman you were supposed to marry,' Renato said. 'I could have told you she had more dignity than that—more dignity than you or any of us.'

'Yes, but—not a single tear, not a word of regret.'

Renato's eyes narrowed. 'By God, she knew how to deal with you!' he said softly.

'Once, I even thought she was laughing at me.'

Bernardo whistled softly. 'An exceptional woman.'

'Yes,' Renato snapped. He poured himself another full tumbler of whisky.

'Haven't you had enough?' Bernardo asked mildly.

Renato swung on him. *'Mind your own damned business!'*

Bernardo shrugged. 'It's nothing to me. But it's not like you to drink heavily—'

'Well, tonight I feel like drinking the cellar dry.'

'You're the one she's mad at,' Lorenzo told him. 'She blames the whole thing on you, and she's right. If you'd kept out of our affairs, who knows what might have happened?'

'Spare me the happy ever after ending,' Renato sneered. 'I'm not convinced.'

'Well, I am,' Lorenzo said with a flash of anger.

'You're out of your mind. It's much too late for second thoughts.'

'You wouldn't like to take a little bet on that, would you? Heather knows we'd have been all right, but for you.

And we might be yet. She's a wonderful woman, and maybe it isn't too late—'

He got no further. Renato's hands were around his throat, choking the life out of him. Renato's eyes, close to his, were glittering, filled with murder.

'*Renato, for God's sake stop!*' That was Bernardo, hauling him off, having to use all his strength, holding him back while Lorenzo choked.

'Get out of here,' Renato raged. 'Get out of my sight!'

'Be damned to you!' Lorenzo said hoarsely. 'Why didn't you stay out of my affairs?'

'Get out, for God's sake!' Bernardo told him. 'You two killing each other is all we need.'

Lorenzo flung Renato a bitter look and departed. Bernardo kept a cautious hold on his brother until the door was closed.

'Oh, the hell with it! Let me go,' Renato said. Bernardo did so at once. 'What are you doing here, anyway? Why aren't you with your lady?'

'I can wait,' Bernardo said. 'She's worth waiting for.'

'Don't tell me this family's actually going to have a wedding after all?'

'I think so. But that's for your ears alone.' Bernardo gave one of his rare smiles. 'As the family head, do you approve?'

'Would you take any notice if I didn't?'

'I'd mind. It wouldn't stop me.'

'For what it's worth, you have my blessing. You're a fortunate man.'

'I know. I can't really believe it. I keep waiting for the snag that will ruin everything.'

'There's no snag.' Renato added quietly, 'One of us, at least, is going to be lucky in love.'

They chinked glasses. Then Bernardo said uneasily, 'Lorenzo is still our brother.'

'I know that.'

'I think you should be careful.'

'Of him?'

'No. Of yourself. Goodnight.'

He went without another word, leaving Renato alone, wishing he could get rid of the tension that plagued him. He poured most of his whisky back into the bottle, knowing that wasn't the answer. Nor was sleep the answer.

He slammed his hand down, realising that there was no answer. There hadn't been one since that evening when he'd met a young woman who'd told him to jump in the river. He'd admired her, been amused by her, but he was so used to planning his life as he wished that he hadn't seen the danger, and had actually encouraged her to marry his brother.

The danger had come in a blinding flash when it was far too late: just before the wedding, when no man of honour could make a move. She'd touched his heart with her vulnerability, an experience so strange that he'd been thrown off balance. And in that confused, blinded state he'd offered her his brotherly help. After that his hands had been tied.

In the cathedral it seemed that Lorenzo had solved the problem. Except that there still echoed through his head the tormenting memory of a young woman, a few hours before what should have been her wedding, her voice carrying sweetly on the night air.

'I just wanted to say how much I love you—love you—*love you*—'

Women had always fallen in love with Lorenzo, and stayed in love with him, long after hope was gone. It wasn't just his looks or his easy good nature. It was a mysterious 'something' that wouldn't let them go, like a magic spell. Renato had never begrudged him before.

And some men, he thought, were just the opposite, as though they carried a curse. Suddenly he saw his mother's agonised face as it had been when he came round after the bike accident. Other faces followed—Heather reading the letter in the cathedral, her love gone, her career destroyed; his mother again, distraught and fainting; even Lorenzo, pale and ashamed at what he'd been driven to do.

All hurt because of himself, because he destroyed whatever he touched.

CHAPTER SEVEN

IT WAS time for Angie to leave. She'd remained a few extra days to support her friend, but now she must leave for England and her work. But surely, Heather thought, she would return to Sicily soon, because she couldn't bear to be away from Bernardo.

She knew this was no light o' love. It had a depth and intensity that she'd never seen in Angie before. Once she'd surprised them in each other's arms, heard the husky murmur of Bernardo's voice speaking words of eternal passion and devotion, and crept quickly away. But the time had passed with no announcement, and yesterday they had both vanished. Of course, they were making plans, Heather thought, and before Angie left they would announce their engagement.

But when she went into their room she knew that something was badly wrong. Angie was packing her suitcase with a kind of fierce purpose, and her face was set in a way that meant she was determined not to cry. In that expression Heather recognised her own experience.

'Darling, what is it?' she asked, taking Angie by the shoulders. 'Have you quarrelled with Bernardo?'

'Oh, no, we haven't quarrelled,' Angie said bitterly. 'There's nothing to quarrel about. He just explained to me calmly and reasonably why he'd *die* rather than marry me.'

'But—he adores you, anyone can see that. What can be wrong if you love each other?'

'That's what I thought, but love isn't enough. He says

he loves me. He says he'll never love any other woman, but it's impossible.'

'But—*why*?'

In halting words Angie told to her why she was planning to go away and leave the man her heart was set on, and whose heart was set on her. She explained it badly, because she was distraught from the day she'd spent with her lover, trying to understand why he was determined on a parting that would break both their hearts—his as well as hers, he'd left her in no doubt of it. But all her love, all her logic, her arguments and frantic pleading, had made no dent on his iron-hard resolution. He might suffer for it until his last moment, but he would not marry her.

'I can't follow that,' Heather said at last. 'To let such a thing come between you—in this day and age.'

'Bernardo's a Sicilian,' Angie said a little wildly. 'He doesn't belong in this day and age. And the bottom line is that his pride means more to him than I do. So I'm leaving. And please Heather, can we not talk about it any more, because I don't think I could stand it?'

Heather didn't answer in words, but she drew her friend close, and they clung to each other.

'How about coming with me?' Angie asked huskily.

'I can't leave yet, not until Baptista is better. But I'll be home soon.'

'I'll keep your room for you.' She gave a wonky smile. 'We haven't either of us had much luck with Sicilian men, have we?'

Heather would have gone with her to the airport, but Bernardo was taking her, so she backed off to give them a last few moments alone together, hoping his mind would change. Perhaps he would even bring Angie home with him.

But he returned alone, with a face of flint. He met

Heather's attempts to talk with courtesy, but it was clear that he'd built a wall around himself. He stayed only long enough for a word with Baptista, before driving away to his home in the mountains, and remaining there.

'What's the matter with him?' Heather stormed to Renato. 'It was as good as settled.'

'I'm as taken aback as you are. Only a few days ago he was set on marrying her. He told me so. But then he made this discovery, and it changed everything.'

'Talk to him, for pity's sake!'

'I have no influence with Bernardo. We had different mothers, and that matters. We have a saying in Sicily. "A man's mother is his soul. If he loses her, he will never find her again." Bernardo feels that if he marries Angie he will lose his soul.'

'Then he's a fool,' Heather said fiercely.

'We're all fools about the one woman who matters.'

'How would you know?' she asked scornfully. 'No woman has ever mattered that much to you.'

'True. And when I watch my brothers I'm glad of it.'

'Yes, you protect yourself from being hurt, don't you?' She sighed. 'Well, you're probably wise. I must try to learn your way. I think it has a lot to be said for it.'

'No, don't do that,' he said unexpectedly. 'It would make you less than yourself, and you mustn't be. These last few days you've been stronger than any of us.'

She shrugged. 'That's because I've lost the power to feel. It's a great advantage. You know yourself how convenient it makes life. We're the lucky ones, Renato. We won't suffer as Angie and Bernardo are doing. Other people, yes, but not us.'

He took her arm to stop her turning away. 'Whatever you do, don't become like me.'

His fingers were touching her bare skin, but she felt no

reaction. How ironically now she recalled the flashes of desire for him that had tormented her before the wedding. All gone now. Dust and ashes. Like her heart.

'But you're the way to be,' she said lightly. 'I envy you.'

His grip tightened. 'Why, because you think I've lost the power to feel? You're wrong. Sometimes I wish—' She felt the tremor that passed through him. He released her.

'No matter,' he said curtly. 'I'll talk to Bernardo, but it won't do any good.'

The day after her return from hospital Baptista summoned Renato and Heather to her presence, like a queen granting an audience.

Heather was reluctant to attend. She was in a strange mood. After several nights of sleeping badly, the armour of unfeeling calm that had protected her so far was beginning to crack. Through the weak places she could glimpse the storm of misery and anger that would overtake her if she gave it a chance.

Worse still were the moments when everything seemed bitterly funny. If she gave way to those she knew she would collapse in wild, uncontrollable laughter. But she mustn't let that happen, so she buckled the armour on more firmly than ever, and hoped for the best.

Baptista had left her bed and was reclining in state on a sofa in her grand sitting room. She looked them both over as they appeared before her, taking up positions at some distance apart.

'We can't leave things like this,' she announced. 'It's all been handled very badly.'

'Perhaps Lorenzo should be here,' Renato suggested.

'Lorenzo is the past. It's the future that concerns me.'

'We know what that has to be,' Heather told her. 'I'll return Bella Rosaria to you—'

'That must wait. If you give it back in the same tax year as I gave it to you, we run into all sorts of problems. We haven't yet discussed what happened in the cathedral.'

Heather took a sharp breath. 'How can there be anything to say? It's over.'

'Over? When such an insult was offered you by my family?'

'That "insult" talk is old-fashioned—' she protested.

'And Sicily is an old-fashioned place, even now. If such a thing had happened to me my father would have shot the man dead. And there wouldn't even have been a trial.'

'Well, I'm not going to start shooting,' Heather declared. She was trying to lighten the atmosphere, but she couldn't resist adding, 'Not Lorenzo, anyway.'

'I sympathise with your feelings, my daughter,' Baptista said, giving Renato a look that would have frozen the blood of a less courageous man. He met it with a grimace in which affection was mixed with hearty respect. It amused Heather to realise that, however he treated anyone else, Renato trod very carefully with his mother.

'Lorenzo and I have already met and declared a truce,' she said.

'And I'm grateful, but that isn't the end of the matter. You have been injured by my family, and you cannot be allowed to suffer.'

'Well, if Renato uses his influence with Gossways to restore me to the training programme, I won't have suffered.'

Renato frowned. 'And that's really your idea of recompense?'

'It'll put me back where I was before you entered my

life,' she said firmly. 'I'll be able to pretend you don't exist. In other words, the perfect solution.'

'Thank you!' he snapped.

'Don't mention it.'

'It's not enough,' Baptista said. 'There is the dishonour.'

'But I told you, Lorenzo's actions can't dishonour me.'

'They can dishonour his family,' Baptista said, so fiercely that Heather was startled. 'He insulted you, and the whole family will bear the shame of it until we have made amends.'

'I won't marry him now.'

'Certainly not. But I have another son. I agree he's done little to recommend himself to you, but Renato is to blame for this and Renato must put it right.' Baptista spoke in her most regal manner. 'Your marriage should take place immediately.'

There was one moment's total, thunderstruck silence. Heather tried to speak but couldn't. The control she'd struggled for was slipping away, releasing the crazy laughter that had been fighting to get out. She gave a choke and turned aside swiftly with her hand over her mouth. But it was useless. A bubble was rising inside her, shooting up until it reached the outside world in peal after peal of mirth. The whole thing was mad. It could only have been imagined in this society that followed its own rules and cared for no other.

'I'm sorry,' she gasped at last, 'but that's the funniest thing you could have said. Me? Marry Renato? A man I can't endure the sight of? Oh, heavens!' She went off into another paroxysm.

Renato regarded her with hard eyes. Then he began to speak in a low, outraged voice. He spoke in Sicilian and Heather couldn't follow it, but she managed to pick out the words for 'crazy', 'unbelievable' and something that she guessed meant 'not in a million years'.

'That's just how I feel, too,' she told him. 'Oh, dear! Don't get me started again.'

'In my day a young woman knew better than to laugh at an eligible match,' Baptista said with haughty disapproval.

'But Renato isn't an eligible match,' Heather pointed out when she'd managed to calm down a little. 'One, he doesn't want to marry anyone. Two, he doesn't want to marry *me*. Three, hell will freeze over before I marry him. It's out of the question.'

'It's good sense. You came here to marry a son of this house, and that's what you must do. Then things will be right again.'

'They'd be very far from right,' Heather said desperately. 'I don't know how you can have thought of such a thing—the last man in the world I'd ever—'

'The feeling is mutual,' Renato said coldly. 'Mamma, I have the greatest respect for you, but you must forget this idea.'

'Your feelings don't enter into it,' Baptista told him firmly. 'You have injured a decent young woman, and must make reparation.'

'One phone call to Gossways will do that very nicely, thank you,' Heather said crisply.

'I'll make it at once,' Renato declared. 'Plus I'll pay all your expenses for your trip here and—'

'Renato, I'm warning you, if you *dare* offer me money you'll be very sorry.'

'I'm already sorry: sorry I ever met you, sorry my brother met you, sorry we welcomed you into our home—'

'Then it's a pity you took so much trouble to get me

here, isn't it? When I got up to walk out of the restaurant in London you should have let me go.'

'If I had, you'd have gone under that car.'

'If I hadn't been running away from you I'd have been in no danger from the car.'

'If you'd been a more reasonable woman you wouldn't have been running away.'

'*I*—? If *I'd* been—? You have a very selective memory. You looked me up and down like a piece of merchandise, decided that I'd just about do, and awarded me your brand of approval. For which you had the nerve to expect me to be grateful. As for poor Lorenzo—remember Lorenzo? The groom?—he didn't know whether he was coming or going.'

'I understood that he proposed to you in the hospital.'

'Only after your majesty made your wishes known. Then we were all supposed to fall into line, weren't we? The way everybody always has for you. The way I'm supposed to today. Only you've miscalculated now, just as you did then. I won't marry you, Renato, and you know why? Because after the way you've behaved you're not good enough. And if the angel Gabriel came down off a cloud with a signed testimonial I would still say you're not good enough.'

'Indeed!' Renato snapped. 'Then allow me to remind you that in Sicily, as, I believe, in other parts of the world, it's normal for a woman *to wait until she's received a proposal of marriage before rejecting it.*'

'I was simply trying to save time.'

'You shouldn't have bothered. Then I wouldn't have needed to say that I would rather swim the Straits of Messina in lead weights than link my life to a woman who is nothing but trouble.'

'Then we're agreed and everything's—oh, Mamma, I'm sorry!'

Shocked, Heather had just remembered Baptista's frail condition, but the old woman was watching them both, bright-eyed, with something that might almost have been enjoyment.

'Yes, I'm sorry too,' Renato said. 'We had no right to lose our tempers—your heart—'

'My heart is well, but you are both being very foolish. I advise you to reconsider.'

'Never.' They spoke with one voice.

'Very well. Perhaps I raised the subject in the wrong way.'

'Mamma, there's no way you could raise this subject that would make Renato acceptable,' Heather pleaded. 'I don't want to marry him, I want to kick his shins.'

'You're perfectly right,' Baptista said at once. 'I never saw a man who needed it more. When you're his wife you can do it every day.'

'This is my mother talking?' Renato enquired grimly.

'I'm not blind to your faults, my son,' Baptista retorted. 'I've found you the perfect wife, someone who won't hurry to agree with you and say, "Yes dear, no dear!" In short, someone who sees right through you to the other side, and isn't impressed by what she sees.'

'That's certainly true,' Heather observed. 'But while I'm reforming Renato's character—and, heaven knows, he needs it—how do *I* benefit?'

'You get to stay here,' Baptista told her. 'You become part of this family, and a Sicilian, both of which nature meant you to be.'

'That's the most tempting thing you've said to me so far,' Heather said. She was recovering her poise and even a touch of humour. 'If you could fix the last two without my having to burden myself with Renato, I'd be delighted.'

'No pleasure comes without pain, my dear. You'll learn to put up with him.'

Heather leaned over and kissed Baptista's cheek. 'Sorry, Mamma. The price is too high.'

'Much too high,' Renato agreed. 'Let us forget it was ever mentioned.' He too had calmed down, although anger still lurked far back in his dark eyes.

'In that case, go away,' Baptista said, seeming to tire of the subject. 'But before you leave, Renato, you can pour me a large brandy.'

Later that day Bernardo returned and went straight to see Baptista. He was calm but very pale, and he politely declined the chance to discuss his troubles. She knew better than to press him.

'Never mind,' she said kindly. 'Things will work out. They usually do. And there's one thing to look forward to. Heather and Renato are going to get married.'

Midnight in the garden. Here, at least, there was the chance for Heather to be at peace, wandering along winding paths, breathing in the scents of a hundred flowers. Here were the rose bushes, created from cuttings from the original garden at Bella Rosaria. She understood so much better now, a symbol of a love that had never died, despite the contentment of an arranged marriage. That was the kind of love she'd wanted, the kind she'd believed she had. And Baptista wanted her to settle for less. She'd thought she'd come to terms with the sadness, but this was a new sadness, showing her the bleak path her life might yet take.

She sat on the stone edge of the fountain and looked

down into the water, seeing the dark shadow of her own head and the silver moon behind. She trailed her fingers, shattering the moon to a thousand fragments, and when the water grew still again, there was another head beside hers.

'You shouldn't have been put through that,' Renato said. 'Mamma gets carried away sometimes. I'm sorry for the things I said—'

'I suppose I was just as bad. There's no point in having a go at you anyway. It's over and done with. I said you were too ready to arrange people's lives, but now I see where you get it from.'

'Don't be angry with her.'

'I'm not. I think she's sweet. But, honestly, what an absurd idea!' She gave a small choke.

'Yes, you've made it clear that you find it funny,' he said with a slight edge in his voice.

'I'm sorry, I'm not laughing at you. It's just—everything—all at once—'

She tried to pull herself together, but suddenly she couldn't stop. She'd thought she'd exorcised the wild mood that had possessed her earlier, but now it was back, worse than ever. Sobs of laughter rose up in her, one after the other, each one bigger than the last, until they weren't laughter any more, and all the tears she'd been suppressing forced their way out.

'That's enough,' Renato said, laying a hand on her shoulder. Then he paused because he could feel the shuddering of her body, and knew that it had changed. 'You're not crying after all this time, surely?'

She tried to say, 'No, of course not,' but the words came out huskily, and then she couldn't manage words at all. She'd controlled herself so fiercely that now she had no control left. She was mortified at Renato seeing her like this but she couldn't do anything about it.

'Heather—' he said quietly.

'No—it's nothing—I'm all right, I just need to—'

'You just need to cry it out,' he said. 'Heather— Heather, listen—' He sat beside her on the fountain and laid light hands on her shoulders and gave her a little shake. 'Stop trying to be so damned strong all the time.'

'I've got to be strong,' she said. 'I'm among sharks.'

'Not really. I'm the only shark, and I'm not biting to-night. Just for once, let's forget that you hate me.'

'I don't—know how.'

'Well, that's honest,' he said, gathering her into his arms. 'Hate me, then, but let's call a truce.'

She couldn't reply. Anguish had taken hold of her com-pletely. She'd told herself that it didn't hurt, but it did. All the happiness she'd dared to enjoy now turned on her, transformed to grief and bitterness. It swamped her, en-gulfed her, and there was no help or comfort in the world, except, mysteriously, for her enemy, whose arms enfolded her.

He held her tightly, murmuring words of kindness that her ears hardly heard, although her heart discerned them, and eased a little. It made no sense, but there was some-thing about his voice that warmed her and made every-thing seem not quite so bad. He drew away to look at her, brushing back the hair from her face with gentle fingers.

'I didn't think you could ever cry,' he said huskily. 'You were so good at shutting us all out of your feel-ings—or maybe just me—'

Her tears still flowed, but his soft caresses against her features were making the jagged edges of the world recede and the misery soften.

'Nothing is worth your tears,' he murmured. He laid

his lips against her wet cheeks, then her eyes. 'Don't cry—*please*.'

She grew completely still, listening to his soft words and letting her body relax against him. With one hand he stroked her hair while his lips wandered over her face. She thought perhaps she shouldn't do this, but the thought was far away, muffled by the warm sweetness that was taking possession of her. She knew that at any moment his lips would find her mouth, and the breath came faster in her throat as she waited for it to happen.

When it did his touch was so light that she had to reach up to him to be sure, slipping an arm about his neck, cupping his head with her hand. It was only a few hours since they'd quarrelled, and soon they would probably quarrel again, but now all the world was upside down, and it seemed natural to let him hold her close while his lips continued the work of consolation.

'Renato...' she whispered, not knowing if she were protesting or simply asking a question.

'Hush! Why should we always be fighting?'

She didn't want to fight a man who could hold her so tenderly. She still didn't trust him, but somehow that didn't matter so much now. What did matter was the slow movement of his mouth across hers, and the sense of sweet contentment that pervaded her.

Her mouth was caressing him back, seeking new sensations. She wanted more of him. He was dangerous, but since coming to this country she'd discovered that she responded to the thrill of danger. She put up her hand and laid it against his hair, thick and springy against her palm. Then his cheek. He needed a shave. That was Renato, not smooth and appealing, but all rough edges and sharp angles. You had to take him as you found him. He couldn't be trusted, but sometimes he could be wonderful.

He slackened his hold, but kept his arms in place, resting his lips against her hair. He was trembling as much as she.

'You said once—I could always ask you for a brother's help,' she reminded him huskily.

'I remember. But neither of us knew this day would come.'

Hadn't they? she thought wildly. Hadn't they?

'Keep your word now,' she whispered. 'Help me as a brother. Help me find my place back in England so that I can go home and forget I ever came to Sicily.'

'Will you forget us so easily?'

He would have held her but she disengaged herself and backed away, trying to put a safe distance between them. But how far was safe?

'Don't ask me that, Renato. You know I can't answer. Just help me go home. That's all I want.'

CHAPTER EIGHT

IT WAS Baptista's idea that Heather should visit Bella Rosaria. 'It's time you were looking over your property,' she said. 'But come to see me often.'

The suggestion appealed to Heather. She could never regard the estate as hers, but while matters were being sorted out it would be the ideal place to stay.

She took a car from the garage and drove out of Palermo, taking the winding road that led up to the village of Ellona, and the pink stone villa that dominated it. It was mid-morning and as she climbed she saw how the fresh, vivid light sharpened the contours of the land, which was freshly harvested and brown after the long, fierce summer. She realised that already she was thinking like a Sicilian. Baptista had been right. She loved this place and didn't want to leave it.

Baptista must have telephoned ahead, because when Heather reached the villa she found they were ready for her. Jocasta, the housekeeper, had prepared the best room in readiness for the new mistress. It was dark and old-fashioned, with crimson tiles on the floor and furniture made of wood that was almost black. But everything was luxurious, and the huge bed was the most comfortable she'd ever known.

She met her steward, Luigi, a small, fierce man, brown as a berry, who might have been any age from fifty to eighty, and who offered to show her over her property. He spoke in a mixture of Sicilian and English. Heather responded in the same do-it-yourself dialect, and they understood each other perfectly.

The villa had its own stables with three horses. Heather had learned to ride while visiting Angie, and now she set out for a ride over the countryside, accompanied by Luigi. Everywhere the land was changing, reflecting the passing of summer and the start of the wet season. Luigi explained that it had been a good harvest this year. She would do well. He didn't seem to notice that she was sunk in embarrassment.

For her first evening Jocasta had ordered what she called 'a simple meal', which turned out to be aubergine salad, followed by squid and macaroni stew, followed by liver with wine sauce. The ride had left her with a good appetite and she had no difficulty doing justice to all these dishes, plus the caramelised oranges. She had the satisfaction of knowing that she'd delighted Jocasta's husband Gino, who did the cooking and was hovering just outside the door. The whole was washed down with half a bottle of a light rosé called Donnafugata, after which she went to bed and slept like a baby.

A strange, dream-like calm seemed to descend on her. The sense of being in limbo was stronger than ever, but now it was a pleasant limbo where she had nothing to do but discover the extent of her new found power. The strained nerves that had betrayed her to Renato in the garden were recovering from their collapse, growing stronger every day.

Some long rides did her good, and her spirits began to be normal again. She made several visits to the Residenza, always choosing a time when Renato was unlikely to be there. To her relief Baptista didn't raise the dangerous subject again. They would talk and discuss Bella Rosaria as though it really was hers. Baptista was full of wise suggestions which Heather duly passed on to Luigi. She was determined to do no more, but little by little she found herself fascinated by the running of the estate.

She wondered what Renato thought of her flight, or the way she'd taken possession of the place he had wanted to own, according to Lorenzo. Doubtless he would soon come storming to visit her. She was ready for him, unafraid.

But when days passed with no sign of him she knew a sense of anticlimax. Then she grew irked at his offhand way of treating her. Something had been left unresolved between them and it had to be sorted. Why couldn't he see that?

It was obvious now that she'd always known he would kiss her. From the moment he walked into Gossways everything he'd said or done had been the actions of a man who would kiss her one day. Her reactions had been clouded by her honest belief that she'd been in love with another man. But behind the curtain of that belief she'd felt like a woman who expected—wanted—to be kissed.

They had almost come to grief the day on the boat, and by the time of the ball her mistake had been staring her in the face. After the aborted wedding she'd retreated into herself, wanting nothing to do with him. But when he'd taken her into his arms by the fountain she'd come to life again so urgently that it had alarmed her. She'd fled because she needed time to think, but now she had to meet him again, and see how he looked when he saw her.

But he didn't appear. Lorenzo seemed almost permanently abroad now, but one day Baptista remarked casually that Renato too was away. She was feeling rather lonely with neither of her sons there, but wasn't it delight-

ful that the two of them could enjoy some time alone
together? In a colourless voice Heather agreed that it was.

Bernardo came to ask if there was anything he could
do for her. He looked ill and wretched, so Heather took
pity on him, invited him to dinner and spent the time
talking about Angie, who'd written twice. He said little,
but she sensed that he was alive to every mention of
Angie's name. She knew that feeling of being haunted.
Something of her sympathy must have shown in her manner, for by the end of the evening they were excellent
friends.

It would have been tempting to drift forever in this
pleasant no-man's-land, but she forced herself to telephone Gossways. As she'd feared, her place on the training programme had gone for ever. She could return as a
sales assistant, but two grades lower than when she'd left.
Renato had made no call on her behalf.

So that was that.

It was another week before she saw Renato's car winding
its way up the narrow main street of Ellona one afternoon,
just as the sun was setting. About time too, she thought
as she descended the stone steps outside the villa. She
tried to arrange her face to suggest the right combination
of welcome and reserve.

But it wasn't Renato.

'Hello,' Lorenzo called cheerily, bounding out and
waving as though nothing was wrong between them. 'I
came to see how you were.'

It took a moment to pull herself together and seem normal. How could it be Lorenzo when it should have been
Renato? How dared he come here when his brother
didn't?

'Fine,' she said, smiling. 'I like it here.'

'All on your own?'

'There are worse things than being alone. Come inside.'

He bounded up the steps, an attractive figure in his light brown trousers and blue short-sleeved shirt, open at the throat. He was smiling and seemed not to have a care in the world. That should have hurt. But it didn't. Those feelings already seemed long in the past.

'I brought you a housewarming present,' he said, flourishing an elegantly wrapped parcel. It turned out to be an alabaster head in the style of a Greek goddess. It was about ten inches tall, delicately made and charming.

'It's a reproduction of a piece in a museum,' Lorenzo explained. 'I chose it because she looks like you. Actually, I'll confess, I bought it for you weeks ago. After what happened—I wasn't sure how to give it to you. But as a housewarming gift—' He gave a deprecating shrug. He was full of charm.

'I love it,' she said. 'And I know just the right place for it.'

She led him out to the rose garden, where there was a little alcove that she'd thought was rather bare. To her delight it harmonised perfectly.

'Lovely,' Lorenzo agreed. 'Do you like this spot, then? I know it's always been a favorite place of Mamma's.'

Perhaps he didn't know the story of Fede, the rose grower. Heather wondered if Baptista would mind if she hinted at it, but Lorenzo's next words killed the impulse. 'Don't you find the house rather gloomy? I always did.'

'Gloomy? Not at all. It's cool and peaceful. I love it.'

'We always had to spend a few weeks here in the summer. I just remember longing to get away.'

So much for her dream of living here with him. A fantasy, born of ignorance, like so many of her thoughts of Lorenzo, she realised. If they had known each other longer she would have seen her infatuation for what it was.

They had wine on the terrace overlooking the garden. Lorenzo was looking mischievous. 'I heard about the row,' he said.

'Row?' she asked cautiously.

'Come on, everyone knows what happened. Mamma tried to arrange a match between you and Renato and you just roared with laughter. I wish I'd been there to see that. My brother, who spends most of his time dodging traps by determined women, actually getting the cold shoulder.'

'It wasn't like that at all,' Heather said firmly. 'Renato and I both felt that it wasn't a good idea.' How dull and prim the words sounded against the explosive reality. But it was best that way. Whatever she might feel about Renato she wasn't going to offer him up for Lorenzo's amusement.

'I'm sure *you* don't like the idea, but *him*? For one thing, you've got this place.'

'Which I'm giving back as soon as the paperwork's sorted.'

'Plus you turned him down. Who do you think was the last woman who did that?'

Me, Heather thought, remembering how she'd told Renato to jump in the river on the first evening.

'Refused him before he'd even asked,' Lorenzo went on with a grin 'I'll bet that got under his skin. He's been in a foul temper ever since he got back from America. Careful! You nearly spilled your drink.'

He was back, she thought. And he hadn't called her.

Well, why should he?

Because he had no right to leave her on hot coals.

Hell would freeze over before she asked when he'd returned.

'Let's drop this subject,' she said. 'I'm not going to marry Renato.'

'I wouldn't care to take a wager on that. You laughed at him. He can't just ignore that.'

'What are you saying? That he'll try to win me over to save his pride?'

'I wouldn't put it past him. He's not used to having to win a woman over. Usually they're only too willing.'

She didn't answer and he gave a rueful half-smile. 'We could have made it, you know—if he hadn't interfered.'

'We'll never know,' she told him. 'It's in the past. Over.'

But he laid down his wineglass on the stone balustrade and reached out to draw her into his arms. Heather had half expected it, and she allowed it to happen because there was something she wanted to know. She even kissed him back. Not out of love. Or passion. Curiosity.

Once she'd loved him so much. The sweetness of his kisses had transported her to heaven. Or so she'd thought. But heaven had turned out to be a rather narrow cul-de-sac. A kiss should open up infinite vistas of joy and passion, even when it was gentle, hovering on the verge of passion, but uncommitted, so that you yearned for...

She sighed and freed herself. It had been a useful experiment and she'd learned what she wanted to know. Lorenzo was basically a pleasant young man, but he still had some growing up to do. It had been like kissing cardboard.

Then she turned her head and saw Renato, regarding them sardonically.

'Forgive me,' he said. 'I didn't realise the two of you would be occupied.'

'Then you should have done,' Lorenzo said cheekily.

Renato advanced and took his arm. 'You were just leaving.'

'Was I?'

'No,' Heather said, furious at this high-handedness. 'I'd just invited Lorenzo to lunch, and he'd accepted.'

Lorenzo caught Renato's eye and what he saw there seemed to decide him. 'Perhaps another time,' he said.

Even knowing it was futile, Heather made an attempt to assert herself as mistress of her own home. 'Not another time,' she said firmly. 'Now. Gino will have prepared food for two—'

'Don't worry, I'm hungry,' Renato said. He regarded Lorenzo with surprise. 'Are you still here?'

'Just going,' Lorenzo said. But he deposited a cheeky kiss on Heather's cheek before vanishing.

When they were alone she turned on Renato, who was looking at her coldly. She even thought she detected a hint of scorn in his eyes, and her temper rose to meet it.

'You've got an unspeakable nerve!' she told him.

'My apologies,' he said, not sounding at all apologetic. 'But I wanted to be rid of him and that was the quickest way.'

'And what about what *I* wanted?'

'It's fairly obvious what you wanted. *Nome de dio*, I thought you had more dignity!'

'How dare you?'

'Oh, please! You were being pretty obvious. No doubt the first step to luring him upstairs to bed.'

She gasped, and would have struck out if he hadn't caught her wrist. 'No, don't attack me just because I speak plainly. If your aim was to get Lorenzo back to the altar, you won't do it that way.'

She was angry enough to speak without thinking. 'If

I'd wanted to trap Lorenzo by taking him to bed I'd have done it before now.'

His grip tightened, and there was a strange light in his eyes. 'Are you saying you never did?'

She drew a sharp breath. 'Let go of me at once.'

'I wondered if you'd slept with him—you denied it the day we met, or I thought you did—but I could be wrong—tell me—' There was a flash of anger in his eyes. *'Tell me!'*

'I'll tell you nothing. It's none of your business.'

'The best thing Lorenzo did was running off that day. He'd have disappointed you. You know that, don't you?'

She did know. The beating of her heart told her, but she wouldn't admit it to him. 'If you thought that, it's a pity you pushed me into his arms,' she said.

'I didn't know then. Neither of us knew. But we know now. He'd have let you down, and then—'

'And then—?'

He didn't need to answer, but it was there between them. And then she would have turned to him.

'Never,' she whispered. 'Never. If I was Lorenzo's wife, I'd have been faithful to the very end.'

'To the bitter end,' he corrected.

'If necessary.'

'No matter how bitter the end would have been for all of us?' His voice became cruel. 'We could all have burned in a self-made hell for all you cared.'

'You needn't have. You have other diversions.'

'Sometimes they're not—' He became aware of what he was saying and stopped abruptly. 'Shall I tell you what hell is?' he asked after a moment.

'I'm sure you know many kinds.'

'It's to love without desire, and desire without love.'

She drew a shuddering breath. 'Let me go, Renato. Let me go now. You have no right to do this.'

She wrenched her wrist free and backed away. But she kept her eyes on him as she would have done a wild animal that might spring either way. This was Renato, a man it was always safest to treat as an enemy. He was still in a state of suppressed anger, his face paler than she had ever seen it, and she knew his control could slip at any moment.

And then Jocasta's step outside the door brought them both out of the fevered dream and they turned forced smiles on her. Somehow the jagged air settled back to normal, leaving only unbelievable memories behind.

Renato greeted Jocasta like an old friend and Heather could see how delighted the housekeeper was to see him. As they exchanged some backchat in Sicilian she mentally stood back, trying not to be aware that she was tingling and newly alive after their brief exchange. Once again they were fighting within a few minutes of meeting, but with Renato fighting held an excitement all its own.

Like Lorenzo, Renato was dressed informally in a short-sleeved shirt, open at the throat, but on him the effect was different. Lorenzo blended into his surroundings. Renato stood out from them. His vital masculinity made him always more noticeable than anything else. Heather found her anger slipping away. He'd been gone so long, and the little ache that had been in her breast for days was explained now, hard though she found it to admit to herself.

'Your favorite wine, *signore*,' Jocasta said, pouring for him.

'Good. And I've had a pressing invitation to lunch,' he said shamelessly.

'Then I'll tell Gino to prepare some meatballs in tomato soup,' Jocasta said.

'Not for lunch, because they'll take time to prepare and we'd like to eat quickly before we go out,' Renato said. 'But I'll have them for supper tonight.'

'I never invited you for lunch or supper,' Heather pointed out when they were alone.

'But you were just about to. I could tell.'

To think she'd actually been glad to see him! He seemed to ruffle her feathers for the devilment of it. Why couldn't it have been him in the car this afternoon, as it should have been? But no, he had to arrive at the wrong moment, teasing and tormenting her, putting her on the defensive, ruining what might have been a delightful visit. And doing all this while looking so vividly alive that something sang inside her and she wondered how she had endured so long without the sight of him. She could gladly have wrung his neck.

'And as for telling her when to serve lunch—'

'We're going out straight after and there's no time to waste.'

As they sat down to lunch they had each managed to slide the polite masks into place, and Renato had done more. He managed to look as though the whole scene hadn't taken place. Heather only hoped her own efforts were as successful.

'Tell me, how have you been while I've been away?' he asked.

'I've enjoyed your absence considerably. Can I hope to have it repeated again soon?'

'Not for a while, I'm afraid. This estate has always been one of our most productive, and it has to stay that way. That means you must know what to do. Luigi will take responsibility, of course, but if you don't know what he's doing he won't respect you.'

'But—' Heather meant to explain yet again that she was going to return the estate to its rightful owner, but gave up. Nobody had listened to her so far, and plainly Renato wasn't listening now.

In fact he seemed to regard her chiefly as an audience. He talked at her rather than to her, and once remarked that she wasn't listening properly. He was totally businesslike and the electricity that had flashed between them earlier might never have been.

'The rains are due,' he told her. 'But with any luck we'll have a few days first. That's why I'm here now. Let's go.'

A small crowd had gathered to watch them get into his open-topped car at the front of the villa. 'Your tenants,' Renato told her.

'You mean some of them live in houses that belong to the estate?'

'All of them live in Ellona, which is yours.'

'But I thought—just one or two houses—'

'Every house in the village. That's why they're watching you. What you do affects them.'

That was only the start. As they drove out that afternoon he showed her vineyards, orchards and olive groves that were all hers. Everything was well kept and flourishing, the tenants celebrating bumper harvests, eager to talk about loans for next year's fertiliser. This was Renato's territory, and Heather had expected him to use his expert knowledge to reduce her to silence. But she had to admit that he behaved beautifully, bringing her into every conversation, treating her with respect, explaining what she needed to know without talking down to her.

At one sheep farm she became fascinated, asking a series of intelligent questions that had the tenant family nodding approval. In a combination of English, Italian and Sicilian she explained that her uncle had been a shepherd.

'We used to spend holidays with him and he'd let me help with the lambing. I loved that.'

'What kind of sheep?' they wanted to know.

'Blackface, some angora—' And she was away, talking eagerly.

They took her to see their best ram and watched as she ran knowledgeable hands over it. They discussed vets' bills. Scandalous. And milking. Did they milk their sheep? They did but they hadn't expected her to know it was possible.

At last the talk died. She looked around and found them staring at her with interest. Renato was smiling as though he'd won something. Heather felt a prickle on her spine as a suspicion came to her.

As they drove back through Ellona Heather's suspicions increased. Every window and door in the main street was open, and they were being studied by curious eyes. The plump little priest stepped out to hail them, and they stopped at his house for a drink. When they emerged they were watched even more intently. It was obvious that this scrutiny had a reason, and she was beginning to fear that she knew what it was.

As they reached the villa Renato said, 'Tomorrow we'll go on horseback.'

'You're coming back tomorrow?'

'I'm staying overnight. You don't mind, do you?'

'Not at all,' she said politely. 'I'll tell Jocasta.'

'No need. I should think she's put my things in my room by now.'

He was right. Clearly he was a favourite with Jocasta, who had not only unpacked his case but ordered the evening meal to suit him. Heather didn't know how to protest about the way he'd taken over. After all, she kept saying that Bella Rosaria wasn't really hers, so it was hard to complain when he took her at her word.

They enjoyed the last of the light wandering in the garden. 'I loved playing here better than anywhere else,' he remembered. 'This was a wonderful place for gangs of bandits. I used to get the boys from the village in and we created mayhem.'

She smiled. 'I wonder how Baptista felt about that in her flower garden.'

'She didn't mind. She said what mattered was that there should be happiness here.' They had reached the rose arbour and sat on the wooden seat. 'I used to come out in the evening and find her sitting in this spot, with her eyes closed.'

'Did you ever find out why?' she asked cautiously.

'You mean did I know about Federico? Yes, the head gardener told me. He'd worked here for years and knew all about it. Apparently there were a lot of rumours when the young man vanished so suddenly.'

'That was the hardest for Baptista to bear,' Heather said. 'Not knowing. You surely don't think—?'

'I doubt it, but I have to admit that my grandfather was a man who wouldn't tolerate opposition.'

They had supper in the library, close to the open French windows. Renato's mood had mellowed and he went on reminiscing about the villa as he'd known it in his childhood.

'I always knew it had a special place in my mother's heart. Perhaps that's why it became enchanted to me too. The Residenza was just a building, but Bella Rosaria was special.'

'Then take it back.'

He gave her an ironic look. 'There's only one way I can do that.'

'No marriage,' she said at once. 'We both agreed.'

He shrugged. 'My mother is a very persuasive woman, and I'm a man with a strong sense of duty.'

She rested her elbows on the table and met his eyes. 'Rubbish!' she said firmly. 'I don't know what game you're playing, but you can forget it. No marriage. Not now. Not ever. You can take that as final.'

He grinned. 'Suppose I don't choose to?'

'Oh, stop this! I know you're only fooling but it's not fair to give the village ideas. Do you think I don't know why they were out in force, watching us? And the priest, practically giving us his blessing. You ought to stop them thinking things. It's not fair.'

'To whom?'

'To them. They obviously like the idea.'

'Yes, you've made yourself popular. And the fact that you know about sheep will be all over the district tonight. Everyone around here sees the propriety of our marriage as clearly as Mamma does.'

She laughed. 'They'd think differently if they could have heard what you said about swimming the Straits of Messina in lead weights.'

He winced. 'I deny it. I never said any such thing. Anyway, a man can grow wiser.'

She refused to rise to the bait. 'I'm going to bed,' she said.

'You're right. We'll make an early start in the morning. Don't be late. I dislike women who keep me waiting.'

This was so clearly meant to be provocative that she said, 'I really will kick your shins in a minute,' in a teasing voice.

'Exactly what Mamma advised, night and morning. You see, we're acting like an old married couple already.'

She began to laugh. She couldn't help it. She ought to at least try to stay cross with him, but the excellent wine and the company of a man who, for all his infuriating behaviour, was still more mysteriously attractive than anyone she'd ever known, was a potent combination. Tonight he'd been pleasant company, making her like him better than at any time before.

'That's better than the last time I heard you laugh,' he said approvingly.

The night in the garden, when she'd laughed on the edge of sobs, and he'd kissed her with a tenderness that had haunted her dreams since. She met his eyes and looked quickly away, confused. She no longer knew what she wanted.

They climbed the stairs together. Outside her door he took her hand, said gently, 'Goodnight, Heather,' and went across the corridor to his own room without waiting for her answer.

When she'd closed her door she stood for a long time, listening to the sound of her own heart beating. He would come to her tonight. She knew that beyond any doubt. Suddenly decided, she turned the key in her lock.

She undressed slowly, torn this way and that, until she crept to the door and unlocked it. Then she got into bed and lay listening to the creaks of the old house, as the night grew quiet around them, staring into the darkness.

Renato wanted to marry her. Or rather, he'd decided in favour of the marriage. That was more accurate. The family needed an heir, and Lorenzo had proved too unreliable, so Renato had reluctantly bowed his neck to the yoke. Marrying her would please his mother and satisfy his sense of duty.

Nothing else?

Yes. She'd challenged him, laughed at him, snubbed him. His pride was at stake. And he wanted to sleep with her. He'd made no bones about it. But she already knew how little physical relationships counted with him. When he'd soothed his pride and gained what he wanted—what then?

Hell is love without desire, and desire without love—desire without love—

At last she fell asleep.

CHAPTER NINE

WHEN they met at breakfast her mood was cool. Naturally she was glad of Renato's restraint the night before. If he'd tried to come to her bed it would have clouded the issue and she would have been angry at his calculation.

But the apparently easy way he'd resisted her was also a kind of calculation, and of the two it was the more insulting. She blushed to recall that she'd left her door unlocked, and he hadn't even tried it. One small victory to him. If she weakened he would control the situation, and that she mustn't allow.

He didn't seem to notice her reserve. His own mood was edgy. Over breakfast he spoke tersely, smiled very little and looked haggard.

The horses were brought round. Soon after they set out she realised that Renato had been right when he'd said the story of the sheep would be all over the district. Wherever they went she found none of the suspicion or hostility that she would have expected, considering that she was a stranger and a foreigner. By some mysterious bush telegraph they knew Renato had chosen her for his wife, they regarded the match as settled, and they approved.

Before long the beauty of the day had its effect on both of them, softening her mood and making him less tense. They stopped at a farm and sat in the sun, drinking rough home-made wine and eating goat's-milk cheese. Heather had been enchanted by Sicily from the first moment. Now she found new things to delight her wherever she looked.

'I love that,' she said, pointing to the ruins of a Greek

133

temple in the distance, with sheep and goats munching contentedly nearby. 'A great, ancient civilisation, side by side with everyday reality. The sheep aren't awed by the temple, and the temple isn't less splendid because of the sheep.'

He nodded agreement. 'It was built in honour of Ceres, the goddess of fertility and abundance. The more sheep the better.'

'And seeing them in harmony like that sums up so much about this country.'

'Do you know how like a Sicilian you sound?' he said. 'Talking as though this was a separate country, instead of part of Italy. We all do that.'

'Yes, I'd noticed. And it's more than a separate country. It's a separate world. There's nothing like it anywhere else.'

'And will you leave it? Turn your back on the welcome it's given you?'

'You're a very clever man.' She sighed. 'You've simply gone over my head again. Your mother has decided, the tenants have decided, Father Torrino tells me how much it will cost to repair the church roof—all because you've let them think it's a done deal. It makes me feel like the last piece in a jigsaw puzzle.'

'That's a very good analogy,' he said, tactfully bypassing her accusations. 'This is a jigsaw puzzle, with all the pieces fitting perfectly. You come into our lives from another country. You have different values, a different language, and yet there's a space waiting for you that's exactly your shape. The differences you bring will only enrich us. We can all see it. Why can't you?'

'Maybe because you come as part of the package,' she said darkly.

He gave her the vivid grin that could so powerfully disconcert her. 'Be brave. I'm not really so bad.'

'You are.'

'I'm not.'

'You are.'

They laughed at the same moment. It was pleasant to be sitting in the bright day, squabbling light-heartedly. In another moment she might have yielded. But then some perverse imp made her ask, 'Why did you change your mind? A couple of weeks ago nothing would make you consider it.'

'Mamma gave me a stern talking-to, and as I'm afraid of her I gave in.' He added outrageously, 'But very reluctantly.'

'Oh, stop it. I'm trying to be serious.'

'Then let's be serious. Arranged marriages can work very well when neither party is burdened with extravagant expectations. We've both seen the dangers of that, haven't we?'

'If you put it like that,' she said with a sigh, 'I suppose we have.'

'Shall we call it a bargain? Come, say yes so that I can call Mamma.'

'I suppose she's sitting by the phone, waiting to hear my answer?'

'Possibly, although I think she knew it was virtually decided.'

She frowned. 'Decided? Now wait a minute. No way was it decided.'

He made a hasty gesture. 'I put that badly. It's just that I told her I thought that when you and I had talked about it calmly—'

'What you told her,' Heather breathed, her eyes kindling, 'was that I was bound to give in. "Just give me a few hours to talk some sense into her, Mamma, and you can start sending out the invitations.'' It was bad enough that you fooled people around here, but how dare you tell your mother it was settled?'

She got hastily to her feet.

Renato swore and rose too. 'Heather, will you listen to reason?'

'No, because I don't like your kind of reason. You pulled my strings to marry me to Lorenzo, only he wasn't there. Now you think you're going to pull my strings again—only, this time, *I* won't be there. Somebody ought to put you in a cage and charge admission, because you come right out of the ark. And you're the last man I could ever marry.'

A look of stubbornness settled on his face. 'But I've given her my word.'

'And *my* word is no.'

'This is Sicily, where a woman's word counts for nothing beside a man's.'

'Well, maybe I'm not as much a Sicilian as we all thought.'

'Why can't you face the inevitable?'

'Because I don't think it *is* inevitable. I'm meant for a better fate than to save you from the results of your own pride. Go back to your light affairs, Renato. Pay them, and forget them. That's all you're good for.'

His sharp intake of breath told him she'd flicked him on the raw. She stormed away to where the horses were tethered. The farmer was there and he smiled at her in a way she was coming to recognise. The sight only increased her sense of being trapped. She thanked him for his hospitality before jumping on her horse and galloping away.

Faster and faster she urged the willing animal, as

though she could outrun all the furies that pursued her whenever Renato Martelli was around. She could hear him behind her now, galloping hard to catch up, shouting something.

She couldn't make out the words, and she missed the signs that would have warned her what was about to happen: the sudden drop in temperature, the darkening of the sky. The first crack of thunder took her by surprise. Her horse was alarmed, missed his footing, found it again and managed to go on. But he'd lost speed, and in the need to control him she'd taken her eyes off Renato. Next thing he'd caught up with her.

'Go on to the temple,' he cried. 'It's nearer than the farm.'

Before she could reply there was another crack of thunder and the heavens opened. She gasped. This wasn't rain as she knew it. It was a flood, a torrent that crashed onto her all at once, pounding like hammers, drenching her in the first second.

'Come on!' he yelled.

She could no longer see the temple in the downpour, and found it only by following him. It loomed suddenly out of the wall of rain, no longer cheerful as in the sun, but almost sinister.

'There,' he cried, pointing to the far end. 'There's some cover.'

But the cover turned out to be too small. There was only just room for the horses, so they put the distressed animals inside, and endured the downpour themselves.

'Damn!' he yelled. 'I thought we had another day at least.'

But now she'd got her second wind Heather was feeling good. The noise of the water, the thunder, the fierceness of the rain against her body, was exhilarating. Renato stared at her, realising that this wasn't the woman he knew, but a new one who revelled in the violence of the elements. She turned and stared back at him, laughing, challenging. The next moment he'd pulled her into his arms.

It felt good to be kissed by a man whose control was slipping, who wanted her almost against his will. There was a driving purpose in his lips that thrilled her. He kissed her mouth, her nose, her eyes, seeking her feverishly as though nothing was ever enough. She gasped and clung to him. The rain had soaked through the thin material of their shirts, making them almost vanish. She relished in the feel of his body, the muscular shape of his arms and shoulders, the heavy bull neck, the sheer primitive force of the man. This was what she'd craved even while she was fending him off, because, like him, she needed her own terms.

But what was happening between them was on nobody's terms: need, craving, curiosity, antagonism. They were all there, mixed up with a desire that obeyed no laws but its own. Her heart was pounding so wildly that he felt it and laid his hand between her breasts.

'Could Lorenzo make you feel like this?' he demanded. 'Can't you feel the difference?'

'There's no difference,' she cried. 'You and Lorenzo are two of a kind. Both selfish, careless of other people's feelings, thinking of women as creatures to be used.'

She wondered what perversity made her hold out against a man who was gaining such a strong hold on her heart and senses. But ancient, wise instinct warned her not to let Renato have too easy a victory. She didn't know what their future would hold, whether it might be love or just desire. But it would be built on what was happening now, and if she didn't stand her ground she would always regret it.

But he too seemed to understand this, because he was making it so hard for her to hold out, caressing her with his lips that murmured seductively of passion and pleasure, passion so intense that it was destiny, pleasure too great to be resisted.

Hell is desire without love.

They shared desire but no love, and a marriage based on that faulty basis could only end in bitterness. She must cling to that, but it was hard when her body clamoured as never before for what only this man could give.

As abruptly as it had started, the rain eased off to a light drizzle. She broke free and turned away from him, but that helped her not at all. Wherever she looked she saw the carvings and statues depicting Ceres and the fertility she demanded. Here was corn, ripe for harvest, there were animals mating vigorously on a frieze that ran all around above their heads. And everywhere were men and women united in a fury of ecstatic creation.

Ceres was a ruthless goddess, sworn to make the little people she ruled fruitful, at any cost. To tempt them she dangled the sweetness of desire, but when her purpose was achieved the desire turned to ashes.

Renato came up behind her. He'd followed her gaze and understood everything she was thinking. 'There's no fighting it,' he said. 'Certainly not in this place, which was built to remind us how helpless we are in the hands of the gods.'

'Do you believe that?'

'I believe there are some forces we can't withstand.'

'And what do you think the gods meant for us?' she asked, turning on him.

'I'll tell you what they didn't mean. They didn't mean

for us to live peacefully. You and I could never do that. There's something in you that drives me crazy, and there's something in me that brings out a temper you never show to anyone else. We've fought from the moment we met, and we'll probably fight until the last moment of our lives. But we'll pass those lives together because *I will not let you marry any other man.*'

Looking into his face, she was swept by a wild mood. It was the same as the one that she'd known on the jet ski when she had incited him to ride on out of sight of the boat. It had almost cost her her life then, and now it might decide the rest of her life.

'Do you understand?' he said. 'Answer me.'

She answered, not in words, but in a slow smile that made him growl and pull her hard against him. 'Are you tormenting me for the pleasure of it?'

'What do you think?' she asked, speaking quietly so that he couldn't hear, had to make out the movement of her lips.

'I think I won't let you torment me any more,' he growled.

She laughed recklessly. 'How will you stop me?'

'Don't challenge me, Heather. You'll lose.'

'I think I've already won.'

She'd won his lips crushing hers, one arm tight around her waist, the other behind her neck, so that she couldn't have escaped if she'd wanted to. But she didn't want to. She wanted to stay in his arms and enjoy her prize to the full. Because afterwards would come the day of reckoning, when she would discover what else she had won with this strange, mysterious, complicated man.

'Tell me that you never slept with him,' he said hoarsely.

'If I did, I had every right to. I was his, not yours.'

'Tell me you didn't.'

'It doesn't concern you. You don't own me. You never will.'

He stepped back from her. He was trembling as though he'd run a long race.

'I do,' he said. 'And I always will.'

He fell silent. He might have been waiting for her response, but she was determined to say nothing. Slowly the stormy look died out of his eyes, leaving bleakness behind. 'The rain has stopped,' he said. 'We should leave before it starts again.'

At the villa he stayed only long enough to dry off and change into some of the dry clothes that were still in his room. Heather went to her own room to change, and when she emerged Renato had already gone.

'He said to say goodbye,' Jocasta explained. 'But he couldn't stay.'

'No, I didn't think he would.'

She ate alone that evening, and picked so delicately at the food that Jocasta privately berated her husband, demanding to know if he wanted to drive the mistress away by his bad cooking.

She was late going to bed. As the moon came up she wandered in the garden, finding her way easily along silvered paths. The rose bush shone in the cool light, symbol of a love that had never really died.

That was what she'd thought awaited her here: the sweetness and tenderness of love. It was the kind of gentle experience that, as a northerner, she had instinctively understood.

Instead, in this country of fierce sun and fiercer rain, she'd found a passion as primitive as time itself, passion as these varied, unpredictable people understood it, and it had revealed that at heart she was one of them.

Very well. If she was to be a Sicilian, then she would meet the problem not merely with Sicilian intensity, but with Sicilian cunning.

She was swept again by the memory of Renato's lips on hers, the way he'd pulled her against him so that her body moulded itself against his. These things had made her want to cry *Yes* with every part of her.

But his mouth had spoken the language of pride and possession, and no woman of spirit could consent to that. So her words had denied him while her senses clamoured for him. It seemed there was no way to solve the riddle.

Unless....

Next day she drove down to the Residenza in the late afternoon, and found Baptista fresh from her nap, bright-eyed and cheerful. They had tea and cakes together on the terrace as the afternoon light faded. The rains had left everywhere looking freshly washed, and now that the hottest part of summer had gone this time of day was cool and pleasant. Encouraged by Baptista, she described how she was spending her time at the villa.

'The local priest paid me a ceremonial visit, and said very anxiously that he hoped I played chess. I assured him that I did, and he went away happy.'

Baptista chuckled. 'Father Torrino is a dear man but the worst chess player in the world. You'll have to let him win sometimes. So you're fitting into the community. That's excellent.'

'Oh, they're all looking me up and down and wondering if I'll "do",' Heather said with a smile. 'They seem to think that I will. It's a happy place. No wonder you love it.' After a moment she added significantly, 'I really don't want to leave.'

'I was sure you wouldn't.'

'But it's not that easy.' Heather sipped her tea and thought for a moment before asking, 'How many men did you turn down before you finally said yes?'

'Five or six. My poor parents were tearing their hair, but they persevered.'

Out of the corner of her eye Heather became aware of a shadow on the curtain, and then the figure of a man appearing. She was sure Baptista also knew he was there, but neither of them took the slightest notice of him. Nor did he speak. He was listening intently.

'It's not just the man who has to be right,' Baptista continued, 'but the circumstances. That's one advantage of using an intermediary. You negotiate the important decisions first, and then there's less to quarrel about.'

'Oh, I don't know,' Heather murmured, still refusing to acknowledge Renato's presence, although he'd poured himself some tea, and taken a seat a little behind them. 'With certain people there would always be something to quarrel about because they're just naturally annoying.'

'I totally agree. A good intermediary takes that into account. Some men are harder to match than others on account of being—how shall I put it?'

'Full of themselves,' Heather supplied.

Baptista gave a delighted snort. 'I love your English idioms. So perfectly expressive. And you have another one—"where to get off!" Such a man needs a wife who can tell him where to get off. As for her, if perhaps she finds her life a little unfocused and lacking in direction, and if he can offer her a life that can remedy these problems—she might well decide to overlook his deficiencies.'

'There's another matter to be settled,' Heather pointed out. 'Fidelity. The party on my side wouldn't want to find herself standing in line behind Julia and Minetta and—'

'Never heard of them,' growled a masculine voice from behind.

'I think he'll decide to forget that he's ever heard of them,' Baptista observed blandly.

'Good,' Heather said. 'My party would expect things to stay that way. Did somebody speak?'

The voice growled again. *'Zoccu non fa pi tia ad autra non fari.'*

'We seem to have been joined by a spirit presence,' Baptista remarked, unperturbed. 'It has just reminded us of a Sicilian proverb: Do not do to others what you don't wish them to do to you.'

'The point is taken,' Heather observed gravely. 'Fidelity on both sides.'

'Excellent. There are certain other matters to be decided in advance. Like, where they are going to live. I refused two suitors because they disliked Bella Rosaria and wouldn't spend any time there. All I wanted was a few weeks in the summer, but they wouldn't budge.'

'A few weeks in summer sounds ideal,' Heather said.

'And the rest of the time here because he does so much business from this house.'

'Of course, he would need to remain at the heart of his business,' Heather agreed. 'But I expect you slipped away to the villa sometimes on your own?'

'Indeed I did. As I'm sure you would wish to do. Although I doubt you'd be on your own because he loves the place too, and might burden you with his company more often than you'd like.'

'I wouldn't mind. He's at his best at the villa.'

'Ah, you've discovered that.'

'Almost human. And it's nice to have something in common.'

'Once that has been decided,' Baptista resumed, 'all

that would remain would be to call in the lawyers and arrange the legal details. As to the dowry—'

'The bride offers Bella Rosaria, a very desirable estate,' Heather pointed out.

'An excellent dowry,' Baptista agreed, 'which will remain her property—'

'But I thought—that is, *she* thought she'd be giving it back to the Martelli family,' Heather protested.

'After the marriage she'll be part of the Martelli family,' Baptista pointed out. 'Besides, a woman is in a stronger position in Sicily if she has some property of her own. You should advise your party to take my word for it.'

Heather nodded. 'She will do so. In fact, she's very aware of how much she owes to your wisdom and judgement in bringing this difficult case to a successful conclusion. Have we forgotten anything?'

'I don't think so.'

'In that case,' Heather said with a sudden air of resolution, 'you can tell your party that my party finds the arrangements quite satisfactory.'

She rose. Baptista held out a hand and Heather helped her to stand. Then the two women went slowly into the house, leaving Renato alone in the gathering twilight, drinking his tea and staring moodily out to sea. Neither of them had spared him so much as a glance.

CHAPTER TEN

FOR her second wedding in Palermo Cathedral Heather chose a much simpler dress than her first. It was of ivory silk, because that suited her lightly tanned complexion better than white, and she borrowed it from a hire shop in Palermo.

'It didn't cost me a penny,' she told Renato and Baptista triumphantly. 'I made them a gift of the old one and they were delighted to let me hire one free.'

Baptista gave a crow of triumph. 'What a business-woman! Didn't I tell you?' This was to Renato.

'You did.' He was grinning. 'Perhaps your suggestion was right, Mamma.'

'Right?' Heather looked from one to the other.

'Mamma thinks you should join the business at once,' Renato explained.

'I shall be retiring soon and you must take my place,' Baptista said. 'Otherwise there won't be a female voice on the board, and that would be disaster.'

'You're on the board?'

'You'll enjoy our board meetings,' Renato told her ironically. 'First Mamma tells us what she wants. Then the meeting begins, she proposes the motion and we all vote according to her instructions.'

'Baloney!' Heather said frankly.

'No wonder Mamma wants you to take her place. You're as big a bully as she is.'

'Take her place?'

'I can't go on for ever,' Baptista said. 'My dear, you

have brains, beauty and business sense. In short, you're a considerable asset. Naturally I was determined to "acquire" you.'

It might have sounded clinical but Heather already knew that her future mother-in-law loved her. The effect, as Baptista had intended, was to make her feel valued, and to show her to herself not just as bride, but as a woman taking her place in a community. This was what arranged marriages were for.

She would have preferred a quiet wedding, but every guest from last time must be asked back, or they would be offended. So the preparations went ahead on the same scale. In the kitchens the chefs worked night and day to outdo their previous efforts. Even the cake had an extra tier.

There was one other aspect which would be exactly the same. Once more Bernardo would be the best man, and on the night before the wedding Heather drove to Palermo Airport to collect Angie, who had flown in to be her bridesmaid. They dined together in a restaurant, and slipped into the house later, unseen by Bernardo.

'He really hasn't suspected?' Angie asked as she prepared for bed in their old room.

'Not a thing. Nobody has mentioned your coming, and the first Bernardo will know is when he sees you walking down the aisle with me tomorrow. You haven't changed, have you?'

'Not by a whisper,' Angie said wistfully. 'And him?'

'He's as unhappy as you are,' Heather said. 'Trust me. I'm going to fix this.'

'Goodness, but you sounded like Baptista then,' Angie said, startled.

'That's what they want me for,' Heather said lightly.

'Pardon?'

'This is an arranged marriage. Very suitable.'

'And that's why you're marrying Renato? Because it's "suitable".'

'Certainly,' Heather said, a little stiffly.

Angie smiled. 'You're kidding yourself.'

The morning came. The family departed. Cousin Enrico, who was giving her away, escorted her to the car, and in a few minutes they'd reached the cathedral. This time there was no breeze to stir her veil, no crowd to cry *'grazziusu'*. No romance, no poetry. Only the certainty that this time her bridegroom would be there, waiting to make the deal. A sensible marriage for sensible people.

Then they had started the long journey down the aisle to the high altar. With a sense of shock she saw Renato's face. Not sensible. Not businesslike. Strangely pale, stunned, exactly as he'd looked on that other day as she descended the stairs to take his arm for him to lead her to her marriage with his brother.

She'd meant to glance at Bernardo to see how he reacted to Angie, but the sight of Renato, his eyes fixed on her with a look she couldn't understand, wiped everything else from her mind. The cathedral vanished, the guests disappeared. There was only herself and Renato, about to become a part of each other's lives for ever.

The whole congregation seemed to he holding its breath as they made their responses, and to heave a collective sigh when they turned to walk back down the aisle, into the sunlight: husband and wife. The arrangement was made, the deal done. Both parties were satisfied.

At the reception in the Residenza they each managed to get through their parts without too much self-consciousness. Heather smiled and cut the cake. They toasted each other in champagne and tried not to seem too aware of what everyone was thinking. There was applause as they took the dance floor together.

Out of the corner of her eye Heather saw Angie dancing with Bernardo. They seemed lost in each other, but their faces were distraught, almost desperate, and her heart sank.

'Did you really think it would work, bringing her here?' Renato murmured.

'I hoped,' she said wistfully. 'They love each other so much.'

'Which is why neither of them can see reason. Not like us.'

'I guess that makes us the lucky ones,' she said, smiling.

He returned her smile. 'I think we might be.'

Something in that smile made her aware of the movement of his legs against hers through the material of her bridal gown. His hand was firm in the small of her back, and he was holding her very close. Once before they had danced, and she'd fought to deny her growing physical awareness of him. But now she didn't have to deny it. Her heart beat a little faster.

At last the guests began to leave, except for the ones who were staying the night, and the bride and groom were free to slip away. Her things had already been moved into the room with the big four-poster bed that for years he had occupied alone.

Now it was hers too. Signora Martelli.

There was only one light in the room, a bedside lamp that cast a small glow over the deep red counterpane and the rest of the room into mysterious shadow. The long mirror showed her to herself, a faint muted figure, still uncertain whether she really belonged here.

Something in the silence made her turn quickly and see

Renato standing just inside the door. She hadn't heard him come in. How long, she wondered, had he been there, looking at her with that strange expression that she couldn't read?

In this light he looked taller and more imposing than ever, except that when he moved towards her there was a new hesitancy in his manner, and she realised that he wasn't really very sure of himself either.

Renato had had champagne set there on ice, to wait for them, with two tall crystal glasses. Renato poured two glasses and offered one to her. She raised it to him, feeling her heart quicken its beating beneath the white dress.

'To us,' he said. They clinked glasses.

She was still in full bridal regalia, but now he lifted off the pearl tiara and removed her veil himself, causing her hair to fall down about her shoulders. Abruptly she set her glass down. Her hand was shaking.

'Are you all right?' he asked. 'It must have been a great strain for you, going through today with all those faces staring at you, wondering.'

'For you too. In fact they were probably wondering more about you, how you felt taking on the woman your brother—ouch!'

'I'm sorry,' he said swiftly releasing her hair where his hand had suddenly tightened. 'I didn't mean to do that. I think we should agree never to refer to that—or to him—again. It's over. It didn't happen.'

Yes, she thought, that was the only way they could live—as though it hadn't happened.

When Renato spoke again it was in a suspiciously cheerful voice, as though he were forcing himself to change the subject.

'Did you see Enrico and Giuseppe vying for Mamma's favours today?'

'Yes. Poor Enrico was hopping with rage when she danced with Giuseppe. If she hadn't danced with him straight after I dread to think what would have happened.'

'Mamma wouldn't have done that,' he said lightly. 'It wouldn't have been proper, and today has been a day of great propriety. We should congratulate ourselves. We've made a wise marriage, bearing in mind the interests of our family and community. This is what sensible people do.'

'It's an excellent business arrangement,' she agreed. 'We both gain.'

'I'm glad you see the position so clearly.'

But as he spoke he was letting his fingertips rest against her neck, setting off a soft excitement deep within her that made a mockery of his prosaic words. She met his eyes, wondering why there was a frown far back in them.

'You haven't changed your mind?' he asked abruptly.

'No, I haven't changed my mind.'

'Ah, yes, you're a woman of your word, I remember.' He drew her close, looking intently into her face as though trying to divine something she hadn't told him.

She had the feeling that he couldn't find it, because the little frown between his eyes didn't abate. If anything it was more intense as he lowered his head so that his lips could touch her neck. She cupped his head instinctively, feeling how well it fitted there.

As his mouth moved persuasively over her skin his fingers were working on the fastening at the back of her dress. It whispered to the ground and she felt the cool night air against her skin.

But she herself couldn't be cool. She was already burning with need for him. Something that had started the day he walked into the department store and challenged her was about to come to fruition, and she would find whether she'd gambled everything on a false dream.

He tossed his jacket and shirt aside and took her into his arms. His kiss was gentle, almost everything held back until they knew each other a little better. Their other kisses had been fierce, antagonistic. Tonight, for the first time, they had time to kiss in peace, giving each other the benefit of leisurely exploration, no rush, no quarrelling, just a man and a woman free to think only of each other.

She tried not to think of all the other, cynical kisses his lips had bestowed, or she would grow too jealous. She wanted him all to herself, now and for ever. Her mouth told him so as she welcomed him inside, relishing the feel of his tongue exploring her, teasing and inciting her. His mouth was warm and persuasive, cajoling her into pleasure. She answered with her own lips and tongue, with movements she hadn't even known she knew, but which seemed to please him because he gave a little growl of pleasure and redoubled his onslaught.

She didn't know where her flimsy slip went, or how she came to be lying on the bed while he tossed aside the rest of his clothes and joined her, pulling her into his arms so that she felt his chest against her, as smooth as the marble of the statues that dotted this ancient island. He was part of it, part of a civilisation that went back almost to the dawn of time, but what she sensed in him now was timeless. Civilisations had arisen from it, yet it was uncivilised, primitive and thrilling.

Once before he'd seen her naked, but she hadn't known. Now she was in his arms again, and this time he was as naked as she, pressing her against his hard body while his hands roved over her. She explored him in turn, tentatively at first, then with growing confidence as she discovered how excitingly masculine he felt against her palms, the tautness of his muscles like sprung steel.

At some point he switched out the bedside lamp so that they were almost in darkness. Only a little light came from the great curtain-hung windows. It might have been any man holding her against him, caressing her body intimately with such skilful hands. But then she sensed the power tempered by gentleness in his embrace, felt the hard, muscular length of his thighs against her own, and knew that this could be no other man but Renato.

She felt his touch along the length of her inner thigh, seeking and finding the heart of her. Shockwaves of desire went through her as she waited for him. In the dim light she could see the gleam of his eyes. She thought they seemed troubled, almost hesitant.

'Renato...' she breathed.

'You're sure—tell me that you're sure—'

It was hard to speak through the tide of warmth engulfing her but she managed to whisper, 'I'm sure—I want you—'

The next moment the world was transformed into a different place as he slowly entered her, and she became his. But she had always been his. If she'd doubted it before she knew it now. She held him tightly, feeling the pleasure mount high and then higher until the world dissolved. Then she was nothing, only heat and darkness and whispered words that she didn't understand, except that they came from the man who had become one with her and made her one with him.

When it was over he didn't release her, but held on as though he was afraid she would slip away. But she didn't want to slip away. She wanted to stay here for ever. She fell easily into a sweet sleep, but awoke an hour later to find him watching her. He smiled and cradled her until she slept again. The last thought in her mind was the memory of his eyes, brooding, watching, never letting her go.

It was too late in the year for a honeymoon on the boat, so they went to the airport the next morning. Angie came with them. Bernardo was still implacable and she was going home. They saw her off to England before catching the flight to Rome. After that they were going on to Paris. It was partly a working trip, as they visited their biggest customers, but Heather enjoyed becoming part of the business. In Paris they toured the couturiers and she acquired a new wardrobe that she wore for entertaining Renato's customers in the evenings. French was one of the languages she'd studied, hoping to rise in Gossways, and she spoke it well enough to get by.

'I shall start getting suspicious,' Renato said as they got undressed in their suite at the Hyatt Regency. 'I keep getting too many compliments about *la belle Madame Martelli, très chic, très merveilleuse.*'

'I'm just trying to do you credit.'

'Hm!' His tone was deeply cynical and she chuckled. He was helping her off with a little black number she'd worn for the first time that night, but something provocative in her laugh made his hands move faster, more determinedly. The next moment the little black dress was lying in ruins on the floor and she was in his arms.

'Renato—'

'Shut up, I'll buy you another,' was the last thing he said before he silenced both of them. And in a few seconds the movement of his lips and hands had driven all else from her mind.

After their first lovemaking she had slipped easily into the rhythm of passion, so that she found herself wanting him at all times, day or night. At first her own eagerness embarrassed her slightly, but that soon passed, and with every day she learned something new about physical love.

She knew that she pleased him as much as he pleased her because nothing was too good for her. He rarely spoke of feelings, never his own. Nor did he often say a word to her that opened doors into his mind. But she had only to express a wish to have it granted.

Once he said a strange thing. As she sat looking at yet another gift of jewellery, he said abruptly, 'You think I overdo it, don't you?'

Thinking only to tease him she joked, 'Not at all. After all, you did once offer me twenty thousand to sleep with you.'

But she regretted it when she saw his brows snap. Renato wasn't without a sense of humour, but he found it hard to laugh at himself. He didn't vent his displeasure on her, but he grew quiet in a way she was learning meant that he was upset. And when she said, 'I was only teasing,' he brightened too quickly.

'Of course,' he said. 'I'm just in a strange mood. Where shall we eat?'

After which the subject was closed, despite all her efforts to raise it and put things right. Nor did she ever wear the jewellery because every time she tried he found fault with her appearance, until it had to be abandoned.

Jewellery was the least of it. Soon after they returned to Sicily she happened to mention the day she'd arrived, when he'd told her Lorenzo was soon flying to New York.

'I was going to turn my pea shooter onto you, but then you said I was going too, so I had to put my pea shooter away.'

'You fancied New York?'

'I'll say. That's one of the really annoying things about you—'

'Among so many—'

'Definitely—the way you take the wind out of my sails when I'm getting good and mad at you.'

They were in bed, relaxing after making love. He grinned at her, curled up in the crook of his arm. 'You enjoy getting mad at me, don't you?'

'It's one of my more enjoyable hobbies, yes.'

'Go on looking at me out of those glittering eyes. It gives me pleasurable thoughts and makes all the effort of landing you worth it.'

'Landing me? I'm not a fish.'

'But you were a challenge.'

'Yes, I know some of the devious methods you used. You were supposed to be persuading Gossways to take me back on the programme, but you never called them.'

Something in his silence told her the monstrous truth. 'It's worse than that, isn't it?' she demanded, sitting up sharply. 'You called some buddy among the big shots and made him promise *not* to have me back.'

'I admit nothing.'

'You don't need to….'

'You've got smoke coming out of your ears again.' He sat up and reached for her. 'Very pretty smoke, mind you….' The last words were muffled as she thumped him with a pillow hard enough to send him right off the bed. He grabbed her as he went, and they ended up on the floor together.

'I thought if I could make you mad enough with me—' he tried to explain as he grappled with her wriggling body '—you'd marry me just for the pleasure of—in my mother's charming phrase—kicking my shins every day. Ouch!'

'Oh, stop making a fuss. I only used my bare foot.'

She managed to get free and climb back onto the bed, but he followed her, pinning her down. She looked up at his face, furious, her breasts rising and falling. 'I'm warning you Renato, I'm good 'n' mad.'

'I know. I've just got a fresh bruise to prove it.'

'Let go of me.'

'When we've had a talk about this—' His eyes roved over her nakedness, and his speech slowed as though something had distracted him. 'It's—important to talk,' he said at last. 'That's what—' his gaze seemed riveted by the sight of her nipples, rosy and expectant '—that's what—good marriages—are made of—'

'Talking?' she said breathlessly.

'Confidence between—' his fingertips brushed one nipple '—husband and wife—trust—where was I?'

'Trust—' she gasped.

'Trust—and shared values—honour—'

'Honour? You? The most devious, conniving, manipulative— *Don't stop!*'

'I wasn't going to,' he whispered against her skin, continuing the work that had driven her half wild. After that there were no more words, no thoughts, just sensations, need and blinding nothingness. The end was explosive enough to blot out the world, leaving only heat and swirling darkness, and somewhere a man with strong arms and powerful loins to bring her joy.

In a sense that was just the trouble. There was joy, bliss, ecstasy, but not precisely happiness. Not unhappiness either, for how could any bride be unhappy with a husband who gave her all his attention and took her to new lands of sensation she'd never dreamed of before? But not to be unhappy wasn't the same as being happy. Especially when she realised that sometimes he would use their sexual harmony to distract her from subjects he wanted to avoid.

She never gave their conversation another thought until a week later he put the tickets for New York into her hands.

'What's this?' she gasped.

'Call it a second honeymoon.'

'But we've barely got back from our first.'

He shrugged. 'I have business in New York. Of course, if you don't want to come—' He reached for the tickets but she seized them and backed away, laughing.

They were in New York for a week, and although he looked in on the odd customer, it never seemed to Heather that this was a vital part of his schedule. She wondered if he'd done it only to please her, but while he murmured many passionate words when they were alone in the night, he never spoke a tender, loving word by day, and his manner, although pleasant, didn't invite her close. Sometimes it was like living with two men.

When they returned home she became more involved in the running of Bella Rosaria. She was wise enough to let Luigi keep the reins in his experienced hands, but subject to his advice she visited her tenants, discussed their problems, and began to make decisions. The revenues that came in were her own. Renato refused to make any claim on them, and even insisted on giving her a wife's allowance. She would have liked to refuse but didn't because she suspected that he would be hurt. It was no more than a suspicion, because she had to guess his feelings, but she sensed that she'd got this one right.

Because of his reticence she couldn't speak out about her fast growing feelings for him. She guessed that it had been growing for some time, but she only discovered its strength when he had to be away for a week. She wouldn't have thought it possible to miss one person so much. It wasn't just her senses that longed for Renato, but her heart craved him night and day. It was their first separation since their marriage and it was almost unbearable.

It was nothing like the gentle pleasure of loving Lorenzo, which now looked more like a feeble infatuation with every day that passed. This love was savage and all-powerful, wiping out lesser feelings, leaving her helpless and desperate.

Their reunion was overwhelming, and somehow she was sure she would find the moment to hint at her feelings and hear something about his own. But his most enthusiastic talk was of deals he had done, and there was something in his cheerfulness that kept her at a distance.

CHAPTER ELEVEN

As with any properly conducted business arrangement the terms of their marriage were adhered to on both sides. Renato had promised Heather a place in the firm, and one day she came home from shopping to find him regarding her with a teasing look.

'How would you like to take a trip for the firm?' he asked. 'I need someone to fix up some deals in Scotland.'

'But isn't that Lorenzo's territory? In fact he's in England right now—'

'He's got some unexpected problems that are going to keep him there,' Renato broke in hastily. 'If you take over Scotland it will ease the pressure on him.'

She was ambitious for the chance. Even so, her first thought had been, I'll have to be away from him. But Renato seemed delighted at the thought of her going.

Next day she was on a flight to Edinburgh. She booked into a newly opened luxury hotel on Princes Street, and spent the next few days selling Martelli produce all over the most exclusive parts of the city, including the hotel itself. Her trip was a triumphant success, but it was spoiled for her by a persistent ache of loneliness that wouldn't go away.

On the last day she called home just to hear his voice, but he was out and wouldn't be back that day. The violence of her disappointment almost winded her. She pulled herself together and went out to work, forcing herself to concentrate, and ending up with a full order book that she was eager to show Renato.

But she saw him a lot sooner than she expected.

Returning to the hotel, she was pulled up short by the sight of Renato and the manager sitting together in the bar. Her first reaction was stunned delight. They rose to greet her, all smiles, and her husband complimented her on the deal she'd done with the hotel.

'Your wife is a true Martelli, Renato,' the manager said. 'She drives a hard bargain.'

'And not only here,' Renato agreed. 'All over town, apparently.'

So that was it. Her brief hope that he'd been missing her died stillborn. He was here as a businessman, finding out the skills of his newest sales rep, 'all over town'.

While the manager was ordering drinks, Renato looked at her glowering face and observed, 'I'd hoped you'd be more pleased to see me.'

'I don't like being checked up on,' she muttered.

He seemed disconcerted, then pulled himself together. 'It's not exactly that—'

'I think it is,' she said with a sigh. 'I don't blame you, but let's drop it.'

No more was said. In the evening they were the manager's guests for dinner, and the two men toasted her. That night in their suite she displayed her order book and received her husband's wholehearted praise. She tried to look behind his eyes, but he wouldn't let her, and when he embraced her, smiling, and said, 'Let me show you just how pleased with you I am,' she stopped worrying about anything else but the delight to be found in his arms.

They stayed another two days, while she finalised her deals. He made a few suggestions but otherwise didn't interfere. On the last night they celebrated over a meal which they had served in their bedroom, 'for the sake of convenience,' as they both delicately put it. And when the time came they were glad there were only a few steps to travel.

As they lay languorously entwined in each other's arms afterwards he murmured, 'You're not really annoyed that I came here, are you?'

'I thought you had important business to see to?'

'What could be more important?'

'Ah, yes, I might have been losing money hand over fist, mightn't I?'

'You forget, I first met you as a demon saleswoman,' he reminded her lightly.

But this sparring wasn't enough for her. Surely now, when they lay so close, she could nudge him towards greater frankness?

'But what do we really know about each other?' she asked. 'In bed, a good deal. Outside, very little.'

'Nonsense. You know a lot about me. Devious, conniving, manipulative—I forget the other words you used but it sounds as though you know me very well. Besides—' he became serious, '—in bed a man and a woman find their greatest truth.'

'Yes,' she said wistfully, 'but not their only truth.'

'How much do you think the other truths matter?'

'Not much now, maybe. But later—as the years pass—'

'Leave the years to take care of themselves,' he said easily.

She made a cynical sound that would have been a snort if she hadn't been a lady. 'That from you—the man who has to plan everything years ahead.'

He didn't say anything for a while, but at last he asked in a strange voice, 'Are we talking about Lorenzo? I'd rather not, but if so, then yes, I admit it. I try to plan too much. Your marriage to him would have been a mistake.

I knew that the day we went out on the boat, but it was too late. What could I do? Seduce my brother's fiancée?'

'*Try* to seduce her,' she said firmly. 'Don't take it for granted that you'd have succeeded.'

He grunted. 'What would you like to bet against my chances?'

She thought of the sensations that had almost drowned her as he rubbed oil into her back. But more than that was the moment of tender understanding between them as she held his wrist and looked at the scar. No passion then. Just an alarmed awareness of each other as people with thoughts and feelings.

'Well?' he persisted. 'If I'd forgotten my honour that day, would you have forgotten yours?'

'It was different. I was in love with Lorenzo.'

'Love is a complication,' he agreed. 'Even when it's an illusion.'

She longed to remind him of his own words about love—'I believed in things I don't believe in now'—and ask if he still meant them. Surely their closeness must have made him feel differently? But her courage failed at the last moment.

'I guess we'll never know the truth,' she said lightly.

'Probably not. But I knew how badly I wanted you, and I kept my distance. When Lorenzo took flight I was secretly glad, except that after that you hated me. I couldn't blame you, but there seemed no way of approaching you.'

'If Mamma hadn't decided to arrange a marriage between us, would you have let me go away?'

'No,' he said simply. 'I wanted you.'

Wanted, she noted. Not loved.

'But when we talked you became angry,' he continued. 'She was the only one you would listen to.'

'You mean—you were behind it?'

'I knew what was in her mind. I could have discouraged her. I didn't.'

'But you hit the roof at the idea of marrying me.'

'Only after you roared with laughter. What did you expect me to say after that?'

She stared at him. It was on the tip of her tongue to demand, But why didn't you just *ask* me to marry you?

But she couldn't say it. It would reveal too much about her emotions, and she was safer not doing that with a man who kept his own emotions hidden.

And that, of course, was the answer. Renato wouldn't risk asking because it meant revealing himself. So he'd sought to negotiate a deal at arm's length.

Now she remembered something else he'd said. 'I would invite betrayal by expecting it.'

Not betrayal. She could never betray him. But withdrawal. A man who kept his heart hidden made it impossible for her to do anything else.

'So Mamma was acting as your emissary?' she asked lightly.

'After the way you'd been hurt, an impersonal approach seemed wiser.'

It was all so reasonable. She wanted to scream at how reasonable it was. Or maybe she just wanted to scream that he had so little to offer.

Baptista was her tower of strength. After the marriage she had never relinquished her role as intermediary.

'That's what I call it,' she observed one day as they sat together at Bella Rosaria, watching the rain. 'Some people would call it being an interfering mother-in-law.'

Heather smiled and squeezed her hand. 'You know better than that.'

'Before you there was no woman who could make him

stop and think, force him to forget his arrogance, and learn to trust and love again. So I ''acquired'' you because he needed you so much. But was I being selfish to you?'

'No, Mamma. We're very happy in many ways. And sometimes I can feel him wanting to reach out to me, but he always pulls back. How can I ever tell him that I love him?'

'Must it be told in words?'

'For me it must.'

'I think his feelings for you were coming alive since before your first ''wedding''. *Maria vergine*, how lucky we all were that Lorenzo had the good sense to abort it!'

'Lorenzo?' Heather echoed with a chuckle. 'Good sense?'

'He saw what needed doing to avert disaster, and he did it. How miserable you'd all be now if he hadn't! He's still rather irresponsible. But he's developing into an excellent and *sensible* young man.' She added with a twinkle, 'But don't tell him I said that.'

'I won't. Besides, if he became too sensible he wouldn't be Lorenzo. Now, Renato is all good sense. It's his driving force. He doesn't love me because he doesn't understand love. He understands need and want and acquisition. But he knows nothing about the heart.'

'You are mistaken,' her mother-in-law said firmly. 'He simply hasn't yet discovered that you matter to him more than anything else in the world. That will take time. Perhaps years.'

Heather said nothing, but in her heart she wondered if she could spend years waiting for what might never happen. She saw Baptista watching her, and knew that she wondered too.

*   *   *

Winter was passing, the rains eased off, leaving the soil rich and black for the spring sowing. Everywhere there was a sense of life renewing. Her first spring. Her first lambing. The harvest that was gathered in this year would be truly her harvest.

She was managing the estate well. Everyone said so, even Luigi, who really did the work of managing it.

'You at least can't be fooled,' she chided him.

'No fooling. You do well. You stand back and let me do my job. That's clever.'

Her revenues were excellent. She spent as Luigi advised, otherwise practised thrift, and built up such excellent credit with the bank that she was able to assist Renato through a minor cashflow problem. There was pleasure in that, but it was lessened by his insistence on paying her a proper rate of interest, 'to keep the books straight'. It was an entirely reasonable explanation, and she couldn't find the words to explain her irrational sadness.

These days she saw little of Lorenzo, whose job occupied him abroad almost permanently. His next visit to England coincided with Renato's departure to spend ten days in Rome. Renato didn't suggest that Heather should go with him.

She spent a couple of days at Bella Rosaria and returned to the Residenza to find that Baptista was out visiting friends, and not expected back until late. In her room she unpacked, trying to ignore the feeling of restlessness that had seized her. She chided herself for being ungrateful. She had everything—almost everything that she could want. But it seemed that all the world was waking to new life and she alone was going nowhere.

From her bedroom window she could see the sea, almost as far as the harbour and the *Santa Maria*, the boat on which she'd first known danger: not the danger of nearly drowning, but the first stirrings of desire and emotion for her fiancé's brother.

How terrible everything would have been if the wedding had gone ahead. Baptista had been right about that. For she no longer believed that making love with Lorenzo would have deadened her to Renato. It would have done the opposite. The more she'd discovered about physical passion, the more she would have craved the man who could make passion absolute for her. And that would not have been Lorenzo.

Instead she was married to the man she wanted, perhaps loved.

She sighed, realising that there was always a perhaps. She was holding back, refusing to admit to herself that she loved a man she wasn't sure was capable of love. Renato lived his life on very precise terms. What he wanted, he found a way to have. Just now he wanted her, and in bed he was as pleased with their bargain as she was herself. But that wasn't love. She'd told Baptista that he knew nothing about the heart. She still feared that was true. And while she believed it, she couldn't open her own heart to him.

There was a knock on her door. It was Sara the maid returning some ornaments she'd taken for washing. As she was laying them out the phone rang on the bedside table.

'Hello,' Heather said, snatching it up. 'Lorenzo?'

He sounded strange and troubled. 'Heather, are you alone?'

'No, just a moment.' She signalled to Sara to leave. 'All right, I'm alone now.'

'I need to talk to you—but Renato mustn't know.' His voice became urgent. 'Nobody must know.'

'Lorenzo, what is it?'

'I want you to come to London.'

'What?'

'I need you. Please, it's important. There are things I—please, Heather, *please*—'

The words poured out of him, frantic, desperate, and her refusal died on her lips.

'All right,' she said at last. 'I'll get the next plane. With luck I should be with you tonight.'

She found her passport and put a few things into an overnight bag, relieved that Baptista's absence gave her the chance to leave without answering questions.

She found Sara and said casually, 'I'll be back tomorrow, or maybe the next day.' Then she got out quickly. She couldn't tell the truth about where she was going or why.

Renato wasn't due home for a week, but the following afternoon he threw the house in turmoil by arriving early, striding into the house like a man with no time to waste. He was smiling, picturing his wife's face at seeing him early, and hearing that he'd abandoned a week's work to return to her. Perhaps she would even relax the slight distance he still felt she kept between them.

'*Amor mia,*' he called, throwing open the door to their bedroom. 'Where are you?'

The room was empty. He shrugged and went quickly downstairs. She would be on the terrace, probably talking with his mother. Or perhaps she was at the estate. Why had he gone first to their bedroom? He grinned, knowing full well why.

'Sara, where is my wife?'

The maid paused as she crossed the hall. She looked worried.

'I don't know, *signore*. Signor Lorenzo called yesterday, and after that she left in a great hurry.'

'Did she say where she was going?'

'No, *signore*. Only that she would be back today, or perhaps tomorrow.'

'Where is my mother?'

'Lying down in her room.'

He opened Baptista's door quietly, but she was sound asleep. He would have to bear his soul in patience. But the question went round and round in his head. What could Lorenzo have said to make Heather leave so quickly?

Renato went to his study and tried to settle to work. For an hour he managed more or less well. At least, he thought he was managing well. Then he put the phone down on a long conversation and realised that he couldn't remember a word of it. After that he gave up and called Lorenzo in London.

Lorenzo wasn't staying at the Ritz this time but at a newly opened luxury hotel that the firm was hoping to supply. As soon as the phone was answered Renato said, 'Lorenzo Martelli's room, please.'

'I'm sorry sir, but Mr Martelli checked out a few hours ago.'

Renato sat up straight. 'This morning? I understood he was there for a week.'

'So did we, sir. But after Mrs Martelli arrived yesterday they decided to leave early.'

'Mrs—Martelli? Do you mean the young English lady?'

'That's right. Mrs Heather Martelli. They checked out of their room this morning.'

The blow over the heart almost winded him. He didn't know how he managed to replace the phone. All the nerves seemed to have died in his hands, and his body was cold with shock.

He ought to have seen this coming. He'd always known that Lorenzo still lingered in her heart, but he'd charged ahead, arranging things as he wanted, as he always did, only to see them disintegrate in his hands.

Suddenly he couldn't breathe. It was like being caught in an avalanche with snow swirling around you from the back, the sides, the top—no way of stopping it—and then it froze solid about you.

He wanted to howl and fight his way out, but he was trapped, unable to move because he didn't know which move was the right one. He only knew that he wanted to turn time back to before this nightmare started. And he couldn't.

His wife had betrayed him with his brother. Thinking he would be away for another week, she'd hurried back to England to be with Lorenzo.

No, it was impossible. If it came out it would break Baptista's heart, and Heather would never do that to her. Renato tried to tell himself that she would never do it to *him*, but somehow the words wouldn't come.

It was impossible because of the kind of person she was, honest, decent, incapable of deceit. But only recently she'd said to him, 'What do you and I know of each other? In bed, everything. Outside, nothing.'

He was brought out of his reverie by the sound of a car drawing up outside. Moving like an automaton, he went out, and was in time to see the taxi door open and his brother emerge, looking dishevelled. Lorenzo, the dandy who would agonise over the perfect tie, was unshaven and his clothes looked rumpled.

He met Renato's eyes, made a helpless gesture, indicating that he couldn't face talking now, and went into the house.

'I need a shower,' he declared, and passed on up the stairs.

Renato made a gesture for Heather to join him in his study. As she walked past him he could hear his heart hammering. His whole life hung on the next few moments, what he would ask and what she would answer.

'What are you doing back so early?' she asked.

'Never mind that. Where in damnation have you been?'

Riled by his tone, she retorted crisply, 'I've been to London.'

'Without telling anyone where you were going, or why.'

'There were very good reasons for that.'

'I'll bet there were.'

Something in his voice made her look at him sharply. 'Be careful, Renato. I'm tired and I'm out of patience. If you've got something to say, say it.'

'Very well. Did you spend last night in his room?'

Heather stared at him in amazement. 'What—?'

'Answer me, damn you! Did you spend last night in Lorenzo's room?'

Her eyes flashed with temper. 'Yes,' she said. 'What are you accusing me of?'

'It's plain enough, isn't it? You always clung onto your image of him, no matter what he did. You're a fool, and I was a fool to marry you.'

'Well, nobody forced you to,' she cried. 'You were the one who insisted on this marriage.'

'Yes, and I'm well repaid for it. I thought you were the most wonderful woman in the world. I thought all beauty and honour lived in you—the one true and honest woman in a world of greedy deceivers. I knew you didn't love me when we married but we had time and I let myself believe—but the minute my back was turned you go to him—to his room, to his bed.'

'Renato—'

'Did you sleep in his bed?'

'Yes,' she yelled.

It was only now that he knew how desperately he'd longed to hear her deny it. It was undeniable, but surely she would find a way to make the terrible truth untrue. There was a roaring in his ears. It was like suffering the agonies of death, except that he stayed alive and died again and again.

Renato was a Sicilian. In this society a faithless wife could cause a blood feud that could last a century. But the only thought in his mind was to implore her to take back her words, let it be as it was before, let him believe in her again. Because if she was a deceiver then nothing in the world was worth anything.

'Do you know what you've just said?' he asked hoarsely. 'No, don't answer.' He held up an arm as if to ward her off. 'Perhaps it was time you said it. Or perhaps I should have listened long ago, when you tried to tell me there was no hope for me. But I'm not good at hearing what it doesn't suit me to hear, as you've often mentioned.'

'Renato—what are you saying?'

He gave a bark of mirthless laughter. 'I'm saying I give in. You've won—you and that boy who's wound himself around your heart so tightly that I can't find a way in. If you want him you can have him. I'll make it easy for you.'

'You mean—you'd free me to marry Lorenzo?'

'What else can I do?'

'What about Mamma?'

'She'll be all right if she sees that I'm perfectly happy about it.'

'And are you—perfectly happy?'

He didn't answer her in words but the truth was there in his eyes. He was dying inside.

'You survived something like this,' he said quietly. 'Maybe you can teach me how.'

'But—happy?'

'That isn't your concern any more. We could have been happy. Or at least I thought we could. I loved you, and I thought in time I could win your love. I hadn't reckoned on your heart being so stubborn and awkward. Why do you think I used my mother as an intermediary? Because I knew it was too soon for you to have got over him. If I'd approached you myself, talking of love, it would only have driven you off further.'

'But you knew—I mean there were things between us even then—'

'Yes, desire, not love. Sometimes I felt you wanted me, but with your body, not your heart. That wasn't mine, and if only you knew how much I wanted it, to have you look at me as I'd seen you look at him. I tried to keep it businesslike, not to alarm you, but that day in the temple—well—' He sighed. 'I couldn't always stick to my good intentions. And all the time I loved you so desperately that I thought you'd see and understand. But you never saw, because you never wanted to. It was all Lorenzo with you.

'We talked, once, about our day on the boat and what might have happened. You said you'd been in love with him, and I said love was a complication even when it was an illusion. If you knew how hard I prayed for you to say then that your love for him had been an illusion. I was holding my breath, willing you to say it—but you didn't. And I suppose I knew the truth.'

His face was as bleak as a winter's day, and for the first time his eyes weren't closed to her, but open, defenceless, letting her see the suffering man within. She put her hand out but he flinched away from it. She couldn't speak. Everything in her was concentrated on hearing what he would say next.

'I should have let you go then,' he said at last, 'and this wouldn't have needed to happen. Well, it's happened. I brought it on myself, and I make no complaint.'

'I don't believe it's you I'm hearing say all this,' she breathed.

'No? Well, I've been unlike myself since I knew you.' He took a shuddering breath. 'I'll make it easy for you, but go quickly. I'm not sure how long I can keep this up.'

'Renato—'

'For God's sake go!' His face was livid. 'Get out of here, and *never let me see you again.*'

CHAPTER TWELVE

SHE took a step towards him. 'I'm not going anywhere. You're my husband and I love you, and I'm staying right here with you.'

'Don't play games with me,' he said hoarsely. 'You've already told me that you slept with him.'

'I said no such thing. I've said that I slept in Lorenzo's bed last night—' in her eagerness she seized his arms and gave him a little shake '—but I didn't say that Lorenzo was there with me.'

'What?' he whispered.

His wretchedness made her heart ache. 'Oh, darling!' She touched his face. 'What a fool you are! While I was sleeping in Lorenzo's bed, *he* was sleeping in a police cell.'

'What—did—you—say?'

'He wasn't with me. He spent the night *under lock and key*, sleeping on a bunk, with a blanket. Why do you think he looks as if he's slept in his clothes? Because he has.'

He stared at her as her words pierced his cloud of misery. And suddenly the sun shone more brilliantly, the steeple bells rang and the trumpets sounded a fanfare.

'A police cell?' he echoed, as though repeating her words was all he could do.

'He called me yesterday from a police station in London. He'd been arrested for driving under the influence and taking a swipe at a policeman. I figured I'd better get over there fast. Mamma was out and I thought the

175

fewer people who knew about it the better, so I just caught the first plane to London.

'I arrived yesterday evening and went straight to the station, but I couldn't get him out because they were afraid he'd skip the country. So he had to spend the night in the cell. I stayed in his hotel room. It seemed silly to pay for another when his was empt—'

She was silenced by the crushing pressure of his mouth on hers. There were no words for the feelings that possessed them. For each the declaration of love had come in the unlikeliest way, catching them unawares, trapping them into admissions that their pride might have made impossible for years. Joy, triumph and blazing, overwhelming relief mingled in their kiss, lighting up the world.

'Tell me it's true,' he said against her mouth. 'Promise me that I won't wake up in a minute—kiss me—kiss me—'

'It's all true, I swear it. I never slept with Lorenzo.'

'No, not that—the other thing you said—about loving me—'

'I do love you, Renato. There's nobody I want but you. But I never thought you'd say you love me.'

'Does a man go insane for a woman, the way I have, unless he loves her?'

'You always had so many good reasons that were nothing to do with love.'

'Fool's reasons. I swore I'd never let a woman matter that much to me again. And then I met you, but it was already too late because you loved another man. I had to tell myself anything except that I loved you.' He kissed her fiercely again and again. 'I've been so afraid...'

Lost in happiness, she was only vaguely aware that she was moving, climbing, somehow they were upstairs. The sudden sound was the door of their bedroom being kicked shut then their clothes being hastily torn off as they reached feverishly for each other.

They made love like people who'd met for the first time. There was pleasure, but also relief and reassurance. Above all there was boundless hope. Only a few minutes ago the future hadn't existed. Now it stretched to infinity, full of joy and fulfilment.

'I suppose we ought to get up,' Heather said at last, reluctantly. 'Mamma will be awake, and she'll wonder why Lorenzo is home. I wonder what he's telling her. We must find out and make sure we don't give him away.'

'You wrong Lorenzo,' Renato said at once. 'He'll tell her the truth. Whatever else you can say about him—and you can say a good deal—he's honest.'

'Yes. Do you realise how much we owe his honesty?'

But Renato didn't answer, and she realised that his wounds were still raw, and he had some way to go yet.

'Tell me the rest of the story,' he said at last. 'What happened? Did you spring him from gaol? Are the two of you on the run?'

'Luckily, desperate measures weren't needed. I got him a lawyer, and first thing this morning he was up before the magistrate. It wasn't very serious. He was only a little bit over the limit, and there was no accident, nobody hurt.'

'What about assaulting the policeman?'

'It was just a little swipe. He barely touched him. He was fined and bound over to keep the peace. I know he has a lot of appointments in England but I thought I'd better get him back here quickly.'

'You did the right thing. I won't send him back for a while. But somebody has to visit his customers, and you're the best person. You did brilliantly on that Scottish trip—'

'Brilliantly? You were breathing down my neck— checking up on me—'

He kissed her. 'It's nice to know I'm not the only fool in the family. I went to Scotland because I couldn't stand being apart from you another day.'

She snuggled against him, wondering if Lorenzo's proximity in England might also have had something to do with it. But she didn't ask. She no longer needed to.

'So there it is,' he murmured, 'the last piece in that jigsaw you were talking about. We fit it exactly.'

'It's odd, I'm not quite sure—' She brooded.

'If we love each other, what else can there be?'

'I don't know. It's just that I have an odd feeling that there are still two pieces missing.'

'Forget it,' he said, holding her tightly. 'We've found each other. I'd nearly given up hope of that happening.'

She let it go and snuggled against him, revelling in her happiness. But the thought wouldn't be entirely dismissed that the jigsaw wasn't quite complete.

Two pieces to go.

She made the trip to England and returned to be plunged into the preparations for Baptista's birthday party, to be given in the Great Hall of the Residenza.

'We can kill two birds with one stone,' Renato said to her one evening. 'You know I've been thinking of branching out into flowers. There are some that we grow here better than anywhere else in the world, and it's an area you might take charge of.'

'I'd love to,' she said eagerly.

'Then you should start meeting some of the specialist growers. 'I'm especially interested in this man,' he said, handing her a business card bearing the name Vincenzo Tordone. 'He has acres of greenhouses that can supply

everything in winter. I'd like you to look him over and
let me know what you think. If his stuff is high quality
we can use him to fill the house with flowers on Mamma's
birthday, and set up a deal afterwards.'

Pleased, Heather visited Vincenzo Tordone in his office
in Palermo. He was a tall, thin man in his late sixties,
with white hair and a gently courteous manner that won
her over at once. He took her on a visit to his glass-
covered acres just outside the city, and she marvelled at
the variety of perfect blooms that flourished under his
hands.

'I have a business in Rome,' he told her as they sipped
Marsala afterwards. 'It's a good business. My wife was
Roman, and when she was alive she helped me to run it.
Now she's dead I've handed the reins to my son and
daughter, and returned to my home.'

'You're Sicilian, then?'

'Oh, yes. I was born in this country, and lived here
until my twenties. One day I shall die and be buried here.'
He sighed with pleasure. 'This is the best land in the
world to grow plants. There's nowhere so fertile, nowhere
else where the flowers raise their heads so eagerly.'

He made her talk about herself, and she gave a carefully
edited description of how she had come from England and
ended up marrying into the Martelli family.

'Do you find our ways strange?' he asked courteously.

'Not really. Everyone has been so kind, especially my
mother-in-law, Baptista. She took me under her wing right
from the start. She even gave me her own estate of Bella
Rosaria.'

'Ah, yes, I've heard of it—who has not? They say the
flowers there are very fine.'

'They are, especially the rose bushes. Some of them

have been there for years. She tends and protects them like children.'

They plunged into a discussion of the best way to make rose bushes long-lasting. She liked the simple old man, and when she got home it was a pleasure to be able to tell Renato honestly that his blooms were first-rate. The deal was duly signed, covering the export of his produce both from Sicily and Rome, with a separate deal covering the provision of flowers for the party.

On the day Baptista spent the afternoon asleep, so as to be at her best for the evening. She rose bright-eyed and cheerful and sat calmly while her maid arrayed her in pearls. When Renato and Heather looked in, she took his hand and said in a pleading voice, 'My son, this may be my last birthday on earth—'

'Mamma, you say that every year,' he reminded her tenderly.

'And it's true every year. But this year there is one special gift that I long for above all others.'

'It's yours if it's in my power.'

'If I could believe that there is truly no more bad blood between you and your brother—'

'Believe it. That was over long ago.'

Baptista smiled, but Heather sensed that she had hoped for something more.

There was a knock on the door, and Bernardo and Lorenzo entered, one carrying wine, the other glasses, to toast their mother privately before the festivities began.

When they had all saluted her Baptista half rose to go, but Renato said, 'Stay a moment. I have another toast.' When he was sure he had everyone's attention he said, 'I drink to my brother, Lorenzo, to whose courage and honesty I owe my happiness. I made a terrible mistake that almost destroyed three lives. When we went to the cathedral, all three of us knew that that marriage ought never to take place. But it seemed too late. The juggernaut was grinding on and nobody knew how to stop it. Only one person found the nerve to halt it in its tracks. My brother, you gave me the woman I love, and for this I thank you with all my heart.'

'And so do I,' Heather said happily.

Baptista was weeping with joy. Lorenzo looked about to sink with embarrassment. Renato set down his glass and seized him in a bear hug while Bernardo thumped them both on the back.

'Thank you,' Heather whispered when Renato had returned to her.

'I should have said it long ago.'

One piece down and one to go.

It was time for the party to begin. As Baptista descended on Renato's arm, to applause from the assembled guests, the profusion of blooms made her stop and gasp with pleasure.

'They are so beautiful, my dears,' she said as she settled in the throne-like chair from which she would preside over the evening. 'Thank you.'

'There is one more thing,' Renato said. 'The man who arranged all this would like to offer you his own congratulations, with a special gift.'

'That is very kind of him.'

'But—' Renato looked a little uncertain. 'Mamma, are you strong enough for a little shock—if it is a happy one?'

'Certainly. You have prepared me. Is Signor Tordone going to give me a shock?'

'I think he just might.'

Renato nodded and a servant opened the door. Through

it came the tall figure of Vincenzo. He walked calmly towards Baptista, never taking his eyes from her.

Nor did she take her eyes from him. As Heather watched she half rose from her seat, then fell back with a little gasp. Her hand flew to her throat as Vincenzo came to stand before her, holding in his hand one perfect red rose.

Baptista didn't seem to see it. All her attention was for the old man's face, and at last a glad cry broke from her.

'Fede!' she said in joyful disbelief. *'Fede!'*

'I don't believe it!' Heather gasped. 'That can't be—'

'It is,' Renato grinned. 'His real name is Federico Marcello. My grandfather was a fearsome character, but never quite the monster people thought. He drove Federico out of Sicily with threats and ordered him to change his name so that Mamma couldn't trace him. But then he arranged for friends to help him get started in his own business, and put quite a lot of work his way.'

'But how did you find him?'

'I set a private enquiry agent onto it. He traced him to Rome and then all the way back here. I was fairly sure who he was when you went to see him, but when you told me about the talk you had, that clinched it.'

'But why didn't you tell me?'

Renato gave her a strange look. 'Perhaps I wanted to surprise you, too. I wonder if I have.'

'Yes,' she said slowly. 'I thought I knew you, but I never imagined that you could think of this.'

He touched her cheek gently. 'It takes a lifetime to know someone, my dearest.'

'And we have a lifetime,' she whispered.

'Do we?'

'Yes. I wasn't sure. But I am now.'

Her heart rejoiced at what she had discovered tonight.

Renato was a proud, difficult man, who would never be easy to live with. But he understood things about love that even she had never dreamed of. This hadn't been only to please his mother. It had also been to prove something to herself that he couldn't have explained in words.

Something caught in her throat as she saw Baptista and Fede sitting side by side, their hands entwined. Moving very quietly, she and Renato crept close enough to hear.

'I returned to Sicily to be close to you,' Fede was saying. 'But I never dared to hope that you would recognise me.'

'I knew you at once,' Baptista said through her joyful tears.

'And I would have known you anywhere. You are just as you have lived in my heart, all these years.'

'All these years.' She said the words slowly. 'And yet I hope you haven't been alone. I would rather think of you having a good life, even without me.'

'Then think it,' Fede said firmly. 'My wife was a wonderful woman. She gave me two fine children, and while she lived we were devoted.' His voice changed. 'But it was not with her as it had been with you.'

'Yes,' Baptista murmured. 'Yes, that's just how it was.'

He kissed her hand. 'We have done our duty to others. Now we may think of ourselves for the time that is left.'

The last guest had gone. The house was quiet as Renato and Heather, arms entwined, climbed the stairs in the semi-darkness.

'They really mean it,' Heather said in wonder. 'When they look at each other they see what used to be.'

'Or maybe they see what truly is,' Renato suggested. 'They see a truth that years and wrinkles can never change.'

'Will it be like that with us?'

'I can only speak for myself. And I tell you that no other woman will ever hold my heart. If you were to die tomorrow I would live alone for the rest of my life, rather than try to replace you. I think Mamma and Fede were each right to marry other people. That's the sensible way. But I can't be sensible where you're concerned. Without you, my life would be only a long wait until we could be together again.'

'And I—'

'Hush!' He laid a gentle hand over her lips. 'Don't say it unless it's true.'

'Do you think my love is less than yours?'

'I don't ask. It doesn't matter. As long as you love me a little. Where you are concerned, I have never been as proud as I seemed. I can live on crumbs.'

It was true. His pride was gone, replaced by a trust in his beloved that made pride needless. She saw it in his eyes, heard it in the gentleness of his voice.

'Not crumbs,' she whispered. 'But a feast.' She took his hand, led him to their room and opened the door. 'Come,' she said as she drew him inside. 'Let me tell you about it.'

The last piece in place.

Lying quietly in her bed that night, Baptista listened until she heard the sound of two sets of footsteps climbing the stairs and going along the corridor. They moved slowly, as if the owners were drifting contentedly, their arms about each other. Outside Heather and Renato's room they stopped. Baptista's sharp ears caught the soft murmur of voices, then the click as the door opened, and another one as it closed.

She smiled to herself in the darkness. She had been

right all along. When her time came, she could go in peace, knowing that her son had found deep, lasting love.

But perhaps her time wouldn't come so soon after all. She had much to live for, including the child that Heather was carrying. Not that Heather knew yet, but she, Baptista knew. A grandson would be nice, but perhaps a little girl would be better. A girl, to wind herself around her father's heart and teach him about love.

And yet, already he'd shown that he knew more about true love than either his mother or his wife had guessed. Who would have imagined that it would be Renato who brought Fede back to her, that he would have understood…?

However much time she had left, Fede would be there. He had promised to visit her every day, and they would sit together talking, or just holding hands. Like hers his body was aged and his face wrinkled, but she had looked into his eyes and known that he was still Fede.

This she owed to Renato, who'd been rescued from harshness and cynicism by the one woman who'd known how to reach him.

And then there was Bernardo, her son and yet not her son, a man with a wild, dark heart that allowed nobody inside. She thought of Angie, the young English woman who had loved him but been defeated by his pride. At least, men called it pride. Baptista called it stupidity. Angie might have saved him. In fact, she still might if certain plans of Baptista's worked out as she meant them to.

A knowing gleam came into her eye. Death could wait until she was ready. There were things to do. Arrangements to make. Heads to knock together. She was feeling stronger every moment….

Kate Walker was born in Nottinghamshire but as she grew up in Yorkshire she has always felt that her roots were there. She met her husband at university and she originally worked as a children's librarian, but after the birth of her son she returned to her old childhood love of writing. When she's not working, she divides her time between her family, their three cats, and her interests of embroidery, antiques, film and theatre, and, of course, reading.

Watch out for Kate Walker's sexy and intense new story:
THE SPANIARD'S INCONVENIENT WIFE
On sale December 2004, in Modern Romance™!

THE HIRED HUSBAND
by
Kate Walker

CHAPTER ONE

'YOU want *what*?'

His expression said it all, Sienna reflected unhappily. He didn't have to speak a single word. Shock, disbelief and sheer antipathy to her suggestion were stamped clearly onto Keir Alexander's hard features, leaving her in no doubt as to how he felt.

'You want what?' he repeated now, the edge in his voice sharpening on every word as his deep brown eyes glared into her anxious blue-green ones.

'I—I want you to marry me.'

It sounded so much worse the second time around. Starker, more incredible, more impossible. She couldn't believe she'd ever had the nerve to ask him once, let alone manage to reiterate her request in the face of his reaction.

If she could have taken it back she would have done so at once, but she had no alternative. She'd tried every other approach, considered every possible answer, but none of them would work. It was Keir or no one. He was her last chance; and if he didn't agree to help her then she was lost. Finished.

'No way, lady!' It was hard, inflexible, adamant. 'No way at all.'

'But—'

'I said *no*!'

'But, Keir...'

But she was talking to the back of his head, and a moment later to empty air as the door slammed to behind him. Keir had walked out on her, rejecting her and her proposal outright, not even sparing her a backward glance. Closing her

5

eyes in despair, her sigh a deep, helpless sound of defeat, Sienna sank down into the nearest chair.

So what did she do now? she asked herself, shaking her dark head despondently. There was nothing she *could* do. No answer presented itself. No fairy godmother appeared to wave her magic wand and put everything right. When she opened her eyes everything was the same as before, the future stretching ahead dark, bleak and with no light at the end of the tunnel.

It had been the worst year of her life so far, and it was still only July. First Dean, and then the loss of her job as an aromatherapist when the beauty salon in which she had worked had closed down. That had been followed by the discovery that her mother, who had clearly been unwell for some time, was in fact suffering from multiple sclerosis. And then, to cap it all, the landlord who owned the small flat she and her mother rented had informed them that he was selling the building. The new owners planned to turn it into a set of offices and they would have to move out— soon.

Oh, it wasn't fair! Sienna slammed one fist into the palm of the other hand in a gesture of frustration and distress. Her mother had to have a home. Somewhere she could live in the comfort and security she needed. The perfect place was available—was hers for the asking. But only if she could meet the conditions laid down. And with Keir's rejection of her proposal her last chance of doing that had been destroyed. She doubted if she would ever see him again.

She didn't know how long she sat there, lost in her misery. She had no idea how much time had passed before the sound of the doorbell pealing through her flat jolted her out of her unhappy reverie. At first she was tempted to ignore it, but when it became obvious that whoever was outside had put their finger firmly on the button and intended keeping it there until they got a response, she forced herself to her feet, dashing down the stairs and wrenching open the door.

She couldn't believe the sight that met her eyes. Keir Alexander stood on the doorstep, dark head held high, his jaw tight, every muscle in his tall, strong body taut with resistance.

'All right,' he said, his voice cold and hard as a sharpened knife. 'Start talking—convince me.'

Sienna talked as she never had in her life before. She couldn't believe that she'd been given a second chance, but she was going to grasp it with both hands, do everything she could—*anything* she could—to ensure it didn't get away from her.

'I know this isn't the way either of us would have done this,' she began, even as they were still climbing the stairs to the first floor where she and her mother lived. 'Not in an ideal world, anyway. It's certainly not the way I ever dreamed of marrying, but beggars can't be choosers. It's the only way I can think of for getting out of a very tight corner indeed, and if you don't agree to help then there's no one else I can turn to.'

She couldn't look at him as she led him into the small sitting room that he had stormed out of such a short time before, painfully conscious of the fact that it was only a few short weeks since the first occasion on which he'd visited her home. Just two months or so since the party at which they'd met.

'You know how ill my mother is—and that it can only get worse. I need to find somewhere for us to live so that I can look after her properly, so...'

'So naturally you want your father's house?' Keir put in harshly.

'Yes.'

Sienna's voice was low and shaken, still carrying the echoes of the way she had felt when a solicitor had contacted her out of the blue. She had been stunned to discover that her father, the man who had abandoned her mother before Sienna had even been born, had had a belated attack of conscience and decided to acknowledge her as his daughter.

As his wife had died some years before, and he had had no other children, he had left her everything he owned in his will. But there was a catch.

'If my—if Andrew Nash hadn't left me all that money, I don't know what I'd have done. And if he hadn't put in the condition, then I wouldn't be forced to involve you in this.'

At last she turned to face Keir, her heart quailing as she saw the heavy lids that hooded his eyes, hiding his thoughts from her. His hands were pushed deep into the pockets of his dark trousers, his shoulders stiff, his very stance declaring hostility and opposition to everything she said.

'The condition being that you have to be married, I presume?'

'That's right. In his letter he said that he'd lived his life wishing he'd chosen differently all those years ago. That he'd realised too late that the love my mother and I could have brought him as a family was more important than the wealth he kept by staying with his wife. And so he made it a prerequisite of my inheritance that I had to be married— happily married—before I could inherit.'

'*Happily* married,' Keir echoed cynically. 'And who's to be the judge of that?'

'My...'

Sienna couldn't get her tongue round the word 'uncle'. After twenty-five years of believing she had no family at all, it was too much to accept that she now had an uncle, particularly one who held her future so securely in his hands.

'His brother, Francis Nash, is to have the final say in seeing that his wishes are carried out. But he knows nothing about me. He's never even seen me. It shouldn't be too hard to—to convince him that... that...'

'That you and I are madly in love and desperate to get married?' Keir finished for her when she couldn't complete the sentence.

'That's right.' It was barely more than a whisper and once more her eyes skittered away from the coldly assessing stare that fixed her like a specimen on a laboratory slide, awaiting analysis. 'W-would you like a drink? There's wine…'

'I think I'd better keep a clear head for this,' Keir returned dismissively. 'I wouldn't want anything to muddle my thinking.'

Did that mean he was actually *considering* the idea? Sienna didn't dare to allow the thought to enter her mind.

'So you want me to play the devoted groom?'

He made it sound like the most repellent task possible. As if he would rather put a gun to his head—anything other than what she had asked of him.

'To lie? Don't you know that lies have a nasty habit of breeding more lies? Before you've time to think you're tangled up in them so tightly that you can't get free and they're dragging you down…'

'But we're not going to lie! Not really. People already know us as a couple. We've been seen out together often enough. It wouldn't be all that different from what we have now. It *wouldn't*!' she declared vehemently when he expressed his disagreement in a harsh sound of disbelief. 'You're here almost every night as it is. What if I'd asked you to move in with me?'

'I'd think you were taking a lot for granted, lady.'

'Keir, it's only supposition!' Desperately Sienna tried to make up the ground she realised she'd lost. 'We both know that our relationship isn't on that sort of footing—that it will probably never be. But we're the only ones who know that. And what we do have is good, isn't it?'

Keir's stony face gave her no encouragement and it was all that she could do not to give up in despair.

' If we decided to say, after a year, that we knew it wasn't working, then we could split—both go our own ways—and it wouldn't matter. There'd be no frayed ends, no regrets, no complications.'

'But this arrangement comes weighed down with complications,' Keir pointed out with cold reason. 'It can't not do that. A marriage certificate complicates things, darling.'

'But it's only a temporary solution, you must see that!' she pleaded with him. 'It won't mean anything to either of us, so you needn't worry about getting trapped in something you don't want! There'll be no commitment beyond that one year—just a twelve month period and then we'll go our separate ways.'

'You make it sound so simple…'

'It *is* simple! It couldn't be anything else. After all, it's not as if you're madly in love with me, or vice versa. And…'

Her voice faded into silence as Keir snatched his hand away from her and moved to stare out of the window, affecting an intent interest in the cars going by in the street.

'It might work,' he said slowly.

Was it possible that he was going to agree? Sienna was past knowing whether she hoped for his agreement or feared it dreadfully. She was so caught up in her own disturbed thoughts at the prospect that she jumped like a startled cat when he suddenly whirled round to face her.

'And what, exactly, would I get out of the deal? Because I presume you were going to offer me something—some remuneration for my co-operation, some compensation for the loss of my freedom by entering into this agreement.'

'Of course.'

Sienna swallowed hard. She had expected this. Had known it must come inevitably. But she hadn't thought he would be quite so cold-blooded about it.

You fool! her heart reproached her. What had she expected? That he would declare that of course he would do it, that he would do whatever she wanted and not expect anything in return?

Of course not. She had known she would have to offer Keir something in exchange for his agreement to help her out. It was just that she hadn't been prepared for the way his demand made her feel that it was that compensation that mattered and not her.

'So?' Keir prompted harshly when she couldn't find the voice to answer him.

'You—you remember what you told me about the shares in Alexander's?'

She had been frankly surprised that he had opened up about so much of his life to her. Keir was the sort of man who kept things very much to himself, limiting the conversation only to uncomplicated, unemotional topics that didn't call for much involvement on either part.

But just three nights earlier he had revealed something of the problems he had been having with the haulage and transportation company of which he was part owner and managing director. Problems that had been caused by his stepmother, his late father's second wife.

Alexander's was a family firm. Originally owned by Keir's father, Don, it had been an ailing, small-scale enterprise when, at twenty-one and fresh from university, Keir had taken it by the scruff of the neck and dragged it forcibly into the late twentieth century. In the following twelve years he had turned it into a huge international success. It was now impossible to travel anywhere in Europe or beyond without seeing one of Alexander's distinctive red and green vehicles somewhere *en route*.

'Did you manage to raise the amount you needed to buy your stepmother out?'

Keir's expression gave her the answer before he spoke, a dark cloud of anger shadowing his face.

'I raised it, but then she upped the stakes again. She says she has another potential buyer in the offing. If that sale goes through then Alexander's as a family firm will cease to exist.'

'And that's so important to you?'

The look her turned on her scorched her from head to toe with its impatient contempt for the stupidity of her question.

'Alexander's is mine, Sienna—*mine*! I'm not prepared to see it the subject of some hostile take-over and swallowed up, becoming just part of another company. I promised my father that, and I'll keep my promise if it kills me.'

'But if your stepmother keeps asking for more?'

Keir's scowl was blacker than ever.

'She knows how much I've invested in modernising things—buying new vehicles, computers, everything over the past year. Given time, that investment will pay off, several hundredfold, but right now it's stretched me to my limit. And Lucille knows that, damn her!'

'How much time would you need?'

'Twelve months, maybe less…'

Sienna knew almost to the exact second the moment that realisation dawned. She saw the subtle changes in his expression, and those dark, knowing eyes slid to her own face, fixing on it in intent appraisal.

'*That's* what you're offering.'

It was a statement, not a question, absolute conviction ringing in his tone, and she could almost hear his astute brain working, weighing up pros and cons, subjecting the idea to shrewd and careful analysis.

'Keir, my inheritance will make me wealthy beyond my wildest dreams. I'll have more than enough to keep myself and my mother in comfort. And I'll be able to help you out too. Oh, *don't* say no!'

He was going to. She knew it just by looking at him. And now that what she hoped for, what she'd prayed might happen, was actually within reach, she couldn't believe that fate would be unkind enough to snatch it away again, right at the last minute.

'Keir, please don't say no! You can pay me back if you like. But I can give you the money you need, and you can help me. I *need* this—we both do!'

Just what was going on inside that handsome head of his? What was that keen, calculating brain thinking? She felt like the accused in some terrible trial. As if she was standing in the dock with Keir acting as both judge and jury, very definitely counsel for the prosecution, about to attack her verbally.

For perhaps thirty of the longest seconds of her life she watched and waited. Watched him consider, debate with himself, accept certain ideas, then just as swiftly reject them. At long last he drew in a deep, uneven breath.

'Two conditions. . .' he said slowly.

'Anything! Anything at all, if you'll just say yes!'

'Condition one...' Keir marked it off on one long finger of his left hand. 'We have a proper wedding. All the trimmings. A church ceremony, flowers, candles, the lot.'

'Whatever you say.'

It was almost impossible to get the words out. Her pulse was racing so fast that her heart seemed to pound against her ribcage, leaving her unable to breathe properly or keep her voice in any way steady.

'And—and condition two?'

'After the proper wedding we have a real marriage. I won't stand for anything else. For one thing, there's no way we'll convince anyone that this is the love-match you're supposed to have by the conditions of your father's will if we don't look really together. It's all or nothing.'

All or nothing. Almost from the moment that they had met she had known that Keir wanted their relationship to be a physical one. He had made no secret of the desire he felt for her, and she had been the one trying to apply the brakes. 'Trying' being the operative word, she acknowledged uncomfortably.

Because she couldn't deny the effect he had on her. From the first moment that he had kissed her, an irresistible, potently sensual chemistry such as she had never known before had sparked between them. It had swept her off her feet, turned her world upside down, taking with it every long-held belief she had ever had about who she was and how she behaved.

It was all the more difficult to cope with because she had never felt like this with Dean. Dean whom she had loved, believed in, trusted. Dean to whom she had given her heart, but even then had never felt the same dangerous, wild excitement that Keir could inspire with simply a look, a touch, a brief caress. She had never understood how she could feel that attraction for a man she barely knew, let alone cared for in the deepest sort of sense.

But perhaps that same excitement would be the saving of her now. Perhaps the unnerving response she felt towards Keir would be enough to turn the fiction of a marriage she was proposing into something that would convince all observers it was actually fact.

But that still didn't make it easy to answer. Her throat closed over a knot of powerful emotions so that all she could do was nod silently, unable to speak a word.

'You agree?' Keir demanded, still in Grand Inquisitor mode.

'I—I agree.'

It was only as she forced it out that comprehension dawned, bright and vivid, blinding her with its brilliance.

She couldn't believe it. Could it possibly be true?

'A proper wedding!' she gasped, struggling to collect what remained of her scattered thoughts. 'A real marriage after a proper wedding! Keir—do you mean—are you agreeing to my proposal?'

The look he turned on her had such a scorching intensity that it seemed to sizzle through the air, sending electrical impulses along every nerve in her body. It spoke of hunger and conquest and passion. But most of all it was redolent with a desire so carnal it seemed positively indecent in the cold light of day.

'Yes, Sienna.'

Hearing his voice, Sienna blinked in disbelief. Suddenly that blazing sensuality was gone, wiped from his face as if it had never been. His tone was emotionless, totally controlled, as blank and indifferent as his eyes, which could have been carved from dark marble they were so cold and lifeless.

'Yes, I'm agreeing to your proposal. Under those conditions, then, yes, I will marry you.'

CHAPTER TWO

'WELL, we did it!'

Sienna's voice was breathless with a mixture of triumph, relief and something coming very close to panic that she prayed the man beside her wouldn't be able to detect. The same emotions were mirrored in the sea-coloured brilliance of her eyes as she turned on him a smile edged with a tension that, try as she might, she was unable to erase completely.

'We did it,' Keir echoed gravely, no answering smile lighting the darkness of his own gaze as it locked with hers. 'But did we get away with it? That's the real question.'

'Oh, don't be silly!'

Sienna made the reproof as careless as was possible when her heartbeat and breathing refused to settle down into anything like their normal rhythm.

'Of course we *got away* with it! Why wouldn't we? And don't say that—you make it sound as if we've done something wrong.'

'And we haven't?'

At his tone, the precarious euphoria that had buoyed her up evaporated in a rush, leaving her feeling disturbingly limp and deflated, like a pricked balloon.

'No, we haven't!' Infuriatingly, she couldn't give the words the conviction she wanted; a quaver she couldn't suppress took all the certainty from her declaration.

'Are you so sure of that? There are those who might label what we've done as fraud, or at the very least an attempt to swindle money from the Nash estate.'

'I'm not swindling anyone! I *am* a Nash, remember? By blood, at least, if not by name. And the only person who

16

might feel defrauded of anything is my father, or rather he might if he was still alive. But, seeing as he never took any interest in my existence from the day I was born, I very much doubt that anything I do now is going to trouble him in the least.'

Moving impulsively, she laid a hand on Keir's arm, her fingers white against the deep colour of his superbly tailored suit as she looked up into the hard-boned strength of his face.

'Don't tell me you're having second thoughts at this late stage?'

'Not second thoughts, no.' Keir pushed one strong hand through his hair, ruffling its gleaming darkness. 'But if we're strictly honest we are pulling a fast one on all those people in there.'

A slight inclination of his head indicated the door at the far side of the room through which the buzz of a hundred conversations could easily be heard.

'Especially your mother.'

'It's because of my mother that I'm doing this,' Sienna reminded him in a vehement undertone made necessary by the need to avoid being heard as the door swung open, revealing the crowded room beyond. 'And you—'

But there was no chance to finish the sentence, because at that moment a loud, stentorian voice broke through the noise, silencing it immediately.

'Ladies and gentlemen—pray silence for the bride and groom!'

'Oh, Lord!'

Taken by surprise, Sienna lurched into a nervous flurry of activity. A hasty glance in the huge, ornately framed mirror over the fireplace reassured her that her veil was still securely anchored, the delicate silver headdress holding it firmly in place in the brown curls of her hair, a couple of shades darker than Keir's.

Her make-up, carefully applied some four hours before, was still almost perfect: a soft wash of beige shadow emphasising the almond shape of her eyes, the long, thick lashes enhanced by a single coat of black mascara. Perhaps the warm pink on the full softness of her mouth had faded just a little, and there seemed to be a surprising lack of colour across the high, slanting cheekbones, but there was nothing she could do about that now. She could only hope that their guests would put her pallor down to excitement or belated wedding nerves.

Patting her cheeks lightly, in an attempt to bring some blood to the surface of her skin in order to make its ivory tones look a little healthier, she turned back to Keir. Meeting his darkly watchful gaze, she switched on what she hoped was a convincing smile, supremely conscious of the fact that it was distinctly ragged round the edges.

'Ready?' he asked, and held out his hand to her.

Sienna could only manage an inarticulate murmur that might have been agreement as she smoothed down her long skirt with uncertain fingers. Made of the finest lace over a delicate silk lining, the dress had originally been her grandmother's, worn on her wedding day almost fifty-five years before. Carefully preserved, wrapped in tissue paper to protect it from the yellowing effects of the light, it had been handed down from mother to daughter in the hope that wearing it as a bride would pass on something of the love that had made the older woman's marriage such a happy one.

But for Sienna's mother, Caroline, there had been no such happy ending. There hadn't even been a wedding ceremony, her daughter reflected bitterly. Her father had already been married. He had had no intention of leaving his wife for the naïve twenty-two-year-old who had been foolish enough to let herself get pregnant as the result of what had, to him at least, been just a pleasant holiday dalliance, with no commitment whatsoever.

'Sienna...' A note of reproof sharpened the edge of Keir's voice, dragging her from her reverie. 'Our guests are waiting.'

The hand he held out moved imperiously, the gesture demanding her instant obedience. For a brief moment the idea of rebellion flared in her mind, but almost immediately she dismissed it.

For now she had to observe all the conventions, play up to everyone's belief that this was the love match of the century. Keir and Sienna, second only to Antony and Cleopatra, or Cathy and Heathcliff in the lists of the all-time great love stories.

Out there, in the elegant dining room beyond the great double doors, was Francis Nash, her late father's brother and only surviving relative. If he was not convinced by their marriage and the whirlwind romance that had apparently preceded it, then the game was well and truly up. One false move and her chance of making sure that her mother spent the rest of her days in the comfort and security she so needed would be ruined.

And so she forced herself to smile again, with rather more success this time, drawing herself up to her full five foot nine as she placed her hand in Keir's.

'I'm ready,' she declared. 'Let's go.'

Hard fingers closed tightly over hers, though whether in encouragement or warning not to take any more risks she couldn't be sure.

'Come on, then,' Keir said, his voice unexpectedly roughened and tight. 'Let's get this show on the road.'

Not giving her time to think, he swung her round and, with her hand held high between them, marched her forcibly across the room, leaving her with no option but to follow him. It was either that or be dragged embarrassingly in his arrogant wake.

In the doorway Keir stopped suddenly, dark head held high, deep brown eyes scanning the elegantly dressed crowd before him as a murmur of interest greeted their appearance. Surprised by his unexpected stillness, it was all Sienna could do to avoid cannoning into the broad, straight line of his back.

Automatically her free hand came out to balance herself, closing over the tight muscles in his arm as she came to an uncertain halt at his side.

'Perfect,' Keir murmured softly, threading the word through with a dark cynicism that she had never heard from him before. 'Now we look just like the model bride and groom on the top of that ridiculously over-decorated cake you insisted on.'

'I…' Sienna began but her muffled protest was ignored as Keir, having caught the eye of the waiting *maître d'*, gave a swift, curt nod as a signal to proceed with the reception.

'Ladies and gentlemen…may I present to you Mr and Mrs Keir Alexander?'

But that was too much. Sienna's head came up sharply, turquoise eyes flashing repudiation of the announcement.

'Mr Keir Alexander and Sienna Rushford!' she pronounced, against the flurry of applause that had greeted the announcement. 'I—'

But the rest of her words were silenced, forced back down her throat, as, with a muttered expletive, Keir caught her in his arms, hauling her up against him as his dark head lowered, his mouth coming down hard on hers.

'Keir!'

His name was a spluttered sound of protest against his lips. It was all she could manage before he kissed her again, with even more ruthless determination.

'Looks like Keir's got a tiger by the tail, all right.'

On the borders of her awareness Sienna heard one of Keir's adolescent stepbrothers make the comment in an aside that was obviously meant to be heard, pitched as it was in a tone that carried clearly in spite of its apparent restraint. The malicious amusement in his voice was impossible to miss.

'Let's hope he's not bitten off more than he can chew.'

Against her slender length Sienna felt the tension that stiffened Keir's hard frame, tightening every muscle into an unyielding wall that seemed to bruise her just to be pressed close to it. So it was almost impossible to equate what all her senses were telling her with the apparently sensual indolence with which he slid his mouth away from hers, trailing it softly over her cheek until his warm breath teased the delicate curves of her ear.

'Do you want this to work or not?' he whispered silkily, his words meant for her hearing alone.

'Of course…'

'Then kiss me!'

'Keir…?' Confusion clouded her eyes, made her voice just a shaken thread of sound.

'*Kiss me!*'

With a raw, uncontrolled sound in his throat, he closed hard fingers over her chin, wrenching her face up to his once more. But this time when his mouth touched hers it was with an unexpected, beguiling gentleness, a voluptuous tenderness that made her senses swim, her heartbeat slow to a heavy, languorous thud.

Against her back, the strength of his arm was all that held her upright. Without its support she felt that she would melt away completely, sliding into a warm, honeyed pool at his feet. Her whole body glowed, heating the blood in her veins until she felt as if she was flooded with molten gold, a burning spiral of very primitive need uncoiling deep inside her. She wanted to feel Keir's mouth all over her skin, not just on her mouth; she longed for the caress of his hands on parts of her body too intimate to be appropriate on this public occasion.

It had been like this from the start, she acknowledged hazily with the little rational thought that was left to her. With Keir she no longer knew herself. She became a stranger even in her own eyes. In her place was a woman who had her own slender height, delicate oval face and thick fall of long dark brown hair, but who acted in ways she had never seen before.

That Sienna rushed into situations that only months before she would have fled from, screaming in panic.

Situations like this travesty of a marriage that was only for show, with no real foundation in fact.

It was several long drawn-out seconds before the realisation that what she had believed to be distant thunder, or even the crazed pounding of her heart echoing inside her head, was in fact another, louder round of appreciative applause from their audience. A couple of the younger guests even added enthusiastic wolf whistles to the chorus of approval.

With carefully feigned reluctance, Keir broke the embrace and turned a slightly rueful smile on her heated face. To the onlookers, it must have appeared quite genuine, but Sienna had sensed the careful judgement that had had him ending the kiss the full space of several heartbeats before he'd lifted his head. She had seen the calculating look he had directed into her glazed eyes, the triumphant twist to that wide mouth as it had abandoned hers, leaving her aching for more.

Straightening fully, Keir slung a possessive arm around her waist as he turned to face the assembly of friends and relations.

'I'm afraid my wife—' a chorus of cheers greeted his use of the word for the first time since the completion of the marriage ceremony '—has strong feminist views that mean she insists on using her own name instead of adopting mine. Some of you may find that rather unromantic, but personally I have no problem with it. After all, when she indulges my every whim in everything apart from this…'

A careful emphasis on the words 'my every whim' left no room for doubt as to exactly what other things he had in mind.

'Who am I to deny her this one wish for independence if it means so much to her?'

Milking the situation for all it was worth, he smiled down into Sienna's flushed face, his appearance to all intents and purposes every inch that of the doting husband.

'Don't be embarrassed, darling,' he reproved softly.

'You're amongst friends here. Everyone knows how we feel about each other.'

Struggling against a crazy desire to kick him hard on the ankle, in order to let him know exactly how she felt about the charade he was acting out, Sienna forced herself to swallow down the anger she couldn't afford to reveal. Painfully conscious of Francis Nash, standing just a few feet away from her, watching Keir's fooling with an intently speculative air, she managed a rather sickly smile.

But she knew that the curve of her lips wasn't matched by the look in her eyes, which were flashing furious reproof and a warning of later retribution into Keir's mocking face. He really was taking things way too far. Nothing like this had been mentioned in their agreement.

But Keir appeared totally unmoved by the silent rage in her eyes. Instead, taking advantage of the fact that a waiter carrying a tray full of glasses of champagne had just come within reach, he appropriated one of the crystal flutes and held it aloft, dark eyes smiling knowingly down into hers all the time.

'If you'll indulge me,' he declared to the surrounding audience, 'I'd like to propose a toast. To Sienna—my beautiful bride, and the woman who has made me the happiest man in the world by becoming my wife today.'

The man really was incorrigible! In spite of herself Sienna found it impossible to hold back a disturbed squawk of protest at this blatant lie. If Keir didn't stop, someone was going to see right through his over-the-top performance and so start to wonder what the real truth was.

'Keir!' she protested softly, knowing that any further show of anger or impatience would only make him worse, drive him to even more dangerous extremes. 'You're embarrassing me.'

Immediately he was apparently all repentance.

'I'm sorry, darling. You're right. There's a time and a place for this, and that's not here and now. We'll finish later...' Deliberately he let his voice drop a couple of octaves, so that it became a husky purr, rich with sensual promise. 'When we're alone.'

Which earned him yet another cheer of enthusiastic appreciation from the spectators, all of whom completely misunderstood the reasons behind the burning colour that suddenly flooded the bride's face.

'I'll look forward to that,' she shot back in swift retaliation. 'But for now we have our guests to see to. Please, everyone—help yourselves to drinks. I'm sure you're ready for them. Lunch will be served in half an hour. In the meantime…'

She directed her attention back to Keir, her voice and her expression hardening as she did so.

'I think you and I had better circulate—talk to a few people… I'll take this half of the room…'

She had nerved herself for further play-acting on his part, perhaps even a downright refusal to do as she asked, but surprisingly it didn't come. Instead Keir simply lifted his glass in a silent, mocking toast before turning and strolling off in the opposite direction from the one she had indicated.

Silently Sienna watched him go, small white teeth worrying at the fullness of her lower lip as she did so. It would all have been so much easier if she could have been in love with Keir, even just a little. After all, that shouldn't have been too hard. He was the sort of man almost any woman with red blood in her veins would have fallen head over heels for. Tall, strong, impossibly good-looking, with the sort of potent hardcore sexuality that turned susceptible female brains to jelly, leaving them incapable of thought.

He was successful too. A self-made man. A man she could be proud to have at her side, proud to call her husband even for such a strictly limited time. But he would never have her heart. That wasn't hers to give. She had already lost it to someone who had proved every bit as unworthy of her love as her father had been of her mother's lifelong devotion.

No, she mustn't think about Dean. Sienna's teeth dug in

harder as she fought against the tears that burned in her eyes. She had thrown in her lot with Keir, and that was the way her future lay—at least for the term of their contract together. It was an arrangement that she had been convinced could work so well for both of them. But today Keir had behaved in a way she'd never seen before.

Sienna's sea-coloured eyes went to where Keir stood, his dark head thrown back, his face alight with laughter at something his companion had said to him. Suddenly she was brought up hard against the truth of just how very little she actually knew about this man who was now her husband.

If looks could kill, Keir thought wryly, catching that turquoise glare from the opposite side of the room, then he would surely have fallen down dead right on the spot, shrivelled into ashes by the force of Sienna's anger. She hadn't liked his teasing earlier, and clearly the thought of it still rankled. He hadn't realised just how volatile his new wife's temper could be.

His *wife*. Carefully he tested the word inside his mind, not yet sure exactly how he felt about it.

'Keir!' A powerful handshake was accompanied by a hearty slap on the back from a tall man with a bushy dark beard and laughing hazel eyes. 'Congratulations, mate! I never thought I'd see the day that you joined the ranks of married men. This Sienna really must be some woman.'

'Believe me, she is.'

Keir could only pray that his words didn't sound as insincere spoken out loud as they did inside his head. Richard Parry had been his friend for over twenty years now, ever since they had first met up at secondary school, and if anyone was likely to smell a rat at his sudden decision to marry then Rick was that person.

'She has to be. I was really beginning to wonder if you were married to that company of yours. You seemed to spend every waking hour of your life in the office.'

'There have been some problems.' The muscles in Keir's jaw tightened, making his reply sound clipped and distant.

'My father's death was so unexpected that it left a lot of things unresolved...'

'But that was—what?—eighteen months ago? Surely you've sorted things out now?'

'Just about.' Keir nodded slowly, his eyes darker than ever as he thought back over the past year and a half. 'There's one last complication I have to deal with, and then everything will be just how I want it.'

In his business world at least. His personal affairs were quite a different matter. But right now all he could think of was the relief that that one 'complication' had been lifted from his shoulders. It had been the bane of his life for ten years, and he hadn't been able to wait to see the back of it. Only now did he feel free to turn his attention fully to the vexed question of his reckless marriage.

'And when can we expect to hear of a whole new generation of Alexanders?' It was Richard's wife who spoke, her voice soft and gentle as her nature, bringing her husband's head round to her at once.

'Give the poor lad a break, Jo! He's barely put the ring on her finger! Let him at least enjoy the honeymoon before you wish the joys of parenthood on him. Not everyone wants to be plagued with the sort of brood we've got.'

The laughter in Richard's voice was belied by the way his eyes lingered on the swell of his wife's stomach, evidence of how close he was to becoming a father for the fourth time.

'But you always said you wanted children, didn't you, Keir? And I think you'd make a wonderful father—if the way you get on with Sam, William and Hannah is anything to go by.'

'Your children are like their mother, Joanna.' Keir smiled. 'They'd get on with anyone at all without any trouble. But I don't think you should look for the chance of a couple of playmates for your gang at any time in the near future. Sienna and I haven't even talked about having kids...'

What would be the point when this charade of a marriage

they had embarked on wasn't meant to last much longer than a full-term pregnancy anyway? But he couldn't admit that to Rick and Joanna, who were so blissfully happy in their own union that they would find it hard to understand the convoluted reasoning that had led to his taking Sienna as his bride.

'Now if you'll excuse me...I'd better rejoin my wife.'

Coward! Keir reproved himself as he turned away and began to weave a path through the crowd to where Sienna stood on the opposite side of the room, pausing occasionally to shake a hand, acknowledge congratulations and good wishes. But his mind wasn't on what he was doing. He knew he couldn't have faced any more of Joanna's gentle questioning without blurting out something that might have given the game away completely.

The trouble was that Rick and his wife had known him for too long. They had been there all those years before when, under the influence of rather more wine than had been wise, he had declared with impassioned certainty that he would never marry unless he knew it was for ever. That only the conviction that the relationship would last for a lifetime, nothing less, would get him up the aisle and put a ring on his finger.

So how had he ended up doing just that, in the certain knowledge that what he had entered into was just a temporary contract? Stopping dead abruptly, Keir looked down at the thick gold band now encircling his wedding finger, twisting it round and round in an uneasy movement. How come he had compromised all his ideals in this way?

Because he was so much older now—and he would say wiser. He knew that such ideals were nothing but fantasies, impossible to achieve. He had been hit over the head with a strong dose of reality that had driven all the dreams from his mind. These days he was realist enough to know that sometimes a pragmatic compromise was the best you could come away with.

'Keir, darling, I'm so glad to see you...'

This time the hand on his arm was much smaller, finer, totally feminine. Adorned with an extravagant display of gold and diamonds, the slender fingers were tipped with long, pointed nails painted in a violent shade of red. As Keir stiffened instinctively a wave of some heavy, musky perfume assailed his nostrils, turning his stomach.

He would recognise that overpowering perfume anywhere, just as he would recognise the sound of her voice and that false-toned 'darling' that they both knew she didn't mean in the slightest. She only used it for the benefit of everyone else around, in order to maintain the illusion—in reality they had never felt anything other than total hatred for each other.

'Lucille.' He bit the word out, her name leaving a foul, bitter taste in his mouth.

Lucille Alexander. The stepmother from hell and his own personal demon. The woman he had described with deliberate understatement as the one last 'complication' he'd had left to deal with in order to be free of all the problems that had been weighing him down over the past ten years. The woman whose greedy demands had forced him into this marriage that was not a marriage but a purely business arrangement.

And as he turned slowly to face her the wave of revulsion he couldn't control left him in no doubt that the prospect of getting her out of his life once and for all made the pretence and subterfuge totally worthwhile.

CHAPTER THREE

'IS SOMETHING wrong?'

'Wrong?'

Keir's voice was distracted, his attention obviously else-where, and the dark-eyed gaze he turned in his wife's direction was hooded, shaded with hidden thoughts that she couldn't begin to understand.

'Why should anything be wrong? After all, we're both now going to get exactly what we want.'

What had put that cynical note into his voice, roughening it until it scraped her already over-sensitive nerves raw? But the truth was that ever since Keir had come back to her side at the start of the formal wedding lunch it had been clear that his mood had changed dramatically. The playful teasing that had so disturbed her had vanished, replaced instead by a darker, brooding distance.

'Well, you could at least act as if you were just the slightest bit pleased to be married to me,' Sienna hissed in the whisper necessitated by her determination not to be heard by her mother at her side and Keir's best man at his. 'If you continue to stare at your plate as if it was poisoned, and push the food around without tasting any of it, people will begin to wonder just what's wrong with you!'

Especially those who had just witnessed his Oscar-winning performance as the most lovelorn and devoted husband of the century.

'Right now you look more like the condemned man who can't even bring himself to eat his last meal...'

No, anger was the wrong approach entirely, drawing a disturbing response from him. Seeing the rejection that flared in his eyes, the way that one long-fingered hand clenched over the starched white damask of his napkin, Sienna hastily adjusted her tone and expression in the hope of appeasing him.

'It won't be long before this is all over,' she tried soothingly. 'There's just the traditional speeches and cutting the cake and then we can call it a day.'

Thankfully, she hadn't given in to the urgings of her friends and planned an evening party to round off the celebrations. She had been unable to square the idea with her already uncomfortable conscience, seeing it as taking hypocrisy way too far. And with Keir in this mood it would have been more like a wake than any sort of revelry.

'We'll soon be able to be on our own again.'

'And that will be so much better, will it?' Keir snapped coldly. 'Mr and Mrs Keir Alexander—oh, I'm sorry, I forgot. You want this marriage so little that you don't even think it's worth changing your name. So I see very little reason why you should be looking forward to our being alone...'

Sienna was astonished at how much his words stung. They were largely the truth, after all, so there was no reason for the sudden twist of pain she was experiencing.

With a sensation like the slow trickle of icy water creeping down her back, she found herself once more in the grip of the appalling unease of earlier that afternoon. It was as if some alien had moved in, taking over the shell of the person she had thought was Keir and replacing him with a total stranger.

But he was a stranger she was now legally tied to. For better for worse. For richer for poorer—in their case, definitely for richer, unless something went terribly wrong. Which it might do if she couldn't jolt him out of this black mood. Already interested eyes were turning their way, obviously made curious by their absorbed concentration on each other, the muttered conversation that was so clearly not made up of words of love.

There was just one way she knew to get through to him.

'Keir…' Deliberately she gentled her voice, making it softly sensual. 'Darling, don't be like this…'

She wasn't sure which startled him the most. The murmured endearment or the gentle hand she laid on his. But she couldn't be unaware of his reaction, seeing it in the sudden widening of his dark eyes. It was there under her fingertips too, in the tension that stiffened his muscles against her, the threat of rejection that he only just controlled in time. She knew how tempted he was to repulse her gesture in a response that would be totally inappropriate to the impression they were trying to create, and she knew just as surely exactly when he decided not to use it.

'I'm sorry.' It was a low, deep sigh. 'I'm just a bear with a sore head today.'

'A sore head!'

It was Sienna's mother who had caught the comment, her laughter-warmed tones lightening the atmosphere dramatically as she echoed his words, leaning forward to smile into Keir's dark, shuttered face.

'Would that be the result of rather too exuberant a stag night last night, son-in-law?' she asked teasingly. 'I would have thought you and your friends'd have more sense…'

'Now don't blame me!' James, the best man, joined in on a note of amused protest. 'Whatever Keir got up to last night, he did it on his own! And as for a stag night, all we had was a very sedate meal together at the beginning of the week, so you can't hold me responsible for the way he's feeling today. Unless you had some sort of debauched evening that you didn't invite me along to, you rogue,' he added, with a none too subtle dig of his elbow into Keir's ribs.

'Nothing of the sort,' his friend returned, switching on a grin that even came close to convincing Sienna, though she was well aware of how very far from genuine it actually was.

Along with the grin went a belated attempt to look affectionate, by turning his hand on the table top until his strong fingers enclosed hers completely, his grip warm and firm. The slow, deliberate movement of his thumb against the sensitivity of her palm dried her throat, the softly sensual circles he was drawing setting her heart thudding and heating her blood.

Keir's wicked, slanted glance in her direction told her that he knew exactly what he was doing. That he had turned her own weapon of the potent effect they had on each other back on her with devastating results.

'I'm afraid what was occupying me last night was business, pure and simple,' he confessed ruefully, his voice revealing nothing of the emotion that Sienna knew would shade hers if she tried to speak. 'A deal that needed finalising.'

'The night before your wedding!' James was obviously disbelieving. 'Keir, man, couldn't it have waited?'

'No way.'

The shake of his dark head that accompanied the flat statement was as firmly emphatic as the words.

'I wanted this particular matter behind me once and for all, so that I was free to concentrate on my bride. It's just that negotiations went on much longer than I had expected...'

Lucille had been as difficult as it was possible for her to be, damn her, Keir reflected grimly. She and her lawyer had held out for every penny she could get away with, and then some. There had been times when he had come close to giving up on the whole thing and walking out, but then, just when he had been about to declare that he had enough, that she could forget it, she had finally capitulated and signed on the dotted line.

'I didn't get to bed until well after midnight, and then I didn't sleep too well.'

'What was the problem?' Sienna inserted rather tartly, the sensual haze that had enclosed her evaporating with a rapidity that left her shaken and disturbingly on the edge of tears.

It was his comment about being free to concentrate on his bride that had changed her mood. She was only too well aware of the fact that it had been inserted solely for the benefit of their audience. It had no grounding at all in reality. In fact the real truth was that, crazily, she didn't even have the faintest idea what they were going to do once the wedding was over.

'Wedding nerves?'

'Something like that.'

'Oh, come on! That's the bride's prerogative, not the groom's!'

She couldn't believe that Keir—strong, independent, determined, cold-blooded, *heart-free* Keir Alexander—had lain awake worrying about the coming day. Refused to even consider that he might have felt as apprehensive as she had about the marriage ceremony and what they were getting themselves into.

Not Keir. He was the one who had been as cool as the proverbial cucumber all the way through this. Once she had convinced him it was the answer to both their problems, he had taken every single thing in his stride, handled each detail, every small hiccup, with the cool assurance that was so much a part of his nature.

'Are you saying that a man can't feel unsure and apprehensive on the night before his wedding—overawed by the prospect of what's ahead of him—the responsibility he's about to take on?'

'N-no...'

The look in his eyes disturbed her. They were darker than ever, shadowed by something she didn't understand. And now that she looked more closely she could see smudges of weariness underneath them, marks that she had never noticed before. The faint lines that fanned out from the corners of his eyes looked more pronounced too, as if etched there by strain and worry.

'Or are you claiming that if I'd rung you when I couldn't

sleep I'd have found you wide awake too, sharing the same
sort of feelings?'

'Well—no, I wasn't.'

The truth was that, worn out by rushing around here there
and everywhere for the past five weeks, she had fallen
asleep as soon as her head had touched the pillow. Even the
last minute butterflies in her stomach at the prospect of the
day ahead had been overcome by the thought that tomorrow,
finally, all her worries would be over.

'I didn't think so.'

Suddenly the thought that had crossed Sienna's mind a
moment before came rushing back with a new and worrying
force.

Once she had convinced him. Keir hadn't wanted this
marriage. When she had first proposed the idea he had rejected it outright. It had only been when he'd made it a
condition that they had a proper marriage, complete in every
way, that he had been persuaded to agree to her proposal.

'Sienna!'

Her name in Keir's voice held a note of warning that
dragged her back to the present. The best man was getting
to his feet, ready to make his speech. Somehow Sienna
found the self-control to appear to be listening. She turned
her head in James's direction, focused her eyes on his face,
and even, forewarned by the ripples of laughter from other
parts of the room, managed to smile at the jokes he made.

But the truth was that she heard little of the witty address,
and registered even less. Deep inside, her stomach was just
a twisting mass of nerves, a knot of fear that made her
stomach heave nauseatingly.

What had she done? She had actually asked this man to
be her husband. To live with her, share her home, her life,
her bed. For the next year, at least, she would have to make
it appear that she and Keir were deeply in love. That they
were no longer two individuals but that indefinable thing
known as 'a couple'.

What had seemed so simple just a few days before now

seemed impossible, unendurable, fraught with pitfalls and traps to catch the unwary. The twelve months that had once appeared such a short space of time now stretched endlessly ahead, three hundred and sixty five days of it, and she had no idea how she was going to live through it.

Fear pounded inside her head, beating at her temples, so that she had to fight against the impulse to push her chair back and run from the room. She had chosen this path, knowing she had no alternative. Married to Keir she would inherit her father's money, and with it all the security and comfort it could bring. Without him she would be once more alone and desperate, with her mother totally dependent on her.

The speeches were over, the toasts completed. At last she was free from the obligation to stay in her seat. The feeling caused a rush of relief that brought her swiftly to her feet, unable to keep still any longer. She had no idea where she was going, thinking vaguely of heading for the huge French windows, now flung open in the late summer heat, of getting some much needed fresh air. Perhaps some deep, cooling breaths would calm her racing pulse, ease the pressure inside her head. But…

'Sienna…' Keir said abruptly, reaching for her. 'Wait…'

His grip on her arm felt like a steel manacle, imprisoning her. Panic flared afresh and, reacting purely instinctively, she tensed, pulling back, away from him, earning herself a dark, disapproving glare.

'What the…? Sienna, just what's got into you? People are looking!'

The savage undertone was somehow more disturbing than if he had actually raised his voice to express the anger he was clearly barely holding in check. The blaze in his eyes terrified her, and suddenly the ground no longer seemed steady beneath her, the thick red carpet shifting unnervingly under the soles of her white satin slippers.

'I won't go with you!' It was a desperate whisper. 'I can't!'

'Sienna, have you taken leave of your senses? Might I remind you that this is our wedding day?'

Remind her! As if she could forget!

'We have guests…people we should speak to.'

Speak! Sienna's tongue felt as if it was glued to the roof of her mouth, preventing her from forming a word. But with Keir's strong hand still clamped on her wrist, the other pressed firmly against the small of her back, she had no option but to follow him out into the room, somehow managing to acknowledge the greetings of the people they passed.

Her face seemed frozen into an expression of feigned happiness, the muscles around her mouth aching from smiling too many false smiles. All she wanted was to get away, be by herself, find peace and quiet in which to try to come to terms with what she'd done. But Keir was unrelenting in his determination that they should greet everyone. Ignoring her murmurs of protest, her obvious reluctance, he steered her from group to group, covering her awkwardness with the smooth ease of his own conversation.

'For God's sake!' he hissed in her ear. 'Now you're the one who looks like the condemned man! Smile, damn you! No one will believe you're madly in love with me if you look at me as if I was some deadly poisonous snake about to strike.'

'I *am* smiling,' Sienna retorted through clenched teeth. 'And as to looking as if I love you—I'd manage that much better if you didn't frogmarch me round the room as if I was either drunk or insane. I can manage to stand on my own two feet, you know. If you'd just let me go…'

'Be my guest!'

She was released so abruptly that she staggered awkwardly, afraid she might actually fall. Instinctively her hand went out to steady herself, and to her total surprise she found it taken by someone new. Soft fingers closed round hers, supporting her.

'Steady!' a female voice cautioned. 'You nearly took a tumble there.'

'Th-thank you.' With her balance restored, Sienna managed to turn to her rescuer with a smile more genuine than anything she had managed before.

'Not to worry,' she was assured. 'Those long skirts can be so very difficult to walk in when you're not used to them.'

'That's true!' The woman's perfume was rather cloying and overpowering, but Sienna struggled not to reveal her response to it. At last she felt something of her earlier panic receding, evaporating in the warmth of this new companion's smile. 'I'm sorry, I don't think. . .'

She didn't recognise the face. This must be someone Keir had invited. Someone she hadn't yet met.

'Keir, won't you introduce me…?'

But Keir stood at her side, stiff and withdrawn, his face appearing to have been carved out of the cold, immobile marble that formed the statues out on the terrace. Even his eyes were blanked off, revealing no emotion.

Why had this had to happen now? Keir asked himself furiously. If he had tried to think of the worst possible moment for Lucille to finally meet up with the woman he had married, then it would have been hard to imagine one that beat this. Sienna had already been behaving like a nervous thoroughbred, fearful of being handled for the first time, so he could just imagine how she was going to deal with this additional development.

The problem was that his new wife couldn't lie to save her life. She had come up with this ridiculous scheme of their pretend marriage, presenting it as the answer to all his problems as well as hers, but the truth was that she didn't know the half of it. She didn't know how appallingly Lucille had behaved—the sort of damage she was still capable of wreaking if given half a chance. And if his stepmother so much as suspected the true reasons behind this hastily arranged wedding, then she was more than likely to pounce on the information like some ecstatic predator. She would use it quite cold-bloodedly to her own advantage, especially if she could work on his own destruction at the same time.

'Keir...'

Just one word from the other woman's lips, but it had a dramatic effect on him. His head jerked round swiftly, his eyes narrowing to mere slits above his high, strong cheek-bones.

'You want to be introduced? Well, fine. It had to be done some time, so I suppose now is as good an occasion as any. Sienna, darling, this is Lucille, my stepmother...' He spat the word out as if it left a foul taste in his mouth. 'Lucille, obviously this is Sienna, my wife.'

Lucille. Sienna couldn't believe what she was hearing. *This* was Lucille, the stepmother Keir so detested that he had finally agreed to their marriage solely because it offered him a way of getting rid of her, expelling her from his life once and for all? This was the monster who, like Medusa, had turned his heart to stone in the moment he had first seen her, and had never let a single redeeming chink of light into it since then.

But this woman was nothing like the one she had imagined. In her thoughts, influenced by Keir's own feelings, she had created a vicious harpy, cold-faced and cold-eyed, not this smiling, bright-eyed creature. And Lucille Alexander was so much smaller than she had anticipated, smaller and lovelier, with her peachy skin, green eyes and red-gold hair. But what rocked her back on her feet, threatening her balance again for a moment, was just how young Keir's step-mother was. She had anticipated some woman in her late forties, early fifties. This Lucille looked barely five or so years older than Keir himself.

'Sienna...' Lucille was holding out her hand. 'It's wonderful to meet you at last. I was beginning to wonder if I would ever get to see you at all. But now that I have I can quite understand why Keir wanted to keep you all to himself.'

'I doubt if you *understand* anything at all,' Keir put in with biting cynicism. 'And if I'd had my way you would never have been invited to the wedding. But Sienna wanted all my family here and, much as I hate to acknowledge it, you are family, if only by marriage...'

'Keir...!' Sienna put in reproachfully.

But Keir ignored her, his attention still fixed on Lucille.

'But, seeing as you are here, perhaps it's just as well. There's a small matter of business we can get out of the way. If you'll just follow me.'

Once again he clamped his hand over Sienna's arm, forcing her to go with him as he turned and marched towards the door. It was either that or be dragged inelegantly and embarrassingly in his wake. He didn't pause to look back and see if Lucille had followed them, apparently totally confident that she would do just that.

And it appeared that his confidence was not misplaced. When he finally came to a halt in the small private room the hotel had put aside for the bride and groom's use, Lucille was only seconds behind them. She was barely through the door before Keir kicked it shut, blocking off the noise and bustle of the reception.

'Now...'

Releasing Sienna abruptly, he reached into his inner jacket pocket, pulling out a long white envelope that he dropped onto the highly polished surface of a nearby table.

'This is what you're really interested in, dear stepmother. Oh, it's all right...' he added, seeing Lucille's curious glance in Sienna's direction. 'My wife and I have no secrets from each other. Quite the contrary. As a matter of fact, it's Sienna, not me, who's buying you out, at the price we agreed last night. Darling...'

It took Sienna the space of a couple of uneven heartbeats to realise that Keir was now speaking to her. And even when she had registered that fact she found herself staring at the fine silver pen he held out to her, unable to comprehend just what he had in mind.

'Sienna,' Keir urged softly. 'I need your signature. The document's all prepared. All you have to do is sign.'

And then it finally dawned on her just what he meant. Of course. This was what she had promised him in return for his agreement to go through with the wedding, his name on the marriage certificate.

But she hadn't expected him to hold her to her promise quite so soon. The ring was barely on her finger, the ink on that certificate barely dry, and already he was pushing her to complete her half of the bargain. She was quite unprepared for how much that hurt.

'Sienna,' Keir urged again, more forcefully this time. 'Sign it please.'

For a second or two Sienna was tempted to rebel. Let him wait for his money! He hadn't done anything to earn it!

But then Lucille spoke, and suddenly Sienna found that her mood had changed dramatically.

'So the little bride is bailing you out, is she Keir, darling? What a generous wedding present—I only hope she thinks you're worth it. But I'm sure you will be—in one important area of marriage at least.'

Her lascivious tone, the way her eyes gleamed, her pink tongue positively licking her lips, made it only too plain exactly what area she meant. Sienna could only stare, transfixed, unable to believe her eyes. It seemed as if the Lucille she had first met had vanished and another woman entirely had taken her place. This was the real stepmother, then, and she was beginning to understand just why Keir detested her so.

'You always did give great value there, didn't you, dearest? But I did wonder what had persuaded you to sign your freedom away like this...'

'I'm not signing anything away.'

Belatedly, it appeared that Keir had remembered the part he was supposed to be playing. Moving behind Sienna, he looped his arms around her waist, fastening his hands together under her breasts and pulling her back against him.

'On the contrary, I'm gaining everything I ever wanted. A beautiful wife, a new life with her, the prospect of a wonderful future...'

The sensual magic of his touch was working its spell all over again. Already Sienna could feel her body respond to the warmth of his, to the strength of his arms around her, the faint crisp scent of his cologne, so subtle and clean in contrast to the overwhelming reek of Lucille's perfume.

Instinctively she laid her head back against his shoulder, feeling his lips brush against her cheek as she did so. In this moment she could almost believe Keir had meant what he'd said. Could almost imagine that this was a real marriage, not the cold-blooded business deal Keir had just proved it to be.

'And naturally you're besotted with him.' Lucille turned a look of scorn on her. 'Well, I just hope you think you've got a good deal on this—that he's worth what you're paying him.'

Behind her, Sienna felt Keir's hard body stiffen in swift rejection. But his face showed no sign of what he was feeling and his hands continued their warm caresses over her arms and tracing the delicate lines of her neck.

'I'm not paying him,' she managed, her voice rather breathless as a result of the heightened, erratic beat of her heart. 'Nor am I bailing him out. What I'm doing is making our partnership a financial one as well as a personal one. An investment for our future.'

She must have sounded more convincing than she had hoped, because against her back she felt Keir's chest move in a silent, secret laugh of triumph.

For the first time Sienna felt a sense of unity with him. A feeling that they were both in this together, united against a common enemy. The sensation sent her spirits soaring, and impulsively she twisted in his grasp so that she could brush a kiss against the softness of his mouth.

'Give me the pen, darling, and show me where to sign. I

want the business side of things over with so that we can concentrate on more *personal* matters.'

In a haze of euphoria she signed her name with a flourish, folded up the document and thrust it back at Lucille, feeling a sense of exhilaration as the other woman took it and deposited it in her smart cream handbag.

'Well, I'll wish you every happiness together.' Lucille's tone implied exactly the opposite. 'You're obviously made for each other.'

It was as the door swung to behind her that Keir moved suddenly and unexpectedly. Sienna found herself gathered up into his arms and enclosed in a bear hug that drove all the breath from her body.

'Brilliant! You were quite perfect! You even had me convinced that you were crazy about me.'

'I did, didn't I?'

The warmth of his approval was doing strange things to her. The light in his eyes, the smile that curved the wide sensual mouth were as intoxicating as the fine champagne she had drunk earlier. She felt as if she was bathed in the warmth of the August sun outside, her skin glowing, her blood heating in response. It was a heady, thrilling sensation and she wanted more of it.

'And believe me, sweetheart, if you can convince my dear stepmother you can convince anyone. We might actually get away with this charade after all.'

Charade. Just one single word but it had an effect like the dash of icy water in her face. Sobering immediately, she felt herself come back down to earth with a sudden and very painful thud. His approval hadn't been for her, but for the performance he believed she had delivered.

Charade. Just for a second she had allowed herself to believe there was something else between them, some unity other than the one that linked them as partners in a scam to enable her to collect her inheritance. Something that would make the coming twelve months easier to live through. But she had only been fooling herself. Keir obviously wanted no such thing.

'So, now that's out of the way we can move on to the next stage...'

'The next stage?' Sienna's uncertainty showed in her voice. 'What next stage is that?'

'Really, Sienna, isn't it obvious?'

The look he turned on her was one of sardonic mockery, mixed with a strong dose of frank disbelief.

'We're married, darling. The wedding's over, the reception's coming to an end. What's the logical next move?'

'You don't mean...?' Sienna could only shake her head in disbelief. He couldn't mean what she thought.

'We do what everyone else does, sweetheart. We go on honeymoon.'

CHAPTER FOUR

HONEYMOON.

The word swung round and round inside Sienna's head as she lingered over a glass of wine on the terrace of the villa, enjoying the cool of the evening after the warmth of the day. Above her head, swallows swooped through the air in pursuit of midges, the swish of their wings the only sound in the silence that surrounded her.

'*We do what everyone else does, sweetheart. We go on honeymoon.*'

She had been frankly stunned by her own reaction to Keir's declaration. It had been the last thing she had expected. The nature of their arrangement was so businesslike and unemotional that she had never even dreamed there would be any place in it for of the conventional pleasures that were supposed to follow immediately after the celebration of a wedding.

So the realisation that they were actually to have a honeymoon had left her quite breathless and surprisingly excited. Somehow the thought of such a holiday had made her feel like a bride.

A *real* bride, she corrected when hard common sense had reminded her that she was actually Keir's bride, even if it was only a pretence at a love match.

'On honeymoon!' she exclaimed, looking up into Keir's dark face in wide-eyed surprise. 'But where…? What…?'

A strong finger laid across her lips silenced her effectively.

'That's my secret,' Keir told her with a grin. 'Isn't that what the groom's supposed to do? Organise everything and keep the destination a mystery until the last minute?'

It was more usual that the bride and groom chose the honeymoon together, poring over brochures and travel articles before deciding on some place they both wanted to visit, Sienna reflected, something of the euphoria that had lifted her spirits fading slightly. Of course there would be nothing like that for herself and Keir.

Discretion warned her that it would be best to make no comment about that. It would only spoil the new warmth that had developed between them. A warmth she very much needed. The last remnants of her earlier panic still lingered in her thoughts, clinging like sticky cobwebs to the corners of her mind, and she wanted desperately to drive them away.

'I didn't think we were having a honeymoon. If I'm honest, it never even crossed my mind.'

'A proper wedding, I said,' Keir reminded her. 'One with all the trimmings.'

'Yes, but this... I mean, can you afford it?'

Big mistake! *Bad* mistake. It was obvious that he didn't like what she'd said at all. The curve to his lips vanished at once, his face hardening ominously. The dark brown eyes took on a dangerous glint that warned her she had overstepped some invisible but firmly defined line that he had drawn around his private affairs.

Swinging away from her, he moved to stare broodingly out of the window into the spectacular garden beyond.

'I may have been forced to into needing a temporary injection of funds in order to meet Lucille's unreasonable demands, but I am still very far from penniless,' he snapped out, so sharply that Sienna found herself taking an involuntary step backwards, away from him. 'And even if I am only a temporary husband, hired for the period of our contract, I trust I know what my duties are—'

'Keir, don't! I didn't mean that the way it sounded!'

'Why not?' he flung over his shoulder at her. 'We both know you wouldn't have proposed marriage to me if you hadn't been desperate.'

'And you wouldn't have accepted if it hadn't suited your business plans!'

'Exactly.'

'You make it sound so sordid—so cold-blooded!'

With an abrupt, savage laugh Keir turned back to face her again, hands pushed deep into his trouser pockets, one black brow raised in taunting mockery.

'That's what business deals are, my lovely,' he told her harshly. 'Rational, hard-headed, and as cold-blooded as possible.'

If only that were really true, he reflected bitterly. If only he could have made *this* decision as coolly and unemotionally as he handled every other problem that he came up against in his working life.

But in this situation his natural control had totally deserted him. And the reasons for that were twofold. Both female. When it came to dealing with either Lucille or the woman now standing before him, the woman he had just made his wife, it seemed that common sense or rational thought went straight out of the window, leaving him uncharacteristically unsure of which way to turn.

As a result he had acted on the sort of impulse that he would have thought was totally alien to him, deciding to act before thinking things through to their logical conclusion. Only time would tell whether that decision would prove to be the best or the worst of his life.

'Why do you look so shocked?' he went on, seeing her big sea-coloured eyes darken in distress. 'You know I'm only speaking the truth. Those are the facts, so why should it worry you to hear them put into words?'

'I…' Sienna could only shake her head, unable to find an answer.

She couldn't deny the truth of what he had said. But it still disturbed her to have it stated so baldly, in the flat, emotionless voice Keir had used to deliver them.

'Conscience problems, sweetheart?' he questioned softly. 'Does it trouble you to discover that you might be every bit as cold-blooded and demanding as I am after all? That when you see something you really want you go for it with all the determination and ruthlessness you can muster up? And that in pursuit of your dream you can drive a harder bargain than anyone?'

His cynical words caught Sienna her on the raw, taking her breath away and making her want to lash out unthinkingly.

'If that was the case then you wouldn't be here right now!' she flashed at him. 'Believe me, if I could have what I *really want*, you wouldn't be the man with a wedding ring on his finger! And if I was to achieve a *dream*, then I would have married—'

'I know. Your precious Dean. The man whose shoes I couldn't possibly fill.'

The temperature in the small room suddenly seemed to have plummeted dramatically, making Sienna shiver convulsively in spite of the late August sun streaming in through the windows. She felt as if Keir's snarled words had been formed in freezing blocks of ice that had fallen brutally onto her delicate skin, chilling her where they landed.

With an effort she brought her dark head up, her face pale and her eyes clouded with remembered pain.

'Leave Dean out of this!'

'I would if I could,' Keir shot back, 'but you seem determined to keep flinging him in my face. I know that he's the one you really love, and that if you could have married him you would have done—but let me remind you of another truth, lady. One you obviously don't wish to face any more than all the rest.'

Keir's voice lowered suddenly, dropping to a low, dangerous whisper that was all the more menacing because of the softness of its tone.

'You haven't married Dean—you married me. As you just pointed out, *I* am the one with a wedding ring on my finger, not your precious lover-boy, who must be cursing his bad judgement in not staying around a little longer.'

'Judgement? Staying…?' Sienna frowned her confusion. 'I don't understand.'

'Oh, come now, darling, you understand only too well. You're not trying to claim that if dear Dean had stayed long enough to discover just how wealthy a young woman you are he wouldn't have had second thoughts about turning his back on you after all?'

Not for the first time, Sienna was thankful that she had never told anyone the full story of Dean's betrayal, but had kept the secret hidden away from prying eyes, especially Keir's.

'You think he would have married me for my money? You couldn't be more wrong.'

'I'm damn sure that he would never have been able to resist the lure of your inheritance, and he couldn't have turned down the opportunity of sharing it with you.'

'As you couldn't…' It was a low, despondent whisper.

'As I couldn't.' Keir confirmed brutally, his narrowed eyes dark and hard as jet, no trace of light showing in them. 'But there's one thing you must remember, my Sienna. One fact that differentiates me from the man you loved and lost and puts me here, with you, when he is who knows where, with God knows who. And that is that *you* proposed to *me*. You came to me with your idea of a marriage contract. *Me*. No one else. And we both know why you did that. Don't we?'

Sienna found it impossible to meet that cold, obsidian gaze. Nervously she dropped her eyes to stare at the floor, fixing them on the highly polished toes of Keir's handmade black shoes, planted firmly on the thick red carpet. But she couldn't block out the ruthless, inimical tones of that softly insistent voice as, seeing she was incapable of speech, Keir answered his question for himself.

'Of course we do. You wanted someone to act as your husband long enough to convince your newly discovered

uncle that you were head over heels in love and to ensure
that every penny of your inheritance was paid over. You
needed someone who people would believe you might actually want to marry, someone who wouldn't disgrace you
in public. But most of all you needed someone who you
could bear to have in your bed...'

'No...'

It was a purely instinctual response, weak and thready, a
protest against the grasping, avaricious picture he was painting with his words.

'Yes,' Keir corrected gently. 'Oh, yes, my darling. Any
number of men would have married you for the price you
were prepared to pay, but you asked me. It's easy enough
to guess why.'

Transfixed, frozen into stillness, Sienna saw those shiny
shoes come closer to her, Keir's footsteps silent on the soft,
rich pile of the carpet. Unable to move away, she felt the
soft brush of his skin against hers as his hand slid under her
chin, his palm warm and hard as he impelled her face upwards. When she would have fought him, he simply applied
a little more pressure, overcoming her resistance as if it had
never been, until her rebellious blue-green eyes blazed into
his, stubborn rejection of what he was about to say stamped
into every line of her face.

'*This* is what you want from me...'

His gentleness was what took her by surprise, defusing
her protest before it even had time to form. His kiss was
the softest drift of his lips across her cheek, barely grazing
the edge of her mouth in a way that had her moaning in
involuntary disappointment.

Because even that featherlight touch was enough to spark
off the hunger inside. Carefully calculated to awaken need,
but not feed it, it was as unsatisfactory as it was enchanting.
Involuntarily Sienna's eyes closed, her head turning in the
direction of that tormenting mouth, seeking more, wanting
a proper kiss, the sort that spoke of urgency and craving,
communicating wordlessly the passion that flickered around

them like the build up of static before a violent thunder-storm.

Close to her ear she felt Keir's warm breath, heard his softly triumphant laughter before she was rewarded with another kiss, only slightly more definite this time. His lips touched against hers, then danced away before she could respond, dropping brief, unfulfilling caresses on her cheek, her forehead, her closed eyelids and finally the dark silk of her hair.

'This is what burns between us, what neither of us can fight or deny. This…'

'*Keir!*'

The protest was torn from her, forming on her tongue before she had time to create any sort of coherent thought.

'What is it, sweetheart?' Amusement threaded through his voice, making it warm and teasing as once more those tormenting lips came close, then paused, only provocative inches away from her own. 'Tell me what you want and I'll give it to you.'

Determinedly keeping her eyes shut, Sienna still couldn't escape the scent of his skin, the faint sound of his breathing. It was more than she could bear, her self-inflicted blindness making every other sense excruciatingly sensitive to everything about him. She had never been more aware of the warmth of his body, the soft brush of his hair against her forehead as he leaned closer.

'Tell me!' he urged again, and the scent of his breath against her face was more than she could bear.

'Keir!'

In spite of herself, her eyes flew open, clashing with the dark intensity of his gaze so very close. Drowning in those chocolate-brown depths, she could no longer listen to the voice of common sense inside her head, heed its warnings, its reminders of the need for self-preservation.

'Kiss me, damn you! Kiss me properly before I go completely out of my mind.'

'Your wish is my command,' Keir muttered roughly, and

the next moment she was enclosed in iron-hard arms, hauled up against the wall of his chest and kissed with a thoroughness that made her head swim.

Without the strength of Keir's hands, clamped tight against the small of her back, she feared she might actually keel over, falling in a swooning heap on the carpet. She was incapable of supporting herself, clinging to the broad, straight shoulders under the fine cloth of his elegant jacket in a desperate attempt to keep herself upright.

Willingly she accepted the hard pressure of his lips, the teasing provocation of his tongue. With a sensual groan her mouth parted to welcome the intimate invasion, her body coming to life under the knowing caresses of his hands.

'Oh, Keir!' she sighed, snatching in a swift, much needed breath.

Her blood was a hot, bubbling stream that spread into every corner of her being, making every nerve, every cell spring into wild, yearning life. She felt that heat pounding against her skull, pulsing down her throat and along her spine, coiling around her heart and making her pelvis throb with molten need.

When his hard fingers curved over the swell of her breasts, their warmth searing into her sensitive flesh through the delicate lace that covered them, she writhed against him, her hunger spiralling as she felt the powerful evidence of his arousal. Beneath the soft silk that lined her dress, her sensitive nipples tightened, hardening in matching response. Simply knowing that he needed her as much as she wanted him made her thoughts spin off into a whirlwind of sensation.

Before I go out of my mind! Sienna thought, when finally the room stopped swinging round and she slowly resurfaced from the depths of sensuality into which she had fallen. She was there already, she admitted to herself. Totally crazed and incapable of rational thought where this man was concerned.

She didn't care if she was confirming everything he had

said about her reasons for marrying him. Couldn't care, because after all it was nothing more or less than the truth. In the first moment Keir Alexander had kissed her he had sparked off a conflagration of desire that was still blazing at white-hot intensity months later. She needed only a look, a word, a caress, or, as now, the touch of his lips against her skin, and she was lost, drowning in a sea of sensation with no wish at all to come up for air.

'Oh, lady, you drive me out of my mind,' Keir muttered against the soft skin of her arched throat. 'You make me forget everything I ever learned about civilised behaviour or gentlemanly conduct. When you're in my arms I feel as primitive as any caveman. I just want to drag you off to my bed, or push you against the wall, or down onto the floor...'

And she would let him, too, Sienna realised hazily. With the taste of his skin on her lips, the scent of his hair in her nostrils, the ragged sound of his breathing in her ears, she had completely forgotten who or where she was, and why. Her own need, urgent and demanding as his, would meet and match any move he made. Already, her impatient hands were under the elegant jacket, tugging avidly at the buttons on his shirt, anxious for the feel of his warm flesh underneath their seeking fingers.

'Sienna...'

Keir too needed more. His hands were under the fall of her veil, fumbling awkwardly with the tiny pearl buttons at the back of her dress, his actions made uncharacteristically clumsy with need.

'Sienna, you're mine—*mine*. You could never be with anyone else, never marry anyone else...'

Both so intent on each other, so absorbed in the elemental force that had them in their grip, they didn't hear the approaching footsteps or register that the door was slightly ajar until a voice they both recognised penetrated the burning mist that filled their thoughts.

'I've no idea where they are! But I've looked everywhere else, so perhaps they're down here.'

Mother!

Realisation hit Sienna in the same moment that Keir's head came up, wide dark eyes looking straight into her stunned aquamarine ones as they both froze into absolute stillness.

'Caroline!'

In instinctive reaction Keir jerked away from her as if he'd been stung, his hands coming up automatically to smooth down his clothing, fasten the buttons she had wrenched open. It was only now, seeing him a short distance away, that Sienna realised just what damage she had inflicted on his usually immaculate appearance. The sleek dark hair was wild and ruffled, his shirt pulled half out of the waistband of his trousers, his elegant tie totally askew.

Hot colour suffused her cheeks at the thought of what she had done, of how close they had come to being caught, the scene that might have met her mother's eyes.

'What's the problem, darling?' Keir had caught her response. 'Why are you so embarrassed.'

'You know why!' Sienna whispered, her hands twisting together in uncomfortable unease. 'If we hadn't heard... If she'd come in...'

'She'd have known that I was kissing you. So what?' Keir's shrug dismissed her concern as utterly unimportant.

'Kissing!' Sienna rolled her eyes in exasperation at the understatement. 'Keir, we were more than *kissing...*'

'And that's such a crime? Sweetheart, we're married! We're supposed to kiss—and more. In fact, I'm sure that's what your mother's expecting—why she's been careful to give us plenty of advance warning. Why do you think it's taking her so long to get down the corridor? I've never known Caroline bump into so many things, even if she does walk with a stick.'

Of course. Now that Sienna was able to think more clearly, she had to admit that her mother was making heavy weather of her progress towards them. And she was chattering at the top of her voice as she came.

But she would be here in a moment.

'Do I look all right?' she asked, suddenly painfully aware of the way Keir had restored his former elegant appearance and was looking totally composed and in control while she still felt flustered and distraught.

'You look fine.'

Keir turned a casually assessing glance on her, sliding from the top of her head down past her over-bright eyes and glowing cheeks and onto the square-cut neckline of her gown, where her struggle to regain control of her uneven breathing showed in the frantic way her breasts rose and fell.

'You look quite perfect—just as a newly married bride should be.'

Then, just as Sienna vented a deep sigh of relief, he added with a wicked grin.

'You look thoroughly kissed, sensually aroused, and bitterly frustrated at having your lovemaking session interrupted.'

'Oh, you…!'

Frantically she whirled round, hunting for a mirror to assess the damage, but too late. Behind her she heard Keir's soft laughter blending with the sound of her mother's voice calling her name.

'Sienna, darling! Keir?'

The door was pushed open and Caroline's thin form appeared in the doorway.

'Ah, there you are! I rather suspected as much. You wanted a little privacy—and who could blame you?' Her smile in Keir's direction was warmly conspiratorial. 'But your guests are getting a little restless, wondering where you are. I think it's time to cut the cake.'

'We were just coming.'

Sienna supposed she should be grateful for Keir's unruffled equanimity. She found herself unable to speak, to form any sort of coherent answer to her mother's questions. And when she turned to face the new arrival any chance of even

thinking straight was driven from her mind. For behind
Caroline, his bulky frame dwarfing her completely, stood
Francis Nash, the man for whose benefit this whole pretence
of a marriage had been staged. Her thoughts a blur, Sienna's
eyes went automatically to Keir, instinctively seeking help.

He stepped into the breach at once, moving to her side
with a smile that was every bit as loving and devoted as she
could have wished as he slipped an arm around her waist
and drew her close.

'We're just coming. I'm sorry if you thought us rude,
slipping away like that, but I had something to tell Sienna,
and I wanted to do it in private.'

'Of course! The honeymoon!'

Her mother's response so startled Sienna that at last she
found her tongue was free to speak.

'You knew!'

'Of course she knew.' Keir's tone was softly indulgent.
'How else do you think I could arrange for your bags to be
packed and your passport ready for us to leave at the end
of the reception?'

The look he turned on Francis Nash was jokingly conspiratorial—men of the world together.

'I've arranged a surprise trip for my bride—one she knew
nothing about. When I told her, she became rather emotional
and—over-enthusiastic in her appreciation. I hope you don't
feel neglected.'

'Er, not at all... I've been well entertained.' Francis returned, all the earlier suspicion Sienna had seen in him melting away in the warmth of Keir's deliberate charm assault.

'But now, my love, we have to go back to the reception.
As your mother says, we've neglected our guests long
enough.'

He was directing that charm at her now, the dark coffee-
coloured eyes gazing deep into her stunned turquoise ones
as if they were once more alone together. Hidden from the
couple at the door by the bulk of his body, Sienna glared
her feelings straight into his smiling face.

Rather emotional and over-enthusiastic indeed! How dared he?

'But first,' Keir went on sweetly, ignoring her silently communicated fury, 'I think perhaps a little repair work would be a good idea.'

Pulling an immaculate white handkerchief from his pocket, he tenderly wiped it around the curves of her mouth. It was only when he lifted it again and she could see that it had come away stained pink that Sienna realised how badly her lipstick had smudged in the heat of their shared passion just moments before.

The knowledge of what a mess she must have looked, and just how deliberately Keir had neglected to warn her of the fact, added fuel to her already burning anger. Struggling against the impulse to administer a smart, reproving kick to his ankle, she had to content herself with glaring even more fiercely at him as he considered his handiwork.

'There, now you look quite perfect.' Bending to brush a soft kiss against her temple, he whispered with laughter warming his voice, 'Don't glower so, darling. You'll ruin the good impression we've already made. Uncle Francis is totally convinced that we just can't keep our hands off each other.'

'And when I next get my hands on you...' Sienna hissed out of the corner of her mouth, only to find that her fury made him laugh even more.

'Promises, promises!' he returned, dropping another, casual kiss onto the tip of her nose. 'But I'm afraid you'll have to wait until we arrive at our honeymoon destination. Now, don't embarrass me in front of your family.'

Embarrass! This time Sienna did kick out at him, only to find that Keir had perfectly anticipated her reaction and, moving surprisingly quickly and neatly for such a big man, easily dodged out of reach. Caught off balance, she was forced to grab at his arm for support, knowing only too well that he was thoroughly enjoying her discomfiture.

Embarrass! The man didn't have an embarrassable bone

in his body, damn him! Her already ruffled mood was made all the worse by the fact that Keir had deliberately raised his voice on the last words, so as to make sure that her uncle and Caroline had heard his laughing comment too.

'It had better be somewhere I like!' she managed through clenched teeth.

'Oh, you'll love it!' her mother put in enthusiastically. 'Keir has been so thoughtful... He's chosen the *perfect* place.'

The warmly approving look she turned on her son-in-law sobered Sienna up in a rush. All anger seeped away from her, leaving her feeling unsettled and prey to disturbing thoughts.

This obvious affection that her mother had developed for Keir, the high esteem in which she so evidently held him, was a complication she couldn't possibly have anticipated when she had started out on this plan of a pretend marriage. But it had happened and there was nothing she could do about it. She could only wonder just how it would affect her mother when, in a year's time, she had to announce the uncontested divorce which was the way they had agreed this farce would end.

'Come on, sweetheart.' Keir's arm around her waist once more urged her out through the door. 'The sooner we get this cake cut, the sooner we can get out of here. It won't be long before we can be on that plane and alone together.'

Alone together. Sienna sat back in her chair, breathing in the warm night air. She and Keir were alone together now. Alone in this villa—this *Italian* villa.

Now she knew why her mother had been so excited, why Caroline had so obviously approved of Keir's choice of honeymoon destination.

Sienna herself hadn't had the faintest idea where she was going. Knowing she had no option but to do as he said, she had followed Keir blindly to the airport. Exhausted by the stresses of the day, the strain of having to pretend to everyone, to put on a show, even in front of her own mother, she had simply slumped in her seat, too tired, too drained even to ask or make any other effort to find out where they were heading. It had only been when their flight was called that she had had the first inkling of where she was to spend her honeymoon.

'Pisa!' she'd exclaimed, turning to stare at Keir in amazement. 'We're going to Italy!'

'That's right—Tuscany, to be precise. I thought you'd like to see the place where your mother met your father— the place you were named after. I've rented a villa just outside Siena.'

She had thought that things couldn't get any worse, but it seemed that fate had had this one final, ironic twist in store for her. Here, in the heart of the Tuscan countryside, where her father had met her mother, seduced her and abandoned her, leaving her pregnant, she was finally alone with the man she had to call her husband—at least for the next twelve months.

A faint movement, a flash of white, caught her vision at the corner of her eye. He was there. Keir had come out of the villa and was walking towards her. Slowly Sienna lifted her head and turned to face her husband. Here, where her mother had fallen hopelessly in love and been left alone and heartbroken, her own travesty of a marriage was to begin.

CHAPTER FIVE

HE HAD been watching her for some time.

In the shadow of the doorway, out of sight and unobserved, Keir had been standing silently, his long body leaning against the wall, just watching this woman who was now his wife.

God, but she was beautiful! With her long dark hair now loosed from the elaborate style that had confined it throughout the long day and tumbling down her back, her high cheekbones and full, softly sensual mouth, she made him think of the first time he had seen her. Then, he had anticipated that her eyes would be as dark as his own. It had only been when she'd turned, and he had seen with a sense of shock their soft, sea-washed colour, that he had fully appreciated the singular nature of her particular loveliness. And that appreciation had grown as he had come to know her.

As he had come to know her! Keir laughed silently, sardonically, at his own foolishness. He didn't know her at all. All he really knew was that instant, blazing physical attraction that had brought them together in the first place. An attraction that showed no sign of palling but which grew stronger with every day that passed.

Simply standing here, just looking at the delicate purity of her carved profile, the sensual curves of her body in the soft lilac dress, was enough to make him feel as he had been kicked hard in the gut, driving all the breath from his body and making him ache with need. But as to what was going on inside that exquisite head of hers—there he was truly groping in the dark.

That was why he had determined on this honeymoon. He

59

had known that she hadn't expected it, that she had believed they would simply go from their wedding to his home until the house she had inherited could be adapted for Caroline's use. And it had been that element of surprise that he had been aiming for, deliberately wrong-footing her.

He had brought her to Italy in the hope that here, on neutral ground, far away from home and the pressures that had driven her—driven both of them—to start out on this counterfeit marriage, he would finally begin to find out just what made this wife of his tick.

But some slight sound he hadn't been aware of making, a movement he hadn't controlled, had alerted her to his presence. Her head had turned; he had no alternative but to join her.

'What were you doing, lurking there in the shadows?'

'I wasn't lurking,' Keir returned cagily. 'I was simply watching you.'

'Watching me?' It was clearly not what she had expected. 'Why?'

'Because I like looking at you. Why not? Can't a man look at his wife?'

Sienna reached for the wine bottle on the table in front of her, her movements edgy and uneven, like her voice.

'We're not the normal sort of man and wife. Some wine?'

'Thanks…'

He took the glass with deliberate slowness, letting his fingers linger on hers for a couple of seconds, meeting her wary gaze head-on.

'So it's not normal for a man to find his wife beautiful?' he asked quietly, lifting his drink to his lips.

Sienna had been about to sip from her own glass, but now she set it down with a distinct tremor that had her hastily reaching to steady it before it fell over, spilling its contents onto the stone flags.

'Of course that's normal! I simply meant that you don't have to put on the big romantic act just because we're on honeymoon. After all, we both know it isn't real.'

'Who said it was just an act? I do think you're beautiful and I want you to know it! And as for romance—we're in Italy. One of the most romantic countries in the world—'

'Not for my mother,' Sienna cut in sharply. 'I doubt if she thinks of her time here in that way. I mean, all it led to was betrayal and heartbreak.'

'You couldn't be more wrong.'

'Oh, so now you know my mother better than I do?'

'Have you talked to her about it?' Keir set his glass down with rather more care than she had used earlier. 'Really talked? I think you'll find that her memories are much happier than you imagine. They're of a time was she was in love and loved in return...'

Sienna's cynical snort of disbelief made it only too plain what she thought about that.

'Okay—she *thought* she was loved. And even though it ended unhappily she doesn't regret having had that experience.'

'"Better to have loved and lost than never to have loved at all"?' Sienna quoted satirically.

'Exactly.'

'You'll have to forgive me if I disagree.'

'You don't believe that having known Dean was worth it?' Keir enquired, with a deceptive mildness that Sienna privately felt hid a very different frame of mind. 'That having known love, even if only once, was—'

'I don't think that anything about Dean was worth it!' Sienna snapped, anxious to cut off that line of questioning once and for all. 'In fact, I truly wish I had never, ever met him!'

She didn't like the look he gave her, or the way one dark straight brow lifted slightly, questioning the truth of her overly vehement declaration.

'And I don't want to talk about him or anything to do with him. Does my mother really have happy memories of Siena?' she asked, because she couldn't help herself.

Keir's dark head nodded slowly as he swallowed another mouthful of wine.

'One of the most memorable times of her life, she told me. She also said that it was impossible to have anything but good thoughts about a time and a relationship that resulted in her having you.'

'You *have* talked, haven't you?' The words came out jerkily, made that way by the unpleasant sensation of unease that was pricking at her, rather like mental pins and needles.

'Your mother is very easy to talk to, and our conversations are always wide-ranging and stimulating. I like Caroline, and I think she likes me.'

'Oh…'

Hastily Sienna reached for her glass again, burying her nose in it so that the dark curtains of her hair fell down on either side of her face, hiding her expression from him.

It was impossible not to think of the way her mother had looked at Keir as they'd left the wedding reception. The warm, approving smiles, the obviously genuine emotion in the hug she had given him as they'd said goodbye. A hug Keir had been only too keen to return, she now recalled. All her anxieties about Caroline's affection for her new son-in-law and the potential problems that might result from that came rushing back in a distressing flood, making her shift uneasily in her seat.

'I wish you wouldn't.'

'Wouldn't what? Talk to your mother? Sienna, I am her son-in-law.'

'Temporary son-in-law. What—?'

She looked up in shock as Keir's glass in turn was slammed down on the table top.

'Well it's true!' she protested sharply.

'*You* know it's true. *I* know it's true.'

The statement was cold and clipped, and Keir's eyes, gleaming disturbingly in the moonlight, were hard, distant and unapproachable.

'But I thought the whole idea was that *no one else* should

know—that everyone should believe our marriage was the genuine thing. It's going to look pretty damn strange, not to mention unconvincing, if I don't even try to make an effort to get on with your mother, especially if she's going to live with us.'

Put like that, there was no denying how right he was. The very reasonableness of his tone made her feel all sorts of a fool for even having raised the subject.

'It's just that I don't want her hurt. She's had enough pain in her life, and now that she's ill I don't want her to put up with any more.'

'I can understand your concern, but really there's no need for it.'

Leaning forward, Keir took hold of her hand where it lay on the table, curling his warm, strong fingers round it.

'Believe me, I would never hurt your mother, Sienna. You must know that.'

'I—I know…'

Sienna wanted to believe that the unsteadiness of her reply was the result of his touch. That the simple contact had sparked off the usual mind-blowing physical response that she experienced with him. But to her consternation she found that the truth was much more complicated.

I would never hurt your mother. She had no hesitation in believing that. But would he offer the same assurance for Sienna herself? Would he be able to say, with the same conviction, I will never hurt *you*?

And the fact that she was even considering the problem was the most disturbing part of it. She would have said that nothing Keir could do could ever hurt her. After all, wasn't that why she had chosen him? Because in their relationship there were no unwanted complications, like emotional involvement of the sort that, after Dean, she was determined to avoid like the plague? So how could anything he did affect her badly enough to cause pain?

'Why the big sigh?'

To her horror she had betrayed the way she was feeling,

and Keir had caught it. Immediately she jumped onto the defensive, too shocked by her unexpected thoughts to try to explain them even to herself.

'I was just thinking of my mother, and—Andrew Nash. I still can't think of him as my father.'

'That's hardly surprising. After all, you never even saw him. And a father is so much more than someone who plays a physical part in your conception. Andrew Nash forfeited his right to that title when he walked out on your mother twenty-six years ago. A belated bequest in his will doesn't alter anything. Did I make a mistake, Sienna?'

'A mistake?'

Sienna frowned her confusion as much at his change of tone as at the question itself. Keir had lowered his voice until it was a softly husky whisper, a sound that brushed over the ends of her nerves in a way that made her shiver in disturbed response.

'In bringing you here? Did I make the wrong decision when I chose Italy for our honeymoon? Would you have preferred France, or perhaps somewhere exotic—a beach and palm trees?'

'No!' Sienna hastened to reassure him, amazed to find that he sounded as if it actually mattered to him. 'No, it wasn't a mistake. Mum's talked about Tuscany so much, and I've always wanted to see it for myself.'

Feeling suddenly disturbed and restless, she got to her feet, moving to lean against the stone wall that edged the terrace, staring out into the countryside, now completely dark except for a few scattered lights.

'Which way is Siena? North or south?'

'South—that way…'

Keir came to stand beside her, pointing away to their right.

'And Florence is in the opposite direction, back on the road we drove along on our way here from Pisa.'

'I can't wait to see the countryside in the daylight.

Everyone I know who's been here tells me it's spectacularly beautiful.'

'It is.'

Keir's response was distracted. This was like making polite conversation with a stranger, he thought uncomfortably. They were pussyfooting around each other in a way that only made his already unsettled mood worse. This was not at all how he had expected to feel on his wedding night.

What *had* he expected? When his mind threw the question at him he had no idea how to answer it. If the truth was told, he was working completely in the dark, unable to see what move to make next.

But one thing he *had* anticipated. He had thought that by now he would be feeling a great sense of freedom. That with Lucille off his back, the debt of honour paid to his father, he would be experiencing a sort of release from the problems that had beset him that would be close to euphoria.

Instead, he felt low and flat, in a way that, combined with the restless unease that had assailed him ever since he had woken, made him as jittery as a cat on a hot roof. Instead of experiencing a sense of liberty, his mood was dark and oppressive, as if he had exchanged one form of obligation for another. And right now he wasn't at all sure that he wouldn't prefer the uncomplicated financial contract with Lucille to the one that he was subsequently tied to.

'You've been here before?'

'A couple of times. The last holiday we had as a family was in Tuscany. That was the year before my mother died.'

Perhaps it was because of the gathering darkness, but the bleakness of his tone sounded disturbingly clear, making Sienna wince inwardly.

'That was when you were how old?'

'Nineteen. I'd just finished my first year at university, and I wasn't at all keen on the idea of going away with my parents. I took a lot of persuading, but I'll always be grateful that I went along in the end. Six months later, she discovered she had leukaemia. Four months after that, she was dead.'

'Oh, Keir…' It was the first time he had ever talked about his mother's tragically early death, and Sienna found that she was deeply touched that he had opened up in this way. 'I'm so sorry.'

Instinctively her hand went out to cover his strong fingers where they lay on the stone parapet. This would partly explain the warmth of his relationship with her mother. Having lost his own parent so early, he must feel the need to revive something of the relationship they had shared with Caroline.

And perhaps it also went some way towards clarifying why he had agreed to her proposal in the first place. He would know how it felt to have a sick mother. Know the feeling that you would do anything at all to make her life easier.

'And how long was it before your father married again?'

'Four years.' His mood had obviously darkened. Asking about Lucille had been a mistake.

But Sienna's curiosity got the better of her.

'She's much younger than I ever expected.'

'Barely forty.' Keir nodded. 'Only seven years older than me.'

Something bleak and disturbing shaded his voice, sending a shiver down Sienna's spine in spite of the warmth of the evening,

'She—'

'Leave her out of this, Sienna,' Keir commanded. 'I don't want my stepmother intruding on my wedding night.'

'*Your* wedding night!'

In spite of herself, Sienna took a small step backwards, unable to control her instinctive response. In her excitement at actually being in Italy she had managed to forget why they were there. She had been able to push from her mind all thought of what was ahead of her, but that possessive 'my wedding night' had brought it rushing back in a way that made her heart jerk in nervous reaction.

'Yes, of course.' To her horror she realised that he had caught the whisper she hadn't been able to hold back, the sudden sharpening of his tone making her mouth dry nervously. 'What is it, Sienna? You're not planning to back out of our agreement, are you?'

'N-no. It's just…'

She couldn't complete the sentence, her throat closing up around the words. It was one thing to agree to the conditions he had imposed in the heat of desperation, when the date of the wedding had still been in the future and the idea of actually going to bed with him had only been just that—an idea, not fully founded in reality. It was quite another to accept that she had used up all her waiting time, that Keir had called in his account, and that right here and now was when she had to start paying.

'Hey!' Keir's voice was surprisingly soft. 'Don't look so panic-stricken. I won't hurt you.'

'I—I know!'

Sienna cursed the quaver in her voice. She had told herself she could do this; convinced herself that, when it came to it, the blazing physical response she felt whenever he touched her would burn away all her fear, all restraint.

But that was when she had pictured Keir literally sweeping her off her feet. When she had imagined him gathering her close and kissing her stupid, driving all thoughts from her mind except the fact that he was a man and she was a woman, and that the need that had brought them together was as old and as elemental as time.

But Keir was making no move to do anything of the sort. Instead of taking her in his arms, he had actually moved a couple of steps backwards, away from her. Instead of the blazing passion she had anticipated, hoped for, there was a cool, unnerving distance, a perturbingly detached sense of circumspection about him. Those dark eyes narrowed thoughtfully, subjecting her to an emotionless scrutiny that made her shift uneasily from one foot to another.

'Do you think I'll force you, is that it? Damn it, Sienna,

don't you know me better than that? I've never bullied a woman into my bed, and I don't intend to start now.'

Perhaps it would be easier if he did, Sienna found herself thinking weakly. At least that would heat the blood that seemed to have frozen in her veins, break through the ice that surrounded her like sheets of plate glass.

She could see Keir's strongly carved face, the softness of his hair stirred by a faint breeze. She could hear his words, blurred slightly by the pounding of her pulse inside her head. But she couldn't make herself move to bridge that gap between them.

'Sienna!'

Her name hissed in between clenched teeth in a sound so expressive of impatience and obdurate demand that she shivered involuntarily. But almost immediately his mood changed again.

'Oh, hell! Look, Sienna, it's been a long day. You're tired. I want you in my bed, yes, but I want you willing. We have twelve months—that's more than enough time.'

'Enough time to take what you want and tire of me?' Sienna couldn't catch the impetuous, unthinking words back, even though she wished she'd never spoken as she saw his proud head go back, brown eyes flashing in bitter anger.

'That really rather depends on you,' he flung back. 'But I for one am not prepared to rush…'

Shaking his head, he raked both hands through the darkness of his hair.

'It's been a stressful day. If you want a little time—a breathing space—I understand. This villa has four bedrooms. If you'd rather sleep alone for tonight, then choose whichever one you want.'

'What?'

Sienna knew she was gaping at him, her confusion and disbelief clear on her face. Did he mean…? Could he mean…?

A tiny, craven part of her mind wanted to grasp at the

opportunity he offered. To take the chance to sleep alone for one last night. But, even as she let the thought slide into her mind, another, more worrying one replaced it.

For tonight, Keir had said, with a deliberate emphasis that left her in no doubt that one night's grace was all she was going to get. Tonight he might be feeling indulgent, generous to a fault because he'd got what he wanted, but tomorrow, and every other night that followed would be a very different matter.

After the proper wedding we have a real marriage. Those had been Keir's terms. There was no way he was going to free her from their arrangement, not without completely retracting what he had promised.

To delay would only make matters worse. The apprehension she felt now would never diminish, only grow worse with each second that passed.

And so she drew herself up, plastered on a smile that she hoped looked more convincing than it felt.

'Don't be silly, Keir!' Her lips felt stiff and wooden, forming the words with difficulty. 'We can't sleep alone. We're married! On honeymoon.'

'But as you've already pointed out, this isn't exactly the normal sort of honeymoon.'

Dark eyes probed hers, seeming to reach deep into her very soul, to try to read what was there. Sienna was sure that he must be able to see the way her heart seemed to be turning somersaults inside her chest, making her breath come in rapid, uneven gasps.

'Though I have to admit I'm forced to wonder just what constitutes ''normal'' under these circumstances.'

Sienna tried to speak, found it impossible, and ran a nervous tongue over her parched lips in order to moisten them.

'I'm sure that any husband would expect to—to sleep with his wife on the first night of their married life. And y-you more than most.'

'And why me more than most, my lovely Sienna?'

His tone had changed, darkened, the emphasis on that 'why me' ominously dangerous.

'We had a bargain. You'll want to claim what you're owed.'

In the gathering shadows it was almost impossible to read his expression clearly. But she couldn't be unaware of the black scowl that distorted his features, menacing as a thundercloud gathering on the horizon.

'You make it sound as if I'm collecting on a bad debt. And besides, you've already given me most of what you promised, so I can afford to be generous.'

Most of what you promised! The words slashed at her like a blunt knife, leaving a raw, bleeding wound. She could be in no doubt as to what he had meant.

He had wanted the money she had promised him to pay off his stepmother, and she had already guaranteed it. Hadn't he had the document waiting, ready to be signed just as soon as their marriage vows had been spoken?

Did she need any further evidence of just how little she meant to him? A real marriage, indeed! He meant no such thing! What he wanted was the best deal he could get.

His coldly calculating mind had assessed what she had offered him, weighed it against what she was asking in return, and decided he could agree to her terms. There was no emotion involved, not even the passion she had been foolish enough to assume. His financial acumen had recognised a good deal when it was offered, and the sexual opportunist in him had added the urge to gain some easy physical pleasure from the arrangement; that was all.

Of course he could afford to be generous! He had her right where he wanted her—and that was very much in second place to his damn business!

The realisation was like a rush of adrenaline in her mind, surprising her by the sense of freedom it brought. If Keir's emotions were so totally uninvolved in their arrangement, then surely she could match him step by step. She could use him as he planned to use her, taking the sexual pleasure their union could provide and giving nothing more.

And at the end of the year she would walk away, as heart free as he was.

'Yes, you have been generous.' Even in her own ears, her voice sounded cold and stilted, bringing the temperature around them down by several calculated degrees. 'After all, you have signed away your freedom in order to help me.'

She knew by the way that the long body before her moved restlessly that he had caught her reference to Lucille's comment at their wedding. Heard it and hadn't liked it at all.

'But we had an agreement, Keir, and I intend to fulfil my part of that deal. That way, no one can ever claim they were short-changed.'

'Oh, I would never claim that, sweetheart,' Keir's tone matched hers ice for ice, making every tiny hair on her skin lift in response. 'So far you've been scrupulous in complying with the letter of our contract.'

There was a distinct bite of acid on the last words that Sienna struggled to ignore.

'And I intend to deliver what I promised.'

'In that case...'

Hard face unsmiling, brown eyes totally lacking in warmth, Keir held out his hand to her.

'Shall we go upstairs?'

CHAPTER SIX

IT TOOK every ounce of courage that Sienna possessed to put her hand into his. The feel of his hard fingers closing around hers made her think of a trap snapping shut, and it was all that she could do not to start nervously, snatching it away from him as if she had been burned.

Without a word he led her into the house and upstairs, to the large, oak-beamed, simply furnished room which, on their arrival, he had declared would be where they would sleep for the duration of their stay. The shutters were fastened over the windows, making the room shadowy and dark, and the cool of the air-conditioning was almost shocking after the warmth of the evening outside. Within seconds, Sienna's skin felt chilled and clammy, and she had to struggle not to shiver openly. To do so would be to risk Keir thinking that her response was one of fear, and she was determined to hide her inner misgivings from him.

The maid had long ago unpacked their belongings and put them away. But some appallingly sensitive instinct, or, more likely, some instruction from Keir himself, had warned her that this was more than a simple holiday, but was supposed to be a honeymoon. And so, as Sienna followed Keir through the door, the first thing that caught her eye was the careful drape of her white silk nightdress, long-skirted, with a delicate lace bodice and shoestring straps, over the pillows on one side of the bed.

The *double* bed, she registered, her heart skipping a painful beat, A bed that, with its soft blue cotton cover, seemed to totally dominate the whole room, making it impossible to look anywhere else. Just the sight of it made her head spin, her legs weaken beneath her, and unthinkingly she tightened her grip on the strength of Keir's hand.

'Steady, my lovely.' His low voice gentled her as if she was some nervous, thoroughbred mare he feared might bolt.

The thought of doing just that had flashed into her mind. Into it, and straight out again, driven away by a mixture of careful rationalisation and fierce, determined pride.

Running away would do no good at all. It would only delay the inevitable. And the thought of the humiliation of being pursued, caught, and dragged back to this room again was more than she could bear. She had made her bed, Sienna thought, gritting her teeth against an impulse to near-hysterical laughter. Made it and must now resign herself to lying in it, with Keir at her side.

'There's no need to be nervous. We can take this as slowly as you'd like. We have all the time in the world.'

Sienna's free hand, clenched into a tight fist, went to her mouth, crushing back the whimper of distress that almost escaped her. How could she tell him that time was not what she needed? That the last thing she wanted was for this to be slow?

Time would give her too much opportunity to think. To register what was happening to her and know that there was no way out. Time would leave her in no doubt at all that this was a business deal and nothing more, offering her no comforting emotions like love or passion to smooth away the rough edges, soften the hard truth of this cold-blooded seduction.

What she needed was the whirlwind of sensation that had assailed her whenever Keir had kissed her in the past. The heated tornado of need that had taken possession of her mind, leaving her incapable of thought, able only to feel, to hunger, to *yearn*. Blinded by that storm of emotion, she could get through this. Any other way and it might destroy her.

But Keir still seemed strangely reluctant to touch her.

Instead, he led her into the middle of the room, dropping her hand and turning to face her.

'Perhaps you'd like a while to yourself? Time to…' the dark-eyed, sombre gaze went to the nightdress on the bed and then to the door of the adjoining *en suite* bathroom '…refresh yourself. Get ready…'

Too numb to speak, Sienna could only nod silently. But as he made a move to walk away the panic that had been twisting in her stomach rose to the surface, telling her in no uncertain terms that this was the last thing she wanted.

'No!'

It was a choked cry, impossible to hold back, and, hearing it, Keir froze before swinging round sharply.

'No?'

'No, I don't want to be left alone like some virginal Victorian bride, while my groom goes downstairs for one last drink, leaving me to get modestly into bed and lie there, waiting. I don't want to bathe, brush my hair, perfume my skin, so that my husband will enjoy taking his conjugal rights—taking me—making me his. That might be appropriate if…'

The words died on her lips, shrivelled into nothing by the fierce blaze in his eyes, the smouldering fury that was so near to the surface he was obviously having to exert all his strength simply to rein it in.

'If this was a real marriage?' he finished for her, with a clipped acidity that made her wince away in misery. 'And you have been so determined to impress on me that it's not. But it *will be* a real marriage, my sweet Sienna, at least for the period arranged by our contract. A real marriage or no marriage—the choice is yours. Are you saying that you want this marriage annulled, revealed as the farce that it is?'

Wide and clouded, Sienna's sea-coloured eyes went to the silk nightdress on the bed. The nightdress that her mother had bought for her, her thin face alight with happiness as she presented it to her daughter as part of her trousseau, telling her to wear it on her wedding night in order to be a beautiful bride for her wonderful husband.

If she called a halt now, how could she face her mother again? And not just because of the inheritance that would then no longer be hers. How could she disillusion Caroline, reveal to her that the wonderful, fairy tale, happy-ever-after marriage that she had believed in was nothing but an illusion, a fantasy dreamed up quite cold-bloodedly for purely materialistic reasons? Not that those reasons could be described as *pure*, she reflected miserably.

'N-no...' she said hesitantly. 'That's not what I want.'

'Then what *do* you want? Come on, Sienna,' Keir urged huskily. 'You've been so determined to let me know what you *don't* want. Isn't it time you started coming clean about what you *do*?'

'I—I...'

His eyes were so deep and dark that she couldn't look away, finding her gaze instead drawn and held, transfixed as if she had been turned to stone.

This must be how it felt to be hypnotised, she thought hazily. This feeling that she had no will of her own, but must wait, quiescent and resigned, like a discarded mario-nette, until the man before her pulled the strings or issued a command that would tell her what to do.

'Say it,' Keir said now, his whisper shivering through the still air. 'Tell me what you want and it can be yours.'

And suddenly it was so easy. Suddenly she knew what she wanted, as if there was nothing else in the world. There was only the hushed silence of the night, and this room, this man and herself, and a communion between them that was as old and as primitive as time.

It was there in the depths of his black, enlarged pupils, in the streak of hectic colour high on the wide cheekbones. It echoed through every uneven breath and in the rapid, jerky patter of her own heart. And in that moment she knew that she had stopped running and that everything she wanted was right here, right now, in this room and nowhere else.

'I want you to kiss me.' Her voice croaked slightly, but it surprised her with the strength and conviction she managed. But still she had to repeat herself, so there could be no mistake. 'Keir, I want you to kiss me…'

'I thought you'd never ask!'

He moved so quickly that she barely saw him. All she knew was that suddenly he was there, with her, enfolding her, surrounding her with the warmth and strength of his body. With one arm at her waist, another at her shoulders, he held her tight up against him, her head bent back while his mouth plundered hers with a fierce hunger that held all the wild heat of the fires burning deep inside him.

And it was just as she had imagined. Just as she had hoped. There was no room for thought, only for feeling. Nothing in her mind but sensation. Nothing in her heart but a flame that matched and outstripped the blaze in his. Nothing in her body but the tempestuous, unbridled hunger that made her shudder with need, her moan a feral, uncontrollable sound expressive of a hunger so deep she had never been fully aware of its existence.

But she knew of it now. It was as if the floodgates inside her had been flung open and she was powerless against the force of the torrent that stormed through, sweeping everything else before it.

'I want you to kiss me,' she muttered again, her voice shaking with a sort of desperation. 'I want you to hold me, and touch me…'

She had no sense at all of having formed the whispered litany of need, only that it tumbled from her lips like a prayer. And that Keir obeyed every request without protest or hesitation.

'I want you to caress me, stroke my skin, make me want you, make me need you.'

'You've got it, darling…' Keir's response was a rough, thickened whisper, his voice muffled against the delicate skin of her throat where his lips blazed a burning trail down towards the racing pulse at the base of her neck. 'Anything you want. Everything you want.'

His hands were at the back of her neck, where the zip fastening of her lilac dress gave him far less trouble than the buttons on her wedding dress had hours earlier. With a faint rustle the delicate material slid down from her shoulders, paused for a moment before she dropped her arms to free it, then slithered all the length of her body to pool in a crumpled heap on the floor at her feet.

This time, Sienna's shiver was one of excitement and anticipation. All the nervousness of moments before had vanished, burned up in the heat that raged through every vein, every nerve-ending, making her skin glow as if it was bathed in the heat of the Tuscan sun and not the cool, shimmering gleam of moonlight.

Her eyes were closed, her body trembling under the onslaught of the sensations that ripped through her. Keir's touch now seemed to be everywhere. On her face, on her arms, smoothing over the rounded curves of her shoulders, sliding down to encircle and cup the warm weight of her breasts.

Against the hard heat of his hands, her sensitised nipples peaked, pressing an urgent message of need into his palms. And lower down, at the core of her most feminine being, the throbbing sensation that started up was like a burning electrical current, sending shockwaves radiating out into every other part of her.

'I want you to make me yours, make me forget about everything else, anything else. I want you to make this into the experience I know it can be. I want you to make it— make it real...'

Make it real! The words reverberated inside Keir's head as her voice choked off on a sigh of delight at some particularly pleasurable touch of his strong fingers. *Make it real!* Dear God, if she only knew!

With his rational mind scrambled by the beating, insistent clamour of every one of his senses, totally at the mercy of the hunger that throbbed inside him, tormenting the most sensitive parts of his anatomy, he almost told her. He almost opened his mouth and blurted out the truth, realising only at the very last moment that to do so would be to ruin everything. Gritting his teeth with the effort, he swallowed down the betraying words.

'Make it real, sweetheart?' he muttered, his tone raw and uneven. 'I can't promise you that. But I can promise you that what we have together will be very special. I promise you a honeymoon you'll never forget.'

'Show me.' It was part request, part command, part sigh of hunger. 'Show me what you—'

The words were crushed back down her throat as once more his mouth fastened on hers, lips fusing hungrily together. Somehow he had shrugged out of the polo shirt he wore, the heated silk of his skin smooth under her hands as she writhed against him in pleasurable abandon. Each second piled sensation on sensation, opening her mouth to him, adding that bit more fuel to the fires of passion they had built between them.

With confident ease he stripped off the wisps of silk that were all she wore, tossing them aside so that they floated like drifts of gossamer onto the polished wood of the floor. Against the yearning sensitivity of her now naked breasts the faint roughness of his body hair was a stinging delight, making her gasp her response into his demanding mouth. She felt the burning power of his arousal pressing against her, and instinctively opened her thighs so that she could accept him into the cradle of her hips.

With a muttered curse Keir gathered her up into his arms, lifting her completely off her feet and carrying her to the bed, where he flung back the covers with a violent gesture, depositing her none too gently on the soft linen sheets. Pausing only to discard his own remaining clothing, he came down beside her, his long, muscular body dark against the pastel bedding, his skin hot to her touch.

'I knew it would be like this,' he muttered thickly. 'Knew

it from the moment I kissed you. You're so responsive to me, and that just blows me away. I can't think straight...'

Watching her intently, he dropped a swift kiss on one pink nipple, then slowly encircled it with his tongue, laughing deep in his throat as she squirmed in breathless, whimpering excitement.

'And neither can you. Do you know what it does to me to see you out of control like this?'

'I—I can see what it does. . .' Sienna managed on a shaken laugh, turquoise eyes widening as she took in the full impact of his powerful nakedness, the potent force of his masculinity. 'How could I be unaware...?'

Her fingers trembling slightly, she reached out to touch him, laughing again, but this time on a note of triumph as his powerful body convulsed at her touch, the shudders of delight that shook him giving her an overwhelming sense of power. How was it possible that this strong, cold-blooded man could be at her mercy like this? How could she have brought him to this state, where each breath rasped into his lungs so painfully, where his eyes were and glazed with uncontrollable desire?

'You witch!' he reproved softly. 'Do that again and I won't be answerable for the consequences.'

'Perhaps the consequences are exactly what I'm after,' Sienna teased, her turquoise eyes gleaming provocatively from behind the silken fall of her long dark hair. 'Perhaps I want—'

'I know *exactly* what you want,' Keir broke in on her. 'You want to know how you make me feel. You want to experience something of the same. Well, when you touch me here...'

Briefly he held her hand against the slick, hard heat of him, then pushed her back against the softness of the pillows, supporting himself on his elbows on either side of her slender frame.

'It feels like this...'

His dark, arrogant head bent to take her right nipple into

his mouth, suckling hard. The warm breath of his laughter feathered over her skin as, unable to control her response, she reared up against him, shifting from side to side as a hot current of need seared along the pathway from the sting-ing tip to the most sensitive point at the juncture of her thighs.

'And at other times it's like this…'

With his mouth still at the tip of her breast, her let his hand drift downwards. Lingering for a moment at the curve of her waist, he traced a delicate circle around the indenture of her navel, before sliding with practised confidence into the hot, moist cleft hidden among the cluster of dark curling hair.

'*Keir!*'

His name was a raw, distraught cry of need, a primal sound that she couldn't have held back if she had tried. The wild, burning rush of pleasure that took possession of her pushed her beyond the edges of her control and into a tem-pestuous, uncivilised territory, where nothing she had ever experienced in the past mattered any more.

'Keir, please!'

Her arms curved around the powerful strength of his back, frantic fingers clenching over his broad shoulders, her nails digging into his skin in mute demand. She wanted him now. Needed to feel him deep inside her, filling her, assuaging the white-hot hunger that burned through every awakened cell in her body.

'Tell me what you want, darling.' Keir's voice was rough with a hunger that matched her own. 'I promised you—anything you want…whatever you want. So tell me…'

'You *know* what I want!'

Restlessly she adjusted her position so that he lay between her thighs. So near and yet so far from giving her what her hungry body craved.

'I want you.'

But still he tormented her by holding off. Still he waited,

watching her face, glittering dark eyes blazing down into hers.

'Say my name, Sienna,' he growled. 'Say it! Say, I want you—Keir.'

She would have said anything he demanded. And why hold back now? After all, it was nothing less than the truth.

'I want you, Keir...'

The words broke on a soaring cry of delight as, with a guttural sound of satisfaction, he moved swiftly, sheathing his strength in her enclosing warmth.

Sienna had barely time to register the glorious sensation of his powerful body filling hers before he began to move. And suddenly she was clinging to him again, beyond thought, beyond knowing even who she was. Every atom of her being was concentrated on the primitive thrusting rhythm that took her out of the known world and lifted her high onto the edge of some undiscovered whirling vortex.

She reached the centre in an explosion of stars, and then suddenly she was crying his name out loud and tumbling, spiralling in a crazy freefall of sensation in which there was no time or space but only herself and Keir and the shattering ecstasy they had created between them.

Above her she felt Keir's powerful body clench, heard his raw cry as he reached his own release before he collapsed on top of her, his broad chest heaving, slowly, slowly coming back down to earth.

It was the start of a very long night. A prolonged, repetitive cycle of awakening desire growing into burning passion, and from there into a frenzied giving and taking of pleasure in all the ways they could think of until at last, satiated and exhausted, they slept in each other's arms, oblivious to the sun coming up, the growing heat of the day.

At that last moment before she finally slid into the depths of sleep, Sienna stirred slightly, managing to lift her head to look into Keir's dark, clouded eyes.

'I'll say one thing for you, husband mine,' she murmured, stretching languorously against him. 'There's no way I could fault you in the performance of those particular conjugal duties.'

She was too tired, too replete, to notice the faint stiffening of the long muscular body beside her. Unaware of the momentary effort he made to bring his thoughts and feelings once more under strict control.

'I aim to please,' he returned, with a carefully casual intonation. 'I promised you a honeymoon to remember. You can believe me when I say that I fully intend to keep that promise.'

CHAPTER SEVEN

'I CAN'T believe I'm really here!' Sienna exclaimed, staring round her in amazement, her mind whirling with the effort of trying to take everything in. 'I can't believe I'm actually in Siena at last.'

Out of the corner of her eye she saw how Keir's mouth twisted slightly, and knew that he was clearly thinking along the same lines as her. There was no way either of them could deny the fact that one of the reasons for the delay between their arrival in Tuscany and the actual visit to Siena itself was the way that they had found it almost impossible to get out of bed.

After that first passion-drenched night, in which they had discovered the mutual delight that their bodies could share, they had indulged again and again in the heady pleasures of the flesh. When they hadn't been making love they had been sleeping off the excesses of the night, just occasionally finding the energy and the inclination to seek the necessary sustenance of food or a cooling, restorative swim in the villa's pool.

But that wasn't all the story. Along with the sensual indulgence of the past ten days had gone Keir's determination that the planned trip to Siena was not to be snatched at too quickly.

'You mustn't gobble the main treat down whole,' he'd reproved gently when, realising that almost half of the allotted days of their honeymoon had passed, Sienna had been desperate to visit the city that had meant so much to her mother. 'You need to take your time, get a feel for the rest of Tuscany too. Believe me, anticipation is a vital part of the enjoyment.' The warm curve to his mouth, the light in his eyes, had told her that he was not just thinking of her expectations of the visit, but other, more intimate pleasures.

And so they had explored other parts of the country together. They had visited such obvious sights as Pisa, with its leaning tower on the green lawns of the Campo dei Miracoli, and Florence, where they had taken in the cathedral, the famous Uffizi gallery and, at the end of a long, steep climb, the beautiful medieval church of San Miniato.

They had crossed the river Arno by the Ponte Vecchio, marvelling at the jewellery in the shops that lined it, and Keir had encouraged Sienna to taste some of the one hundred different variations of ice cream that contributed to Florence's claim to be the ice cream capital of the world. On other occasions they had lingered for hours over coffee or glasses of good red Chianti in some of the many fine restaurants, and Sienna had enjoyed those times as much as any. The slow, desultory conversations they had shared had helped her to relax, to allow herself to believe that perhaps, after all, this fabrication of a marriage might actually work out.

'It all seems so timeless, so unchanging,' she said now. 'It must have looked exactly like this when my mother was here.'

'Well, I don't suppose that twenty-six years or so means very much to a city whose palaces were built according to ideas laid down in the thirteenth century,' Keir returned on a note of amusement. 'With a history like that, the odd quarter of a century must seem like little more than the blink of an eye.'

'Being here now, I can believe that—and yet it's all of my lifetime.'

'Sometimes things change very slowly; sometimes they happen in an instant,' Keir commented cryptically, thinking of the impact she had had on him in the moment they had first met. He had been knocked completely off balance mentally, in the blink of an eyelid, and he had been unable to recover ever since.

Simply to look at her as she was now, tall and slim in a sleeveless turquoise sundress that matched the colour of those amazing eyes, made his body tighten in hungry response. With her dark hair tumbling loose around her shoulders, long, tanned bare legs revealed by her provocatively short skirt, delicate strappy sandals on her feet, she had only to smile in his direction and his temperature shot skywards.

He regretted the revealing comment as Sienna swung round to face him, her eyes bright with frank curiosity.

'That's a very enigmatic comment. Are you thinking of anything in particular?'

Keir's dark eyes wouldn't meet her enquiring turquoise ones as his gesture took in their surroundings in Siena's main square.

'If we'd been here a little earlier in the month, we could have seen the Palio—the horse race held in this square. All the riders and officials dress up in medieval costumes. It's an amazing spectacle.'

It was obvious that she was being distracted from what was actually in his thoughts, but Sienna found that genuine interest got the better of her wanting to pursue that original subject.

'A horse race? *Here?*' Once more she surveyed the uneven shape of the Campo, slightly sloping and irregular, and surrounded on all sides by high buildings of glowing rose-coloured brick. 'It doesn't seem possible—or very wise.'

'The stones are sanded over and the walls are padded. Even so, there are plenty of stories of jockeys—or even horses—flying through the air. But the Sienese say that no one has ever been killed at a Palio. That's because it's supposed to be under the direct protection of the Virgin Mary, but perhaps the fact that the race itself only lasts for a minute and a half has something to do with it.'

'It sounds quite terrifying.' Sienna found it hard to imagine the noise and the excitement of such an event in the sleepy atmosphere of this quiet morning.

'Did your mother never see the Palio? After all, she was

here in June, and the first of the races is run on the second of July.'

'No, she never... How did you know exactly when my mother was here?'

Keir's grin was wide in response to her mystified expression.

'She told me she named you for the place and the month in which you were conceived, and I learned your full name—Sienna June—at the wedding ceremony, of course. We go this way,' he added, catching hold of her hand and leading her down one of the shadowy streets at the west side of the square. 'How did she meet your father?'

Sienna forced herself to ignore the by now so familiar quickening of her pulse that was her automatic response to the touch of his hand on hers. Simply to have his long, hard fingers coiled around her own flooded her body with a glowing warmth that had nothing to do with the heat of the day. Casually dressed, in a white short-sleeved shirt and lightweight black trousers, and with his golden tan enhanced by days in the Italian sun, his tall, lean body had a sensual impact that took her breath away.

'Mum was nanny to a wealthy Sienese family, and my father was here on business—he was a wine importer. They met when he came to dinner with the Lorenzettis. He charmed her, and she fell head over heels in love.'

'He never let on that he was married?'

'Not for a moment.' Sienna shook her dark head in disbelief. 'Mum never suspected a thing until she discovered she was pregnant and he refused to have anything to do with her and the baby—with me.'

Keir's comment on that fact was short, succinct and very rude, making it only too plain how he viewed the selfishness Andrew Nash had displayed.

'He took advantage of her naïveté. She was only— what?—twenty-one?'

'Twenty-two.'

Sienna's response was low-voiced. She was uncomfortably aware of the fact that, although her mother had had the excuse of youth on her side, she herself had been older, infinitely more worldly-wise, when she had met Dean. And yet he had still deceived her just as easily as her father had her mother. More so, in fact. Because not only had he had a wife and a child back home in Brighton, but he had also been seeing someone else, one of Sienna's workmates at the beauty salon.

'Where are we going?'

She forced the question out in order to distract herself from the distress that thinking of Dean caused. She couldn't believe she had let herself be conned in that way. Had always believed that, with her mother's story as a warning always in her mind, she had developed a natural scepticism and instinctive distrust of men who were intent only on trying it on. And yet she had succumbed to Dean's blandishments, his outrageous compliments, his apparent devotion, with the sort of blind foolishness that she now found impossible to believe.

She had swallowed every one of his lies and been enticed into breaking her own careful rules for self-preservation, seduced into his bed with the ease of a practised angler landing a very gullible fish.

'This is Via del Capitano. It leads to the *Duomo*—the cathedral. I warn you, you'll either love it or hate it—there's no in between.'

'You're right!' Sienna could only gasp a short time later as she stared in amazement at the effect of the black and white stripes of marble stretching from floor to ceiling in the nave and the aisles of the huge Gothic cathedral. 'It's amazing! It looks like nothing so much as a huge mint humbug!'

She was thankful to find the cathedral so fascinating, grateful for the opportunity it gave her to be distracted from the pain of her memories. She was able to push all thoughts of Dean from her mind until at last they wandered back down into the centre of Siena, to lunch on bread and cheese and black olives, sitting in the sun on the pavement outside a small *trattoria*.

'I'm surprised your mother didn't name you Catherine, after Siena's very own saint,' Keir commented, breaking off a crust of bread and spreading it liberally with butter. 'After all, she was born not so very far from here—on Vicolo del Tiratoio.'

'She said she thought about it, but as a name it didn't have the special significance that Siena had for her, though in the end she decided she preferred a slightly different spelling. You know, this is totally crazy!'

Intrigued by her tone, Keir looked up, brown eyes frowning into the sun.

'What is?' he enquired mildly.

'All this talk of my mother and her past, when I know nothing about yours—and I'm married to you!'

Broad shoulders under the immaculate white shirt lifted in a dismissive shrug.

'There's nothing much to tell,' Keir stated off-handedly.

'I don't believe that. A man with your looks—your money—there must have been women...'

'There have—plenty of them.' It was an emotionless statement offered in a flat tone that erased any suspicion of boasting. 'But no one who really mattered.'

'You never fell in love?'

'Love?' He seemed to be considering the word, his expression thoughtful as he sipped at his wine. 'Rick Parry always says that my one true love is my work. And I suppose in a way it was true. Certainly from the time that I came back from university to discover that Dad had almost reduced Alexander's to the state where the next step would have been to call in the receivers, getting the firm back on its feet again was something of an obsession. Any women in my life took strictly second place.'

He didn't sound in the least bit penitent about it, Sienna reflected. Instead, his almost casual delivery spoke of indifference to the effect his actions might have had.

'So there was no one special?'

'There was one girl I thought I cared for more than all the rest.' Keir swirled the wine round in his glass, staring down into its ruby depths. 'But when it came down to it, I cared about my work more.'

'It strikes me she had a lucky escape!'

Those dark-chocolate eyes lifted to meet Sienna's blue-green gaze, and Keir's sensual mouth twisted at the indignation in her tone.

'What I felt for her wasn't the real thing.'

'And would you know the *real thing* if it bit you on the nose?'

'If I'd truly loved her, then nothing else would have mattered. I would have given her all the time she needed, given up work—even the company—to be with her.'

Which put her right in her place, Sienna told herself bitterly. He hadn't been prepared to give anything up for her. On the contrary, the only reason he had married her was in order to obtain the money he needed to save that precious company of his. She didn't even rank as highly as the girl he'd thought he'd cared for.

'So what about you?'

'What about me?' Still struggling at the smart of facing up to just how little she truly meant to Keir, Sienna didn't trouble to adjust her tone, earning herself a quick, dark frown of reproof.

'Are you going to tell me the gory details of your love-life?'

'Nothing to tell.' She aimed for airy insouciance and missed it by a mile, fingers clenching tight over her knife until her knuckles showed white.

'Not even about your precious Dean?'

The sarcasm of the question caught Sienna on the raw. Turquoise eyes flashing angrily, she lifted her head and glared defiance straight into his still, watchful face.

'Dean is none of your business!'

'I'm making it my business,' Keir shot back. 'Dean hurt you and humiliated you...'

She didn't need reminding of that! But what shocked and stunned her into blank confusion was a new realisation, that came with a rush that made her head spin dizzily.

Dean had beguiled and seduced her. He had enticed her into his bed with soft words and softer lies, and, foolishly, crazily in love with him, she had offered no resistance. But never once in all that time that she and Dean had been lovers had she ever experienced the sheer mind-blowing, soul-shattering physical ecstasy that she had known with Keir since their wedding day.

She had never been able to respond to Dean as she did to Keir, never wanted him as she wanted this man who was now her husband. And Dean's lovemaking had never left her exhausted and satiated, yet knowing that he had only to touch her and her whole body would come alive once again, desperately yearning, needing more.

'It's nothing to do with you!'

'You're my wife.'

'Your *wife*!' Sienna echoed, pain shading her words with black cynicism. 'And we both know just how much—or rather how little—that means, husband dear.'

'I'm a better damn husband than your precious Dean would ever have been, sweetheart! Would he have brought you here, to Siena? Would he have provided this honeymoon?'

'You didn't have to lay on a honeymoon! No one asked you to!'

She regretted the impetuous words as soon as they had left her lips, urgently wishing them back as she saw the black scowl that darkened his handsome features.

'You're wrong there, my lovely Sienna,' Keir put in, his coldly clipped enunciation freezing the impulse to apologise before it had time to fully form. 'I may only be the husband you hired on a temporary basis, but, believe me, I know

what's expected of me. And I have every intention of fulfilling my contract to the letter.'

'Keir, please. You know you're—'

'Know I'm what? More than that? Don't kid yourself,
darling—and don't try to pretend to me because it won't
work. But one thing I do know…'

Pushing back his chair so violently that it scraped over
the pavement with an ugly grating sound, Keir got to his
feet in a swift, angry movement.

'One thing I'll never be is second best—not to your precious Dean, or anyone else. And if you want proof…'

'Keir…' Sienna, tried but her voice failed her as he
moved to her side, towering over her threateningly, a wild,
dangerous look in his coffee-coloured eyes. 'I…'

Her second feeble attempt at remonstration went un-
heeded as Keir reached down and clamped powerful fingers
on her arms, pulling her out of her seat and yanking her
close up against the hard strength of his body. She was lifted
half off her feet, only the very tips of her toes still retaining
contact with the ground as she swayed against him. With
one arm holding her tight, his other hand came under her
chin, forcing her face up to meet his as his mouth swooped
downwards.

In such a public place, his kiss was almost shocking in
its fierce sensuality. Instantly a river of golden heat raged
through every nerve and cell in Sienna's body, sending her
thoughts spinning off into a wild fever over which she had
no control at all, her mind hazing as if she was in the grip
of some delirium. Her soul seemed to be drawn out of her
body, the electrical current of need that pulsed at the centre
of her being making her whimper with a hunger that was
dangerously close to pain.

It was several moments before she became aware of anything other that Keir. And it was only when she was released
and set down, blinking hard in the sudden brightness of the
sunlight, that she became aware of the interested and very
approving audience his actions had earned for them.

'Now tell me I'm second best,' Keir challenged menacingly. 'Tell me your Dean can match that.'

And when she could only shake her head, her eyes glazed with desire, unable to speak, his smile was positively fiendish in its dark triumph.

'I thought not. Forget Dean, Sienna. He's the past—gone. I am your present, and you are mine—for this year at least. And I'll have no third party intruding into this marriage. Is that understood?'

'Understood,' was all that Sienna managed to croak in reply.

'Good.'

With a gesture of supreme arrogance, Keir tossed down a handful of notes in payment of their bill before linking his hand with hers so firmly that, even if she had thought of resistance, she would have had no chance of getting away.

'And now, my lovely wife, we're going home. Back to the villa and to our bedroom, where I will prove to you once more that I am all the husband you need.'

He didn't give her a chance to argue, obviously not expecting any hint of objection from her. And the problem was, Sienna reflected, she was incapable of making any. The excitement his kiss had aroused still spiralled deep inside her, fed by the anticipation of just what awaited her when they reached the villa.

Feeling like this, she admitted to herself, she would go anywhere Keir asked her to, do anything he commanded. Somehow over the past ten days he had enslaved her sexually, and right now she doubted if she could possibly break free of his sensual mastery ever again.

CHAPTER EIGHT

'Sienna, darling, do you know that there's still a film in here?'

'Hmm?' Frowning distractedly, Sienna dragged her attention away from the list she had been studying. 'I'm sorry, Mum, what did you say?'

'I wanted to know if you'd realised that there's a film in this camera.'

Caroline Rushford waved the article in question under her daughter's nose.

'Do you know when it was last used?'

'Oh. . .'

Sienna chewed the end of her pen as she thought about answering. Not because she needed time to think, but for exactly the opposite reason. She was only too well aware of when anyone had last taken a photograph with that particular camera, just as she knew precisely why it had been put away with the film unfinished rather than taken to be developed.

'That'll be the camera I took on honeymoon,' she said carefully.

'But that's over three months ago! I would have thought you'd have wanted to see the pictures you'd taken before now.'

'I—forgot about it. There's been a lot going on.'

'But your *honeymoon*, darling! Surely you and Keir would want to look back at the pictures and remember?'

That was precisely what she *didn't* want to do, Sienna reflected privately. She still couldn't look back at the days she had spent in Italy with Keir without feeling distinctly uncomfortable. And, even after three months, she still wasn't prepared to contemplate any evidence of that time, even if only in a photograph.

She felt that she had lost something of herself while she had been away. Or did she mean she'd found a side of herself she hadn't known existed? She didn't know and couldn't begin to work it out. All she did know was that she had gone to Italy as one woman and come home another.

And that woman was addicted to Keir Alexander.

There was no other way to describe how Keir made her feel. He was in her blood, in her mind, in her *soul*. When he was with her, she couldn't keep away from him, but was constantly drawn to his side as a needle to the most powerful magnet. She had to watch every expression that crossed his stunning face, every movement of his sexy body. Her hands, too, wouldn't stay by her side but had to keep reaching out, touching his shoulder or his arm, her fingers tangling with his.

And when he wasn't there—which, she had to admit, was more likely the case these days—she missed him unbearably. The emptiness of the space where he should have been was like a reproach to her, the feeling of incompleteness she felt like an ache in the very core of her being. It was as if some part of her, an arm or a leg, had been amputated and she hadn't yet learned how to function without it.

The only time she felt fully whole was when she was in bed with him. When his arms were round her, his mouth on her skin, his powerful body linked possessively with hers...

'Smile!'

Sienna started nervously, her head coming up, eyes blinking frantically as she reacted to a sudden, unexpected flash of light.

Her consternation grew as a whirring sound from the camera revealed that the film was now used up, and the rewind mechanism had come into operation.

'Mum, what—?'

'There was only one frame left, so I took your picture to finish it. You looked like a startled rabbit, but who cares! Now you can take the film to be developed and we can all have a look at the honeymoon photos.'

'There won't be time,' Sienna objected. 'We have too much packing to do.'

The alterations to her father's house had been completed, and they were due to move out of Keir's apartment and into their new home by the end of the following week.

'And just how long does it take to drop a film in at the shop? We're only moving house, Sienna, not leaving the country! And if you won't have time, then I'll get Keir to do it.'

'If you can catch him.' Sienna's tone was dry, blending into cynical. 'I don't think he's been home before ten once this month.'

And on several nights it had been well past midnight before she had heard the sound of his car drawing up outside, his key being inserted in the lock. On those late nights she had made herself go to bed, hating the thought of Keir finding her still up and waiting for him. She had even tried to force herself to sleep, but had been unable to do so.

On the one rare occasion when, exhausted by a very long day of organising and packing, she had actually drifted into a light doze she had woken instantly at the feel of him sliding in beside her. He hadn't even needed to touch her. Just the faint sound he'd made, the scent of his skin reaching her, had had her turning to him, her body raging with a hunger that would have been far more appropriate if they had been apart for fourteen days instead of as many hours.

'Yes, he does seem to be working very hard.' Caroline frowned her concern. 'There isn't any problem, is there?'

'What sort of problem?'

It was impossible to erase the uneasy edge from her voice. Had she put a foot wrong somewhere, so that her mother had begun to suspect the truth about her marriage? Had Caroline, after three months of seeing her daughter and son-in-law together at the close quarters necessitated by their sharing the same house, come to realise that it was not, after all, the love match she believed?

'Oh, not between you two—that's obvious! Anyone who's not completely blind can see that you're absolutely besotted and that you can't keep your hands off each other.'

'*Mum!*'

'Now don't go coy on me!' Caroline laughed, regarding her daughter's flaming cheeks with an indulgent smile. 'I may be middle-aged, and a bit wobbly on my pins, but I hope my mind is still as broad as it ever was. I would have more to worry about if you and Keir *didn't* fancy the pants off each other, seeing as you're still such newly-weds. No, it was Keir's job I was thinking of. There isn't anything wrong at Alexander's, is there?'

'Nothing I know of,' Sienna hastened to assure her.

Not that she knew much more than her mother. The only time Keir had ever really talked to her about his company had been in the days before their marriage, when his account of Lucille's hostile negotiations had first put the idea of proposing into her head.

But once the wedding ceremony had been performed, and she had signed the documents he had produced so precipitately at the reception, he had never said another word on the subject. Alexander's success or failure was a closed book as far as she was concerned.

'You know Keir. The original workaholic, that's my husband.'

'Well, see if you can't get him to ease up a bit. I'm surprised you haven't made some sort of protest at the way he's neglecting you. It's not good for a husband to work so hard in the first months of marriage.'

Caroline shot her daughter an arch glance.

'After all, you don't want him too tired when he gets home, do you?'

'Mum, really!'

'Oh, don't give me that look, Sienna! I can still remember

how it felt to be head over heels in love, even if for me it didn't work out as well as it has for you and Keir. Which reminds me...'

Reaching for the camera again, she opened the back and took out the finished roll of film.

'I can't wait to see your pictures of Siena.' The faint shimmer of tears in her blue eyes betrayed just how much it meant to her. 'So promise me you'll get this developed as soon as possible.'

Did she have any alternative? Sienna asked herself. How could she possibly turn her mother down?

'Of course I will,' she sighed. 'I'll take care of it first thing tomorrow.'

'And tell that husband of yours to ease up. I'm sure he doesn't have to spend quite so much time at the office.'

'My mother's worried about you,' Sienna flung the words at Keir as soon as he came into their bedroom later that night.

Much later, she registered with a strange sense of unease. In a series of late nights, this was one of the latest. Just what did Keir find to do until almost midnight almost every night?

'She thinks you're working too hard.'

'And good evening to you, too,' Keir returned satirically, slumping down onto the end of the bed and tugging his tie free at his throat.

My mother's worried about you! This wife of his really knew how to stick a knife in without appearing to do so. Her mother! Did she know what it did to him to come home and find his wife in his bed, wearing only the sexiest slip of a nightgown he had ever seen, and be told that *her mother* worried about him? Which begged the implication that Sienna herself didn't give a damn.

'So do you agree with her?'

The narrow-eyed look he turned on her had a disturbingly

appraising quality about it, one that made Sienna shift uneasily under the soft, downy duvet.

She was painfully aware of the fact that she was wearing only an oyster-coloured silk nightdress, its deep vee neckline exposing more of the creamy curves of her breasts than she was comfortable with in the present situation. Keir on the other hand was still fully dressed in an exquisitely cut dark grey suit, white shirt and what had once been an elegant burgundy silk tie but which was now hopelessly mangled by the careless way he was pulling at it.

'You have been staying out late a lot.'

'I'm a grown man, Sienna. I stopped obeying a nighttime curfew on my eighteenth birthday.'

'I realise that. But would it be asking too much for you to let me know when you're going to be really late?'

'Why, sweetheart?' It was a soft, silky hiss. The sort of voice that the serpent must have used in the Garden of Eden. 'Missed me have you?'

'Of course not!'

The retort had come too swiftly, Sienna reproached herself. It had been far too vehement as well.

'I know you can look after yourself,' she amended hastily. Understatement of the year. He could more than look after himself. She couldn't imagine anyone who, coming under the influence of that charisma, the aura of authority and total self-assurance that he wore with the ease of a natural right, would even dare to *think* of trying it on.

'Then what's the problem?'

He was tugging at his tie again, his movements rough and impatient. When it finally came loose in his hand he tossed it in the vague direction of a chair, totally ignoring the way it fell short, slithering onto the thick bronze carpet instead.

'I—she—we were afraid you'd wear yourself out.'

Even as she spoke the words she saw how ridiculous they were. She'd rarely, if ever, seen Keir even slightly tired, never mind worn out. He was one of those men who seemed to have endless reserves of stamina and was able to pace himself perfectly. When other, weaker people were falling by the wayside he just kept on going, never looking hurried or flustered, always in control.

'How very thoughtful of you.' Keir's tone said exactly the opposite.

He was shrugging himself out of his jacket now, the elegant garment following the tie in the direction of the chair, with rather more success this time. No sooner had it landed than Keir pushed off his shoes, not even bothering to unfasten the laces first, then moved to lounge against the pillows on his side of the bed, legs stretched out before him, crossed at the ankles.

'So what's the problem, darling? Are you not getting enough?'

'No!' It was an indignant squawk. 'I mean I...'

Sienna struggled to collect her whirling thoughts. But it was hard—almost impossible—to concentrate on what she was trying to say. Sprawled beside her, his long body indolently at ease, Keir had now begun to unbutton his shirt, displaying a tantalising amount of smoothly muscled chest, the tanned skin hazed with fine dark hair. Just the sight of it dried Sienna's mouth painfully, so that she had to swallow convulsively to ease the tightness in her throat.

Dear God, was he planning on doing a complete striptease? He was so close to her that the warm scent of his body, subtly mixed with the clean, crisp tang of the cologne he wore, tantalised her nostrils. Did he have any awareness of the effect he was having on her? The way that her heart now beat in double-quick time, her blood singing a restless incantation of delight in her veins?

But then Keir slanted a lazy, heavy-lidded glance in her direction, and, seeing the provocative gleam in the dark-chocolate colour of his eyes, she recognised that of course he knew what he was doing. Knew it and was playing on it quite deliberately, aiming for just the effect he had created.

'Are you sure?' he teased now, his voice low and rich so

that it made her think of dark honey running smoothly over gravel. 'Because I wouldn't want my precious bride to feel that she was being short-changed. If I'm skimping on my husbandly duties…'

'Oh, to hell with your husbandly duties!' Sienna exploded in exasperation. 'Why do you have to bring everything down to sex?'

Keir's dark eyes rounded in a display of hurt innocence that was so obviously make-believe Sienna had to grit her teeth against the impulse to lash out and wipe it from his handsome face.

'Did I mention sex, darling?' he asked, his tone as wounded as his expression. 'I don't believe the word ever crossed my lips. But if that's what this is all about…'

'You know very well that it's nothing of the sort!' Sienna flashed, moving swiftly to one side to dodge the kiss he was clearly planning on planting on her mouth.

She knew only too well what would happen if she let him touch her. One kiss and she would go up in flames. The potent sensuality that he could trigger with just one caress would swamp her mind, leaving her incapable of thought. And then tonight would follow the same voluptuous pattern as every other night of their marriage. He would take her down the entrancing paths she had come to know so well, give her the physical delights that she craved so greedily, reduce her to an exhausted, satiated wreck, and any opportunity to talk would be lost.

'I'm not the one with a cesspit for a mind.'

The mocking angle of one straight black brow clearly questioned the truth of that unwise declaration, a wicked, derisive smile curving the corners of Keir's mouth.

'What I meant was…'

She couldn't complete the sentence; her mind totally distracted by the sight of Keir pulling open the narrow leather belt at the waistband of his trousers in order to free his shirt completely.

Under cover of the bedclothes, she clenched her hands

into such tight, rigid fists that her nails dug painfully into her palms. It was either that or give in to the appalling temptation to touch. To push aside the soft white material and let her wanton fingers explore the warm, tight contours of his muscles, the hard frame of his chest.

'What you meant was...?' Keir prompted softly as she swallowed hard.

'What I meant was...' Sienna struggled to ignore his wicked, sexy grin. 'Is everything all right—at work. Is there some problem with Alexander's?'

If she had thrown a bucket of icy water right in his face she couldn't have destroyed the seductive mood any more completely. Keir's face froze, carved features hardening into rigid rejection, his eyes taking on an obsidian glitter that made them look like dark shards of ice.

'That's my business!' he snapped coldly, jack-knifing out of his relaxed pose and into a stiffly upright position, every tight muscle in his long frame speaking with dangerous eloquence of the strength of his rejection of her. 'My business and mine alone.'

The force of his reaction startled and worried Sienna. Was her mother right after all? Did the long hours that Keir had been working mean that, in spite of the injection of cash she had made into Alexander's, the company was still in difficulties? She knew how much that company meant to Keir. It was his only link with his late father, and she couldn't bear to contemplate the effect losing it would have on him.

'But it isn't just your business,' she protested, flinging back the bedclothes and reaching for the silk robe, an exact match for her nightdress, which lay across the foot of the bed.

She would feel much more in control if she covered up, she told herself as she belted it tightly around her slim waist. A seductive sliver of silk and lace might be suitable for a passionate night; it was totally inappropriate for a serious business meeting.

'I'm involved in Alexander's too.'

Could he ever forget it? Keir asked himself. All these months ago, on a mad, foolish impulse, he had snatched at the offer she'd made him, seeing it as his only way out of a tricky situation. Alexander's or Sienna. The woman or the company. That had seemed to be the choice he'd been faced with then.

If he put in the concentrated effort his company needed, then he would have to neglect his relationship with the woman who had knocked him for six in the moment he'd first seen her. And everything about her attitude had said that if he did just that then she wasn't likely to stay around for long. But if he went with his emotional instincts, and focused solely on his developing feelings for Sienna, then Lucille would make her move and he could lose everything.

And then Sienna had come up with the astonishing proposal that had seemed to be the answer to all his problems. He could rescue Alexander's and at the same time win himself a breathing space with Sienna. At the time, the year she had declared their marriage should last had seemed like an eternity—more than enough time to win her round, seduce her into wanting him, needing him, and, hopefully, falling in love with him so that they could turn their temporary marriage into a permanent relationship.

Well, he'd sorted the work problems. More than sorted them. After three months' concentrated effort, Alexander's was well and truly back on track, with the potential to be even more successful than ever.

But three months with Sienna seemed to have had no effect at all. If anything, it seemed he was further from winning her heart than when he'd first started. Oh, she *wanted* him; there was no doubt about that. The physical side of their relationship was everything he'd ever dreamed it would be, and then some! But sex was all it was. There was no trace of a possibility that she had come to care for him at all.

And if he'd needed any further proof of that, then she'd

just thrown it right into his face. Just the suspicion of any problem on the financial front and she'd switched immediately from bedroom to boardroom mode. Though he supposed he ought to be grateful for the fact that she'd put on her robe. At least now he'd be able to think straight, without being constantly distracted by the sight of her creamy skin, the rich curves of her breasts.

'What's wrong, Sienna?' Disappointment put a caustic bite into his voice. 'Are you worried about the return on your investment? Afraid that I might actually go under—that you could end up married to a man who isn't as wealthy as you thought? One who may even be *poor*?'

'Is that possible?'

Shock and consternation showed in her face. How could this have happened? Could she really have been so blind that she hadn't noticed the difficulties Keir was facing?

But of course she had. She'd been only too aware of the long hours he was working, the length of his absences from the house. She just hadn't realised the reasons for them. Instead she had attributed his preoccupation to a need to be away from her, to put a distance between them. How could she have been so stupid—so selfish!

'Keir, are things really so bad?'

'Depends on what you're looking for,' Keir returned laconically.

Stretching lazily, he linked his hands behind his head, leaning back against them and half closing his eyes. The movement pulled his shirt open wider over his chest and the way his heavy eyelids drooped at the outer corners gave him a sleepily sensual look that tugged at her heart with disturbing appeal.

'If you want to be married to a man who can match your father's money pound for pound, then stick around, you might strike lucky. But if you're looking for a way out of our agreement, then tough—no deal, lady.'

'Keir, don't be silly!'

Confusion mixed with a half-formed sense of relief to

create an exasperation she couldn't explain. Did he mean that things were okay with Alexander's, or just the opposite? She had no way of knowing, and Keir's body language gave her no help at all.

That apparently indolently relaxed position could be just what it seemed, or it could be a deliberate front, nicely calculated to hide a very different set of feelings, ones he was determined not to let her see.

'Why on earth should I want out of our arrangement? I still need your co-operation, remember! My uncle Francis has only handed over part of my inheritance—the rest of it is dependent on our staying together for the year we agreed on. I have to keep you as my husband until then.'

Well, that's told you, Alexander, you fool! Keir mocked himself. She couldn't have spelled it out any more clearly if she'd tried. And the irony was that just for a moment, a weak, crazy moment, he had actually let the idea of telling her the truth slide into his mind.

What the hell could he have been thinking of? Admitting that he cared for—that he loved—there, now he'd admitted it to himself—a woman who saw him only as the key to her father's fortune? He needed to have his brain examined. Keir could only shake his head in disbelief at his own foolishness. Did he plan to lie down on the floor in front of her and let her walk all over him with those dainty, narrow feet?

'No?'

To his consternation he realised that Sienna had caught his unthinking shake of the head and had interpreted it in a very different way.

'What do you mean, no, Keir?'

Sienna wished she could bring her voice down an octave or two. It sounded far too shrill and accusatory at this pitch. And if she wasn't careful then the high, tight sound might even reach to where her mother lay sleeping at the far end of the corridor.

'Are you trying to say you don't intend sticking by our contract?'

Sienna felt as if her stomach was turning summersaults inside her. What would she do without him? The future suddenly seemed unbearably bleak when viewed from the perspective of having to face it alone.

'Do you want out? Is that it, Keir? Have you...?'

The truth was suddenly unnervingly bright, like a brilliant spotlight concentrated onto previously concealed corners of her mind, illuminating things she would prefer to have kept hidden away.

'Have you found someone? Is that it?'

Just for a moment Keir's gaze slid away from hers, intensifying her unease one thousandfold. He looked decidedly shifty, as if he very definitely had something to hide.

'Have you—have you fallen in love with someone else?'

'Don't be so stupid!' Keir exploded, all traces of the lazy mood burning away in the heat of the dark fury that blazed in his eyes. 'I gave you my word and I intend to stick by that, no matter what!'

'Oh, thank God!'

The rush of relief was so intense that she almost sagged against the side of the bed, and only just disguised the moment of weakness by transforming it into a none too elegant drop onto the padded stool in front of her dressing table.

'Yeah, thank God!' Keir echoed with black cynicism. 'Oh, don't worry, my lovely, your inheritance is quite safe with me! You paid for a year of my life, and that's what you'll get, right down to the very last second.'

Suddenly too restless to stay still any longer, he flung himself to his feet and strode round to where she perched on the stool, her slender arms folded tightly around herself. The wary look in her brilliant eyes as she watched him approach only inflamed further the volatile mixture of emotions he was already prey to.

She didn't trust him; that was the real problem. Didn't trust him not to take the money and run, leaving her in the lurch once again, all alone and with a sick mother to care for. That rat Dean Hanson really had done a number on her!

It was just as well he couldn't get his hands on him right at this moment, because he would be strongly tempted to do something very foolish indeed. And it would be nothing less than the repellent louse deserved!

'That's all I want.'

Sienna's voice was as coolly distant as her expression, but he would never know the effort it had cost her to keep it that way. Keir had looked positively murderous marching towards her just now, and it had been all she could do to keep her composure when every nerve in her body was screaming at her to get off the stool and run. Put as great a distance as possible between the two of them as quickly as possible.

'At least we both know where we stand.'

'So we do.'

His expressive mouth curved into a bleak travesty of a smile, one that had no trace of humour in it and which did nothing at all to warm the arctic bleakness of his eyes.

'But let me just clear up a couple of final points—or rather, correct some misconceptions you seem to hold about just what our original agreement entailed.'

One strong hand was held up between them, only inches away from her face, and Keir's voice was coldly emphatic as he marked off each point on a finger as he made it.

'One—you paid me to marry you; what I do with the money is none of your business. Your investment was in *me*, not Alexander's. Two—the state of my company is no concern of yours, nor will it ever be. I handle my own affairs as I see fit, and I won't answer to you about any of them. And three—I agreed to be a husband, not a lapdog. I'll act like your husband in public, be at your side when you need me, but that's all. I'm not at your beck and call. I come and go as I please, do what I want when I want. Is that understood?'

'Perfectly.' Sienna was proud of her control over her voice as she answered him. It matched his cold enunciation perfectly. So much so that she almost expected to see the letters form in shapes of ice on the carpet between them.

'Because if there's anything there you can't live with, then I suggest we dissolve our partnership right here and now.'

'There's no need for that! What you're offering is precisely what I want from you. Nothing more; nothing less.'

'Then at least we understand each other.'

Keir flexed his broad shoulders, pushing both hands through the dark silk of his hair. The movement ruffled its usual sleek smoothness, causing one wayward lock to fall forward onto his forehead in a way that Sienna found dangerously appealing. Before she had time to think of the possible consequences of her action, she had reached out and brushed it gently back into place.

'Sienna...'

The sound of Keir's voice told her immediately how his mood had changed in an instant. Dropping an octave or more, it had become a huskily sensual whisper, one that curled like smoke around every nerve, making her toes curl in instant response on the soft, thick pile of the carpet. Chocolate-brown eyes locked with aquamarine, and Keir's intent gaze held her mesmerised, unable to look away, incapable even of breathing as she froze into immobility.

'When I came into this room you were decidedly peeved. I have to wonder why you were in such a bad mood?'

'I—I told you why,' Sienna managed with difficulty. 'My mother...'

Keir's arrogant flick of a hand dismissed the mention of Caroline as the irrelevance it was.

'Correct me if I'm wrong, but I suspect you were feeling neglected. "You have been staying out late a lot..."'

Sienna blinked in shock as he mimicked her own petulant tone with distinctly unnerving accuracy. Her sense of disbelief deepened as she saw Keir's smile, the way the pupils of his eyes had enlarged until there was only the tiniest rim of brown at their edges.

'If that's the case, darling, you only have to say. Because if you're not getting what you want…'

One long-fingered hand slid under her chin, lifting her face up towards his, his hard palm warm against her cheek. The temptation to turn her mouth into that palm, press a lingering kiss against it, was almost overwhelming. But then, just as she was about to succumb, a very different thought struck her, changing her mood abruptly.

'I'd be only too happy to put things right. After all, I am your husband…'

'My husband as defined by the strictly narrow business terms you detailed only moments ago!' Sienna flared, wrenching her head away from his beguiling caress.

She refused to allow herself even to register the screaming protest from every awakened nerve in her body as she sprang to her feet, facing him defiantly from a safe distance of several metres.

'This isn't a real marriage, and we both know it!'

'We have a certificate that says otherwise,' Keir pointed out imperturbably.

'But there's a whole lot more to a marriage than just a piece of paper! Important things. Things that make the difference between a union that will last and one that's already past its sell-by date!'

Tell me about it, Keir reflected broodingly. It was the lack of those important things that chafed at him day and night, eating into his heart like acid. His only antidote was work, the long, wearing hours that he spent in the office every day.

Or sex. Only in bed could he express anything of the way he felt for Sienna. And only in bed would she respond in kind.

'Come to bed, Sienna.' He spoke without thinking, cursing his foolish tongue when he saw the stormy rejection in her sea-coloured eyes.

Come to bed! She couldn't believe the arrogance of the man. He had just spelled out to her in no uncertain terms the fact that she meant nothing to him except as part of a purely mercenary deal, and now he thought he could click his fingers and she would jump into bed with him without a second's thought. She had far more respect for herself than that, and even though her wanton body hungered for the feel of his against it she was determined to defy it.

'Sex won't change anything!' she tossed at him, magnificent in her disdain. 'And even a *proper* wife can say no.'

A faint smile touched her lips as she saw his proud head go back in surprise.

'Yes, Keir, I'm saying no to you. Is that a first? Am I the only woman ever to have resisted your all-conquering charms?'

The only one who'd ever mattered. But he'd be damned if he let her see it.

'That's your prerogative, sweetheart.' He smiled, his smile a masterpiece of indifference. 'But if you change your mind, just come and find me.'

'Come and...' He was already halfway towards the door by the time her mind had cleared enough to let her speak. 'But where are you going?'

Keir spared her only the briefest of glances, not even slowing his long, smooth strides.

'I'll sleep in the spare room tonight, darling,' he threw over his shoulder at her. 'I think we'll both find it more comfortable that way.'

Beyond speaking, beyond thought, Sienna could only stand and stare as she watched the door swing to behind him. She was totally unprepared for the rush of distress that assailed her as she heard Keir's angry footsteps moving swiftly down the corridor.

She had meant every word she'd said, so why should she feel so lost, so bereft, so desolated by the way he had left her? Somewhere during the course of tonight the balance of their relationship had shifted disturbingly, leaving her shocked and bewildered by her own response.

She had always known that Keir had only married her for

the money she had offered him. Known that there was no emotion in the role he played, that he was a husband in name only and would never be anything more. It was what she had wanted from him after all. So why should that suddenly prove to be so out of synch with her feelings? Why did his indifference now have the power to hurt her so terribly?

CHAPTER NINE

SHE got her answer just thirty-six hours later.

If she was honest with herself, Sienna had to admit that she'd known all along. But she couldn't bring herself to acknowledge the truth, even to herself. It created too many problems, complicated things impossibly. And the consequences for her own future were more than she dared to contemplate.

But when she saw the photograph she knew, absolutely and finally, without any hope of redemption. There was no denying anything any more. No way of dodging round the truth. It was there, right in front of her, as clear as day.

'Oh, no!' she whispered weakly, fighting against the tears that burned in her eyes. 'How could this have happened? And what on earth do I do now?'

She hadn't been able to get out of taking the photographs to be developed. Her mother had insisted on it.

'And make sure you ask for the twenty-four hour service!' she'd added as Sienna had reluctantly left the house to carry out the errand. 'I've waited over three months to see those pictures. I don't intend to delay any longer!'

And of course the first thing she'd done this morning was to remind her daughter to collect the prints just as soon as she could.

She didn't really understand what instinct had driven her to open the package of photographs as soon as she'd got back to her car. If pressed, she would have said that seeing them was the last thing she wanted right then. After the argument she had had with Keir, her thoughts had been so unsettled, her mood swinging violently from one extreme to another, that the last thing she needed was any more to worry about.

Keir had come home later than ever last night. So late that she had no idea of what time he had actually arrived home. She had waited and waited for him, but in the end exhaustion had got the better of her and she had fallen fast asleep. In fact, the only indication she'd had that he'd been in the house at all had been the indentation left by his head in the pillow beside her when she'd woken, and the discovery of the clothes he had worn that day lying discarded in the washing basket.

By the time she'd surfaced from a restless and unsatisfying sleep he'd already gone. She had had no chance to see him, hadn't spoken to him since he had walked out on her the night before last.

So it had been the foolish thought that she desperately needed to see his face, even if only in the flat, one-dimensional form of a photograph, that had driven her to wrench open the envelope and pull out its contents.

It was the first one she saw. Lying on top of the pile, clear and crisply defined, undeniable in its impact, the picture had a shock value that winged straight into her heart, like an arrow thudding into the gold at the centre of a target.

She remembered the scene only too well. It had been on the afternoon of their visit to Florence, when she and Keir had made their way through the narrow, straight streets around the Piazza della Repubblica to the Mercato Nuovo.

'You can't leave Florence without seeing Il Porcellino,' Keir had announced.

'Il Porcellino? The piglet?' Sienna was proud of her growing knowledge of the Italian language. 'What on earth is that?'

And when she was confronted by the large bronze statue she exclaimed in amused surprise.

'That's no *piglet*! It's a fully-grown boar!' she said, eyeing the strong body, the dangerous looking tusks at either side of the snout. The end of the creature's nose looked more polished than the rest of him, rubbed smooth and shiny, obviously by much handling.

'You have to rub his snout,' Keir told her, a grin surfacing in response to her bemused expression. 'Go on,' he urged, when she hesitated.

Unable to resist that smile, Sienna had done as he asked, looking up at Keir for an answer as she did so.

'Can you tell me exactly *why* I'm doing this? I presume it has some special significance?'

Keir nodded his dark head in response. 'It's supposed to bring good luck, but more especially make sure that one day destiny will bring you back to Florence again in the future.'

'Oh, well, in that case...'

Sienna rubbed the bronze muzzle once again, with renewed enthusiasm.

'I've fallen in love with Italy, with Tuscany in particular, and I'd love to come back to this beautiful city any time fate wants to bring me here.'

It was the uncomfortable little skip of her heart, making her breath catch unexpectedly in the middle of the sentence, that warned her. Suddenly she couldn't take her eyes from Keir, standing so tall and strong just to one side. His casual elegance, in a black polo shirt and smart chinos, had a heart-stopping impact, but what suddenly made her shiver, in spite of the heat, was what she saw in his eyes.

The smile on that handsome face seemed strangely forced and unnatural, and the dark pools of his eyes remained bleak and shadowed, no warmth lighting them at all.

One day destiny will bring you back to Florence again in the future. Yes, but *when* in the future, and with whom? In twelve month's time she and Keir would be divorced, and would probably never see each other again.

Sienna shivered again, a cold, creeping sensation slithering down her spine. She couldn't imagine ever coming here without Keir. His presence was so much a part of her enjoyment of the place, her delight in Tuscany, that she couldn't think of it without him.

'Keir!'

Impulsively she reached out and caught hold of his hand, pulling him forward.

'You must do it too! You must stroke Porcellino's snout!'

When for a moment it seemed that he would resist, that he would refuse to move, she felt the faint feeling of unease grow worse, developing into a disturbing near-panic that made her heart race.

'*Keir!*' she tried again, disconcerted to find her voice quavering on his name. 'Don't you want to come back to Florence? I can't believe that!'

At last he moved, stepping forward and giving the bronze boar a desultory pat on the muzzle.

'*Ciao*, Porcellino,' he said, and it was the cool flippancy of the response that told Sienna just what had been going through his mind.

He didn't care whether he came back to Florence or not. He was totally indifferent to the fact. Or rather, he didn't care if he never came back *with her*.

And now, all these months later, Sienna was confronted by the evidence of just what that had meant to her. Lying in her lap, where her nerveless fingers had dropped it, was a photograph of herself in the Mercato Nuovo, her hand still resting lightly on the bronze statue of the boar.

She remembered exactly when it had been taken. While she had struggled with the unsettled thoughts Keir's response had brought to her mind, he had stepped back quite coolly, and, with a casual command of 'Smile!', had captured her image before she'd had time to protest.

He had captured much more than that too. Sienna sighed, looking into the image of her own face. He had caught her look of uncertainty, the confusion as she'd struggled with her thoughts, a confusion that her carefully switched-on smile had done nothing to hide. And there, behind the pretence at happiness, was something darker, something Sienna wouldn't have recognised if she'd seen it earlier.

But she knew it now. Now she recognised the shadow of

the same pain she had felt when Keir had walked out on her to go and sleep elsewhere. And blending with the sense of loss was the most devastating thing of all. This was a photograph of a woman deeply in love, but as yet unaware of what she really felt. It was there in her eyes, in the yearning that she hadn't been able to conceal, the need that was etched onto her face.

'Oh, *no!*'

Sienna's hand clenched over the photograph, crushing it impossibly. When had this happened to her? *How* had it happened to her? How could she have fallen in love with Keir when she had been so totally convinced that she'd loved Dean? And yet now, somehow, what she had felt for Dean seemed so alien, unfounded, light-years away from the way Keir made her feel.

So what made the difference? Sienna started the car, manoeuvring it out of the parking space with far less than her usual attention to what she was doing. Her mind was whirling, struggling to cope with the conflicting memories and emotions her heart was throwing at it, forcing her to look at them squarely in a way that she had never done before.

'Believe me, if I could have what I *really want*, you wouldn't be the man with a wedding ring on his finger!'

Her own words, spoken in anger on her wedding day, came back to haunt her.

'And if I was to achieve a *dream*, then I would have married—'

I would have married Dean. That was what she had meant. She had thought herself in love with Dean. Believed that his cruelty, his faithlessness had broken her heart. So how could her affections have swung from one man to another, with barely so much as a heartbeat in between?

Because she had never truly loved Dean.

The truth dawned with the effect of a blow to her head, making her stall the car at traffic lights, earning her a reproachful blare of the horn from the driver behind her. Moving off hastily, she drove on automatic pilot as reality finally took the place of the self-delusion she had suffered from for so long.

Dean had set himself to win her over. He had been un-failingly pleasant and cheerful, always apparently kind, con-siderate—always so damn *nice*. He had never been impa-tient, never angry, always gentle, always agreeable. And he had always been *lying* to her, manipulating her with charm into getting her exactly where he'd wanted her—in his bed.

Keir, on the other hand, didn't try to be nice. He was always himself, whether his mood was good or bad. And none of it mattered. She didn't need charm or kindness, was indifferent to his temper. She loved being with him no mat-ter what sort of a mood he was in, even when he was cold or downright cruel. And she missed him when he wasn't there.

And Keir had never needed to entice her into his bed. She would have fallen into it without a second thought right from the very start if her mind hadn't been so determined to hold onto her memories of Dean. She had been so ashamed, so confused by the passion she'd felt for Keir, which had been so unlike the gentle emotions she had had for Dean, when in fact those feelings had been telling her the truth about the difference between the two men.

She had been in love with Keir almost from the start. She had just been too blind, too deceived, to see it clearly. She wasn't exactly sure when it had happened, but somewhere along the line she'd fallen totally, irrevocably in love with her temporary husband. Like her mother before her, she'd found the love of her life in Italy, and, like Caroline's doomed relationship, hers too was destined to fail.

But how was she going to face Keir now? Sienna asked herself as she swung her car into the underground parking space beneath the block where Keir had his apartment. She felt as if one complete layer of her skin had been scraped away, leaving her feeling raw and unnaturally sensitive to pain. So how could she face the man she loved and not reveal her feelings?

In the end it turned out that Keir himself had solved that problem for her, temporarily at least, because of—what else?—his work.

'He rang while you were out,' Caroline informed her. 'Some problem at the Belgian depot. He had to fly out straight away. He couldn't say when he'd be back.'

But the reprieve was only temporary, Sienna knew that. Before long Keir would be back, and she would have to continue to pretend that their marriage was nothing more than the business arrangement she had insisted on at the start. There were still almost nine months of the year they had agreed on ahead of her. How could she live through them and not give herself away?

She knew it would be harder than she could possibly imagine. That the layer of skin that she'd felt had been stripped off would never grow back again. That, as a result, a simple look from Keir's dark eyes, a touch, the softest kiss, would leave her feeling painfully bruised. She would never be able to settle in his company. Her mind would be split into two, one half wanting to drive her to throw herself into his arms and beg him to hold her tight, never let her go, the other urging her to keep her distance, reveal nothing of what was in her thoughts.

And she would feel herself constantly hanging back, frozen by indecision, unable to make any move one way or another.

It was like coming home to a different woman, Keir told himself with a sense of something close to disbelief. He had only been away for six days, less than a week, and yet when he returned Sienna was very definitely not the wife he had left behind.

Those aquamarine eyes watched him warily from behind the shield of long, luxuriant lashes, and her soft mouth rarely curved into the wide, brilliant smile that turned his heart over inside his chest. She had put a strict curb on all those impulsive little gestures too. No more gentle touches on his arm or his cheek, no tantalising trail of her fingers over the back of his hand that seemed to say she couldn't keep her hands to herself, and which drove him crazy with the flaring hunger for more.

Her speech was quieter too, with fewer of those fiery, provocative moments of defiance that had so delighted him from the start. A week ago she had been like a nervous, half-tamed thoroughbred, one that trusted no man, acknowledged no one as master, but who allowed him and him alone to touch her, as long as he took care not to startle her. But now it seemed that even such a tentative understanding as they had reached had been destroyed at a stroke. She eyed him warily, starting nervously if he came close unexpectedly, and he didn't like the way that made him feel.

By the time his mother-in-law had made tactful excuses about needing an early night and left them alone together he was definitely spoiling for a fight.

'What is this?' he demanded, hiding unease with impatience. 'What are you sulking about?'

'Why would I be sulking?' Sienna asked, at last showing some spark of the woman she had been a week before.

'Perhaps because I've been concentrating too much on my work? Because I've been away...?'

'It doesn't trouble me at all,' she returned, with an indifferent shrug of her slim shoulders.

'It did before I went,' Keir reminded her pointedly. 'You said you were concerned. . .'

'I said my *mother* was concerned. As a matter of fact, I've been far too busy organising the move to even notice you weren't here.'

Not true! Her conscience reproached her sharply for the blatant lie. She had missed him desperately every single second he had been away.

'Is that a fact?' One dark, mockingly lifted brow questioned the vehemence of her retort. 'Well, that takes care of the days, I suppose. But what about the nights?'

Keir's voice had lowered to a sexy, smoky whisper that

coiled beguilingly around senses already beleaguered simply by having him so near. After the desert of empty days that had passed since she had last seen him, his presence had thrown her responses into sensory overload. She felt like someone who had been starving and was now suddenly presented with a banquet, and didn't know which course to concentrate on first.

If she looked into his eyes, she couldn't see the hard, lean strength of that stunning body. If she let her gaze dwell on the width of his shoulders, the strong wall of his chest, she missed the softness of his mouth, the smooth silk of his hair. She wanted all of him, every glorious, stunning inch, and yet fear of betraying herself and revealing the force of her feelings forced her to impose a distance that was the last thing on earth she wanted between them.

'The nights?'

She aimed for airy unconcern and almost managed it. The nights had been the worst. She had been unable to sleep for hours, lying awake lost and desolate, supremely conscious of the empty space beside her, the inanimate cold of the sheets where there should have been the living, breathing warmth of Keir's body.

And when at last exhaustion had overcome her she had drifted into a restless, unsettled doze. Her shallow, unsatisfying sleep had been filled with burning dreams, dreams filled with heady, erotic images of Keir, of his kisses, his caresses, and the blazing, scorching passion that they lit in her responsive body. She had tossed and turned, waking drenched in sweat and with her body aching, crying out for the fulfilment it longed for and for which her wanton dreams were no possible substitute.

'I got some decent sleep at last,' she managed, with a dark flippancy that she hoped hid the bitter reality from him.

'Did you indeed? Then you'll be well rested.'

'And just what is that supposed to mean?'

His sigh was a masterpiece in its balance of resignation and exasperation.

'What do you think it's supposed to mean? Perhaps foolishly, I had hoped, in the depths of my cesspit of a mind, that you might be glad to see me back. That you would be happy to welcome me…'

She was. Oh, but she *was* glad to see him. And how she wanted to offer him the sort of welcome she knew he meant. But fear held her back. Fear of betraying herself, of letting her new-found feelings show.

Her love was the last thing Keir wanted from her. He had agreed to a no-strings, purely business deal, and any emotion could only complicate matters immeasurably. He was her husband for the year only, and when the time was up he wanted to go, be set free to walk away without a backward glance.

'So I'm going to have to work a little harder, am I?'

The casual way Keir slipped his hand into the pocket of his jacket deceived Sienna completely. She had no sense of anticipation, no suspicion at all. And when he waved his fingers under her nose she stared in total incomprehension at the beautiful piece of jewellery that dangled from them.

The gold bracelet was the most delicate piece of work she had ever seen. Each link was made up of a tiny flower at the heart of which, brilliant as a dewdrop, glistened a perfect, dazzling diamond.

'An early Christmas present for my beautiful wife.'

'Keir!' Sienna breathed in shock and disbelief. 'I don't know what to say! You shouldn't have!'

Until Alexander's was secure, he should be ploughing all his money back into the company, not wasting it on extravagant fripperies for her! But as Keir dropped the bracelet into her upturned palm and closed her fingers over it she couldn't suppress the rush of excitement and delight that came from knowing he hadn't completely forgotten her while he had been away. He had thought of her. And he had taken the time to select this lovely, perfect gift.

'Oh, Keir!' Impulsively she pressed her lips against the

lean plane of his cheek. 'You're so generous! I don't know
how to thank you!'

'Don't you?' he questioned huskily, the dark fires in his
eyes blazing down into hers in an eloquent declaration of
intent. 'Well, this will do for a start...'

His arrogant dark head swooped down and the hard, confident mouth captured hers, his kiss a demand more than a
caress as it crushed her lips beneath his. It took just the
space of a single, jolting heartbeat for that kiss to light the
fires already smouldering in her heart, melting away any
thought of resistance and setting her blood thundering
through her veins.

Keir parted her lips to invade her softened mouth, thrusting, tasting, demanding, communicating without words the
fierce, impatient need that had him in its grip. His urgent
appeal to her senses cut straight through what remained of
her defences, pushing her into an open, yielding admission
of her own desire. She trembled hungrily beneath that devouring onslaught. It made her feel wanted, dominated, and
weak with hunger.

Her hands snaked up to coil around his strong neck, shaking fingers tangling in the crisp, short hair at the nape. An
instinctive, sinuous movement of her hips against his
brought her into close contact with the heated force of his
erection, taut against the close fit of his perfectly cut trousers. She had no way of knowing whether her moan of need
preceded Keir's or vice versa, only that the two blended
together into a single sound of longing.

'Upstairs?' Keir muttered roughly against her ear, his
voice thickened and rough, a flare of heated colour searing
his strong cheekbones.

'Upstairs,' Sienna whispered in confirmation, unable to
find the thought to form any further words.

They weren't needed. Keir looked for no further encouragement, instead swinging her up into his arms and carrying
her bodily towards the stairs.

'If you knew how I've missed you!' Keir declared huskily

as he tumbled her onto the bed to lie in a splayed heap of limbs. He gave her no time to adjust her position, coming down beside her and tugging impatiently at her clothes.

For once he seemed to have lost all his finesse as a lover, too aroused, too ardent to take his usual care in easing her clothing from her. But Sienna welcomed this new clumsiness as she had delighted in that unevenly voiced 'I've missed you.'

With her own love so desperately close to the surface, needing only the slightest urging to come tumbling out, she revelled in even the slightest hint from Keir that he too was more emotionally involved than before.

'Keir…' she whispered shakily, the longing for him a tight knot of pain low down in her body.

'I know, sweetheart.' His soft voice soothed. 'I know. It's been a long, long six days, but I intend to make up for that now.'

'Yes… Oh, yes.'

It was a sigh of contentment, cracking in the middle as his hands stroked over her body, making every inch of her throb in intense arousal. She had likened her need of him to an addiction, and now she knew how true addicts felt when, having endured the pain of withdrawal symptoms, they were once again able to feed their craving.

Hard fingers splayed across her spine, crushing her close against the heated length of him, and his mouth seemed to be everywhere, on her hair, her mouth, the wild pulse at the base of her neck, then, hungrily demanding, back on her lips again. And all the while his hands roved over her skin, leaving burning, erotic trails where they touched, making her moan her delight out loud.

Cupping her breasts, he lifted them to his mouth, caressing the hardened buds with his lips and his tongue. But when she would have caught his head in her hands, fingers tangling in the luxuriant dark hair in order to drag his mouth back to hers, he tugged himself gently free. The next moment Sienna froze into stunned stillness, her body arched to meet the tormenting trail of his kisses over the soft skin of her stomach and down to the most intimate spot of all.

'*Keir!*' she gasped, pushed to too high a pitch to know or care what she was saying. 'Keir, my—'

Realisation dawned just in time to have her swallowing down the incriminating word. *My love*, she had almost said. *Keir, my love!* And the realisation of how close she had come to giving herself away put a new exigency into her caresses, her hands sliding down between their two bodies and closing over the hot, hard length of him. She knew a sense of very feminine triumph as she heard him groan aloud.

'Sienna!' Her name was just a raw, hungry sound. 'Darling, if you do that, I... You drive me wild; I can't...'

'Do you think I mind?' Her own whisper feathered laughter against his ear. 'What if I want you wild?'

Above her, Keir's eyes closed and his dark head fell back, hectic colour burning across his cheekbones.

'In that case, my lady...'

The heated, wild invasion of his body into hers was so intensely welcome that Sienna felt scalding tears spill from the corners of her eyes and trickle down her cheeks. This was the fist time she had truly made love with Keir, knowing that he had her heart, and the heightened pleasure that secret knowledge brought was almost more than she could bear.

'Sienna?' To her horror Keir had sensed the change in her, the dampness of her tears against his face. 'What...?'

But Sienna couldn't bear the searching intensity of his dark eyes. Moving her head restlessly on the pillow, she tried to avoid that probing stare.

'Don't stop!' she pleaded feverishly. 'Please don't.'

And then, when it seemed he would ignore her, when he didn't move but simply looked down into her flushed face, frowning his confusion, she balled her slender hands into tight fists, pummelling them against his strong shoulders in angry reproof.

'I said *don't stop!*'

Taking the initiative herself, she writhed underneath his imprisoning body, exciting herself every bit as much as him. She knew the moment that Keir lost all control. Heard it in the muffled groan of surrender, felt it in the unruly movement of his powerful body. With a raw, guttural sound in his throat, he took up the rhythm she had started and built on it, with a raw, forceful timing that built to a wild crescendo, driving her onwards and upwards until she felt herself explode into a thousand brilliant stars as she tumbled into total oblivion.

A long, long time later she surfaced from the exhausted sleep that had claimed her to find the room shadowed by the darkness of the night. It was as she stirred restlessly, slowly becoming aware of the coolness of the sheets at her side, the empty space where Keir should have been, that the cool, unearthly light of the full moon slid between her half-closed lids.

Forcing them open, she focused blearily on the window at the far side of the room. The heavy velvet curtains were drawn back on one side and Keir, his navy towelling robe pulled on against the chill of the early December night, stood staring out into the darkness, his hands pushed deep into his pockets and his shoulders hunched as if against some unwanted burden.

'Keir?'

His dark head whipped round at the sound of her questioning use of his name, and she smiled sleepily, waving one hand in a gesture of invitation, willing him to come back and join her in the bed once more.

But Keir simply shook his head, and turned back to whatever held his attention beyond the glass.

'Go back to sleep, Sienna,' he instructed quietly. 'You have a busy day ahead of you tomorrow. You need your rest.'

Too tired to disobey, Sienna tried a half-hearted sound of protest, but without any force behind it. Already her eyes were closing once more, warm, drugging waves of sleep reaching out to enfold her.

'Tomorrow...' she managed, surfacing just long enough to catch the faint twist of his beautifully shaped mouth.

'Yes, tomorrow,' he responded flatly, a note she had never heard before shading his words. 'Now go to sleep.'

Turning on her side, Sienna nuzzled her face into the pillow once more, wrinkling her nose in annoyance as a fine strand of hair fell forward, tickling her cheek. It was only as she lifted a lazy hand to brush it away that she realised that the gold and diamond bracelet Keir had brought her, and which she last recalled holding tight in her fist as he carried her upstairs, was now fastened securely around her slender wrist. How...?

But sleep claimed her before she could think of any explanation of its presence.

Hearing her contented sigh, Keir turned once more to study her sleeping face, illuminated by the moonlight that slanted softly across her pillow.

In some ways it had been the homecoming he had dreamed of. But in others it had been everything he had ever feared. Their lovemaking had been so intense, so wild, so unbelievable. And Sienna herself had seemed like a different woman. Herself, and yet not the Sienna he had known up to now.

She had been so passionate, so responsive. He might almost have let himself believe that she had missed him as much as he had her. That the six days apart had made her look at him and their marriage in a different light, so that he could almost imagine there was a future for them after all.

Almost.

If he had fallen asleep when she had done he might have deluded himself completely, seeing what he wanted even though it wasn't there.

But when Sienna had curled up against him, her head resting on his chest, sighing her gratification, he had forced himself to stay awake to enjoy the sensation of having her so close, holding her tight against him. And so he had seen how, as she'd succumbed to the exhaustion that had claimed her, the arm that she had flung around him had relaxed, her clenched fist loosening, fingers uncurling softly.

As she'd done so something had slithered from her grasp, landing in a soft, metallic coil on the warm skin of his chest. The bracelet—presented to her downstairs and clutched in her greedy grasp ever since. An expensive trinket that had brought about a dramatic change in her attitude, transforming it from spiky reluctance to willing co-operation in the space of a heartbeat.

Well, if he left it like that, she might lose it somewhere in the bed, and that would be a pity after the effort she'd gone to to earn it, he'd told himself cynically. And so he'd fastened it round her slender wrist, where she couldn't miss seeing it as soon as she woke.

Face it, fool! Keir now reproved himself angrily, dragging his gaze away from Sienna as she settled back to sleep, and turning to stare into the bleak, cold light of the moon that so perfectly matched his mood. Face the fact that this marriage is still based firmly on commercial lines. With every transaction paid for strictly in hard cash.

CHAPTER TEN

'I HAVE something for you,' Keir said casually. 'Happy Valentine's Day.'

'For me?'

Sienna's head came up sharply from the book she had been reading to stare at her husband in blank confusion.

'But I would have thought that the roses were enough...'

The roses were more than enough. Peach and gold, they exactly matched the flowers in her wedding bouquet, and just to think that he had troubled to remember sent her heart soaring in a singing reaction to his thoughtfulness. She tried not to pin too much on it, but all the same it was impossible not to let herself wonder, to dream. He had been so very generous at Christmas, and now this. Was it possible that perhaps, slowly, Keir was coming to care for her in a way that was more than sexual?

'I still wanted you to have this.'

Belatedly Sienna realised all that Keir held out to her now was a white envelope. Just a card, then, not the extra Valentine's gift she had been foolishly anticipating.

'Well, you obviously don't believe in pretending to be a secret admirer,' she joked as she took it from him.

She had tried that, she recalled, hot colour washing her cheeks. Too scared to send him a Valentine's card that came anywhere near the truth about the way she felt, she had chosen instead one with a jokey inscription and had put it in the post, carefully disguising her handwriting as best she could.

The joke had fallen painfully flat when Keir had opened the card along with the rest of his mail at breakfast time. He had barely skimmed over the words inside, his sensual mouth managing only the faintest flicker of a smile, before he had turned to her with a 'Thanks' so off-hand as to be positively indifferent.

'You want me to know exactly who it's from?' she said now.

'With this, I do.'

Something about his attitude set her nerves on edge. This felt all wrong. It was no light-hearted card for Valentine's Day. Not even a slightly risqué joke, as hers had been.

Sienna's fingers trembled as she ripped open the envelope. It was impossible to hold back the irrational hopes that flooded her mind. Could it be that the roses had just been the start, that they were meant to test the water, so to speak? Keir wanted her to know that this came from him, and so...

Not a card. All the nervous excitement that had buoyed her up left her body in a rush, so that she actually sagged back into her chair. Then what?

It took several more uncertain seconds before she recognised the slip of paper she held as a cheque. Much longer to make out the amount written on it as the figures danced before her eyes.

'What...? I don't understand.'

With a determined effort she blinked hard to clear her blurring vision, forcing herself to concentrate. She recognised Keir's handwriting, the firm, upward slash of his signature, heavily underlined, but nothing else made sense. The value of the cheque was impossibly large, for one thing.

'Keir, what is this?' Shadowed with confusion, her turquoise eyes sought his, meeting head-on a gaze that was dark as jet and every bit as unyielding.

'Can't you guess?' Rough and hard-edged, his tone scraped over already raw nerves, making her shiver unhappily. 'That cheque is for every penny I owe you, plus some extra to cover the interest.'

Every penny I owe you. But why? Afraid to ask the real question, the one that was pounding in her head, she dodged the issue cravenly instead.

'But, Keir—it's so much. Can you afford it?' she asked, affecting a calm she was a million miles from feeling, and finding herself quite pleased with the result. She sounded cool and in control, not the twisting mass of nerves that she was inside.

'Of course I can afford it!' Keir exploded, slamming one fist into the palm of the other hand in a gesture so expressive of his mood that Sienna flinched back in her chair, watching him with wide, wary eyes.

She had known something was up from the moment he had come home. Normally when he got back from the office his first action was to change his clothes, casting off the conformity and restrictions of his work-wear and putting on something more casual and comfortable. But today he had acted completely out of character, keeping on the superbly tailored navy blue suit and matching shirt and tie all through dinner.

Sienna found the formality of his appearance thoroughly disconcerting. So much so that she had found it hard to eat the delicious meal put in front of her. Dressed this way, he looked stunningly handsome, the severe lines of the tailored clothes enhancing the forceful appeal of his lean body, the striking, dark good looks. But he also looked icily remote and intimidating, a sleekly groomed predator whom she watched uneasily from behind the protection of her long black lashes.

She didn't even have the shield of her mother's presence at the table with them in order to dilute the impact of Keir's disturbing presence, deflect the more pointed remarks, fill the most uncomfortable silences. Caroline had found the cold, damp winter particularly wearing, and Keir had insisted that she take a holiday, visiting some friends in Spain, until the weather improved.

'I'm sorry. I didn't mean...' Sienna got to her feet in a rush, feeling far too vulnerable sitting down while he towered over her in this way. 'But, Keir—how?—why?'

The beautifully shaped mouth twisted into a cynical grimace as he lifted broad, straight shoulders in a dismissive shrug.

'How? Hard work, careful investment. Some calculated speculation on the stock market. As to why—well, I'm sure you can guess the answer to that.'

'To pay me back? But the money wasn't a *loan*!' And what did it mean for her, now that he had paid it all off? Where did that leave the two of them?

'I saw it as such—a temporary loan to get me out of an unexpected tight spot. And I knew I'd never rest until it was all paid back. So I took a couple of calculated gambles.'

'Keir, you might have lost everything!'

'It would have been worth it.'

'It mattered so much to you? But why?'

'Oh, come on, Sienna!' It was a low savage growl. 'You understand better than that. You knew I was never going to be a tame lapdog of a husband, someone who would be at your beck and call, come when you whistled. I took your money because I was forced to, I needed it. But I don't need it now, and so—'

'And now?' Sienna prompted nervously when he unexpectedly broke off the angry tirade. 'What happens now?'

Her hands were damp with perspiration, and she wiped them as inconspicuously as possible down the skirt of her deep red, long-sleeved dress. Just what did Keir have in mind for their future?

What happens now? Keir echoed her question in the privacy of his own thoughts. Did he really know how to answer that?

If he was strictly honest, then he hadn't thought things through properly. In fact, he hadn't considered beyond the moment that he handed over the cheque to her. For nearly six months now, all his attention had been concentrated on the prospect of this one moment. The point where he could pay back every penny of the money Sienna had given him and know that, with Alexander's in the clear and the debt he owed to her discharged, everything was on a completely different footing. They could start again.

But nothing had gone as he had anticipated. For one thing, Sienna hadn't even seemed pleased by the gesture he had made. Her amazing eyes had been as cold and unwelcoming as the North Sea on a winter's day, her expression coolly indifferent.

'Have you thought about making this marriage of ours into the real thing?' Keir asked, with a nonchalance that took her breath away. 'After all, we both get on well enough together—and you have to admit that the sex couldn't be better.'

'Is that a proposal?' High and tight with something close to hysterical laughter, Sienna's voice perfectly expressed the disbelief she was feeling. 'Because quite frankly I've had more flattering put-downs! What on earth makes you think I'd agree to any such thing?'

What indeed? Keir was forced to ask himself, shaking his head at his own stupidity. He could only be grateful that he'd managed to hide the way he really felt. This way, he'd asked the question, but without putting himself on the line. He could just imagine what her response would have been if he'd been fool enough to do that!

'Why not?' If he could have managed to sound more detached, he didn't know how. 'Plenty of other marriages have been built on a whole lot less. It's a start.'

'Not much of one!' Sienna used scorn to disguise the pain she felt. 'And what, precisely, would I get out of this marriage you're proposing—other, that is, than a raging sex-life?'

The dreadful thing was that she was tempted! If he had been just the tiniest bit more gentle. If he had couched his offer in terms that were even the slightest bit less insulting, she might actually have said yes.

'A rich husband—because, believe me, Sienna, I *am* rich now. The problems I had are all behind me. A good life-style—a child...'

A child. A baby with Keir's dark hair and big brown eyes. Her own private fantasy come true. But she could never admit as much.

'No way! A baby should be brought into the world by two people who truly love each other. A child deserves to have parents who can teach it by example what love is, what it means. They shouldn't just be two people brought together by a temporary difficulty who decided to stay together because they had a great *sex-life*!'

Well, now you know, Keir Alexander! Do you want it spelled out any more clearly than that? *Could* she make it any plainer? Did he really want to stick around and see what little was left of his ego taken and trampled into the ground under her dainty, arrogant little feet?

'Then there's not much point in continuing with this farce, is there? We might as well call it a day.'

Sienna felt all the blood drain from her face, leaving it cold as ice. Twice she opened her mouth to speak, only to have her voice fail her at the last moment. With a struggle, she tried one more time.

'You—you can't mean that!'

He couldn't! Not now. Not yet. Cold and callous and totally unfeeling he might be, but he'd stolen her heart, and if he walked out of the door he'd take it with him, leaving just a raw, gaping hole where it should be.

'I mean it,' Keir returned dangerously. 'Every damn word.'

He was turning towards the door as he spoke. He had every intention of carrying out his threat unless she did something drastic. But what? Desperation forced inspiration into her panicked mind.

'Well, that's just typical!' she flung after him. 'Typical male selfishness! Now you've got everything you want, you don't even spare a thought for me!'

It stopped him at least. Froze him halfway across the room, before slowly swinging round to face her again.

'Everything—' he began, but she was too distraught to

let him speak. Instead she rushed on, the words pouring out of her, totally beyond her control.

'You know what my situation is! How I have to convince my uncle this is real! I must stay married to you or I'll lose everything!'

And he would never know just how true those words really were. Without Keir she would never inherit the rest of her father's money, but then without Keir she wouldn't care about anything like that at all. Nothing would have any meaning.

'If the money matters to you that damn much, I'll give it you. I told you, I'm rich...'

'It's not just the money!' Was he so desperate to be free of her? 'There's this house—my mother's home—and how do you think people will talk if you walk out on me now?'

'By "people" I presume you mean your precious Dean Hanson?'

Dean had never even crossed her mind, but it would be safer not to admit that.

'You owe me a year! That was what we agreed on! I want that year—no more, no less! As I said before, that money wasn't a loan! I—bought you—paid for you...'

She was saying all the wrong things, she knew that by the black, savage scowl that had descended on his stunning features, the blaze of yellow fury in the depths of his eyes.

'The hired husband.' Bleak cynicism lashed at her like the cruel flick of a whip but she forced herself to ignore it.

'You agreed to stay for twelve months, not six. You must stay!'

'Must?'

Must was quite the wrong word to have used.

'You—you promised...'

Abruptly Keir's mood changed. The tension in his shoulders vanished, leaving them with a disturbingly despondent slump as he raked both hands through the dark silk of his hair in a gesture of angry frustration.

'I promised,' he echoed flatly. 'And I should keep my promise.'

He couldn't summon up any emotion to inject into the words. The emotion was all in his heart. How in hell was he to stay in the relationship feeling as he did and knowing there was no hope of a response? How was he to survive when he could only get in deeper and deeper, as the past months had already proved to him?

He'd thought he could have it all. Keir almost laughed aloud at his own foolishness. The company and the marriage. But nearly six months down the line Sienna showed no sign at all of coming to care for him. If anything, she was further away than ever.

But he had promised, and, recognising an Achilles' heel when she saw one, Sienna had gone straight for it. He would never renege on a promise and she knew it. So now he was caught, trapped into living with a woman who saw him only as the key to the money she would inherit. When the year they'd agreed on was up and he'd outlived his usefulness to her she would let him go without even waving goodbye. The real problem was whether he could last another six months without betraying himself. Without her finding out what he really felt.

'All right, Sienna, you win. I'll stay.'

All right, Sienna, you win. He was conceding defeat, Sienna told herself. But if she'd won, why did it feel so much like a total failure? Why did she feel so despondent, so totally desolate, as if something very special, something precious and valuable had just died right there in front of her eyes?

Because she'd won the battle but lost the war. She'd persuaded Keir to stay, but so much against his will that he must always hate her for it. She had used moral blackmail on him, left him with no alternative, and he would never forgive her for that. He would stay because he was obliged to, but he would resent every second he spent with her.

And when the year was up he would escape, throw off

he bonds that he saw as forcing him to be, in that detested phrase, the hired husband and leave without a backward glance. And she would have to let him go. She had no reason to justify keeping him with her any longer. Just to think of it made her heart ache as if it was bruised.

When the year was up! Sienna had to force back the cry of distress that almost escaped her, biting down hard on her lower lip to keep herself silent. The end of the year might be the least of her worries. The real problem was whether she could survive the next six months or so and keep the truth of her feelings for Keir hidden all that time.

CHAPTER ELEVEN

SIENNA wasn't asleep when Keir finally came to bed, jus
half dozing. But when she felt the bedclothes lift slightly
the bed dip under his weight, and the warm, intensely per
sonal scent of his body coil around her she came wide
awake at once. For a few moments she lay absolutely still
wondering whether to speak or take the more diplomatic
route of keeping quiet. The past weeks had been hard
enough. Was she about to make them more difficult fo
herself?

In the month since Valentine's Day, it had seemed as i
Keir barely existed in her life. If it hadn't been for the fac
that he came home every night, then she would never have
seen him. He was out early in the morning, often before she
even woke, and he stayed out all day, only reappearing late
than ever before, often only just in time to collapse into bed
and fall fast asleep.

But she knew that he no longer needed to work so hard
Alexander's was going from strength to strength, the in
vestments Keir had made bringing in a small fortune in in
terest. And so the only conclusion she could come to was
that he was deliberately distancing himself from her, staying
out in order to avoid having to come face to face with her

And she couldn't bear it. The few months that were lef
of their marriage were steadily going by. All around her
the signs of spring's arrival were slowly starting to appear
Before she could blink it would be summer, and at the end
of that summer she and Keir would go their separate ways
This was all the time with him that was left to her. She
couldn't possibly let it go to waste.

Beside her, Keir stirred restlessly, and, unexpectedly, she

heard him sigh deeply. Just what was the reason for his despondency she didn't know, but she *had* to talk to him—and now.

'Keir?' she said softly, and instantly felt the long body at her side stiffen.

'I didn't realise you were awake.' Coming out of the darkness, his voice was far from welcoming, with no trace of warmth in it.

Not the best beginning, but she forced herself to ignore the tension in him so that she could continue.

'My mother will be back next week. Can I hope that you'll at least make some effort to be home once in a while when she's here?'

Keir lifted his hands and linked them behind his head, staring up at the ceiling.

'So that's what's so important it's kept you awake half the night,' he drawled sardonically. 'Well, you needn't worry your pretty head about things any more. I'll be here.'

He'd be here for Caroline, the moment her mother set foot in the house. But he hadn't been here for her, for his wife, for ages.

'Thanks.'

There was no way she could control her voice. She sounded as ungracious and ill-tempered as a hibernating bear woken far too early from its sleep. And, to judge by the way Keir's head turned swiftly in her direction, he was well aware of the fact.

'You don't sound too pleased with the idea,' he commented satirically. 'Was that the wrong answer? Was I supposed to say, No, I'll make myself scarce so that Caroline will be forced to wonder what's up?'

'Of course not! But that's just what she'll do if you continue the way you've been behaving. Don't you think it's a little too early to start laying preparations so that people won't be too surprised when we finally divorce?'

'That wasn't what was in my mind at all.'

It was impossible to interpret Keir's tone, and the way he

had pulled himself up onto his pillows, leaning back against the bedhead, meant that his face was way above hers, impossible to see. So she had no clues at all as to exactly what *had* been in his thoughts.

'But then I don't think you'd want to know what I was really thinking.'

'Wouldn't I?'

Sienna copied his movement of a moment earlier, levering herself up until she was sitting against the pillows. She caught the flash of his dark eyes, eerie and disturbing in the moonlight coming through a chink in the curtains, glancing at her just once, then away again, with a speed that slashed at her heart in its total indifference.

'And what would you know about it, *husband*?' She emphasised the word with a sarcasm that matched his own. 'When have you been around to learn anything about the way I was thinking? To see anything beyond the needs of that damn company of your—'

'Well, well, what is this?' Keir interrupted her tirade mockingly. 'Are you claiming, dear wife, that you've actually been missing me? That, unlike the last time, this protest is actually on your own behalf and not just your mother's?'

The cynical intonation of that 'dear wife' turned the endearment into an insult that twisted the knife in the wound he had already inflicted on her.

'Don't call me that!' She was beyond thinking if her response was wise, beyond caring how much it gave away. 'Don't you dare use the word wife in reference to me!'

'Why not?' Keir returned with deceptive mildness. Sienna was only too well aware of the way that that ominously quiet voice hid a ruthless temper, only barely reined in. One false move and he would loose his grip on it altogether. 'I understood that was what you are—for now at least.'

Suddenly a fierce, liberating anger filled Sienna's thoughts, obliterating rational thought. She didn't care if she drove him to lose his temper. Perhaps, after all, that was what she wanted him to do. It would be such a change to see some emotion, some passion in him, even if it was only anger. For the past few weeks he had been so controlled, so coolly distant, that at times she had been ready to scream. It would be a relief to let out some of that tension, like hot air escaping from a pressure cooker.

'A wife in name only! A wife who hasn't been treated like a wife! Do you know how long it is since we—since we made love—or did anything together! You're out all day and half the night; I hardly ever see you! If you were a different man, I might think you had a mistress, but I can't even tell myself that! Instead my rival in the…the…'

Desperately she caught herself up as her wayward tongue almost gave the game away completely. *My rival in the love stakes* she had been about to say and her heart clenched in panic at the thought of just how Keir would have responded to *that*!

'My rival for your attention,' she amended hastily, 'is your company!'

Her words died away into the silence of the night. A silence so still and profound that it tugged sharply at her nerves, making her skin feel cold. Say something! she pleaded silently, willing Keir to speak. But still the silence stretched out, tightening her nerves with every fearful beat of her heart. And still Keir said nothing.

She was so tense with expectation of his angry response that when he moved suddenly she flinched away nervously. But Keir had only lifted his hands to rake them through his hair, shaking his head slightly as he did so.

'I had no idea you felt this way. I—'

'Well, what way did you expect me to feel? Was I supposed to sit quietly at home while you were out playing at being the businessman of the year?'

'I was not *playing*!' It came out with a snap from between clenched teeth. 'I was earning the money to pay you back.'

'Money I didn't want!'

That brought his eyes round to her again, studying her so

intently from beneath lowered lids that she shifted uncomfortably against the softness of the pillows. Now that her eyes had grown accustomed to the darkness, she could make out the strong, clean lines of his chest, the wide, straight shoulders, and her fingers itched to stretch out and touch. She had to clench them tightly out of sight under the covers so that they didn't smooth over the skin she knew felt like heated satin, trace the tantalising line of body hair down to where it vanished out of sight under the duvet.

The moonlight played on the carved lines of Keir's face, throwing it into planes and shadows that emphasised the purity of the bone structure, the deep pools of his eyes. Against the immaculate white of the pillow covers, the darkness of his hair was almost shocking. The restless movement of his hands a moment before had ruffled it softly, so that a single wayward lock had fallen forward over the high forehead, just asking to be stroked back into place.

But she didn't dare. His mood was too dangerous, too unpredictable. From wanting the release of his fury, she was now desperate to do anything to avoid it. It was impossible to tell which was worse—the fire of his anger or the coldness of his indifference. Both were brutally destructive in their own way.

'Here we go again,' Keir muttered roughly. '"I don't want…I don't want". Will you ever tell me what you *do* want?'

Oh, but that was easy. If only she had the nerve to say it.

Did she dare? Sienna stared up into the impenetrable darkness of his eyes and drew in a ragged, uncertain breath. Her lips were too dry to speak, and she slid her tongue over them to ease the feeling.

It was as she saw Keir's gaze drop to follow the small movement, the sudden tension in his jaw, that she knew he was not as unaffected by her as he seemed. Was his indifference, then, all just an act? Had he felt the past weeks' separation as badly as she had? Was the hunger that she had experienced even now eating away at him as it was inside her?

'Oh, Keir, don't you know...' A blend of uncertainty and undisguised desire, touched with a hint of soft amusement lowered her voice by a husky octave, and she knew from the way Keir's head went back slightly that he was not unaware of it. 'Surely you can guess.'

His breath was dragged into his lungs with an effort, as if they were raw and uncomfortable.

'Tell me.'

His command was even more rasping than hers had been. The sound of it made Sienna's mood lift dramatically. In this way at least they could still communicate.

With a small smile tugging at the corners of her mouth she finally gave way to temptation. Lifting her hand, she touched it lightly to the strong curve of one shoulder, the smile growing as she saw the shudder he was unable to control. Very gently she trailed her fingertips across his chest, her gaze fixed on the path she was taking so that she couldn't miss the response he fought.

Just for a second she let her fingers rest against the pulse at the base of his throat. Finding it satisfactorily heightened, the blood throbbing beneath the delicate pressure, she let the smile become a grin of triumph. If she couldn't keep him with her any other way, there was always this. Sex had been their way of connecting from the start. It wasn't perfect. It wasn't what she wanted. But it was better than nothing.

'You know what I want, Keir. I want you.'

The breath he drew in was even deeper, rawer, than before. He was weakening. Whatever wounded pride or determination to make his company the best in the world had kept him from her over the past weeks, it was weakening rapidly. The wall he had built between them was cracking apart, coming down brick by brick. A little more encouragement was all it needed.

Her fingers traced delicate, heated patterns down over his

impressive torso, making small circles in the softness of the fine dark hair, feeling the powerful muscles clench and tighten underneath her touch. Her own heart was thudding painfully, her blood heating until it created a fire of need at the most feminine core of her body.

'Did you hear me, Keir?'

His lack of anything to say was surprising. But perhaps he wanted her to carry on persuading him. Perhaps he wanted to carry out this game of provocation to the very limit. Perhaps he wanted her to tantalise and torment him until he could take no more.

'I said I want you.'

Her wandering hands had reached the line of the bed-clothes and she hesitated, then ran them backwards and for-wards along the top of the soft barrier, as if debating whether to go any further. Keir was totally still now, he almost seemed to have stopped breathing.

'I want you to—'

She broke off on a squawk of shocked surprise as Keir moved at last. But not in the way she had anticipated.

A hard hand clamped onto hers, strong fingers closing tightly, stilling her teasing movement.

'I heard what you said,' Keir growled savagely. 'But you'll have to forgive me—I'm not in the mood tonight.'

'Not—not in the—' Sienna turned wide, stunned eyes on his face, finding it closed and shuttered, as cold and un-yielding as if it was that of a marble statue. 'I don't under-stand.'

What had happened to the response she had been so sure of? The passion she had believed was just under the surface, needing just the faintest encouragement to be set free?

Not in the mood? Dear God, Alexander, who are you trying to kid? The hunger was like a pain inside him, claw-ing at him. But he'd been caught that way before and the inevitable kickback had become harder and harder to en-dure.

Oh, he could let himself make love to Sienna quite easily.

Let himself! He almost laughed aloud at the bitter irony of the thought. It was all he could do to stop himself from grabbing her and throwing her back on the bed and... But it was no longer the same.

The pleasure—the *physical* pleasure—was still there, intense as ever. If anything, it grew more intense each time he made love to Sienna. He was always fully *physically* satisfied. But deep inside was an emotional black hole that was growing wider and deeper with every day of this façade of a marriage that passed.

He hated the way it made him feel. Feared that one day he might weaken and say what he really felt, reveal his heart openly to her. He was afraid that one night, in the throes of passion, or, worse, when he had had rather too much to drink, he might just let down the barriers he'd lived with for so long and tell her that he loved her.

And so for weeks now he'd held back, making excuses. He'd stayed out as long as he could and come to bed later and later, waiting until he was sure that she was asleep. Or he'd protested a tiredness he was far from feeling. Anything so that he could avoid being in bed with her when she was awake. It was bad enough having to endure the long wakeful hours with her warm, soft body curled so close to his, the perfume of her skin filling his nostrils.

'I don't understand.' Sienna's eyes, pale in the moonlight, were sheened with tears she wouldn't let herself shed. 'What is it? Don't you fancy me any more?'

Fancy her! 'Fancy' didn't describe it. He ached with hunger. Wanted her as he had never wanted any woman, and that hunger never eased, was never appeased.

But he couldn't bear the emotional backlash any longer. Couldn't handle the thought that making love meant nowhere near as much to her. That with her it was only physical. That her mind and her heart were not involved in the way that his were. That perhaps she was even comparing him with Dean and wishing he were the man she loved.

'Sienna, I told you I wasn't in the mood.'

If her tormenting fingers wandered an inch or so below the covers she'd soon prove that statement for the outright lie it was. Silently Keir cursed his wilful body for the all too obvious signs it was betraying.

'But you haven't made love to me for weeks!'

Not with his body, perhaps, but in his mind…! In his thoughts he had been with her, loving her, more times than he cared to count. His thoughts had produced the most erotic, most carnal, positively X-rated films for his own private viewing. But the most fantastical element about them had been that in every one of his dreams Sienna had been avowing her undying love for him.

'We don't have to be at it every second of the day!'

'Keir, we're not *at it* any time. And we're supposed to be—we're newly-weds—we're married.'

'Yeah, we're married,' Keir echoed cynically. 'And this is what happens when you get married. Romance flies out of the window. You sign that piece of paper and everything changes. Reality intervenes…'

'But ours isn't exactly the usual sort of marriage. You're not really my husband, are you? And I'm not anything like a wife. It's not even a *real* marriage.'

'You said it, lady.'

If she'd kicked him right where it hurt most, it couldn't have been more painful. But it had had one welcome effect—it had successfully doused his ardour in a second. At least now he would be able to get out of bed and walk away without revealing the lie he had been telling all this time.

And he had to walk away. He couldn't stay. Couldn't talk to her any more. But he had to make sure she didn't come after him.

'Real marriage or no, Sienna darling, the magic's gone out of it. I mean, look at what you're wearing…'

The flick of his hand that indicated the soft cotton of her well-worn tee shirt was arrogantly contemptuous.

'This…' Sienna caught herself up in a panic, painfully aware of the way that she had come close to admitting that, feeling lost and abandoned, she had pulled on the old tee shirt for comfort. 'It's a cold night!' she substituted hastily.

'In a centrally heated house.'

As if to prove his point, Keir flung back the duvet and swung his long legs out of bed with obvious indifference to the chill of the night. Proudly naked, he strode across the room to snatch up his robe and shrug it on, belting it tightly round his waist.

'You can't walk out on me like this!' Sienna protested wildly. 'I won't let you.'

'You can't stop me.' Keir's contradiction was formed in ice.

And before she had time to recover enough from that final cutting comment he was gone.

Left alone, Sienna wrapped her arms tightly round her slim body, as if to hold herself together. Deep inside she felt as if she was falling apart. As if everything that was truly her was crumbling to pieces, never to be put back together again. The pain of Keir's rejection was almost more than she could bear. And it was so much worse because it had been done so coldly, with absolute control, no trace of anger or any other emotion in his voice.

Somewhere along the line she had foolishly allowed herself to become complacent. Because Keir had desired her so much at the start of their marriage, she had convinced herself that he would always feel that way. That if nothing else, the blazing physical passion they shared would keep him by her side for what remained of their marriage. She had relied on that and allowed herself to hope that perhaps in that time there might be a chance that he would come to feel something else, something much deeper.

Now it seemed that both dreams had been trampled in the dust. Keir didn't even want her any more. So she might as well give up.

No! Even as the thought formed in her mind she rejected it. She still had over five months of her marriage left. She would use them to win Keir back to her, one way or another.

It was either that or face the prospect of a future living with a vital part of her cut away.

And passion would be the easier approach to take. If sex was the way to keep him interested then she'd give him sex, sex and more sex. All she had to do was relight the fires that seemed to have subsided from their original blaze to a mere flicker. This grotty old tee shirt would have to go for a start.

Pulling the duvet up over the offending item, Sienna settled down to some serious planning.

CHAPTER TWELVE

'THERE! That should do it.'

Sienna smiled with satisfaction as she replaced her credit card in its holder and pushed it back into her handbag. It could do with a rest. She'd really given it a battering today! But in the end it would all be worth it.

Or at least she prayed it would be worth it. If the full-scale assault on Keir's senses that she planned, with the help of a morning at the hairdresser's and a beauty salon and the contents of the various carrier bags with which she was now laden, didn't work then she had no idea at all what her next move would be. But there would be one; she was determined on that. She was going to win this battle or at the very least go down fighting.

But first she was in urgent need of refreshment. Her feet were throbbing and her throat was dry. She needed a cool drink before she made her way back home.

The wine bar was crowded and noisy, buzzing with a hundred different conversations as Sienna hunted round for a space to deposit her bags. She didn't find one. What she saw instead had her frozen to the spot, turquoise eyes widening in shock, her blood running cold in her veins.

'Keir!' she breathed, her voice shaking.

She'd forgotten that this bar was a favourite of his. Just a short walk from his offices, it was where he and his employees gathered to celebrate a birthday or a particularly successful deal.

But it wasn't any member of Keir's staff who was with him now. It wasn't even a client or one of his friends. Even though the woman seated on the far side of the crowded room had her back to her, Sienna would have recognised her anywhere.

The red-gold hair was unmistakable, as was the tinkling laugh that now sounded through a sudden drop in the conversation as she leaned forwards to take one of Keir's hands in both of hers. And, in spite of knowing it was impossible at this distance, she actually thought she could catch a waft of Lucille's sickeningly sweet trademark perfume.

Keir and his stepmother, here! Sienna's first coherent thought was that she might be seen if she stayed any longer. Keir, at least, with his back to the window, was facing in her direction. If he looked up, glanced this way…

Panic put wings on her heels, and after a couple of moments' frantic pushing and shoving she was once more outside on the pavement, breathing hard, as if she had run a sprinting race.

Keir and Lucille. Keir and Lucille. The names ran like a litany of horror through her mind. Keir and his stepmother, the woman he professed to hate. But if that was the case, then why was he meeting with her secretly like this?

Sienna gave a low moan, swaying back against the wall and closing her eyes in despair. Was this, and not the demands of work at all, the reason why Keir had been out so late so often? Were assignations with Lucille what had kept him away from home? And, if so, what sick sort of a plot had he been hatching all the time—perhaps even from the moment that he'd agreed to marry her?

'Excuse me, my dear…' A concerned voice penetrated the whirling haze inside Sienna's head. 'But are you all right?'

'Oh, yes!' Hastily she forced her eyes open, staring straight into the anxious face of the elderly gentleman in front of her. 'Thank you, yes, I'm fine. Truly I am. I—just felt rather tired. The crowds, you know.'

'That's London for you. Perhaps you should go in here…' a wave of his hand indicated the wine bar behind her '…and sit down for a moment.'

'Oh, there's no need for that!' Sienna assured him, barely suppressing a shudder at the thought. What she should be doing was getting on her way, so as to be well out of sight as quickly as possible just in case Keir and his companion came out of the wine bar on their way home. 'I really have to be on my way. But thank you for your concern...'

She was already moving as she spoke, not daring to look back in case she saw the tall, proud figure of her husband, or Lucille's smaller, curvier form, trim in the elegant cream suit.

On their way home. And what if their destination wasn't separate—two homes—but they were heading in exactly the same direction? What if Keir's plan was to head for Lucille's house... Because he had to be spending all these late evenings *somewhere.*

From some hidden corner of her memory came an image from her wedding day, the lascivious expression on Lucille's face when she had looked at Keir. Once again she heard that double-edged, 'You always did give great value there, didn't you, dearest?'

No, she wouldn't let herself think it. Desperately Sienna hailed a taxi, wanting only to be home, away from the tormenting images that preyed on her thoughts. But of course leaving the wine bar behind did not mean freeing herself from the memory of what she had seen. That pursued her all the way home, and fretted at her thoughts throughout the evening.

And things were made so much worse by the fact that once again Keir was late. Once more it was almost midnight before Sienna heard his heavy footsteps on the stairs.

By then she was in bed. For a long time she had debated with herself the wisdom of staying up and confronting Keir over what she had seen, having it out with him. But in the end reason had won. She didn't know *what* she had seen, did she?

And, even if things were as bad as she feared, surely it was better to stick to her original plan? Even if Keir's attentions had strayed—to his stepmother of all people!—she could still win him back if she just put her mind to it. She didn't allow herself to consider the possibility that Keir's attentions had never *strayed*, but in fact Lucille had been the one he had been interested in—and possibly his mistress—all this time.

'Waiting up for me again, my darling wife?' Keir's drawling voice, blackly cynical and very slightly slurred, challenged her from the doorway.

Dark hair tousled, brown eyes impossibly bright, and with a day's growth of beard heavily shadowing the strong line of his jaw, he looked totally unlike the elegantly groomed businessman she had seen in the wine bar. The wild, gipsyish look was emphasised by the way that his shirt hung loose, his tie unfastened and dangling round his neck, the tailored jacket slung over one shoulder, a finger hooked into the neckline.

'How very devoted you are…'

'And how very drunk you are,' Sienna returned sharply.

Foolishly, crazily, her heart had lifted as she'd realised the state he was in. To have got this drunk then surely he couldn't have had any sort of enjoyable time with Lucille, could he? Or, if he'd stayed with her, then surely he would have been incapable…

'I trust you didn't drive home in that state.'

'I'm intoxicated, not stupid! Of course I took a taxi.' With his free hand he executed a rather wild salute. 'But thank you for caring all the same.'

'It was the other people on the roads I was thinking of,' Sienna returned tartly, reverting to schoolmistress mode in order to hide the sense of horror that gripped her at just thinking of the possibility of that glorious body being damaged in any way. 'I would hate the thought that you'd hurt anyone.'

'Now that's more like it. For a moment there I wondered if I'd got the right room.'

There would be no talking to him tonight, Sienna reflected wearily. He was past listening to anything she said. And, knowing how volatile his temper was these days, even when sober, she wasn't prepared to risk the nuclear explosion that must inevitably result if she provoked him in this mood.

'I wasn't sure if you were in fact my beloved and loving wife…'

'In the flesh, as you can see.'

That comment had been a mistake, she realised, as in response to her words Keir's polished onyx eyes slid downwards from her face and moved lazily over the amount of creamy skin, the flushed curves of her breasts exposed by the black satin and lace nightgown that had been one of her purchases earlier that day.

'And what flesh,' Keir muttered, the words thick with sensual appreciation as he levered himself upright from the doorpost against which he had been lounging. 'Sienna, you look…'

As he paused, seeming to hunt for the right word, Sienna's heart skipped first one then several beats at the thought that the first stage of her plan had succeeded. Perhaps it wasn't quite as she would have wanted it. She would have much preferred it if Keir had been completely sober, so that she would have known his comments came from the heart, but it was a start.

'Devastating…' It was dragged out into a long, aching sigh.

But a second later a change came over Keir's face. His jaw tightened, dark eyes suddenly focusing more clearly, and he drew himself up with an abrupt little shake of his proud head, as if to drive away some unwanted thought.

'What are you up to, darling?' His voice was different too. Clearer, curt, and only faintly ragged round the edges. Evidently he was really nothing like as drunk as he had first led her to believe. 'Trying to tempt my jaded appetites?'

The pain burned like acid in her heart. From being what she had wanted so desperately, the desire she saw smouldering in his eyes was now like an image from a nightmare. She had longed for this, dreamed of his finding her desirable and wanting to make love to her, but not like this. Not like this!

'Keir, don't!'

'"Keir, don't!"' he echoed, bleakly mocking. 'Oh, now I know that you really are my wife. Now...'

She couldn't take any more. 'Are you coming to bed or not?'

For the space of a long, drawn-out heartbeat, he paused, narrowed eyes searching her face, his gaze seeming to scorch where it rested. Sienna felt as if her heart was beating high up in her throat, pounding painfully against the tangled knot of feelings that had gathered there, choking her.

Then, just when she knew she could take no more, he shook his head again, more slowly this time.

'No,' he pronounced, slow and deep and inflexible, turning a look of violent antipathy on the inoffensive divan on which she lay. 'No way. Not in *that* bed, not tonight. If I'm to sleep at all tonight—and it's really rather important that I do—I'll have to—'

'Why?' Sienna questioned, interrupting him. 'I mean, why is it important that you sleep tonight?'

'Oh, didn't I tell you?' It was impossible to tell whether his surprise at her question was affected or genuine. 'I'm driving one of the lorries to Carlisle tomorrow morning.'

'A lorry! But why?'

'There's no one else. This flu epidemic has had drivers going down like flies. This consignment has to be delivered tomorrow without fail, and I was the only person available with the necessary licence.'

Or it was another excuse to avoid spending time with her.

'I'm coming with you!' The impulsive words were out before she had even fully formed the thought of uttering them.

'No.' Flat and hard, the single word brooked no argument. He didn't want her with him; resistance was etched into every line of his strong face

Sienna simply ignored it. '*Yes!* Oh, please, Keir! I've never been in one of those huge cabs and I've always wanted to…'

When she turned those huge, pleading eyes on his face like that it was impossible to refuse her anything, Keir thought despairingly. If only he was a little more sober he'd be able to think of some argument against the idea, say something that would put her off.

'*Please!*'

'I'm leaving at six.' His back was against the wall and he knew it.

'I'll be there.'

'This is fun!' Sienna couldn't contain her enthusiasm. 'It's amazing being so high up like this. You can see for miles.'

Keir couldn't hold back a swift grin in response to her exuberant gesture, which took in the expanse of rainswept motorway visible through the huge windscreen of the truck's cab.

'I can still remember the way I felt the first time I drove one of these on my own. It felt like being at the wheel of a tank.'

If he was honest, he had never expected that Sienna would manage to get out of bed to join him in the early dawn, particularly when the weather was so foul. But she'd surprised him by being up and ready by the time he'd made it downstairs.

One look at her determined face had told him that there was no point in trying to dissuade her from coming with him, and anyway he hadn't had time to argue. He'd already been running late, and it had been easier simply to go along with her resolve to accompany him. There was nothing he could do but make the best of it. At least the concentration required in handling the heavy vehicle in the unpleasant weather conditions distracted his attention from the way her tight jeans hugged the rounded shape of her bottom and hips, and the turquoise cotton sweater echoed the colour of her eyes.

'I never realised you actually *drove* for the company. I've always thought of you as management.'

'It was a matter of necessity at the beginning. Alexander's was so run-down that we just weren't making enough to pay the number of drivers we really needed. I got my licence as soon as I could, and went out on the road with the rest of them until things got better.'

'And you enjoyed it.' Sienna didn't disguise the surprise she felt. She was discovering a new and very different side to this man who was her husband. A side that she had never dreamed existed.

The man sitting beside her in the cab, casually dressed in an elderly grey sweatshirt and black jeans, strong fingers firm on the wheel, every movement sure and confident and in control, was light-years away from the sophisticated, immaculately groomed businessman she had thought she was married to.

This Keir seemed years younger, his brown eyes alight with something close to excitement, the long body relaxed and yet always alert, ready to cope with any problem that presented itself. He looked powerfully, vibrantly alive, vital energy crackling through him, seeming to play around him like an electrical storm. And Sienna felt herself caught up in his enthusiasm with him.

'I loved it. Loved the freedom, the hours—days—when there was just me and I didn't have to answer to anyone else.'

'Was that so important to you? I thought you got on well with your father.'

'With my father, yes.'

The emphasis on the word 'father' brought Sienna's head round to stare at him, a faint frown creasing the space between her brows.

'But not with...?'

The sudden memory of the scene in the wine bar the previous day made her tongue falter nervously, fearful of the repercussions if she actually framed the question. But Keir supplied the remainder of the sentence, completing it with surprising equanimity.

'Not with my stepmother—or my own mother, for that matter.' His mouth twisted into a cynical grimace. 'I never seemed to be able to manage any sort of a real rapport with the female side of my family.'

Which was such a loaded comment that it had Sienna moving restlessly in her seat, painfully aware of the way it could be made to apply to her. But her courage failed her at the thought of questioning him further on either that or the subject of Lucille, and so, acknowledging her cowardice, she stuck to the least contentious topic.

'You didn't have an easy relationship with your mother?'

'That is very definitely an understatement, my dear Sienna. No one had an *easy* relationship with my mother; she was a very demanding woman. Just because she died appallingly young, it didn't make her a saint. At times she made my father's life hell with her unceasing complaints, her extravagant spending—'

Keir broke off in order to concentrate on manoeuvring the truck around a roundabout, but when they were once more back on the straight road he continued as if his speech had never been interrupted.

'That was why the company was in such bad shape when I left university—the money she took out of it, and the fact that my father completely went to pieces after she died. It took us years to pull things round again, and I'm sure the stress of those times took their toll, contributing to the stroke that finally killed him.'

Keir's expressive mouth twisted sharply again, revealing his feelings only too clearly.

'The only thing I can say is that at least she was nowhere near as bad as the second Mrs Don Alexander.'

'Lucille...' Sienna's uneasy whispering of Keir's stepmother's name earned her a slanted, narrow-eyed look, swift and assessing.

'Lucille,' he repeated when she couldn't continue. 'What is it, Sienna?'

'I—I saw you with her yesterday.'

At first she thought he hadn't heard her. His face betrayed no response; he changed gear every bit as smoothly as he had done everything up to now. It was only when he expelled his breath on a hiss of exasperation that she realised that the calm he displayed was only on the surface, and what was underneath was far more complex than she knew.

Abruptly Keir indicated left, swinging the truck into the lane that led to the motorway services. It was only when they had parked and he had switched off the engine that he turned to her, his expression icily distant.

'You saw Lucille with me,' he corrected coldly. 'Not the other way around. There is a difference.'

She wanted desperately to believe him. Everything in her heart cried out to accept his version of the story and so ease one of the causes of the unhappiness that she had endured for the past weeks. But was she being gullible and naïve to let her emotions rule her head? Uneasily she ducked her head in order to avoid that intently probing, dark-eyed gaze.

'She was holding your hand...' she muttered, unwillingly to give him an easy victory.

'Exactly. *She* was holding...' with a suddenness that made her jump, Keir reached out and closed his hand over Sienna's, where they lay in her lap '...*my* hands... Do you see?'

And of course she did. Looking down at Keir's strong fingers folded over hers, in exactly the same position as Lucille's had been, she could recall only too clearly how the older woman had reached for Keir in much the same way as he had just demonstrated to her. Though that still didn't mean their meeting was totally innocent. Still unable to meet his eyes, she could only nod in silent acknowledgement.

'Sienna.' Keir's voice was suddenly surprisingly soft, gently cajoling her out of her withdrawn mood. 'Could it be that you were the tiniest bit jealous?'

But that would be admitting too much. With a jerky, peevish movement, Sienna snatched her hands away from Keir's, pushing them restlessly through her hair.

'And why exactly would I to be jealous of her? It's not as if she's got anything I want…' Or anyone, if Keir's story was to be believed. 'Seeing as we've stopped here, have we time to have a drink? I'm dying for a coffee.'

She waited only long enough to see his curt nod of agreement before opening the door and clambering down from the high cab. Keir was close behind her as she marched towards the coffee bar. In the queue to buy their drinks he was a dark, silent figure whose presence lifted all the tiny hairs on the back of her neck in instinctive awareness, but he didn't say a word until they were actually seated at a table inside the café. Only then did he turn to her, a frown drawing his dark straight brows together.

'I'm having trouble believing that you could actually think I would make a secret assignation with Lucille…'

'Did I mention secrets—or assignations?' Sienna tried for flippancy, praying that her expression, the anxiety in her eyes, wouldn't give her away.

'You didn't have to.' Keir was stirring sugar into his coffee with unnecessary force. 'It was all written there on your face. You thought I'd arranged to meet her…'

'You didn't?' It came out too quickly, destroying her earlier pretence at carelessness.

Keir looked deep into her troubled turquoise eyes, his expression unexpectedly serious.

'No, I didn't. Look, Sienna, let me tell you a few home truths about Lucille. About this woman who you choose to believe I would dally with at the risk of yet more damage to our marriage…'

'Choose to!' Sienna protested indignantly. 'You make it sound as if I'm looking for—'

'Well, aren't you? Sienna, I made a commitment to this marriage when we first started out on it. A husband for a year was what I promised, and I have no intention of putting that in jeopardy.'

It was truly terrifying how easy it was to believe him. When those dark eyes held her mesmerised, and his voice rang with conviction, he could have told her *anything* and she would have accepted it. The noise and bustle of the café around them blurred to an indistinct haze and in that moment it seemed as if there was only herself in the world with Keir, this man she loved so desperately and yet dared not tell.

'Lu—Lucille…?' she managed to remind him, in a voice that sounded raw and husky, as if from overuse.

'Lucille,' Keir repeated, scowling darkly. 'The woman who broke my father's heart but wouldn't let him go. She didn't want him, but she wanted his income, and so she clung like a limpet to that marriage certificate even after it ceased to have any meaning whatsoever. She had numerous affairs when they were married, bled him dry with her spending. And even when he was dead she didn't let go, but lingered like a vulture, picking over what was left.'

He picked up his coffee cup and drank from it, but Sienna was sure that he never even tasted the dark liquid.

'Legally she was still his wife, and as he'd never got around to changing his will when she ran out on him, she was entitled to everything he'd left her. And that was to have been her last revenge. She knew exactly to the penny what I had available to buy her out, and so she asked for that plus half as much again. If I didn't pay she would sell to someone else, and Alexander's—the company Dad had put his life into—would be no more. I was desperate.'

So desperate that he had taken the offer *she'd* made to him. He'd signed away his freedom for a year in order to save Alexander's in his father's memory.

'Keir…' Sienna's eyes were soft as she looked at him, seeing the proud head downbent, that dark gaze staring broodingly into his coffee cup. 'You don't have to tell me this.'

That brought his head up sharply, brown eyes blazing into sea-green.

'Oh, but I do. Don't you see? I want you to know that nothing on this earth would force me into meeting with that she-wolf ever again. That if she hadn't come up to me in that wine bar yesterday and—'

He broke off abruptly, shaking his dark head as if to rid himself of the memory.

'I would never have sought her out.'

Sienna felt as if her emotions were on some violent out-of-control seesaw. Just as her heart was soaring in delight, hearing the vehement conviction of his declaration, a tiny, more rational part of her mind noted a disturbing tension about Keir's shoulders and jaw, an unexpected wariness in his eyes. She was seized by the sudden conviction that he was holding something back. Something vital to her peace of mind.

But she didn't have time to go back over their conversation and try to place exactly when the change had first come over him. Because Keir's next words drove every other thought from her mind.

'You have to see that I would do *anything*—anything at all—to get Lucille out of my life for good.'

Which was a real backhander, Sienna reflected miserably, fighting to force back the bitter tears that burned in her eyes, refusing to let them fall. Because in the same moment that Keir had given her peace of mind on the subject of his meeting with Lucille he had also blasted apart any chance of hope she might have had on another, far more important matter.

'I would do *anything*—anything at all…' Even, it seemed, accept Sienna's proposal of marriage.

Just when it had seemed that she was beyond feeling any more pain, it was clear that Keir could still find new ways of twisting the knife in even deeper.

CHAPTER THIRTEEN

'I NEVER realised that Carlisle was so close to the Scottish border!'

Sienna was studying the book of maps she had discovered amongst the collection of bits and pieces in the cab.

'I've never been to Scotland—do you think?—could we…?'

'I can take a hint!' Keir's tone was dry but suprisingly mellow. 'Yes, we can make a trip over the border, just to say you've been.'

'Great!'

As the day had gone on she had found it increasingly difficult to maintain the level of bright, inconsequential chatter that she had decided was the best way of hiding from Keir the real way she was feeling inside. But this new discovery made things rather easier, and Keir's unexpectedly easygoing mood helped immeasurably.

'What's the nearest place in Scotland I might have heard of?'

'Gretna. It's just over the border.'

'Gretna Green?' Sienna consulted the map again. 'Oh, yes… Is it as romantic as it sounds?'

'Romantic?' Keir's laughter was a sound of pure cynicism. 'You can forget any delusions you have on that score. It's pure commercialism through and through. Oh, don't look so disappointed, darling, I'm sure a believer in true love like you will be able to find some romance in the place somewhere.'

It was so loaded with hidden significance that it was like an actual blow to her stomach, leaving her incapable of breathing for a moment. But she couldn't get her mind round what exactly Keir was driving at.

'True love?' she questioned uncertainly, her heart racing in double quick time. Did he know? Had he guessed? How—*how*—had she given herself away?

'Oh, come on, sweetheart! You must be the last of the really great romantics. After all, you've held on to your precious Dean's memory all this time...'

'Dean!'

The rush of relief was so intense it was like pure adrenaline, making her head spin.

'You mean *Dean*!'

'Of course.' The look he slanted in her direction was swiftly assessing, his frown revealing the danger she was in, how close she had come to blasting her whole subterfuge wide open. 'Who else?'

Who else!

Sienna took a deep breath, knowing she had to go for broke. She had to find something to tell him in order to distract that calculating mind from thinking back over her reaction, putting two and two together and coming up with an answer that would destroy the balance of their relationship for ever. And she had to make it good.

There was only one thing for it. The truth. Or at least a part of it. Enough to convince Keir and make him stop questioning her.

And besides, she wanted him to know. Wanted it all out in the open once and for all.

'Let me tell you about Dean,' she said carefully. '*Everything* about Dean.'

'Everything?'

Keir's eyes were on the road, but Sienna could tell that every nerve in that long, lithe body was attuned to her, his mind concentrated on her words.

'Yes, everything! It's not a pretty story—and not one I'm proud of. You see, I was duped, deluded—conned. Dean Hanson was a liar and a cheat, a deceiver through and through, but I let him trick me. I was easy prey because I was stupid and gullible and I ignored all the warning signs until it was far too late.'

Bending her head so that the dark fall of her hair hung like sleek curtains around her face, hiding it, she stared down at her hands clasped tightly in her lap.

'I met him at the salon where I worked. He was a salesman for one of the cosmetics firms. We—we hit it off straight away. He was good-looking, witty, charming…' The word tasted sour in her mouth. 'So charming. He told me I was beautiful. That he'd never met anyone like me before. That I'd knocked him off balance in the first moment he'd ever seen me…'

'All the usual garbage,' Keir put in when her voice failed her. 'The sort of thing a guy spouts automatically when he wants to get a woman into bed,' he added sardonically when she turned to him, a question in her eyes.

The sort of thing he would have said to her at the start of their relationship if she hadn't flattened him with the crazy marriage idea. Only with him it would have been true, and not just his hormones talking.

Okay, not *entirely* his hormones talking, he amended with painful honesty. He had wanted her in his bed—fast! The rest had come later.

'The usual garbage,' Sienna echoed in a thready voice that twisted something painfully in his guts. 'Well, I fell for it. Hook, line and sinker. He had me wrapped round his little finger so fast that I didn't know night from day. I was dreaming of rings and wedding bells and happy ever after— and then I found out the truth.'

'Don't tell me. He was married.'

Despondently Sienna nodded, aquamarine eyes dulled and shadowed.

'Married with a kid and another on the way. And…'

Beside her, Keir swore violently as a gear change resulted in a totally uncharacteristic crunching sound.

'There's more?'

'I wasn't the only one.'

This was what she had found so hard to cope with. She couldn't believe that she had been so naïve, so gullible, so totally, senselessly blind. Dean's wife and child had been miles away, but his other woman—apart from Sienna herself, of course—had been right there under her nose all the time.

'Jacqui worked in the salon with me.' It was a cry of pain. 'I saw her every day. Talked to her. Had lunch with her. And I never suspected!'

This time the black savagery of Keir's response, the brutally eloquent stream of curses, made her flinch in the same moment that her heart soared at the thought that at least he cared enough to react in this coldly furious way.

'I was luckier than Jacqui,' she managed, on what was supposed to be a laugh, but one that broke painfully in the middle. 'She ended up pregnant, and when she told him she couldn't see Dean for dust—what was that?'

The growl of the engine had hidden Keir's muttered words, so now as she turned her pale face towards him, he repeated more clearly, 'I said, you really choose your times, lady.'

'Times?' Sienna frowned her bewilderment, turquoise eyes clashing with deepest brown. 'I don't...'

'Sienna...' Her name was a sound of pure exasperation. 'Do you know what it does to me to listen to you pouring your heart out like that and not to be able to do anything about it because—'

His fist slammed down on the edge of the steering wheel in a gesture of burning frustration.

'Because you have to concentrate on your driving,' Sienna finished for him. 'Don't worry, I understand. I mean, what else could you do?'

'If I could just get off this damned motorway, I'd stop this truck at once...'

The vehemence of his response was startling, the suppressed anger in his tone mixing with some other, inexplicable note to create the emotional equivalent of a Molotov cocktail.

'I'd take you in my arms, hold you, keep you safe. Let you cry out all the hurt until you were ready to face the world again…'

'It's—it's all right. I'm not going to cry.'

Not true! her conscience reproved her. Hot tears were pricking at her eyes, threatening to fall and prove her a liar. But they weren't the sort of tears Keir believed she would shed. Not tears of loss and pain at the way Dean had treated her. Instead they were tears of joy and delight, mixed thoroughly with a strong sense of disbelief at the thought that Keir even wanted to comfort her like this. Just to imagine him taking her in his arms and holding her made her blood sing in her veins.

'I've wept all the tears I'm ever going to waste on Dean Hanson. I'm over him. I'm never going to think of him again.'

I'm over him. Keir had to force himself to keep his eyes on the road as Sienna's declaration reverberated inside his head. *I'm over him.* If she only knew how long he had waited for her to say those very words. And now the moment was here but he had no idea how to react. He *couldn't* react or the result would be a very nasty accident on a crowded motorway.

So what did he do? His hands clenched so tightly over the wheel that his knuckles showed white as he was suddenly a prey to the terrible despondent thought that perhaps, after all, those words had come too late. That the past seven months had already inflicted so much damage on what had only been a very fragile relationship to start with that it would be too difficult to repair it. Certainly it seemed impossible that they could ever think of starting again.

And, to make matters worse, he was developing a headache that was making it difficult to think straight. Wearily he sighed, massaging the back of his neck with one hand.

'Is something wrong?' Sienna was quick to notice his reaction.

'I'm tired,' Keir hedged. 'Didn't sleep too well last night.'

And when he had dozed at all his dreams had all been of Sienna, beautiful, sensual Sienna, her creamy skin flushed with warmth, in the stunning black nightdress she had worn last night. How he had ever managed to stop himself from getting into bed beside her and ripping it from her glorious body, he would never know.

'But it doesn't matter. We're nearly there. Just another ten miles or so and we can stop for the night.'

The night. Sienna, you idiot, you hadn't thought of that!

'What—I mean, where do you normally sleep when you're on the road?'

The grin he turned on her lacked something of its usual megawatt brilliance, but at least it contained genuine good humour.

'In the cab.' His amusement grew at the sight of her stunned expression. 'There's plenty of room, and it's cosy enough with a duvet… But don't worry, I won't expect you to share. I expect you'd find it rather too intimate for comfort.'

If only he knew that intimacy was exactly what she hungered for. But Keir was concentrating fiercely on his driving, so much so that he completely missed the play of emotions over her face.

'I rang ahead from the first services we stopped at and I've booked us into a hotel together.'

'Together?'

Dark brown eyes were slanted in her direction, and in spite of the brevity of that glance she was shocked to see how dilated his pupils were. He looked pale too, worryingly so.

'The hotel only had one room. So I'm sorry, you'll have to share with me tonight.'

There had been no need for that 'sorry' Sienna told him

blithely in the privacy of her thoughts. 'Together' was exactly what she wanted for tonight.

But by the time they finally reached their hotel it was obvious that any plans she might have would have to be shelved. Keir was evidently decidedly unwell. He had lost all trace of colour and it seemed that he could barely open his eyes. His skin was faintly sheened with perspiration and felt damp and clammy under Sienna's fingertips when she touched him.

'Keir, what is it?' she asked anxiously as the lift moved upwards towards their floor. 'Are you ill?'

'Migraine.' His voice was rough and hoarse, as if it came from a painfully dry throat. 'I don't get them often, but when I do...'

The words trailed off and he swayed on his feet.

'Here...' Stepping forward hastily, she took his arm. 'Lean on me.'

The unexpected ease with which he complied, when she had expected at least a token protest, was more worrying even than his pallor. His arm around her shoulders was warm and heavy, and she had to stiffen her back to support him.

The short trip down the corridor seemed to take an age, but at last they reached their room. Sienna had barely got him inside before he lurched to the bed and collapsed facedown, burying his head in the pillows.

'Keir...' It was shocking to see him like this. She had always thought of Keir as being so strong, so capable, someone who could handle everything. 'Do you have any medication? Tablets you can take?'

'At home, in London,' he managed, his voice muffled by the pillows.

Not much use to him there, Sienna told herself. But there had to be something she could do to help. Suddenly inspiration struck.

'I have to go out for a minute, Keir. But I won't be long, I promise. Half an hour at most.'

By a lucky chance she found a chemist still open in the very next street so in the end she was less than half that time. The small pile of discarded clothes on the floor beside the bed told their own story. Keir had just had enough strength to strip them off before subsiding back under the covers.

'Well, that'll make my job easier. Here, take these...'

Compliant as a tired child, Keir swallowed the painkillers she held out to him, opening his eyes just wide enough to eye the two bottles she held with faint curiosity.

'What...?'

'Lavender essential oil and almond oil as a carrier. I'm going to give you a massage. I *am* a qualified aromatherapist, remember,' she added, when he looked slightly sceptical. 'I used to do this for a living. Now lie down on your front so I can do your back.'

Kneeling beside him on the bed, she blended the oils together then poured a little into her cupped hands. When it was slightly warmed she smoothed it over the length of his back, wincing as she felt the tight knots of tension in his muscles just under the surface of the skin. He really must be in pain, she thought in some distress.

Fired by a determination to help, she swept her palms up the long straight line of his spine to the nape of his neck and out across his shoulders, kneading firmly on the taut muscles.

'Mmm...' Keir sighed softly. 'That feels good.'

Already he was beginning to relax a little, something of the strain easing out of him under the pressure of her trained movements.

'Don't stop.'

She couldn't if she had to, Sienna admitted to herself. The feel of the warm satin of his skin under her fingers, the scent of his body combined with the perfume of the lavender gave her a very real sense of pleasure, one that carried a potently erotic charge. She had never been more intensely aware of the strength of the muscles in those broad, straight shoulders, the width of his ribcage, the supple texture of his skin.

She could feel the effect she was having on him and sensed an answering response in her own body. Her breasts felt full and heavy, aching faintly, and her blood heated swiftly, flooding her veins with a golden warmth.

'Sienna...' Keir's voice was barely audible, so that she had to bend closer to hear it. 'Something to tell you.'

'What's that?'

'About Lucille...'

'What about Lucille?' The steady rhythm of the massage never faltered, in spite of the new and disturbing tension she suddenly found she was prey to. She didn't want to hear a word about his stepmother.

'Those affairs she had...'

He was clearly having to make an effort to get the words out. But it was obvious that this was something he wanted her to know, no matter what it cost him.

'She tried it on with me.'

'What?!'

Just for a second Sienna lost her timing, her hands freezing in mid-stroke. But then she collected her scattered thoughts, bringing her attention back to the job in hand. Concentrate! she told herself fiercely. Keep your mind on what you're doing. Don't let him know how upset you are!

'She came on to me. One night when my dad was away. She came to my room wearing just a robe, with nothing on underneath. Said she was tired of Old Alexander, and thought she'd try the young one out instead.'

'But you told her no chance.'

It was a statement, not a question. She didn't even need to think to know that that would have been his reaction. After all, she'd seen enough of his hatred of his stepmother, the supreme contempt in which he held her, and his heartfelt loyalty to his father to know he would never have considered anything else.

'Yeah...' It was a sigh of relief, and under her massaging

fingers rather more of the tension eased from his tight muscles. 'She went then. But I always worried...'

'Worried?'

'That my dad would find out. That he'd believe I'd taken an active part in her scheme. It would have destroyed our relationship. And she never gave up. Even on the day the will was read—and yesterday, in the wine bar.'

'She—*Lucille* sought you out?'

'She still has a contact at the office. Someone who'd told her that I was there every day. She thought that our marriage was in trouble. That she could take her chance. I always suspected that might happen if she even got a whiff of a suggestion of our arrangement...'

The weary voice trailed off, and Sienna wondered if he'd drifted asleep. But a couple of seconds later Keir obviously forced himself back to consciousness again. There was clearly something he still wanted to say.

'Obviously I told her to go to hell...'

It was all he could manage. This time he did fall asleep. Deeply asleep, his breathing even and relaxed, the long body finally at ease.

Not daring to risk waking him, Sienna continued with the massage for a few minutes more, ceasing only when she knew he wouldn't stir when she removed her hands. Easing herself away from him, she pulled the blankets up over Keir once more before lying down beside him, staring up at the ceiling, her mind buzzing. The things Keir had said had given her plenty to think about.

At some point, much later in the night, Keir finally stirred, surfacing from the deep sleep which had claimed him. His headache had gone and he felt totally different. He felt wonderful, he thought, stretching luxuriously, then freezing as the movement brought him into contact with the warm feminine softness of the woman lying next to him.

'Sienna...'

It was just a whisper but it brought her instantly awake, wide turquoise eyes flying open to look straight into his.

'What is it? Are you all right?'

Keir's smile was gentle, warm. If she'd been weak and foolish she might even have described it as loving. She wasn't as stupid as that, but even so she couldn't stop herself from allowing herself the indulgence of savouring the word just for a moment.

'I'm fine. Your massage worked wonders.'

The kiss he dropped onto the end of her nose was soft as thistledown and heartbreakingly brief. It was there just for a second, then it was gone, and her heart cried out at the pain of its loss.

But then in the space of a heartbeat she saw Keir's face change. Saw the sudden stillness, the swift darkening of his eyes. And she knew what he was feeling because it was happening to her, too. The swift awakening of every sense. The quickened beat of the heart flooding every inch of her body with heat. The spiralling hunger that scarcely seemed to be born before it grew to uncontrollable proportions, impossible to suppress, making her move restlessly at his side.

'Sienna...' he said again, but on a very different note this time, one that drew a deep, heartfelt sigh from her because she knew there was now no going back.

Not that she wanted to go back. Ever. This was all she wanted, all she had ever dreamed of. Everything she had ever longed for was right here in this room, in her arms. She was lost, drowning in the deep dark pools of his eyes, and she never wanted to be rescued because this was what she had been born for, and without it she would always be incomplete.

Keir's smile was slow, surprisingly hesitant, his gaze holding her mesmerised as his hands slid over the curves of her shoulders, down her arms, and across to support the soft weight of her breasts against the heat of his palms.

'Can we do this?' he whispered, and the unexpected, unbelievable note of uncertainty in his voice was the last thing she had expected.

'Can we do this?' she echoed softly, knowing with absolute certainty, without hope of salvation, that if they *didn't* she would die, or at the very least shatter into tiny pieces, impossible to put back together again. 'Oh, Keir, of course we can! We're husband and wife.'

Her encouraging smile was crushed under the force of his kiss, and with a sense of having truly come home she willingly surrendered to their mutual passion.

CHAPTER FOURTEEN

SIENNA stared at the calendar and sighed deeply. It didn't matter how many times she checked the dates, it still said the same.

Of course it did! With a despairing gesture she tossed the pen down onto the kitchen work-surface and sighed again. If only she could throw away her worries as easily. But that was impossible, as, deep down, she had always known it would be.

June the twenty-second. In another two months exactly it would be her first 'anniversary'. The first and last. The day that she and Keir had agreed would mark the end of the agreement that bound them together. So what exactly would they be celebrating? A year together or the start of their lives apart?

Just over three months ago they had been in a hotel room in Carlisle. In bed. That night Keir had made love to her as never before. She had been caught up in a whirlwind of sensation, lifted higher and higher, away from all reality, everything that bound her to the earth. She had given herself to him without restraint, without thought of control or hesitation, and he had responded in kind—or so she had believed.

But only the very next day that idyllic interlude had been exposed as the fantasy that it was and she had come tumbling back down to earth, landing with a very definite and very painful thud.

The truth had dawned on—what else?—the morning after. True to his promise, Keir had taken her over the border into Scotland, into Gretna Green. And while they were there a bride had arrived for her wedding. White dress, heather in her bouquet, even a Scots piper walking before her, escorting her to the ceremony.

And it had been as the piper began to play, as the first haunting notes had sounded in the cool spring air, that Keir's mouth had twisted and he had muttered with black cynicism, 'There she goes. Another lamb to the slaughter. The triumph of optimism over reality.'

She'd needed that, Sienna told herself. Needed the cold splash of realism in her face, driving away the last foolish remnants of fantasy that had still clung to a mind so stupefied by passion, drunk on sensuality, that it had been in danger of being unable to see the truth when it jumped up and bit her.

After all, she'd been there before. Hadn't she already had far too much bitter evidence of the fact that, where Keir Alexander was concerned, passion was a substitute for love, not a vital component of it? To Sienna their lovemaking had been an expression of a deeper feeling, of true sharing, and a promise of a more permanent commitment. But Keir had no idea at all of for ever. To him the ardour of the moment was just that, for the moment, and when it was over, having taken his fill of pleasure, he was perfectly capable of turning and walking away.

But for Sienna that could never be. And not just because of the way she felt about her husband. Because the passage of time had forced her to face up to another reality, one she had at first only feared, but now knew to be a definite fact.

That night in Carlisle, for the first time since their marriage, Keir had made love to her without the use of any form of protection, and now she knew just what a mistake that had been. She was three months pregnant by a man who showed no sign at all of reconsidering his determination to end their marriage once they had reached their first anniversary.

Unobserved, Keir watched Sienna from the doorway, his heart sinking as he saw the way she studied the calendar. It was obvious that she was counting off the days to the end of their marriage, and to judge by the expression on her face it clearly couldn't come soon enough.

'Why the big sigh?'

The casual question made Sienna jump like a startled cat, whirling round to face him.

'Oh—nothing! I was just thinking how the calendar says it's summer, but the weather doesn't seem to agree.'

'It's an English summer,' Keir laughed. 'Rain, rain, and more rain. How about if I take you away from it all?' he added unexpectedly. 'Somewhere warm. What about Italy again?'

'No thanks!' Sienna answered hastily. How could she go back to Italy when her memories of that first time, of her honeymoon, were still so vivid in her mind? She doubted if she would ever set foot in that magical country again, because if she did her pleasure would be tainted by images of herself and Keir during those strange, unreal first days of their marriage. Days when she had still been able to hide behind the protective armour of pretending to herself that she wasn't in love with her husband.

'Well, then, what about dinner, at least? Caroline is visiting a friend tonight, so you needn't worry about her being on her own. We could make a night of it. Say yes, Sienna,' he urged, seeing the uncertain, hesitant look that crossed her face. 'I have something very important I want to talk to you about.'

'You do?' Sienna's heart seemed to turn a somersault inside her chest. What could Keir want to talk to her about that he would describe as 'very important'? 'What is it?'

But Keir simply adopted a mysteriously evasive expression, shaking his dark head adamantly.

'Tonight,' was all he would say. 'I'll tell you everything tonight.'

This was how it had been for the past three months, Sienna reflected as she began her preparations for the evening ahead of her. Ever since they had returned from

Carlisle Keir had almost seemed to become a different person. He had changed his behaviour completely.

The long working hours, the late nights were now just a memory. Keir came home every evening; he took every weekend away from the office. But it was more than that. He had never been so attentive, even in the early days before they had married. He took her out—to restaurants, to the theatre, to concerts. And as the days had grown warmer and longer he'd organised outings—picnics, days by the sea, countless special treats. If she had been asked to describe his attitude in a single word, she would have said that he *courted* her.

Except that courting usually led to something. An engagement, or a marriage, and she and Keir already had both of those behind them. All that this change in Keir's behaviour was leading to was their divorce; because never once had he suggested that they didn't stick to the plan she had originally detailed when she had proposed to him, almost a year before.

But she enjoyed this new way of living, and went along with it, making no protests and asking no questions. She welcomed any crumb of warmth, any attention he was prepared to offer her. After the devastating experience on Valentine's Day of thinking that she had lost him, that he was ending their marriage right there and then, she certainly wasn't about to look any gift horses in the mouth.

'Ready?' Keir appeared in the doorway as she was putting the last touches to her make-up.

'Just coming.'

She slid her feet into high-heeled court shoes, smoothed down the rich blue silk of her elegant vee-necked dress, and turned to survey herself in the mirror.

'You look wonderful.'

In the glass her eyes met Keir's, and she saw the warmly sensual approval in their ebony depths. Immediately her heart gave a nervous flutter, like the wings of a dozen butterflies beating inside her chest, as she fought to control her instinctive response to his smile.

Because over the past few months, while her days had been peaceful, warm, filled with unexpected delights, the nights had been so very different. The hedonistic sensual indulgence of the night in Carlisle had never been repeated. Clearly Keir saw it as a mistake and had moved to clamp down on such unrestrained behaviour. Or it had been just the last throes of a passion already waning that had now burned itself out completely?

'You're not so bad yourself,' she managed, with a lightness she was far from feeling.

The sober dark suit fitted his superb physique like a glove, the fine material of his cream shirt clinging to the muscled lines of his chest, its pale colour bringing out the darkness of his hair and eyes. The superb cut of his trousers emphasised the impact of sleek hips and long powerful legs, a narrow leather belt cinching the slim waist. Seen like this, Keir was every inch the sophisticated, successful business-man she knew him to be.

But she had also known, all too briefly, another, very different Keir. A relaxed, more informal man, casual in sweatshirt and jeans, who had driven a powerful truck with easy confidence and evident enjoyment Or the less con-trolled, more vulnerable man who had opened up about his past, about some of his own inner fears when she had mas-saged his back. Her heart ached for the loss of those other sides to her husband, carefully concealed once more behind the worldly mask he displayed in public.

And the public Keir was very much to the fore now, as he drove her to a favourite restaurant, encouraged her to choose the dishes she most enjoyed from the spectacular menu, entertained her with the sort of light, witty conver-sation that had her laughing out loud in delight. In fact he played his role as escort to perfection, so much so that it was not until the very end of the meal, when they were actually preparing to leave, that she suddenly remembered the reason they were out together at all.

'You said you had something you wanted to talk to me about, Keir. Something very important.'

It was as if she had thrown a switch, turning off a light deep inside him. Abruptly his mood changed, all amusement fading from his eyes, leaving them shuttered and distant. The muscles in his face tightened, the smile that had danced on his lips all night vanishing in an instant.

'Not here,' he said, scrawling his signature on the credit card slip with such an aggressive pressure that it ripped through the top layer of paper. 'We'll talk about it when we get home.'

Which was guaranteed to set Sienna's heart pounding in panic, a cold hand seeming to twist her nerves into knots, destroying all her pleasure in the evening. As Keir escorted her out to the car and all through their homeward journey her mind was racing, trying desperately to think back, find out just when she had made a mistake, when things had gone wrong.

Because something had gone terribly wrong. Everything about Keir's withdrawn silence, the stiff, antagonistic set of his shoulders, the tension that held his long body stiff in the seat beside her, all communicated the fact that he wished he was anywhere but here.

And so when they were once more inside the house, and Keir had ushered her into the elegant sitting room with its cool cream and beige décor, she couldn't control herself any longer. Already wound up so tight that if she didn't say something she felt she might actually snap in two, she turned to Keir in something close to desperation.

'Keir, what is it? What do you want to talk to me about?'

He didn't answer her, didn't look at her. Instead he crossed the room to select a bottle of brandy and pour himself a drink. Then, as he was about to replace the bottle, a thought obviously struck him and he turned to her again.

'Would you like one?'

'N-no thanks.'

Sienna's response was distracted. Because in those few seconds something had happened to stop her thought processes dead, and then start them off on a very different track indeed.

When Keir had lifted the brandy bottle to fill his glass she had noted a totally uncharacteristic tremor in his hand. It had been there again when he'd replaced the bottle, making it clatter faintly against the tray.

Keir was *nervous*! And that was something she had never seen before. Something had put him very much on edge, and that simple fact was so incredible, so unexpected that it threw her thoughts into turmoil, making her reassess everything that had happened and come up with a totally new interpretation of events.

'Won't you sit down?'

'Do I need to?'

She tried for a joking tone, saw it fall desperately flat, the unresponsive twitch of Keir's lips into a travesty of a smile adding fuel to the fire of speculation that was now blazing in her mind.

Was it possible that she'd got it all completely wrong? Had Keir not wanted to tell her something dreadful, but quite the opposite? Earlier this evening she had likened his behaviour over the past weeks to the old-fashioned tradition of courting. What if that had been exactly what he had been doing, and now...now...

The idea was too important, too fragile, for her to want to risk tempting fate by actually letting it form, even inside her head. So instead she turned to Keir again, unable to wait any longer.

'Keir, please! What is it?'

Still he prevaricated for a few more long drawn-out moments, taking first a sip from his brandy, then another, deeper swallow, as he came to sit in the chair opposite her. He seemed to be hunting for a way to begin, and that was so unlike the cool, confident Keir she knew, the man who always knew what to say, that it seemed to confirm her happier suspicions, warming her heart.

'Keir...' she prompted softly.

Keir's dark head came up, chocolate-brown eyes clashing with turquoise, and in that moment Sienna's new-found conviction faltered, a sliver of her earlier panic sliding in through a chink in her mental armour.

'I think it's about time we stared thinking about the future. We need to think ahead, decide what explanation we're going to give...'

'Explanation?' Her voice was just a raw croak, total incomprehension clouding her eyes.

'For splitting up.' Each word was clipped, coldly enunciated, falling like controlled blows on her sensitised nerves. 'We need to have some reason to get divorced. Something to tell friends—your mother—when they ask.'

When she had actually come round to expecting exactly the opposite, the realisation of the true horror of reality was like the destruction of her soul. If Keir had reached into her chest and ripped out her heart, it couldn't have hurt any more. Her eyes blurred, there was a sound like the buzzing of a thousand angry bees inside her head, and she knew with a sickening sense of conviction that if she hadn't been sitting down she would have collapsed in a limp, lifeless heap on the thick carpet right at Keir's feet.

'We—I...'

No words would come. None at all. Her mind was just one terrible scream of agony. She had thought—hoped—Oh, God, what did she do now?

'If you like, I'll take responsibility for it.'

Keir seemed oblivious to her distress. He was talking in a strangely distant, toneless voice. It was as if he had embarked on a speech that he knew he must finish no matter what. And he had no intention at all of diverging from the script in any way.

'For...?'

'Grounds for divorce. I'll provide you with just cause—adultery, perhaps.'

'Adultery!' How could he articulate such an appalling word with such a total lack of emotion? And how could he even think of suggesting such a thing?

'It's probably easiest.'

'Ease—' Sienna swallowed hard, trying to ease the painful constriction in her throat. 'Adultery with *who*?' she demanded hoarsely and ungrammatically, and watched in horrified disbelief as Keir shrugged broad shoulders dismissively.

'Someone. Anyone. Does it matter?'

'Oh, yes, it matters! It matters like hell! I have a right to know who you're going to be unfaithful to me with…'

The words tumbled out faster than a racing stream, clumsily tangling up in each other in her desperation to have them spoken.

'I need to know who you're going to involve in helping you destroy our marriage.'

'But we don't have a marriage to destroy. You know that,' Keir stated with deadly calm. 'The arrangement was—'

'I know what the arrangement was!' Sienna yelled, unable to express her misery in any other way. Seeing the swift reproving frown he turned on her, she hastily adjusted the volume downwards as she continued, 'You don't have to spell it out for me. I know what we agreed.'

'Then you'll also agree that we need to start making plans…'

'No…'

She was getting to her feet as she spoke, spinning away from him, unable to look into that cold, emotionless face any longer.

'What? Sienna, what did you say?'

On the mantelpiece in front of her, in a silver frame, was a colour photograph of their wedding day, placed there by her mother. Sienna's eyes flinched away from it, unable to bear the sight of her own wide, brilliant smile, the tall, impossibly handsome man at her side.

Slowly she forced herself to turn and face Keir again.

'I said no. I don't want to make any plans. It's too early.'

'The year is up in two months' time,' Keir reminded her cruelly, emphasising the point by slamming the side of his hand down on the arm of his chair in time with the last three words.

'I know that, but…'

What could she say to dissuade him? How could she hope to change his mind?

She couldn't. If he was so desperate to be free of their marriage, he would break away from her no matter what she did. Wasn't it better to agree, to let him go easily? That way at least they might have some chance of remaining friends.

But, *oh*… A cruel hand twisted her heart, so that she had to bite back a whimper of pain. She didn't want them to be just *friends*.

'All right.' She had to force the words out, but even so he had to strain to hear a voice that was little more than a whisper. 'All right, we'll do as you say. But have you thought about my mother?'

'Caroline?'

For the first time Keir's resolution faltered. His head went back sharply, onyx eyes widening in something close to shock. His movements suddenly strangely jerky, he lifted his glass to his lips, downing what was left in it before pushing himself to his feet and crossing to the tray to refill it.

'What about Caroline?' he asked, the hoarseness of his voice betraying the way his composure had cracked wide open.

It was a further cruel body-blow amongst so many devastating hurts to realise how much Keir cared for her mother. To see in his face his concern for Caroline where there was none for Sienna herself. But that affection was the only weapon she had left in her arsenal, and she was determined to use it against him as ruthlessly as she could.

'Don't you see it would hurt her terribly to think that you could be unfaithful to me so soon after our wedding? It would devastate her to find you so shallow, so selfish. She respects you, admires you… She loves you, Keir!'

'Do you think I don't know that?'

The brandy glass was slammed back down onto the tray with such force that Sienna fully expected to see the beautiful crystal shatter under the impact.

'Do you think I don't know how Caroline feels? But I can't afford to think of her—I have to concentrate on you. On what you want. Otherwise I can't do this. I—'

'Just a minute!'

Sienna's vehemence shocked Keir into a silence that lay thick and heavy around them. Slowly she shook her head, trying to clear her thoughts, before turning to look at him again.

'What did you say?'

Had Keir suddenly changed dramatically, or was she actually looking at a totally different man? Had his face always been so pale, his eyes so shockingly dark? Why hadn't she noticed the way his skin was drawn tight over the wide cheekbones, etching white marks of strain around his nose and mouth? Was it possible that, caught up in her own misery, she had been reading him all wrong?

'What did you say?' she repeated more emphatically when he didn't answer her.

'That I have to do this for you. That—'

'But what if I don't want it?'

She would have thought it was impossible for him to lose any more colour, but now his face was ashen with shock. He took a single step towards her, then stopped, his eyes never leaving her face.

'You—?'

'I don't want it, Keir. I want to stay married to you. I want us to try and make a go of things together.'

The words were hopelessly inadequate to describe the way she felt but she didn't dare to be any more revealing, to expose her true emotions without some idea of what he thought.

'I don't think so.'

Keir shook his head firmly enough, but there was something in his eyes that didn't tally with the emphatic negative. A tiny spark of vulnerability that lit a flare of hope in Sienna's heart.

'It wouldn't work.'

'Why not? Surely we have something special…'

'What? *Sex?*' She had never heard such raw anger in his voice. 'Is that really so very special? Do you think that's all that matters to me? Or that it says anything about the way you feel? Do you think that just because I can bring you orgasm, because I can make you shudder in ecstasy underneath me, that I'm fool enough to believe it means you love me?'

'It's part of it. Keir…' Drawing a deep, uneven breath, she took a calculated risk, her heart clenching in tension as she spoke. 'Dean could never make me feel that way.'

She had his attention now, with a vengeance. But she didn't know how to build on it. The problem was that she was working blind, unable to gauge just what he was thinking. And those dark, unreadable eyes gave her no clue at all.

'Would you stay if I told you I was pregnant?'

She had invested so much emotional importance in the certainty that he would say, yes, of course he would stay, that it rocked her world to see the way he shook his head.

'A child should have two parents who love each other, not two disparate people yoked together purely in name. I'd always be there for any child, Sienna; I'd want to be a true father. I've always believed that I would have to be married to the mother of my child. It was what I *wanted*. But I couldn't force you into something like that. I couldn't tie you to a marriage you didn't truly want.'

And that was when Sienna knew. When she realised with absolute certainty that Keir loved her. That he would even go against his own needs, his own beliefs, if he thought it would bring her happiness.

'You need to be free to find someone to love.'

'But, Keir, I already have.'

The look he turned on her was so numb, so bruised that it wrenched at her heart.

'You have? Who…?'

'Who do you think? Keir, you must know it's you!'

Looking into his handsome face she saw the shock, disbelief, the slow, unbelieving dawning of understanding.

'I know nothing of the damn sort!' he exploded, with a touch of the old Keir that brought a delighted bubble of laughter to her lips.

'Then let me put it into words of one syllable,' she said, at long last having the courage to come forward and take him by the hand. 'I, Sienna, love you, Keir, with all my heart, and if you'll let me I'll be your wife for better for worse, for richer for poorer, for all those other things, if only you'll let me be your wife *for real*.'

The last words came out on a gasp of shock as she was whirled into his arms and crushed close up against his chest. One strong hand came under her chin, lifting her face until her eyes met his deep ones, that blazed with a devotion so fierce and true that any last remaining fears were shrivelled up in the stormy heat of it.

'If you love me, I'll never let you be anyone else's wife as long as there's a breath left in my body.'

With a sigh of pure happiness that seemed to come from the depths of his soul he brought his mouth down hard on hers, expressing his feelings in a way that mere words could never manage. Her head spinning, her legs weakening beneath her, Sienna could only cling to him and respond in kind, willing him to know from her kiss the overwhelming strength of her feelings for him.

When at last he wrenched his lips away they were both

trembling with emotion and need, and she knew that the flare of colour high on his cheekbones was matched in her own face as he stared down into it.

'I really think that we should get a divorce, my love,' Keir said when he finally gathered the strength to speak.

That 'my love' told her there was no way he meant what he had said at all, but still his words confused her.

'But, Keir, why?'

'So that we can start again. So that I can propose to you as I always planned to do. So that we can get married all over again, properly this time…'

'As you always planned to?' Sienna pounced on the part of his impassioned declaration that had surprised her most. 'Keir, are you saying…?'

'That I always meant to ask you to marry me,' he confirmed her suspicions easily. 'Right from the start I knew I wanted to marry you, but I wanted to give you time to get over Dean. And I wanted the problems with the company sorted out too, so that I could promise you a secure future.'

She had never guessed that he felt this way. 'That wouldn't have mattered.'

'It would have mattered to me. I thought I had time. That I could sort out my own problems first and then come to you free of all of them. But then you pre-empted me with your proposal, and I was so afraid that if I said no you'd look elsewhere, find someone else, that I jumped in with both feet. I was arrogant enough to think that a year would be more than enough time to make you come to care for me…'

'It didn't take half that long,' Sienna whispered, resting her head against the firm, secure support of his shoulder. 'I knew I was crazy about you before six months were up.'

'You…? Valentine's Day,' Keir declared perceptively, and Sienna nodded confirmation of his assumption.

'I couldn't let you out of our agreement because I was terrified you'd walk out of my life and never come back again.'

'That was not what I had in mind at all,' Keir told her softly. 'What I wanted was a chance to offer you marriage on equal terms, without my being just the hired husband.'

'You were never that,' Sienna assured him. To her, Keir could never be 'just' anything. 'But if you felt that way, why did you stop sleeping with me?'

'The sex was getting in the way. We were falling into bed instead of talking to each other. Making love instead of loving. I wanted to take our relationship back a couple of steps, so that we could learn to get to know each other properly. And I couldn't bear to make love to you when I thought that for you it was only sex.'

'That I can believe. What I don't understand is why you said what you did that day in Scotland.'

'At Gretna?' Supremely sensitive to her moods, Keir had picked up at once on her train of thought. 'Oh, Sienna,' he groaned, shaking his head in amazement at his own actions. 'If you knew how much I regretted that afterwards. But it was either that or admit the way I was feeling—that I was jealous as hell of that wedding being a real one. The sort of marriage I had always dreamed of having for myself.'

'Well, we can have that now,' Sienna told him, smiling up into his face and seeing the love shining in his eyes, so clear to see. 'We can begin again.'

Keir nodded slowly, his expression thoughtful.

'How do you feel about having a private ceremony on our anniversary? Just the two of us, renewing our vows, making them real and lasting this time, a marriage that will be for ever.'

'I'd love that,' Sienna whispered. 'But only if you don't mind a pregnant bride.'

'I don't mind—' Keir began, then broke off in shock as the impact of what she'd said hit home fully. 'You *meant* it!'

'I meant it,' Sienna admitted, her pale skin colouring in response to the blazing, ecstatic force of his smile. 'So I'm afraid it won't be "just the two of us" for very much longer.'

'Do you think I mind? I couldn't be happier.'

Keir hugged her even closer, pressing his mouth lovingly to the corner of her smiling mouth.

'I lied, you know,' he whispered against her ear, his warm breath feathering over her skin. 'I could never have let you go to find someone else. I wanted you all to myself. I always believed that if ever I married it would be for a lifetime.'

'Oh, Keir…' Sienna sighed against his lips as his mouth captured hers once more and the heated waves of passion washed over her, threatening to drive away all rational thought. 'That agreement we made. Do you think we could extend the contract beyond its original term—say for the rest of our lives?'

'That might just be long enough,' he told her huskily, swinging her up into his arms and heading for the stairs and their bedroom. 'And the rest of our lives starts now.'

MILLS & BOON

Strictly Business

When the fun starts...
after hours!

Liz Fielding

PENNY JORDAN

Hannah Bernard

On sale 3rd September 2004

Available at most branches of WHSmith, Tesco, Martins, Borders, Eason, Sainsbury's and all good paperback bookshops.

It only takes a second to say 'I do'...

Marriage
for Keeps

KAREN YOUNG GINA WILKINS MARGOT DALTON

MILLS & BOON

On sale 1st October 2004

Available at most branches of WHSmith, Tesco, ASDA, Martins,
Borders, Eason, Sainsbury's and all good paperback bookshops.

0904/03b

MILLS & BOON®

Volume 4
on sale from
1st October
2004

Lynne
Graham

International Playboys

An Insatiable

Passion

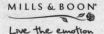